# SHAW

To Janice,

Peace and Blessings!

Thank You

Sonia Swayze

AKA Cora Mack

# SHAW

CORA MACK

| Library of Congress Control Number: | | 2013906360 |
| --- | --- | --- |
| ISBN: | Hardcover | 978-1-4836-2267-5 |
| | Softcover | 978-1-4836-2266-8 |
| | Ebook | 978-1-4836-2268-2 |



This book was printed in the United States of America.

Rev. date: 05/06/2013

**To order additional copies of this book, contact:**
Xlibris Corporation
1-888-795-4274
www.Xlibris.com
Orders@Xlibris.com
114443

For Ruth, Dot, Sam, and Gloria

It's done . . .

# CHAPTER 1

Death promised big money, and William Taylor had made a bundle. He'd vowed to do right by people once they were dead, and as a result, he'd come by plenty of business as an undertaker. It's not that he was entirely motivated by money, though for a black man in the 1950s, money was an issue. The fact is, his father and his grandfather were undertakers, and they both taught him to show respect for the Negro dead. White undertakers, if they took them at all, handled black bodies like a lynching after-party. They were dragged, hidden, and funerals were conducted in secret to protect the temperament of white customers. William Taylor's funeral home offered Negroes in Washington, DC, an opportunity to look their personal best when they went to meet their maker. It also offered him a chance to make a very good living. The fact that both he and his wife, Naomi, were licensed undertakers gave rise to a booming business. Black people in the community respected his professionalism and appreciated her compassion. Naomi was, in fact, the only licensed female undertaker in DC at the time, white or black.

Since he stayed busy, William Taylor had seldom an occasion to exalt in the revelry and excitement of the living, except in autumn of every year, he'd join the ranks, lie back, and watch his favorite sporting event—the World Series. Dressed in his usual white shirt and striped tie, as he did every single day since he never knew when a customer would come by, Taylor, most people called him Taylor, stretched out in his parlor and watched game 4 with Naomi. It happened to be a Sunday afternoon, October 7, 1956, and the New York Yankees were playing the Brooklyn Dodgers.

"Hey, baby, where's the beer?" Taylor hollered to Naomi.

"Coming, I've got Mildred on the line," Naomi replied.

Taylor knew Naomi and her girlfriends had a baseball pool going. What he didn't know is how much money she bet on Jackie Robinson hitting a home run. You couldn't tell her that ball wasn't going in the stands.

"Don't worry, Mildred. It's going to clear the fence. I'll be downtown shopping tomorrow," he heard Naomi tell her friend.

Now, most men in DC gambled trying to hit the big one, but quiet as kept, women in the city played the numbers, bet on the horses, and organized their own baseball pool to make a little extra for the household. Any issues of religious conscience were assuaged by the knowledge that even the reverends were playing the numbers, reconciling any sin by using a portion of the winnings for the church—buying suits and cars with the rest. Naomi rushed into the parlor with the beer and sat on the edge of the sofa, waiting for the home run.

"Come on, Jackie, I've already picked out a new bathing suit to wear to Chicken Bone Beach!" Chicken Bone was the nickname of a restricted area of Atlantic City Beach for Negroes on the New Jersey Shore. Folks gathered on the beach and feasted on baskets of fried chicken all day, leaving behind the bones in the sand.

"The score is 2 to 1 in the fourth, New York on top," the announcer said.

The Dodgers' manager sent Gil Hodges to the plate ahead of Jackie Robinson, originally on the roster to bat next. Naomi hit the ceiling.

"That bigot . . ."

"Naomi, calm down. There's still five more innings in the game," Taylor reminded her. "Is that food I smell burning?"

"Oh lord, my beans!" Naomi jumped up and ran to the kitchen. The half-cooked green beans from her garden had stuck to the bottom of the pot. She scooped up the ones that weren't burnt, put them in another pot on low heat, and hurried back to the game.

* * *

Around two o'clock, the doorbell chimed. Taylor shoved himself from his seat, grumbling, and crossed the parlor to the front door. At five foot eight, clean shaven, with a hint of gray at the temples, he appeared short next to most men. And his deep-set eyes mimicked his mahogany-colored skin, which was as smooth as a baby's behind. He adjusted his tie and opened the door. Before him stood two women, and the elder introduced both of them.

"I'm Ida Pickett . . . this my sista, Grace."

Taylor noticed that Ida Pickett's pink lipstick had smeared around her mouth and her eyes were swollen half-shut. Suddenly, tears gushed from her eyes, faster than a sudden downpour of rain. Now in a frenzy of emotion, she began to shake. Before Taylor opened his mouth to speak, she'd collapsed on the porch, sobbing and ranting about her dead daughter. This display was not something new for Taylor. People went to his house all the time distraught with a family member close by to help hold them up.

"Now, now . . . Mrs. Pickett," Taylor said, "come inside and tell me what happened to her."

Mrs. Pickett's sister helped Taylor hold up the distressed woman, and they led her to his office across the viewing room in his house, which doubled as a funeral home. They settled her into a comfortable chair. Mrs. Pickett dropped her pocketbook on the floor. She hunched over, mumbling, then wiped her eyes with a handkerchief, already soaked with moisture from her tears.

"My daughter's dead . . . I don't have no money and no insurance to bury her." Mrs. Pickett began to sob louder. "Jesus took her! He took my baby!" She picked up her pocketbook then dropped it again, loose change falling out and rolling on the floor. Grace kneeled down, gathered up the coins, and put them in her pocket.

Taylor turned away and looked back toward the door, where Naomi stood. He shook his head, knowing what little comfort either of them might offer the grieving mother. He focused his attention back to Mrs. Pickett, who told him in the midst of her moaning and weeping that she'd rushed her eight-year-old daughter Lilly Mae to the Children's Hospital emergency room nine o'clock that morning because her ears were infected.

"Pus ran down Lilly Mae's neck like wata," Mrs. Pickett said, her voice quivering. "The doctor, he checked her ears, then the nurse shot her with pen'cillin. Next thing I knowed, Lilly Mae stopped hollerin' . . . couldn't catch her breath and she just fell across my lap . . . She died. They tried to bring her back, save for the fact she'd already gone over." Mrs. Pickett threw up her hands in disbelief, while her sister stood by silently weeping. The train taking her husband home from his railroad job had broken down; that's why Grace went with her and Mr. Pickett didn't. He was still making his way home.

Taylor grasped Mrs. Pickett's hands in his, close fitted, like somebody trying to lock hold of a firefly, and looked into her eyes. "I'm so sorry you lost your baby." In the back of his mind he wondered if the Yankees had scored.

Mrs. Pickett slumped forward, shaking her head back and forth. Then she said, "Grace called my insurance company. I wasn't up to talkin' to nobody. The insurance girl told Grace I didn't make no payment for three months so they canceled my policy. I told Grace to tell her I had money order receipts to prove I made all my payments."

Taylor knew that most families didn't buy separate insurance policies for their children. They'd attach a clause to their own. "Did you have coverage for Lilly Mae on that policy?"

"Yes, sir, I did!" she snapped. "That girl, she wouldn't listen to Grace, so we took a cab down there to show 'em my receipts." Mrs. Pickett sat up straighter now, as though anger had blocked out some of her grief. "A man answered the door, and his sorry behind wouldn't let me in. Said Family Life didn't conduct business on weekends. Told me to go home and call for an appointment. Those people were some nasty. Didn't care one way or anotha Lilly Mae died and I'd no money to bury her. If I'd a gun, I would've shot 'em all." She slumped forward again. "Me and my husband . . . we work every day tryin' to make ends meet, 'cept we don't have savin's and no money to bury our child." She breathed heavily now. "Please help me."

Grace wrapped her arms around her sister and cried with her. And Taylor, after many years in the business, never did find words to make bearable the pain brought on by a child's death. And he didn't have a playbook for it, though over time he'd learned to maneuver through it.

"Mrs. Pickett, I'm going to help you." He patted her hands, striving to maintain some calm. "Tell me about your baby."

"Oh lawd, help me, please help me," she said, exasperated. "My baby . . . Lilly Mae. She named for her granny on her daddy's side. They both born with the same big brown eyes and mouth that peaked at the top . . . a pretty girl . . . the color of peanut butter. We called her Peanut. She liked dancing, even tried to sing. I'd just started teachin' her to sew clothes for her doll." Tears flowed from Mrs. Pickett's eyes. Her body shook. She drooled at the mouth and mucus dripped from her nose. She wiped away the spittle and the snot with a tissue Naomi had stuffed into her hand and stared down at the wood floor, whimpering.

"You need me in here?" Naomi asked Taylor.

"No . . . where's Ruth?" Ruth, Taylor's twenty-three-year-old stepdaughter, Naomi's daughter by her first husband, worked as a nurse. She might be needed if Mrs. Pickett required more than comfort.

"The hospital," Naomi replied.

Taylor hesitated. "We'll be all right."

Naomi left the room.

"This is difficult, I know," Taylor said to Mrs. Pickett.

Mrs. Pickett didn't respond.

"Are you listening to me?" Taylor asked her.

She raised her head straining to see him. "Yes, sir."

"I need to ask you . . . Who held your policy?"

"Family Life," she answered.

"On Fourteenth Street Northwest?" he asked.

"Yes . . . . yes, sir, Mr. Taylor," she replied.

Taylor cracked his knuckles, something he did when he got angry. The sound of his finger joints popping echoed in the room. His mother had warned him, ***You gonna end up with arthritis if you don't stop that.*** Sure enough, his knuckles had already started changing shape and ached when it rained or snowed or when the temperature went below forty degrees.

He knew Family Life well. A Negro-owned business, it had tripled its client base over the years as more Negroes migrated to DC from the South, found work, and bought into their disability and life insurance. He knew the company executives and suspected that they had falsely accused Mrs. Pickett of missing her monthly payments in order to keep the death benefits owed her. He'd heard similar stories from six other families he'd recently done business with. He believed Mrs. Pickett made those payments. Families like hers worked hard to hold on to life insurance even if it meant buying chicken livers and neck bones for dinner, instead of lamb chops or roast beef, assurance they or their family members would be put away proper.

At a Negroes in Business meeting in March, he decided not to put up with it anymore. While there, he'd accused the company president, Rutherford Daniels, of stealing money from his clients when they tried to collect on their dead. Of course he denied any wrong doing. Taylor had left the meeting disgusted at how indignant Daniel's behaved. Remembering the incident, he heaved himself from his chair, his face rigid, and pounded his desk so hard the desk lamp fell over, startling the women. Marching across the room, his hands clenched, he tried to get a grasp on his fury. He turned toward the window as if to look out at the street. Instead, he closed his eyes and took in a deep breath.

"Please forgive me, ladies, I didn't mean to frighten you. Losing a child is painful enough, and to have to go through this," Taylor muttered. His baby sister, Pansy, had died trying to come into the world. He'd remembered it like yesterday, his parents and grandparents grieving like Mrs. Pickett did. Words didn't ease their pain either. He'd buried Pansy and all the other children in his heart, though they'd stayed alive in his mind, and each time another child died, he'd recall the last. This time, infant Sara. She'd come out the womb with her heart sitting atop her small chest, a rare occurrence that graced the front page of every local and a few national newspapers. She'd died in her mother's arms the same hour she was born. An extraordinary event, and for a Negro child to receive such national attention made it even more noteworthy.

Research institutes around the world offered to buy Sara's body, instead, her parents went to Taylor's to plan her funeral, so he had made the front page too: "Sara Tool's Body at William T. and Naomi Taylor's Funeral Home." It had been a year since Sara died. Taylor still shuddered at having to put her tiny heart in the hollow space where it belonged. Lilly Mae would be the first child he'd bury since Sara. The truth of the matter is, the death of a child was never easy for Taylor. If there were ever an event to test a man's prowess, this had to be it.

After being deep in thought, Taylor spoke, "I need to bring Lilly Mae here this evening. I want you to come back tomorrow at ten o'clock and we'll plan everything." He called a cab to take the women home. As they shuffled through the door, Taylor said, "Mrs. Pickett, I know you're hurting, and I know you're in pain. All the same, your baby's up there dancing with the angels now. God needed another angel." While holding on to her sister, Mrs. Pickett cried so hard her body shook.

Taylor thought about other grief-stricken mothers like Mrs. Pickett, and fathers who tortured themselves trying to figure out which sin they were being punished for. Their worlds seemed to get smaller as hopes and dreams died with their children, and in a marriage where problems already existed, the child's death literally tore the family apart. That's what happened to Sara's family. After she died, her parents separated, unable to labor through the pain together as they did during her birth.

* * *

"Sara's family didn't have money or insurance," Taylor reminded Naomi, who had joined him on the porch. He eyed Naomi, expecting her to say something. She stayed quiet with a worried expression on her face. He wondered what bothered her. "Do you remember, Naomi?"

"Oh yes, I remember," she replied. "But I'm concerned about you. No parent wants to bury their child, we both know that. Still, you let anger stop you from giving Mrs. Pickett what she needed, your sympathy and trust. So the next time we get a child, I'm working with the family."

"You're right," Taylor said. "I'll apologize to her tomorrow. You know she can't pay either."

"I heard her. We'll have to close down soon if we keep taking on all the Mrs. Picketts of the world. We need paying customers and soon," Naomi said.

"So you want to send our poor people to white morticians, is that what you want?" Taylor said, shaking his head. "Negroes deserve a decent funeral, rich or poor, and to look like Negroes before the Good Lord, not painted with white makeup to look like clowns. And you know what'll happen to Lilly Mae. If some sick fool doesn't rape her, they'll make light of her."

"I'm not arguing that, Taylor. You don't seem to understand, there's no money coming in to pay for the caskets, the graves, or the material for the shrouds and slippers I make," Naomi argued.

"I've heard people say that when you finish with the women, they look better dead than they did alive." Taylor chuckled.

"Don't change the subject," Naomi said, frustrated. "You keep taking on these cases, I'm getting a second job as a seamstress somewhere."

Taylor leaped from the glider, angry as a hornet whose nest had been disturbed. "My wife isn't working two jobs!"

"You won't have a say, if you don't bring in paying customers. I'm not losing everything we've worked for because of your pride." Naomi stormed into the house.

Taylor banged his hands on the porch rail so hard, his finger pained from his gold wedding band pressed into his skin. He examined the band and his class ring from Howard University, the Negro college in DC, nationally revered by blacks across the country. He sighed—no damage. He'd replace the class ring, if need be, but Naomi, already irritated with him, would give him the blues if he had to replace his wedding band.

Taylor knew if he refused to help the impoverished and cash-poor families and those without life insurance, white morticians would. Although tension between the races had heightened because of forced integration, now in its second year in DC, white funeral-home directors were relentless in going after colored business, motivated by competition and the potential income from grateful families who'd go yet again with more black bodies.

# Chapter 2

Taylor stood alone on the front porch long after Naomi stalked into the house. He glanced down at her flowerpots on the porch steps, housing witch hazel and crocuses, both in full bloom. Autumn had debuted, and Taylor delighted in the spell of warm weather, yet just two weeks ago, the temperature had dropped below freezing. Ice crystals had formed on Naomi's carrots and beets she'd grown in the backyard, killing them. He'd watch her throw a tantrum because she'd have to buy from the market, instead of canning her own vegetables for winter. She'd spent her first marriage farming the land with her first husband. The fact that he was a mulatto, half-white and half-Native American, made it easier for him to own land in those days. The fact that Naomi was half-Negro and half-Native American made it easier for him to marry her.

Naomi's threat to work a second job bothered Taylor. He knew she would. Yet how would it look . . . the wife of the director of the second-largest Negro funeral home working a second job? He cringed at the thought of it. He had to do something to improve their finances. No matter what, he'd still take care of Lilly Mae.

He leaned against the porch rail, gazing at the brilliant display of red, gold, and orange-colored leaves fluttering in the warm breeze. The rich, beautiful hues of autumn seemed to ease the sting of Mrs. Pickett's situation, at least for the moment, for in the distance loomed a dark cloud threatening to pounce the earth with her tears. Taylor prayed that the cloud would pass over. He turned to open the door. He stopped when he heard the distinctive drone of the engine in his black Packard cruising down Sixth Street, where he lived, in the Shaw district, the center of the nation's capital. Mostly Negroes lived in Shaw, which spanned streets north of Penn Quarter, east of DuPont Circle, and south of Adams Morgan. Taylor waved as Leroy, his driver and his wife's adopted brother, pulled into the paved driveway. Ruth jumped from the car and rushed up the steps.

"Hey, Dad, where's Mom?" Ruth gave him a quick peck on the cheek.

Taylor followed her into the house. "I'm fine, thank you. She's in the kitchen. Why such a hurry?"

"I've got a date."

"With whom?"

Ruth turned and looked at him. "Easton, of course, who else?"

"Where you going?"

"Dinner . . . and to see ***Carmen Jones.***" ***Carmen Jones***, a film adapted from the opera ***Carmen***, featured an all-black cast.

"Me and your mother are going to see Billie Holiday this evening," Taylor said. "We have a body to pick up, so I hope Leroy can do it. I don't want to be late for the show."

"Mom will have a conniption if you're late. Can't it wait until tomorrow?" Ruth asked.

"Afraid not," Taylor said. "Hospitals are already peeved because undertakers don't pick up bodies fast enough. They claim space is a problem."

"I'm home!" Ruth called to her mother from the hallway.

"Your dress is hanging on my closet door," Naomi answered.

Ruth ran toward the staircase, tripping on the hall rug as she always did when she became overly excited, and cursed. "Damn it," she mumbled.

"I heard that," Taylor said, standing at the doorway to the parlor.

"I know, I know, nobody's allowed to curse in this house except you," Ruth responded.

Taylor chuckled as he watched Ruth climb the stairs, the complete opposite of her mother as she had full lips, olive-colored skin, and midnight-brown hair that hung almost to her waist; not kinky hair that needed a hot comb or a lye perm. It looked loose and curly, a fair combination of her Native American and Negro roots. Like Naomi, she had the same pointy nose and brows that held shape above hazel-colored eyes that slanted upward so much, some black folks believed she originated from a foreign country. White folks did too.

"Where are you from?" black people would ask her.

"Virginia," she'd reply.

"No, where are you from?" they'd ask again, meaning what country.

Ruth would simply say, "I'm a Negro."

Ruth had just turned eight years old when Taylor married Naomi. At that time, Thomas, his son by his first wife, spent most weekends at the funeral home. Taylor enjoyed seeing the two riding their bikes and playing baseball or marbles in the dirt. When Thomas hit his teens and made known his interest in girls, Taylor often found Ruth sitting alone on the porch, Thomas out and about with his new friends. After Thomas graduated from college, he moved to southeast of the city, though he went by the funeral home at least once or twice a week.

Taylor scurried into his office, called Leroy to pick up Lilly Mae's body, filled out the form he needed to claim the body, and left it in an envelope on his desk. He headed for the kitchen, wondering why Naomi insisted on cooking dinner since neither of them planned to eat it today; they were dining at the club. The doorbell rang. Taylor did an about-face. ***Please don't let it be a customer,*** he said to himself.

* * *

"Good evening, sir," Easton Priest said to Taylor, stepping inside. "Is that pound cake I smell?"

Taylor smiled. "Yeah it is, except you won't be eating any. I heard you're going out to dinner."

"Yes Sir, we are, can't we still eat dessert here?" Easton asked, chuckling.

A young investigative reporter for the ***Negro News***, Easton had started his career at the newspaper right after graduating from Howard University five years earlier, and now he wrote his own weekly column. He'd spent the last three months covering protests against integration in DC and just published his report, which stimulated a lot of conversation among self-professed authorities on the subject, who failed to acknowledge the inconsistencies in how ***Brown versus the Board of Education*** had been enforced in DC and throughout the country. But the Montgomery, Alabama, boycott had taken center stage in the battle for black equality. Led by a young minister in Montgomery, it had been almost a year since it started. Montgomery had lost a fortune in revenue, and angry white leaders were fighting against the boycott.

"What do you make of the boycott in Alabama?" Taylor asked Easton.

"If we managed to pull ourselves up from slavery, we can walk our way out of discrimination," Easton replied. "I wish I could be there and help move people where they need to go and encourage them to keep walking, just a little while longer."

Ruth strolled into the parlor.

Easton stood with a glint in his eyes as she moved closer to him. He bent down and kissed her on the forehead. He often slouched, trying to find a comfort zone between his height and Ruth's short stature. A muscular six-foot-tall young man with a cleft in his chin, dressed in a pin-striped suit, he looked as if someone had sculpted him from bronze, the color of his skin. His small wire-rimmed glasses covered eyes so dark they looked black, as black as the bow tie clipped to his shirt collar.

"Me and Easton were talking about the boycott in Alabama," Taylor told Ruth. "If the city wins the injunction against the car pools, Negroes may go back to riding buses. I tell you, I never imagined I'd witness any of this in my life."

"And we're going to see a lot more," Ruth responded. "Give me a minute, I'm going to say good night to Mom." Ruth smiled at her beau and strutted to the kitchen.

* * *

"Wow, you look fabulous!" exclaimed Naomi at the sight of Ruth. "Why, your lipstick is the exact, same color as the dress!" The red silk dress that Naomi had made accentuated a twenty-two-inch waistline most women Ruth's age only dreamed about. The V-cut dress had cropped sleeves and a ballerina skirt that hid most of her bow legs. She had draped a blue, gold, and red-flowered shawl around her shoulders and clipped on gold-studded earrings. She swung around in her red sling-back heels, which added three inches to her height.

Naomi stopped shucking corn off the cob and leaned against the sink to eye Ruth as she posed, hands on hips, back arched, the shawl now draped over her arm. "You pose better than some of those models I see at fashion shows."

"This dress can make any woman feel she belongs on a catwalk. I saw this dress in my mind, and you made it real. You're a genius."

"Anything for you, sweetie pie," Naomi responded.

"I can't wait till we start designing my wedding gown. Princess Grace will drool when she sees me dancing down the aisle with ***my*** black prince." Grace Kelly had married the Prince of Monaco in April.

"Ruth, I'm not buying an ounce of thread until I see a ring on your finger," Naomi responded.

"Soon, it's coming soon. Wait . . . I just realized, Easton didn't say a word about how I look," she said, as if a light bulb just clicked on in her head. "You'd think he'd say something."

"Some men don't know how or when to compliment women," Naomi responded, not giving Easton any slack for being slow on the uptake.

Ruth hugged her mother.

"My goodness, you're almost up to my nose in those shoes," Naomi said. The two women giggled. Together they went to the parlor, and then Ruth cut loose.

"It's party time!" Ruth swung around in a circle and grabbed Easton's hand.

"You look gorgeous!" Easton said.

"Yes, you do," Taylor said a look of approval on his face.

"Thank you. A Naomi Taylor original." She twirled slowly, like a ballerina wound atop a jewelry box. When she stopped, she winked at Easton, clasped her hand in his, and led him out the front door.

# Chapter 3

Taylor missed the last innings of the baseball game dealing with Mrs. Pickett, though he knew Jackie Robinson didn't hit a home run, because Naomi had been as quiet as a mouse. "How much did you lose?" he asked her.

"Doc called while you were on the porch. I have to get ready for the show." She strode off down the hallway without answering Taylor.

"Save some hot water for me too!" Taylor yelled, his appeal falling on deaf ears. A bit subdued, he went to his office. He didn't like Naomi gambling, then again she'd become paranoid about the business because he'd taken on so many charity cases. Not only did he struggle watching poor bereaved families suffer, he had to admit he was struggling financially too, the Family Life scam affecting his business and his family. When Mrs. Pickett showed up with her story, it had plucked his last nerve. Death provided plenty of business to go around, so why would Family Life need to steal her money?

* * *

Taylor returned Doc Nelson's call.

"Doc, what's on your mind?" Taylor asked his best friend.

"Whiskey for the poker game tomorrow night, don't forget it. And bring plenty of that cold cash you keep hidden away," Doc said, chuckling.

"Liquor, not a problem, cash, now that's a different story," Taylor said. "Remember the family where the husband died and Family Life had canceled their policy without telling them? Well, it happened to another Family, today. They lost a child and can't pay a dime for the funeral because Family Life stole their money."

"Say what . . . how so?" Doc asked. A pharmacist by trade, Doc owned a drugstore in the city. He also had a policy with Family Life.

"The family goes to collect what they're owed, and out of the blue, the company tells them their policy is canceled. The first they'd heard about it. To hear the company tell it, they only cancel policies after three or more payments are missed."

"Did they miss three payments?" Doc asked.

"Hell no! The families showed me their contract agreements and money order receipts for the monthly payments," Taylor replied. "They didn't miss any payments. The company is scamming these people."

“What are you going to do?” Doc asked.

“Call the police if the insurance board doesn’t do anything,” Taylor replied. “Even though the police probably won’t do a damn thing either. Family Life has been running this scam for at least seven months, that I know of. No telling who else is involved.”

“You’re talking fraud,” Doc said. “You need more than receipts to prove it. Back off until you get something that’ll stand up in court. Keep me posted. I haven’t had problems with the company myself.”

“You’re not poor,” Taylor said. “And you haven’t had anyone die on you lately.”

As much as Taylor respected Doc Nelson, he had no intentions of backing off. He’d pounce on Family Life like an eagle swooping down on a rat until they stopped stealing from their clients, and from him.

# Chapter 4

Taylor and Naomi arrived at the Jazz Room thirty minutes before show time. The Jazz Room, on U Street in the northwest part of the city, hosted many of the great jazz vocalists and instrumentalists of the '50s. Neon lights dazzled from it and other bars, restaurants, and all-night dance clubs along U Street. The vibrant lights electrified the narrow sidewalks crammed with club goers, who were dressed to the nines. Men pimped in double-breasted suits, and women strutted in stiletto heels, wearing red, emerald green, and flame-orange crepe, silk, and satin dresses. They bounced from one nightclub to another, and with the sound of each blues number or jazz improvisation, they fell in step, tapped their feet, or nodded to the pulsating rhythms of instruments vibrating in the air.

U Street extended from Ninth Street Northeast to Eighteenth Street and Florida Avenue Northwest. Like many other commercial establishments on the block, the Jazz Room had been there for several years. The area had been predominantly white and middle class up until the early fifties. When DC became more segregated, the area became the focal point for Negro-owned businesses and entertainment. The jazz singer, Pearl Bailey, called U Street Black Broadway, though it only had two theatres.

Taylor and Naomi sat two rows from the stage in the small cavernous room, smiling at each other and holding hands. You'd never know they'd had a disagreement earlier in the day. By the time their drinks arrived, all the tables were full. Some folks resigned to stand at the bar to hear Billie Holiday sing because the club sold more tickets than they had seats. The tickets were a hot commodity. Lady Day had published her autobiography, ***Lady Sings the Blues***, earlier in the year and released a new LP of the same name a few months later in June. Plans for a film about the songstress were in the making, and Dorothy Dandridge was being considered to play her. So the first day tickets went on sale, Taylor had rushed to the Jazz Room before the doors opened.

"You look beautiful this evening," Taylor said to Naomi, smiling at the plunging neckline that framed her rounded breast. She'd made the sapphire-blue satin dress after she'd finished Ruth's, and unlike Ruth's, hers showed a lot more skin, the back of it plunging into a V. Her sapphire earbobs were a perfect compliment to the dress, which Taylor saw as simply elegant.

"Thank you." Naomi turned away, blushing.

Taylor took a swig of his whiskey and observed the red fade from Naomi's face as he held her hand and brushed it with his lips. When the white lights dimmed, Taylor cut his eyes toward the soft blue illuminating the center stage. The band began playing the melody to "Good Morning, Heartache." The emcee appeared, and without a lot of ceremony, he introduced the "magnificent Billie Holiday."

Everybody in the room stood and clapped as Lady Day sauntered on stage wearing a slinky pale-blue strapless evening gown with a white gardenia in her hair. Throughout the evening she sang her most popular recordings, including her newest one, "Lady Sings the Blues." When the song ended, an elated Taylor leaped from his seat, and along with others he chanted her name and shouted a few amens. Suddenly the room darkened with a spotlight on Billie's face. The sultry voice began singing the most controversial song she'd ever recorded, "Strange Fruit."

When she finished, the room went pitch-black. The only sound heard, Billie Holiday stumbling off stage, a low moan escaping her lips. No one stood and clapped, no one whistled, no one yelled for an encore. All Taylor heard were his great-grandparents, former slaves, howling in despair at his great-uncle Brotus swinging from a cypress tree, his wife and children at his feet, begging Jesus for mercy. He shuddered. He couldn't see Naomi caressing his hand, except there was no mistaking her touch. When the dim light came on, he gazed around the room, as his eyes adjusted to the light. Some heads were bowed as if in prayer, others looked down at the stone floor with blank faces. Taylor believed lynching had to be the most evil and soul-wrenching crime against the black man, a cold-blooded murder that ripped apart a mother's heart, and white men celebrated it.

# Chapter 5

Taylor woke to a gloomy Monday morning. As a rule, he'd snooze like a newborn baby after making love to Naomi. Not last night. He'd tossed and turned troubled by Family Life's corrupt business practices. He rolled off the bed and trudged to the bathroom. He lingered in the hot tube of water, and when it cooled, he'd heat it up more. It irritated him that Family Life had stolen money yet again from another bereaved family. Negroes had enough worries trying to survive in a world embittered by the evils of racism and segregation, worn down by anger and riots, and now this. After thirty minutes or so, he dried off, dressed, and went downstairs for breakfast.

* * *

Naomi stood in the kitchen, glancing out the window at the red and purple mums she'd planted near the backyard fence, while humming an Ella Fitzgerald tune, "In time the Rockies may crumble, Gibraltar may tumble, they're only made of clay, but our love is here to stay."

"***Good morning***," she sang to Taylor, and set a plate of creamed chipped beef on toast and black coffee in front of him.

"Just get the paper!" he demanded.

"Oh no!" Naomi exclaimed. "Oh no!" She juggled her cup of coffee, dripping some on herself and on the floor. She put the cup down, placed her hands on her hips, and cut into Taylor. "Have you lost your right mind? Don't you ever, ever ask me for anything that way again, never!"

Taylor looked at her narrowed eyes, fixed on him, creamed chipped beef dangling from his fork like a dried leaf covered with white gravy. "Naomi, I'm sorry." He stood and grabbed her hands. "Family Life's got me riled. We wouldn't be worrying about money if they hadn't stolen from their clients. I know one thing, when I finish with them, they'll be lucky if they can sell candy."

"I don't give a darn about who riled you! You better be careful how you talk to me," Naomi told him, "what you say to me."

"You're right, baby. I know better than to disrespect you." Taylor kissed the palms of her hands.

"Don't play with me, because I'm not putting up with it," she said.

Taylor held Naomi close to him. "It won't happen again. When I'm through here, I'm calling the insurance board and paying Family Life a visit. Don't forget Mrs. Pickett is coming at ten o'clock to make arrangements for Lilly Mae's funeral. Offer her the least-expensive casket. We've got to cut back."

Still agitated, Naomi peeled away from him. "You plan to take on every company that steals from their customers." Not waiting for an answer, she said, "You can't fight for everyone who comes through these doors, Taylor. And I'm not talking about this one company, there's always going to be others."

Taylor shot back. "What do you mean? People are fighting and dying for us every day, or have you forgotten about the lynching and murders still going on down South?" Naomi didn't answer, and Taylor didn't force her to. They ate in silence. When he finished, he kissed Naomi on the cheek and went to call the insurance board. Customer service directed him to mail his complaint in writing, saying it would be passed on to the complaint department.

"Connect me to the complaint department, I'll speak with them now," Taylor said.

"Sir, your complaint has to be in writing, it's our policy."

Taylor slammed down the receiver. He stomped upstairs to the bedroom like a rejected kid. He donned his suit jacket and brushed lint off the sleeve. He ran back down the steps to the kitchen. Naomi had left. ***Probably in the morgue.***

* * *

Gray clouds covered the entire sky, not leaving a hint of blue anywhere, unlike the day before when rays of sun had brightened the heavens like fireworks on the Fourth of July. Because of light traffic, it took Taylor less than the usual thirty minutes to reach Family Life offices on Fourteenth Street. The company occupied all three floors of a corner row house that had a large red, black, and green sign in the picture window that read, "Family Life Insurance Company, You can depend on us." The slogan had sucked in so many people.

Taylor remembered the Negroes in Business meeting he'd attended in March. He'd almost caused a riot when he stood up in front of everybody and said Family Life had made a lot of money stealing from their clients. Afterward, Rutherford Daniels, the company president, had threatened to sue him for libel. Taylor realized a meeting with him might be testy. He wondered if Daniels was still fuming at the mouth.

The receptionist recognized Taylor immediately from his picture in the ***Negro News*** society page. He'd been featured in the paper a few times, most recently because of infant Sara. She buzzed Daniels, and a few minutes later, he offered Taylor a seat in his office. Suited up, Daniels appeared not much taller than Taylor, with a lanky build. He gave Taylor the once-over, not a bad thing except his thick eyebrows met in the middle, giving the impression he only had one long eyebrow.

"I won't need to sit as what I have to say won't take a minute, Mr. Daniels," Taylor said. "We talked before, and it didn't go well. Let's be reasonable now. White folks have done everything they can to keep us down. The harder we work, the more prosperous we become, the more bitter they get. They don't want us to have nothing. You and me, we provide a service to our people. They trust us because we're one of them. But when one has been cheated by us, we lose business from others. I just had a distraught mother come to me whose child died, and your company canceled her insurance policy. The sad part about it, she didn't even know the policy had been canceled. You can imagine how she felt."

"Listen, I told you before, we do everything we can to help people keep their coverage. Maybe her payments were late," Daniels said.

"I saw the receipts, she paid on time," Taylor said. "Why are you all stealing from your own people?"

"We're not stealing from anybody! I told you, if you make that claim in public again, I'll sue you for everything you're worth," Daniels responded.

"You just refuse to admit it," Taylor said. "Why would seven families swear on the Bible that they paid you every month, show you receipts, and you still cancel their policies?" Taylor took a step toward Daniels, cracking his knuckles, the distinct popping sound resonating in the room. "In spite of the fact you've committed fraud, you're a liar, sir!"

Taylor was the most-talked-about Negro undertaker in DC because he'd helped so many people in the city. They loved and respected him. His word meant something, and Daniels knew it, lawsuit or not. The only reasons he agreed to see him without an appointment were his connections in the community and the fact that he'd cofounded the Funeral Directors and Morticians Association, an important resource for his business. Daniel's face reddened. He swung away from Taylor and sat behind his desk.

"You better be careful what you say about us, Taylor. We're not letting anyone, not even you, destroy our business. You may not be as successful as you are if we didn't cover your people. You need to concern yourself with your own business before you end up with nothing. I know people who can get at your pockets," Daniels said.

Daniels threatened Taylor's business, not him, though Taylor wondered if Daniels knew how much money he'd lost covering expenses for the families Daniels's company had stolen from. "Don't threaten me, Daniels. I'm not one of the poor people you like to steal from. I'm not afraid of you. I told the insurance board that your company is stealing from your clients. You can expect to hear from them soon."

Taylor stalked out of Daniels's office. Anger boiled inside him like hot water in a steam donkey, ready to explode because of too much pressure inside. He slammed the door behind him, furious at Daniels for treating him like some kind of fool. Daniels knew damn well he'd stolen from his clients. Taylor wasn't through with him yet.

# CHAPTER 6

It was only Tuesday, and Taylor had dealt with more crap in the past two days than he'd bargained for. The World Series had always created an air of excitement for him, not today. Fooling with Daniels had put a damper on his enthusiasm. He'd wanted to knock the daylights out of him, instead he left the man sitting behind his desk, fuming at the mouth. Taylor mulled over the incident. ***Daniels thinks it's all right to steal from poor grieving families. I got news for him.***

Taylor drove to the ***Negro News's*** office on Twelfth Street Northwest. When he entered the one-story building, a haze of stale cigarette smoke met him at the door. Water quickly pooled in his eyes, and he wondered how anyone managed to breathe, let alone work all day in the smoke-filled room. And it seemed as if all the telephones in the room were ringing off the hook. Copyboys slid from one reporter's desk to another, collecting stories that would eventually connect readers to the best and worst moments in DC, while typewriter keys vibrated throughout the room, sounding like tap dancers out of sync with each other.

Taylor perused the hectic office, no one at the receptionist's desk and no sign of Easton. To his left a man sat in a wheelchair, pounding away on a typewriter, his back to Taylor. "Excuse me, sir." Taylor touched the man's shirtsleeve. The man swung around, almost bumping into him. "I didn't mean to startle you, son." He peered down at the empty space where a leg used to be. "Is Easton Priest here?"

"Mr. Taylor, it's a pleasure meeting you. I remember you from your picture in the ***Negro News.*** I'm Lloyd B. Cooke." The man extended his hand toward Taylor. "I'll get him for you. You can sit here, sir." He pointed to a chair beside his desk.

Taylor watched Lloyd roll away to find Easton.

* * *

"Your girlfriend's father is here to see you. Be careful, I think he's got a shotgun with him," Lloyd said, snickering.

Easton dropped a handful of papers and hurried into the newsroom. "Mr. Taylor, how can I help you?" Easton shook his hand.

"I have a situation that needs investigating," Taylor replied. "Can we talk in private?"

"The meeting room, we can talk there."

"Did you enjoy ***Carmen Jones***?" Taylor asked as they walked together.

Easton smiled. "Yes, I did. Dorothy Dandridge, Pearl Bailey, Harry Belafonte all in one movie. They can sing and act."

"You telling me," Taylor exclaimed.

Eager for Easton to hear his case, Taylor painted a picture of a corrupt company that had stolen money from poor people at one of the most venerable times in their lives, leaving them even more saddened and hopeless. "I feel confident that you can unearth more details about the company's appalling practices if the paper agrees to conduct an in-depth investigation of the company. When can I expect to hear from you?"

Easton agreed to help, promising to call him after he talked with his boss. "I'll need names and phone numbers of the families involved."

"They're in my office," Taylor replied. "I'll call you when I get home."

* * *

Taylor went straight home to his office, gathered the information Easton requested, and called him. Easton hadn't spoken to his boss yet, so Taylor still didn't know if the ***Negro News*** planned to investigate the company. He strolled into the kitchen to find his son, Thomas, and Naomi at the table, eating. William Thomas Taylor IV eased halfway out of his seat.

"Hey, Daddy," Thomas said, his mouth full of food. Elaine, Thomas's mother, wanted to call him Thomas instead of William so he'd have his own identity. It didn't bother Taylor too much. Thomas's lack of interest in the funeral business disappointed him more. He chose accounting as a profession and serviced small-business owners in the city. Thomas often stopped by Sixth Street during the day since he set his own schedule.

Taylor glanced at his watch. "You working today?"

"I quit my job," Thomas answered. "My boss and I didn't agree—on principle." He twirled his fork around on the table.

"Principle, what the hell are you talking about?" Taylor's brow puckered. He threw his sandwich on the plate. "Thomas . . . my office now."

Thomas glimpsed at Naomi grinning. "Here we go again." He pimped into Taylor's office.

Taylor slammed the door behind him. He beat down on the wooden floor with his feet and gave Thomas the blues for quitting yet another job.

* * *

After ten minutes or so, Naomi heard a loud thud. She ran to the office and tried to open the door. Someone had locked it. She heard Thomas whimpering. "Is everything all right in there?"

"Everything's fine, Naomi, leave us be," Taylor said in a gruff voice.

Naomi had never known Taylor to be violent or to use physical force against anyone. But he'd been pushed to the brink, angry with Family Life for stealing Mrs. Pickett's money, and now, Thomas had quit a job, yet again. She sat in the telephone chair table in the hall and waited. A half hour later, the two men went through the door. Seeing Thomas in one piece, she returned to the kitchen.

Taylor started for the front door. "I'll call you later," he said to Thomas. Taylor believed his heart had flipped a few times during the fight with his son. He sat in his car and took in a deep breath, taken aback at what Thomas had told him. He gunned the engine and sped off to confront Doc Nelson, his ace boon coon, his son's godfather, about supplying Thomas with drugs to get high.

* * *

Doc's Pharmacie, on New Hampshire Avenue in Northwest DC, sat between Edith's Beauty Shop and Michael & Sons' Printers. The beauty shop doors were propped open, and the odor of burnt hair from the hot combs used to straighten it hovered outside, causing the hair in Taylor's nostrils to bristle. He heard the cranking sound from the printer, housed in the rear of Michael & Sons', even with the door closed, and in the Pharmacie window, old relics used to mix medicines, and porcelain figurines of doctors and nurses, were displayed, along with bottles of aspirin, seltzers, and jars of Musterole and VapoRub, medicines TV ads had encouraged people to buy for the aches, pains, and upset stomachs from the flu. Taylor raced past the counter, the clerk fast on his heels.

"Dr. Nelson isn't here!" the clerk shouted at Taylor.

Taylor burst into Doc Nelson's office. No sign of him anywhere.

"I told you, Dr. Nelson isn't here," the clerk repeated himself. "He's at Saint Elizabeth's."

Taylor didn't mouth a word. He didn't even look at the clerk. He just left.

* * *

Taylor drove through the Anacostia neighborhood of southeast to Asylum Road and Saint Elizabeth's Hospital, once called the Government Hospital for the Insane. The red brick buildings that comprised the mental institution covered three hundred acres split on both sides of the road. There was no reason to be on Asylum Road, unless you had business at the hospital, since the road came to a dead-end. Taylor remembered the four people who'd disappeared on the road, one each year for the past six years, their cars found abandoned in the same spot. The two men and two women were never found. None of them were connected to patients at the hospital. All of them were Negroes. Most Negroes believed the Klan kidnapped them. The elder Negroes believed that demons roaming the grounds of the hospital got hold of them. Taylor didn't know what to believe, except he didn't want to be on the road any longer than necessary. He sped up the hill to a three-story building that housed the pharmacy where Doc Nelson worked part-time.

Taylor barged into Doc's office. "Thomas said you're giving him illegal drugs. Why you trying to poison my son?" Taylor yelled.

"What?" Doc shut the door, looking alarmed.

"Now I know why he can't keep a job. Why you trying to kill my son?" Taylor's hands clenched, ready to strike.

"Keep your voice down, my workers can hear you," Doc begged.

"The hell with them." Taylor spun around and hit the wall with his fist. "I trusted you with my son."

"He told me he hurt his back playing baseball, so I gave him pain pills. I tried to help him, or didn't he tell you that part?" Doc Nelson asked.

"He told me about his back. He didn't tell me you were treating him," Taylor replied, moving within inches of Doc's face. "What else are you giving him?"

Doc stepped back and replied, "I haven't given him anything for three months."

"So where's he getting the drugs?" Taylor asked. "Let me guess . . . you hooked him up with someone else to keep your hands clean, right?"

"Man, what's wrong with you? I wouldn't do that to Thomas!" Doc yelled. "If he's on something, he's not getting it from me. Go back and talk to your son."

"I will, then I'm coming back here," Taylor responded, cracking his knuckles. "Until I do, don't give Thomas another damn drug, not even aspirin, unless it's a matter of life or death. Do we understand each other?" Taylor pointed his finger right between Doc's eyes.

Doc looked down at his friend. "I'm sorry." He reached to shake Taylor's hand. "I should've said something to you. I love you and Thomas, you know that."

"Don't give me a reason to doubt you. It hurt me to think you, of all people, would mess up Thomas with drugs," Taylor exclaimed. "And don't mention this to his mother, Naomi, or anyone else. They don't need to worry. His problem stays here, between us." He started toward the door then stopped and looked back at Doc. Doc turned away.

* * *

Two hours and two shots of whiskey later, Taylor sat at his desk, staring at a picture of him and Doc Nelson on a fishing trip. He pulled a pint of whiskey from a drawer and poured another shot. He smiled, reflecting on their boyhood days, flirting with death—jumping from huge oak trees onto barren earth, racing their bikes alongside speeding cars, and jumping onto soda trucks to grab a few cold ones. And as young men, how Doc had intervened more than once to save his ass from an irate husband or jealous boyfriend after he'd carried on illicit affairs with other men's wives and girlfriends. The community forgave him; his first wife didn't. She divorced him. Doc merely told the jilted men, "You want him, you got to come through me first." Fortunate for Taylor, no one wanted to take on Doc. He'd been known to throw a mean punch. A rather dignified-looking brother, the same height as Easton with broad shoulders and long arms. Red freckles covered cinnamon-colored cheeks, and a pointed goatee accentuated his triangular face.

Doc Nelson and his wife, Dorothy, who happened to be Naomi's first cousin, had done more than enough to help Taylor with Thomas after his divorce. ***Somebody is lying,*** Taylor thought. Doc said he gave Thomas something for his back pain, nothing more, though Thomas had been adamant about Doc supplying him with all kinds of drugs. In spite of Thomas's irresponsible behavior, Taylor had never known him to lie.

Naomi strutted into the office. Taylor didn't budge. She slithered around his desk, her body poised in front of him. Lured by the smell of her perfume, he rested his head on her breast, his hands around her waist. "Maybe he'd be more responsible if I had raised him myself," Taylor said.

"Stop blaming yourself. Let him go and let God take over. He already knows how to help Thomas," Naomi said, caressing his face.

"He's my boy, I have to take some blame," Taylor said, his voice weary.

"Well, you can do that later," Naomi said. "Come on, I need help in the kitchen now."

Taylor followed Naomi, a heavy feeling in his heart for her. He swore he'd heard birds singing in his head the first time he saw her. After nineteen years, she still captivated him. Simply being close to her lessened his anger and the sick feeling in his stomach after learning that his best friend may have been doping his son.

# Chapter 7

Easton moved through the room like he had wings, flying high after Taylor left his office. Unsettling as the allegations sounded, the prospect of investigating a million-dollar company planted a big smile on his face. He believed exposing fraud in one of DC's most successful Negro businesses might pay off in a handsome raise, boost his career, and impress his future father-in-law. He quickly jotted down all the sordid details Taylor had disclosed about Family Life Insurance Company. If they are stealing from their clients, Easton wondered what else they were doing. He had a policy with the company too, and if the allegations turned out to be true, he'd be the first person to cancel his policy, and he expected everyone else would once they read his report.

While reaching for his cigarettes, Easton knocked over his coffee. He jumped up, a stream of the hot liquid running down his pant leg. "Shit," he said, brushing the coffee off his pants with a handkerchief. He looked at his watch. He didn't have time to go home and change before his date with Ruth. He hurried to the john. He patted his wet slacks with a towel, trying to absorb the moisture. Other than the clinging wet feeling on his legs, he saw no visible stain on his black slacks. He rinsed out his hanky, returned to his desk, and draped it on the back of his wooden chair to dry. He then kneeled on the speckled linoleum floor dotted with brown burn circles from cigarettes stamped into the pattern and soaked up the small slurry of coffee muddled with black dust particles from carbon paper.

Easton rang his boss, Aaron Holt, proprietor and chief editor of the ***Negro News***, at home sick with the flu. He had acquired the newspaper from his late uncle after no other Holt in the family expressed an interest in it.

"Aaron, Easton here. Sorry to bother you. I need to tell you about a conversation I just had with William Taylor . . . please."

"It can't wait?" Aaron asked.

"I'm talking fraud in the largest Negro insurance company in the city," Easton said.

"I'm listening," Aaron said.

Easton gave an account of the questionable dealings of Family Life Insurance Company that, according to William Taylor, had left several families without coverage or money to bury their dead. He let Aaron know that he wanted to lead the investigation on the alleged corruption. Even though Aaron considered Easton one of his top investigative reporters, he had reservations about him taking the lead on this one.

"I'm giving it to someone else, someone who can be objective," Aaron said.

"You're implying that I can't be objective because Mr. Taylor is Ruth's father?" Easton asked. "Aaron, he's the victim here."

"That's my point," Aaron replied. "You've already decided that he's right and the company is wrong, and you haven't even started the investigation."

"Okay, okay, you're right. I'm not thinking," Easton responded. "I know better."

"I know you do." Aaron sighed. "And I know what this means to you, so I won't stand in your way this time. Understand me now, I won't accept anything less than your best, and I know what that is. And remember, this investigation is not just about Family Life. It's about Taylor too. If the allegations are true, the company will try and bring Taylor down with them. You're bound to hear things about him that might curl your lips. Don't let your relationship with him cloud your mind."

"Thanks, Aaron, I won't disappoint you."

"Don't disappoint yourself," Aaron replied, and hung up.

"All right now!" Easton shouted. He immediately called William Taylor. "Mr. Taylor, the ***Negro News*** has agreed to investigate the allegations of fraud in Family Life Insurance Company that you brought forward to us today, and I will be leading the effort."

"Thank you, son. I have no doubts that you'll be thorough in your investigation," Taylor said.

Easton rushed over to Lloyd's desk. "Lloyd, drop what you're doing, we've got a new assignment, ***Black-Collar Crime***." Easton gave him a rundown of Family Life's alleged activities and a list of former clients affected. "If the allegations are true, we can bank on a criminal investigation down the road. Remember, we aren't lawyers or cops, so we can talk to any agency or person about this company. We're not legally bound to anyone, just to the truth, so don't feel limited in your inquiries. Now if we mess up, we might end up in jail or sued with the bad guys still on the street. Our biggest challenge is getting people to talk with us, let alone tell us the truth. Sometimes you can win them over just by being charming."

"You want me to smile a lot?" Lloyd asked.

"Something like that," Easton replied, laughing. "I need to cancel my date with Ruth this evening. I'll be right back." The hospital where Ruth worked had strict rules about personal calls. Immediate family only, so he dared not call her at work, he called Naomi instead.

"Taylor's Funeral Home, may I help you?"

Easton hesitated as he always did when Ruth or Naomi answered the phone. In truth, they sounded alike on the phone, and he had to be careful what he said. "Mrs. Taylor, this is Easton. Can you please call and tell Ruth I can't pick her up today? I have an investigation I need to start working on now. I won't finish what I need to do before three thirty. I'll call her this evening."

"I'll let her know," Naomi promised.

Next, Easton called Odean, one of his contacts on the street. "Do you have life insurance with Family Life?"

"Why you asking?" Odean asked.

"Investigation I'm conducting," Easton replied.

"No, I don't. My sister does," Odean replied. "What do you want to know?"

"If Family Life ever canceled her policy and why," Easton responded. "As a matter of fact, if anybody tells you the company canceled their policy, I want to know . . . I need to talk to them."

"Since you aren't telling me why I'm asking the question, I guess I have to make up something," Odean replied.

"Didn't you tell me you used to be a big liar?" Easton asked.

"You don't forget nothing, do you?" Odean asked.

"No, I don't," Easton replied. "Thank you, brotha."

# Chapter 8

On Wednesday morning, October $10^{th}$, Easton began interviewing the alleged victims of Family Life's scam he and Lloyd had tracked down the day before. He'd interview one family, and they'd tell him about another family who'd suffered the same pain and humiliation. Some were reluctant to talk because they didn't want their names in the paper. Others didn't care as long as they got their money in the end.

Easton also drove to Baltimore and met with Carson Zeb, president of the Funeral Directors and Morticians Association, who affirmed Taylor's accusations against Family Life.

"Let's be honest, sir," Easton said. "Were you afraid if you reported them to the insurance board, undertakers in the area might lose business?"

"I'd expected they might lose some business," he replied. "Mind you, people have to go somewhere to funeralize their dead, so they weren't going to lose all their business."

"Thank you for your time, sir. You've been most helpful. I believe retaliation will be the least of your worries." Easton shook his hand and left to meet with a former classmate from Howard University, now an attorney, at the Baltimore City Courthouse. Easton had called and asked him to search for possible civil suits or lawsuits filed against Family Life. The attorney had uncovered three lawsuits filed against the company and its executives over the past four years. In three of the lawsuits, the families had sued the company for half a million dollars for stealing their money and causing extreme suffering. When the attorney briefed Easton about the suits, he figured the three complainants had the same lawyer; they all read the same.

"It's all here." Easton's friend handed him a large brown envelope.

"Thanks, brotha. When you coming to the city?" Easton asked.

"Next Friday's payday . . . the eagle will be flyin'. I'll call you."

Easton shook the brotha's hand and slipped him a couple of dollars. Information cost: ***you take care of me, I'll take care of you.*** It didn't matter if the information came from someone on the street, sitting behind a desk, or an old friend from school; they all got paid. Sometimes he'd spend almost a whole week's salary buying information. In the end, Aaron reimbursed him for what he'd spent and gave him a small bonus too, depending on the outcome of the investigation. And he never turned down favors from well-connected people like Taylor, a living encyclopedia of the rich and powerful, poor and humble, charitable and hustlers, and those on the take. And as Taylor once told Easton, "A dead body can tell you a lot, so don't ever believe that your secrets go to the grave with you. If I see something that ain't right, I write it down, just in case I need to use the information later."

"Sounds like blackmail," Easton had said.

"Blackmail . . . of course not, Easton," Taylor had replied. "I'd only reveal what I know for business reasons."

* * *

The blue sky had turned gray, and rain began to drizzle as Easton left Baltimore and headed back to DC. Traffic going South on Route 1 crawled for only a few miles, then the rain stopped. Bright rays of sun peered through the clouds, and cars revved up to the seventy-five-mile-an-hour speed limit as if they were racing for the finish line. Easton arrived at Superior Court in no time.

"Easton Priest, it's good to see you, man," his contact said, shaking Easton's hand. "When you called yesterday, I requested the documents you wanted as soon as we hung up, so I expect the courier to walk through that door in thirty minutes or so. The cafeteria is still open for business, if you want coffee while you wait. I'll have everything ready when you get back."

* * *

Before Easton entered the small eatery, he smelled the distinct odor of burned coffee. The smell reminded him of wood burning in the smoke pits used to deliver smoke to the old smokehouses in Tennessee, where his family and many others paid to preserve and house their meat, because they didn't have enough money to buy a refrigerator. The smoking would take two, maybe three weeks, depending on the meat, and after it is cooked and served on his plate, he'd savor every bite. He wondered how long the coffee had been sitting. He bought an orange soda instead and a bag of potato chips.

Easton nodded at familiar faces though he grappled with where he'd seen them. He talked with other reporters who were waiting to cover a hearing involving a woman who shot and killed her husband. Before he got up to leave, he spotted Samia Cox, his college love, though the sparks hadn't flown both ways.

"What a surprise," Easton said, hugging Samia. "Looking good, looking good, woman! What have you been up to since graduation?"

"I'm in my second year at Howard's Law School, clerking for Judge Hammond this semester," she said, beaming at him. "What about you?"

"Reporter for the ***Negro News***."

"Oh yes, I've read some of your articles."

"Do you represent clients in the courtroom?" Easton asked.

"Not yet. I assist where I can," she replied. "Are you married?"

"I'm involved," Easton responded, giving no clear indication that he planned to marry Ruth. "Are you still with Ross 'the Boss' Stewart?"

"Hell no!" Samia replied. "He loved himself more than he loved his mother. He didn't have room for anyone in his life unless it was on his terms." She looked at her watch. "Sorry, I need to run. It's been so good seeing you." She kissed him on the cheek and whispered in his ear. "Call me if you become uninvolved."

"I'll do that," Easton answered. ***Temptation is a bitch.*** He had been infatuated with Samia his sophomore year—missing classes, halfway doing homework, and almost failing his English class trying to keep up with her. He smiled, thinking how foolish he'd acted running after her and she'd wanted someone else. Before he knew it, thirty minutes had passed. He rushed back to his contact's office.

"It's all here." His contact handed him an envelope.

Easton thanked him with the last five bills in his pocket.

* * *

Around eight o'clock that evening, Easton interviewed the last victim of Family Life's scam that he knew about and hurried back to the ***News*** room, where Lloyd waited for him. Stacked in front of Lloyd were notepads and papers containing information from his inquiries.

"Whoa . . . look-ka here, me and you gonna be working all night, brotha," Easton said, eyeing all the documents. "And I haven't laid my papers out yet."

The two men worked past midnight, sifting through all the information they'd gathered. When they finished, Easton stood and stretched his arms and legs. He lit a cigarette, turned up the radio and sang along with Muddy Waters, "Still a Fool." He tapped his foot in time to the music, and when it ended . . .

"Damn, there's no solid evidence Family Life committed fraud, just the policyholder's word against the company, and that's not enough," Easton said, disappointment in his voice. "Taylor is going to hit the ceiling, and Aaron won't be happy either if the report doesn't sell a lot of papers."

"What now?" Lloyd asked.

Easton glanced at his pocket watch, a graduation gift from his parents. "It's one o'clock in the morning. Let's split."

# CHAPTER 9

Wednesday evening, October 11, five days after Lilly Mae Pickett died, Taylor moved her coffin to the family's small apartment for the evening wake. He positioned the coffin in front of the living room window and watched the sunbeams bounce off her death mask, back to the sun. Later that evening, Lilly Mae's parents sat beside her. Taylor watched as her teachers, neighbors, family members, and schoolmates paused and stared at the little girl, tears streaming down their faces. Some gently placed stuffed animals and dolls around her, not wanting to disturb her it seemed. It made Taylor's heart ache. He toddled over to Naomi, who sat cradling two little girls, one on each knee, as they wept. Ushers from the Picketts' church also comforted the little ones as they struggled with their friend's death. When the wake ended, he assured Mr. and Mrs. Pickett that he'd pick them up at ten o'clock in the morning for the funeral.

* * *

When Taylor and Naomi returned home, Taylor found a note taped to the phone.

"I see Thomas came by," Taylor said, holding up a piece of paper. "Carson Zeb called, I wonder what he wants."

"For you to run the next meeting," Naomi replied.

Carson Zeb, president of the Funeral Directors and Morticians Association, often asked Taylor to run the quarterly meetings because he had a knack for sticking to the agenda, unlike Carson Zeb, who placated members and very little got done. Taylor called him.

"Easton Priest, from the ***Negro News***, came all the way from DC to meet with me about Family Life," Carson Zeb said to Taylor. "Did you send him here?"

"No . . . no," Taylor replied. "I'm glad to hear he's on the job though. Family Life knows they're under investigation, it's no secret. They may try to steer some of their clients to white undertakers for spite. Mind you, most coloreds will still come to us to funeralize their dead, if that's what you're worried about."

"I don't want trouble," the president responded.

"Trouble! Zeb, the company is stealing from your clients, you already got trouble," Taylor responded. "Wake up, man . . . this is bigger than you." Taylor questioned Zeb's understanding of the problem. ***Either he's ignorant or pocketing***

***a piece of the action.*** He called Easton at work. “I just talked to Carson Zeb. You must’ve scared the shit out of him. He doesn’t want trouble.”

Easton chuckled. “How does he plan to get around it?”

“He’s not,” Taylor replied. “Unless he’s in on the scam. How’s the investigation going?”

“We heard stories similar to yours from other undertakers and policyholders, and we reviewed a few lawsuits filed by Family Life’s former clients accusing the company of stealing their money. Unfortunately, the suits didn’t go anywhere because the policyholders were too poor to pay the lawyers. I believe once we determine who cashed the money orders for the monthly payments, there might be a strong case for fraud. Please hold on to those money order receipts. We shared what we learned with the insurance board this morning, and they reluctantly agreed to audit Family Life. We’re still going to print a report, hoping other people will come forward with more information we can work with,” Easton told Taylor. “Look for my report in the morning paper.”

“Hold on a minute,” Taylor said. “Did you find any evidence of fraud or not?”

“No, we didn’t,” Easton replied. “No concrete proof of fraud.”

“Dammit . . . You mean to say we have to bow to the devil and allow those crooks to keep stealing money from poor people?”

Easton hesitated before answering. “No, sir. We plan to continue the investigation.”

Taylor acknowledged Easton’s efforts despite the fact they weren’t going to help the least of God’s children or his pocketbook. “Maybe you don’t have any concrete evidence right now, but when you get it, and I believe you will, we’re all going to be surprised at just how deceptive Family Life is.”

* * *

After the report went to press, Easton met his friend Toast at a joint on U Street. Toast, birth name Ray, had come by his nickname because his skin looked like toasted bread. Easton and Toast had attended high school together in Tennessee. Toast went on to graduate from a college in Knoxville, Tennessee, then moved to DC, got a job teaching, and coached varsity basketball at Dubois High School. Though Toast was married and had a two-year-old son, he and Easton hook up at least once a month for drinks.

“What you drinking?” Easton asked, shaking his hand.

“Gin and tonic,” Toast answered. “They don’t have anything stronger.”

“Bad day?” Easton asked.

“My mother-in-law is sick in Mississippi, so Yvonne is upset, Malcolm is irritable. The whole house is in turmoil. I told her to go see her mother so she’d stop worrying. I just might be free this weekend,” he answered. “Whatcha been up to, man?”

"I almost had a big story," Easton replied.

"About what?" Toast asked.

Easton sat on a stool next to Toast and ordered bourbon straight up. "Alleged fraud in Family Life Insurance Company. Taylor asked the ***News*** to investigate the company because he believes they stole money from their poor clients. Apparently, when they tried to collect their death benefits, Family Life had canceled their policies because they missed payments, even though Taylor showed me money order receipts saying otherwise. I begged Aaron to let me lead the investigation and didn't prove squat."

"You couldn't use the receipts?" Toast asked.

"We have to prove that Family Life actually cashed the money orders, and since they won't talk to us, we can't prove shit," Easton replied. "Is your life insurance policy with Family Life?"

"Yeah . . . life and disability, in case I'm injured on the basketball court or pass out and break my neck when I leave here," Toast answered.

"Well, you aren't poor, so they won't mess with you." Easton laughed. "My gut tells me they're shady as hell, and I for one don't believe Taylor would ask us to investigate the company on a hunch."

Easton burned another cigarette and changed the subject to Ruth. He talked nineteen to the dozen about marrying her and the engagement ring he bought. "Will you be my best man?"

"What took you so long to ask? I'll be honored to stand by you, Mr. Priest," Toast replied. "Ruth is a beautiful spirit." Their glasses clinked for what was to be.

Easton's mood slowly disintegrated into self-pity, his mind now foggy from all the alcohol he'd poured into his body. Two hours and five drinks later and high as a kite, "They're no good, you hear me," Easton hurled at Toast.

"Whoa . . . slow down, brotha, it's me, Toast."

Easton took another swig of bourbon. He lowered his voice and said, "Sorry, man, I let Taylor down, and I was banking on a nice bonus this year . . . for my honeymoon. My report will be in the ***Negro News*** tomorrow. Read it."

"Whatever you say," Toast replied.

Two honeys strutted into the bar.

"To be single again," Toast said, grinning. One of the women sat at the bar next to him.

"Down, boy, down," Easton said. "You want to change seats?"

"I'm allowed to socialize," Toast exclaimed.

"As long as you keep your hands to yourself. Now me, I'm not married yet." Easton, with a little swagger in his step, left his barstool and approached the other woman. "You sure are fine. Can I buy you a drink?"

"Yes, you can. Rum and Coke, thank you," she said, smiling.

"Bartender, give the ladies what they want," Easton said.

"Easton, you're drunker than me. Let's split before we both get in trouble," Toast said.

"I'm buying the ladies a drink. It's nothing wrong with that," Easton said.

"Tell Ruth that when the woman knocks on your door and says she's pregnant with your bambino," Toast said.

Easton stared at Toast as visions of Ruth making love to another man raced through his mind. "Hey, man, this will take care of the drinks." He handed the bartender a few bills and turned toward the women. "You ladies have a nice evening."

The two men staggered out of the bar and into the cool night air. Suddenly Toast grabbed Easton's shoulder and lowered his head as if in prayer. "I'm sick!" he exclaimed, and stumbled to the curb. It appeared as if everything he'd eaten that day gushed out of his mouth like water from a hydrant and splattered on the road. People passed by Toast, shaking their heads. Others moved as far away from him as possible.

Easton stayed with him until he regained his composure enough to drive home, then Easton slid into his ride. He leaned his head against the car window. He didn't know if his eyes were going around in circles or the globes on the lampposts were. He swore he saw images of dead bodies spinning in the night light. He straightened upright, his eyes stretched open. He had a whirling sensation in his head, and his hands trembled from the cool air or maybe from too much alcohol. He wasn't sure. He rummaged through his jacket pocket for a cigarette and took a long drag. He squeezed his eyes shut and lay back on the seat.

In the midst of Easton's drunken fog, he recalled one woman's sad story about her parents' death. They were alleged victims of Family Life, Iroquois from Louisa County, Virginia. The father had developed gangrene after a nail went through his soft-soled moccasins and penetrated his foot. Even though they amputated the infected foot and leg, it was too late. The gangrene had ravaged his body and he died. The daughter went to Family Life to collect his death benefits, only to learn that his life insurance policy had been canceled, supposedly because of missed payments. The daughter showed them receipts and pleaded for the benefits; they ignored her. Her mother fell deeper into sadness, and the next day, at the rising of the sun, she killed herself with a steak knife. Apparently, in her culture, the wife assumed responsibility for paying for her husband's funeral, and the insurance policy was all she had.

Easton's stomach gurgled from anger brewing inside, just like beer boiling and fermenting over time. ***People shouldn't have to go through this.*** He paused for a moment. "Damn . . . I'm beginning to sound like Taylor." He revved the car engine and crept home.

# Chapter 10

At six o'clock Thursday morning, Taylor hurried to his office for the ***Negro News.*** His eyelids still heavy from a restless sleep, he found Easton's report on page 3 of the paper:

**Audit Requested on Family Life Insurance Company's Cancellation Policies**

The president of the Negro Funeral Directors and Morticians Association has asked the DC Insurance Board to conduct an audit of Family Life Insurance Company Inc. to determine if the company is prematurely canceling their client's policies. According to William T. Taylor, director of William T. and Naomi B. Taylor's Funeral Home, "When some beneficiaries have contacted Family Life to claim death benefits, they're told their policies were canceled because they didn't pay premiums for three consecutive months. The families are telling me it's not true, they didn't miss any payments, and they never received a notice of the cancellation." Mr. Taylor shared with the ***Negro News*** that he had seen money order receipts for the monthly payments that prove the families made payments to Family Life. In all, Mr. Taylor claims that seven families came to him over the past year, families who he believes were victims of this alleged fraud. He says the families did not report Family Life to the insurance board because they felt threatened by the company and were afraid if they went public, they might get sued and lose what little they had. Like Taylor, other funeral-home directors voiced similar complaints about the company and reported thousands of dollars in lost revenue burying deceased members of the families affected.

Family Life's president, Rutherford Daniels, had this to say about the allegations: "Family Life Insurance Company is a decent, law-abiding company providing services to hundreds of families in the Washington, DC, area. It's unfortunate that a handful of our clients who failed to pay their premiums, felt the need to levy these charges [stealing their money] against us. By all accounts, when a family is having trouble paying their premiums, we meet with them to work out a payment plan so they can keep their policy. These allegations are not only unfounded, they are absurd."

> The request for an audit comes after the ***Negro News*** conducted an investigation of the alleged fraud. According to Easton Priest, the ***News*** lead investigative reporter, he asked Daniels if the beneficiary's money orders were cashed. Daniels refused to answer. Priest was also denied review of the "notices of cancellation" the company claimed they mailed to families. The insurance board is reviewing the request for an audit of Family Life.

Taylor cracked his knuckles. It wasn't the story he'd hoped for. He wondered what it would take to bring Daniels to his knees. Since he had to conduct Lillie Mae's funeral in a couple of hours, he chose not to dwell on it. He went into the kitchen, a look of disappointment on his face. "Easton's report on Family Life is in the paper . . . no evidence of fraud," he told Naomi. "It doesn't mean they aren't crooks, though. Daniels pretends he's an upstanding citizen, but I can see right through his sorry ass. He's a thief and a scoundrel, and I'm not letting this go until he or somebody in that company is behind bars. Payday will come for everybody they stole from, and when it does, I do intend to collect what we're owed."

Naomi nestled in close to Taylor and wrapped her arms around him. "I read the report, darling. Don't worry, the truth will come out soon enough. It always does."

Taylor's voice crackled as he stared into Naomi's eyes. "Everything—buying caskets, opening graves for poor people-it's costing us a fortune. We need to cut back on spending until this is all over."

"What about the fish fry tomorrow night? It's our turn," Naomi asked. One Friday evening each month, the Taylors and their friends got together for a fish fry. They'd eat, play bid whist, or dance all night.

"We're not canceling the fish fry. Besides, we still have to eat," Taylor replied. "A little music, dancing, we deserve to have some fun."

Taylor brushed the strands of black hair away from Naomi's face. His heart stepped up a beat, and his breathing quickened. He leaned in and pressed his mouth hard on her soft, wet lips. His body forced her back against the kitchen counter. Proud below the navel, he started to sweat. She eased away to breathe. He unbuttoned the front of her dress, loosened her bra, and cupped her smooth, firm breast in his hand.

"Upstairs," Taylor said.

"Taylor, we have a funeral this morning and we haven't eaten breakfast yet," Naomi said.

It had been a while since they had stolen time to make love before their workday began. Taylor had his way, and minutes later, they collapsed beside each other, gasping with pleasure, exhausted from the energy released after long, intense moments of passion. They wallowed in the closeness, listening to the music of Count Basie on the radio; neither spoke. When the news came on, the lovers forced themselves out of bed.

Taylor asked, "Will Ruth be around to help cook tomorrow?"

"No, indeed. She'll be at a bridal shower. It'll be just me and you frying fish," Naomi replied. "Do you want balloons?"

Taylor walked out of the bedroom, laughing. "Sure, why not." ***I love that woman,*** he said to himself, as he walked to the bathroom, though the laughter quickly faded to outrage as he contemplated the possibility of Family Life getting away with fraud. He cracked his knuckles until they hurt. He wanted to go back to Daniels's office and confront him again, to unleash his fury upon the man, to destroy him and all that he stood for. Daniels thievery had affected his family, his livelihood, and Taylor didn't want to let him off the hook. There would be backlash, no doubt, if he struck him or, God forbid, killed him. He didn't believe in the death penalty. It didn't matter what he believed, if convicted of murder, Taylor was going to fry in the electric chair.

# Chapter 11

Friday morning, October 12, Taylor watched Naomi from the front porch, stroll up O Street to the market, pulling a grocery cart behind her. She fell in step with other women heading to the market. His eyes shifted to the top of the marketplace, peeping through the trees lining the neighborhood streets. It happened to be the tallest part of the structure, painted a dull gray, it was triangular, and the windows—taller than they were wide—jutted out on either side of it. Known as the Northern Market, it had served the Shaw community since the late 1800s. One of the largest open-air shopping areas in DC, the market occupied the entire corner of Seventh and O Street Northwest. Built with faded red bricks in a style from the Victorian era, not unlike many other structures in DC, it featured arches and columns around the windows and doors. On sunny days, streams of bright light poured through the windows, temporarily blinding anybody standing in its path. Rain came through too if the windows weren't shut fast enough. Taylor had offered to drive Naomi to the market; she wanted to walk instead. "I need the fresh air," she'd said.

Taylor went to his office and pulled the files on the seven families victimized by Family Life and reviewed their financial statements, something he seldom did since Naomi and Thomas always kept the books. Then he looked at the balance sheet for the business. He cringed, the loss much higher than he'd realized. Naomi didn't lie; they might have to declare bankruptcy if they keep taking on charity cases. If Family Life's fraudulent activities were ever proven, he'd help the families get their money back and leverage to get his.

* * *

Not ten minutes later, Taylor's lawyer, Collin Dewitt Unger, Esq., called him after reading Easton's report. "Since you're quoted in the paper, Family Life may come after you, so be careful what you say in the future and watch your back. I know you well enough to believe that you encouraged Easton Priest to conduct the investigation. With him dating Ruth, don't be surprised if Family Life accuses the ***Negro News*** of bias. Be prepared to explain yourself."

"I'm not worried about those jackasses," Taylor replied. "Let them come after me if they want. I got something for them. And I didn't encourage Easton to do nothing. His boss assigned the case to him."

"Taylor, keep your cool," Unger said. "You really don't know who or what you're dealing with. The investigation may have pissed off the company more than you think. Now . . . what about your losses?"

* * *

An hour later, Naomi returned with the grocery cart loaded to the top. Taylor lugged the heavy cart into the house.

"Everybody is talking about Easton's report," Naomi told Taylor, while putting away groceries. "It seems as if they believe you more than they believe Family Life. They all said thank you. I got my catfish half price and a free cup of coffee, they were so grateful."

"Well, I'll be damned. I guess I'm not the only one who sees through those fools. The Good Lord knows what he's doing. You just wait. I'm going to get back every penny I've shelled out because of them."

"If you remember, Taylor, the families did offer us the money their friends and relatives gave them. You refused to take it," Naomi said.

"They needed it more than we did," Taylor replied.

"Well, next time I'm accepting it since you can't say no to these poor folks," Naomi said, still pulling food from the cart and handing it to Taylor.

"What did you do, buy enough for the whole neighborhood?" Taylor asked.

Naomi laughed. "No, that's something you would do."

"What all is in here?" Taylor asked.

"Dinner," Naomi replied. "By the way, I stopped by Leslie Ann Penny's table. She told me to tell you hello."

Taylor smirked.

"I wonder when she has time to make hats, the way she travels around. And they are absolutely gorgeous. I didn't have time to try any on today. Ruth and I need hats to match the coats I made this summer. She's such a talented young lady."

* * *

Naomi waved through the screened door as their first guests approached the house. "You're here already! I expected you at colored people's time," she said to Yancey and Mildred Jenkins.

"You know we're always on time for a house party at the Taylors'," Yancey said, laughing.

The Nelsons and Parkers arrived a few minutes later. Taylor popped open a bottle of champagne he'd bought for what he thought would be a celebration. He poured some in each flute and raised his for a toast. "To Easton and the ***Negro News*** for investigating Family Life . . . thank you. And to the Good Lord, your poor people don't have much to begin with, and to have Family Life steal what little they do have, please help Easton find evidence to put those crooks away."

"Taylor, helping those people is all well and good, but as far as I'm concerned, a man's business is his business," Ivy Parker said.

"Ivy, if the business is corrupt, what are people to do?" Taylor asked.

"If I'm not mistaken, the investigation didn't prove they were corrupt," Ivy replied.

"Ivy, the investigation is not over," Taylor said.

"Then I guess we'll have to wait and see what happens," Ivy replied.

"What they've done is a disgrace to the Negro race, and I'm going to see to it that they pay for their wrongdoings. They ought to know better than to play with good people!" Taylor said, raising his voice higher than his glass of champagne. When he paused to drink it, Naomi quickly ushered everybody to the dining room to eat.

Naomi lit the two candles in the center of the table and turned down the radio so they'd be able to hear one another talk. Two crystal lamps on the buffet gave off soft light. A homemade pound cake and a bowl of sliced peaches sat between them. She served fried catfish, collard greens, red beans and rice, baked corn muffins, and brewed tea sweetened with sugar and garnished with lemons. She asked Taylor to say a quick prayer over the food and then . . .

"Let's eat."

Everyone praised the meal to high heaven.

"Woman, these collard greens are delicious," Yancey said.

"You aren't kidding," Mildred chimed in. "You must've put your foot in them."

"I did," Naomi replied. "I threw those seeds in the dirt and danced them in the ground with my bare feet."

* * *

With their bellies stuffed, they moved to the parlor. While Taylor pushed the coffee table against the wall, Doc Nelson rolled up the area rug, making room for the four couples to slide across the wood floor when they danced. Naomi blew up five balloons. Taylor laughed like a kid as the eight grown adults knocked them about like children.

After Naomi replaced the white lightbulbs in the lamps with red ones, she shouted, "Are you ready to dance?" She put a stack of 45s on the record player, and before the first one dropped, she started shuffling her feet. The others got in the spirit and did the boogie-woogie to the lively beat of "Straighten up and Fly Right," "Roll with Me, Henry," "What a Little Moonlight Can Do," and "What Is This Thing Called Love?" among others.

After midnight, Taylor begged off the fast tunes. He couldn't cut a rug the way he used to. All the shuffling, spinning, and dipping tired him out. He slowed the tempo with a love song by Nat King Cole, "(I Love You) for Sentimental Reasons," and drew Naomi to him. They pressed close against each other, grinding slowly to the rhythm of the music. "***I love you for sentimental reasons***," Taylor sang in Naomi's ear.

"I love you too," Naomi whispered. "I'll always love you."

Taylor gently stroked Naomi's face, amazed at how glamorous she looked when wearing colors other than black or navy blue, her uniform colors. Her turquoise crepe dress cut low in the front had three rhinestone buttons on the bodice that glimmered when she moved. He knew she'd been sewing something for herself. He didn't expect such elegance. Large silver hoop earrings dangled from under a thick mane the color of coal, and to him she was the most beautiful woman in the world—light, bright and almost white, as Negroes would say, and deep red colored her lips. An imposing five foot nine with long legs, she equaled the height of most men and towered over Taylor with high heels on.

Taylor and Naomi had both experienced their share of pain, sorrow, and broken hearts before they met each other through Dorothy, Naomi's cousin. Two years after they met, they married. They'd just celebrated their nineteenth wedding anniversary in June.

Around one thirty in the morning, Naomi turned off the record player. She sat at the upright piano Taylor had bought her for Christmas one year, and played "Autumn Leaves." Mildred sang the lyrics.

Taylor sat with his mouth open, surprised at how long Mildred held the last note. He wondered how she managed to breathe, in awe of her amazing talent. Doc Nelson felt the same way.

"Watch out, Billie Holiday, Mildred Jenkins is in the house," Doc Nelson shouted.

Yancey raised his shot of whiskey and praised the duo's performance. "Lawd, today, you two need to go on the road and make some money so Taylor and I can retire."

"I'll carry your luggage," Parker said.

Laughter filled the room. Soon after, the party petered out and their friends left.

* * *

Naomi headed for the kitchen to wash dishes, leaving Taylor to put the parlor back together. She'd finished drying the last of the pots and pans when Taylor snuck up behind her and wrapped his arms around her waist.

"Boy, your catfish tasted sensational. You outdid yourself, woman!" Taylor said, laughing.

"Thank you, darling, but we both know you were hungry."

"That's true. The food still tasted good, baby." He held her tighter.

"The dishes . . . I'm not waking up to a dirty kitchen," Naomi said, and wiggled from his grip.

Taylor went into the pantry and fetched a bottle of sherry. "A little night cap for us." He filled the two sherry glasses Naomi had set on the table.

Naomi put away the last of the dishes and sat next to Taylor. "What a fabulous party. Did you see the moonlight coming through the window with that cool breeze?"

"That's when I fell in love with you again." He grinned, sipping on his drink.

"Well, I love a good time," she said, blushing. "We have to do this more often."

Taylor nodded in agreement.

After Naomi finished her third glass of sherry, she stood, a bit tipsy, and said in a sexy voice, "Darling, I'll be waiting for you, don't take too long." She leaned over, kissed Taylor on the lips, and left him at the table.

Taylor imagined her lying back in the claw-foot bathtub, her feet hanging over the edge, her skin glistening from the moist heat. She'd put on either the blue satin nightgown or the red one trimmed in black lace, his favorites. Three glasses of sherry always knocked Naomi out, so he knew he had to hurry and close up the house if he wanted to make love to her; otherwise he'd have to wait until morning, which wasn't such a terrible thought.

The wood floors creaked in the quiet of the night as he scurried from room to room, closing windows and turning off lights. Before flicking off his desk lamp, the ***Negro News*** caught his eye, still folded open to Easton's article, "Audit Requested on Family Life Insurance Company's Cancellation Policies." He hated what the company had done to poor Negroes. Someday soon their fraudulent activities would be exposed. Only then might he move on. He looked at his watch, two thirty in the morning. He returned to the kitchen and downed the last of the sherry. As he walked toward the pantry to trash the empty bottle, he heard footsteps clicking on the linoleum behind him. Smiling, he turned around. "Baby, you missed me?"

* * *

A loud noise, glass breaking, voices. Naomi sat straight up in bed. She felt for Taylor—not there. She switched on the light by her bed, rubbed her eyes, and squinted at the clock—two forty in the morning.

"Taylor!" Naomi called out. "Taylor, where are you?"

Taylor didn't answer. She put on her robe and ran downstairs. The light in the kitchen still on, a whiff of cold air greeted her at the door. ***He forgot to close the pantry door.*** She tightened her robe. When she reached the kitchen, she froze in her tracks. Taylor lay sprawled on the floor, the front of his white shirt now red. She screamed to the top of her lungs. Her legs buckled and she crumpled to her knees.

"Oh lord! No, Lord!" she bellowed, crawling to him. After she reached him, she cupped his head in her trembling hands. Blood spurted from his neck onto the floor. "Taylor!" she yelled in his ear. Her eyes filled with tears, and for a few seconds she couldn't see, then they rushed out dropping on Taylor's face. She leaned closer, waiting for him to breathe—nothing. She grabbed a dish towel from the counter and pressed it on Taylor's neck to stop the bleeding. His blood quickly soaked through the towel. She screeched, straining to get up, and stumbled across the room to the telephone. Shouting into the receiver, she told the operator how she'd found her husband—bleeding, not breathing. She gave her address, hung up, and hurried back to him. She'd seen enough dead bodies to know . . . Taylor was dead. She cradled his head to her chest and screamed out to God, calling out Taylor's name. His blood covered her body, and she trembled at the sight of it.

* * *

Ruth had left the bridal shower, dropped off Caroline, and sped home. She pulled into the driveway at two fifty in the morning. She hoped her mother hadn't waited up for her. For out of respect, she'd have to bite her tongue and listen to her go on about how terrible it looked for a young woman to go home by herself at this hour of the morning. She jumped from the Packard and quietly shut the door. In the distance she heard the sound of an ambulance. ***Probably heading to the hospital,*** she thought. She almost slipped on pieces of her mother's clay flowerpots shattered on the ground, mangled blossoms and crumbs of dirt scattered about. ***What happened here?*** The sirens were louder now. She turned to see an ambulance a couple of blocks away coming down Sixth Street. She skipped steps to the door. She fumbled with the key, trying to get inside. When she opened the door, she heard someone crying in the kitchen. "Mom!" she called out, racing down the hallway to the kitchen. Her purse fell from her hand onto the blood-soaked floor as she screamed, "Oh god!" Naomi was kneeling on the floor, holding Taylor, his face ashen, his body still, like the large pool of blood Naomi knelt in. Ruth didn't hear the first knock on the door.

# Chapter 12

A half of dozen police cars had quickly lined up and down Sixth Street Northwest where Taylor lived and died. Blue lights flashed from beacons mounted atop the black-and-whites, a signal to everyone that Sixth Street belonged to the police now, although their presence didn't stop Taylor's neighbors from congregating on one another's front porches and in the street outside his house, on the corner of 6th and O Street.

Awakened by the piercing wail of the ambulance and police sirens, neighbors had jumped from the comfort of their warm beds for the cold October air to find out what went wrong in their usually quiet neighborhood. They shuddered when they heard Taylor had been murdered. They huddled together in small units, seeking solace from one another. It didn't matter that the sun was still asleep. The moon and the lampposts provided all the light needed for the painful vigil.

"Did you hear the sirens? William Taylor's dead." His next-door neighbor had gotten on the phone and called everyone he knew in the neighborhood and beyond. "Somebody killed him." The neighbor's friends and family called others, which sparked off phone calls as far away as South Carolina.

"Who in the world killed him?" one woman had cried.

"Lawd help us," another said.

"Easton!" a voice yelled.

Easton squinted in the faint streetlight. He looked around until he spotted the top of his cousin Jimmy's sand-colored head. He answered, "Trying to get to Ruth . . . catch you later!"

Easton and Toast had been hard at it partying in a bar on U Street. Toast's wife and son had taken a train to Mississippi to see his ailing mother-in-law, and Ruth had gone to a bridal shower, so the two men had been doing what single men do on a Friday night in DC, clubbing. The usual Saturday night revelry of loud music, constant chatter, and laughter had suddenly faded to a murmur. The high some patrons had nursed all night came crashing down at the news of William Taylor's death, sobering them to a painful reality. Word of Taylor's murder had raged through Shaw like a California wildfire, reaching U Street even before all God's angels got the news. Easton had dropped his shot of bourbon on the bar counter and ran to call Ruth.

"Is it true?" Easton had asked Ruth.

"Yes," Ruth had replied bawling uncontrollably.

Easton barely understood her. She had told Easton how she'd arrived home from the bridal shower and found her mother in the kitchen, holding on to Taylor, blood spatter all over her and the floor. Somebody had stabbed Taylor to death.

Easton inched his way through the maze of people. His six-foot-tall frame towered over most of the people around him, which made it easier for him to raise a camera above their heads and snap photos of the crime scene, Taylor's house, which sat on the corner of Sixth and O Street. It looked bigger than the other brick row houses on the block because of the morgue built off the rear, now obscured by police standing guard around it.

After Ruth told Easton that Taylor had been stabbed to death, he felt numb then fear hit him like a bulldozer—fear for Ruth. Fortunate or not, Ruth was not home at the time of the murder. ***Who's to say the killer might not come back, for her and Naomi. Will she be next, or did the killer just want Taylor dead?*** Easton continued to rub shoulders toward the house, maybe a little too hard.

"Nigga, don't push me." A young boy turned and faced Easton. "The man ain't goin' nowhere, he's dead."

Four other brothas togged up in stocking caps and black do-rags tied in knots at the back of their heads surrounded Easton. Each time one opened their mouth, talking shit mostly, a whiff of the Friday night mix hung in the air—whiskey, stale cigarette breath, and marijuana.

"Come on, man, cut me some slack," Easton said. "I'm trying to hook up with my woman . . . Taylor's daughter."

One of the brothas cocked his head to the side and leaned back. He nodded to the others. "You cool . . . you cool, man." He held out his hand.

They slapped palms, and Easton moved on, nudging his way through a cluster of women who weren't quite as hostile as the men. They just stared him down. When he reached the curb, a string of yellow crime tape laced the black wrought-iron fence surrounding Taylor's house. Trimmed hedgerows along the inside of the fence stopped briefly for a red brick path leading to the front steps, where Naomi's mangled blossoms lay amid shattered pieces of the clay flowerpots still on the ground. Easton saw Ruth clinging to Naomi on the covered porch in front of the fluorescent window sign announcing "William T. and Naomi B. Taylor Undertakers and Embalmers." Its blue light shone bright in the darkness. Taylor's son Thomas, Leroy, and Doc Nelson and Dorothy were there too. Easton supposed Ruth or Naomi had called them soon after she found Taylor's body.

Easton joined the other newspaper reporters, who were positioned along the curb lane, already snapping pictures and shouting questions at the police, trying to get the 411 on Taylor's murder. Easton reached into his coat pocket for a cigarette and lit up.

"When did you get here?" Easton asked one of the reporters, surprised to see so many of them. He thought he'd had an edge on the news.

"About three forty-five," one reporter replied.

"Same here," another answered.

"Twenty minutes ago," said another.

Easton skirted his way toward the front of the house. He spotted Aaron, his boss, leaning against a huge oak tree, writing on his notepad. Easton stepped onto the treed lawn, acorns and leaves crunching under his feet.

"Aaron, what you know?" he said, shaking his boss's hand.

"I called you a couple of times," Aaron replied.

"Clubbing," Easton said. "One of the bartenders got a call and told everybody. I called Ruth, and she confirmed it."

"What did she say?" Aaron asked.

"Naomi found Taylor dead in the kitchen, sliced up."

"Did Naomi see who did it?"

"Not even a shadow."

"Did Ruth?"

"She was at a bridal shower."

"Till three o'clock in the morning? It must have been some kind of shower."

Easton smiled. "Yeah, I guess so." For a fleeting moment, he too had questioned Ruth's whereabouts until three o'clock in the morning, though the thought left him as quickly as it came. Taylor's murder took center stage, on the other hand with Aaron bringing it up again, he'd ask her about it later.

Aaron looked up from his notepad. "We're getting zilch from the cops. We need to . . ." He stopped talking in midsentence. The eerie moans and sobs from the large crowd that had assembled on the street hushed as the paramedics took Taylor's body out the front door, covered with a black tarp and strapped on a gurney. A profound stillness filled the air. Only the wispy, wheezing, gasping, labored breathing of the people and the sound of camera shutters clicking vibrated in the night air. Aaron pointed toward the porch. "Good God, Naomi just keeled over."

Easton eyed Naomi, who had fallen over on Ruth, thrusting her up against the house. Doc Nelson and Leroy were lifting Naomi off Ruth. "I'm going up there."

"Try to get inside and take pictures if you can," Aaron urged him.

A policeman refused to let Easton past the roped-off area even though he stretched the truth somewhat and claimed Ruth as his fiancée. They were, in fact, planning to marry in the spring. He just hadn't given her a ring yet. Easton waved Ruth toward him. She pounded the four steps down to the yellow tape where Easton stood on the other side.

"How you holding up?" Easton asked Ruth as she fell in his arms, crying.

"It's so hard," Ruth replied. She then turned toward one of the policemen. "Please let him through, please . . . he's my fiancé."

The policeman stared at Ruth and Easton. He walked away and turned his back to the couple. He spoke in a whisper into his walkie-talkie. As close as they were to the man, neither Easton nor Ruth understood a word he said because of the loud crackling noise coming through the speaker. When the policeman finished talking on the Handie-Talkie, he lifted the tape for Easton to go under it.

"Thank you," Easton said. He wanted to say more, perturbed that the man had turned his back on him. Since he got what he wanted, to be with Ruth, he left it alone. When they reached the porch, another officer built like a linebacker went out of the house. Easton knew from the look on his face that he recognized him.

"Reporters don't belong up here," the officer hollered at Easton.

"The chief gave the okay," the officer's colleague yelled to him.

The officer did not try to hide his repulsion. "You must think you're a special nigger." He stormed back inside.

The second time in less than an hour, Easton had been called out of his name, a racial epithet for sure this time, having come from the white officer. Easton grasped the door handle to go after him. Ruth grabbed Easton's arm.

"No, Easton . . . he'll kill you!"

"Let it go, son," Doc Nelson said. "We already have enough to deal with."

Easton relented, for now. Ruth was right. He might have been shot and killed had he laid one finger on the officer. DC police were known to shoot Negroes first and ask questions later.

"What happened to your mother's feet?" Easton asked as he glanced down and saw the white bandages wrapped around Naomi's feet and ankles.

"She cut her feet on broken glass in the kitchen. From a wine bottle, I believe," Ruth replied. "She didn't know they were bleeding until the paramedics told her. I think she's still in shock."

They watched as the coroner's men loaded William Taylor's body in an ambulance. Ruth let go of Easton's arm and held Naomi as she grabbed at her chest, gasping.

"Nooo! Nooo! Nooo!" Naomi screamed. Her weakened body slumped over onto Ruth, again. Easton gently held her up and guided her onto the glider. Dorothy, Naomi's cousin, plopped down beside her. She embraced Naomi so tight, Easton questioned Naomi's ability to breathe.

Easton, grappling with his own grief, embraced Ruth. He smothered her limp body, trying to shield her from the pain of losing a father a second time. She'd told him that her biological father had met his fate the day after her fifth birthday. To hear her talk about him sometimes, you'd think he had died yesterday. He closed his eyes.

When the door of the ambulance closed, a loud, deep, roaring sound vaulted through the air. Easton would never try to explain it, though he did understand it—the sound of sorrow and woe. The same sound he had uttered when his grandparents died. He opened his eyes. It had come from Thomas, who'd almost wrapped his entire body around one of the pillars supporting the roof. He slowly slid down toward the concrete porch. Doc Nelson rushed over and caught him right before he touched down. Easton shook his head and turned away.

"So many people here," Easton said as he perused the crowd, the night-light illuminating the street just enough to see blank expressions spread over the faces of every color Negro you can imagine—chocolate, coffee, caramel, copper, cinnamon, bronze, mocha, olive, ebony, and high yellow. He watched as some folks fell on their knees, arms stretched to the sky, calling on the Almighty.

"Help me, Jesus!" they pleaded.

Others held their heads, hearts, or stomachs and begged, "Lawd, have mercy!"

Still others stood whimpering, looking toward the house where evil had crept in and encroached on one of their own. They cursed and prayed at the same time, angry at Taylor's killer, whoever he was.

Easton had heard stories of Taylor's overzealous behavior as a young man, though no one ever denied his success as an undertaker. A staunch businessman, one whom Negroes sought during the most vulnerable times in their lives, he had been very good to the residents of Shaw. Easton had also seen him in action as am active member of the NAACP, not afraid to speak out against segregation and for black equality. And he'd helped the poor and disenfranchised all year round, not just at Thanksgiving or Christmas as some do-gooders did. He practiced what he preached. "No one should go without food, a roof over their head, or clothing," Taylor used to say. "It's too many of us to give . . . to help . . . there's no excuse. If we don't reach back and bring others along, we won't move forward as a people."

Easton moved to the edge of the porch and snapped a picture of the ambulance rolling down the street, mourners in step alongside it. When the moving coffin sped up, sorrowful cries followed it out of sight. Sixth Street grew quieter as people lingered in the road, appearing lost and bewildered.

* * *

Easton followed Ruth inside. She went upstairs for clothes she'd packed for her and Naomi's stay at the Jenkinses', while police processed the crime scene. The police officer fell in close behind her.

"You stay here," he directed Easton.

Easton wanted to kick his ass. Instead, he waited until the officer was out of sight and eased along the wall to the kitchen. Another cop blocked the doorway.

"Ira, you're here," Easton said, surprised to see him. Ira, one of four Negroes on the DC police force, had recently been promoted to detective. The other three cops were assigned to precincts in Northeast, Southeast, and the Shaw districts, the area of Northwest where Taylor lived. Precincts on the other side of the park in Chevy Chase and Georgetown, where most white folks in the city lived, were assigned to white cops only. "Let me get a picture, one picture. I won't touch a thing."

"No pictures," Ira said. "You know the rules. How did you get in here, anyway?"

"A cop let me in. I'm Ruth's fiancé, remember?"

"Yeah, okay. Take a quick look. No pictures. They're watching every move I make." Ira motioned for Easton to move in closer. He stepped aside long enough for him to see where Taylor had lain.

Easton peered through the door. "Oh god!" He breathed. He didn't know how much blood a person's body possessed and wondered if all Taylors had pooled into the massive puddle on the floor. Some had dried in clumps and turned dark, like small pieces of beef liver before they're cooked. He covered his mouth. He quickly turned away at the sight and putrid smell of it. He breathed shallow, trying to take in as little as possible; the air of death still filled his lungs. He thought he might just vomit right then and there.

"Who did this?" A hand still over his nose and his mouth.

"Damn, Easton," Ira said, with a nervous smirk on his face. "Remind me not to let you look at another crime scene, if I ever get another chance to be at one."

"Sorry," Easton said, staggering, somewhat dazed, past Ira. He leaned against a wall and wiped off sweat oozing from his brow. He'd never seen so much blood in all his life, and hoped never to see it again. Recovered somewhat, he went in search of Ruth. The officer leered down at him from the top of the staircase. Easton guessed she hadn't gone down yet. "Ruth!"

"Coming," she responded. She started down the stairs, carrying two suitcases. Easton skipped steps and grabbed them from her. He eyed the policeman, annoyed that he hadn't bothered to help her.

"He won't let me take my jewelry box," Ruth said to Easton. "I wish I could lock my bedroom door. My suit bag is still upstairs."

Easton loaded the suitcases into the trunk of Doc Nelson's black Desoto, because he had to park his car three blocks away, too far to carry heavy luggage. Doc Nelson had agreed to drop the luggage off at the Jenkinses' on his way home. When Easton went back into the house for the suit bag, Ira met him at the door. Not much older than Easton, he already sported a large beer belly.

"Naomi Taylor said she doesn't know who killed her husband. She did say Taylor and Rutherford Daniels had gone at each other a couple of times. If you hear something different, give me a ring."

"Yeah," Easton responded. "You do the same."

Ira and Easton needed each other. Investigative reporting proved to be a daunting task sometimes; that's why Easton had contacts on the street, in the courthouse, and the precincts. And being the only Negro detective on the force, Ira had to walk a fine line. Ira told Easton that his partner sometimes held back information on cases they were supposed to work on together, and Ira didn't know shit from Shinola until his partner briefed the boss, trying to make himself look good and Ira look stupid.

* * *

Easton slammed the trunk shut. He watched Doc Nelson drive off with Dorothy and Thomas, past double-parked cars and people milling around in the street. Police cars had lined both sides of Sixth Street, creating a narrow path for other cars. Residential streets in Washington, DC, weren't wide anyway, and at a crime scene, forget it.

Moving about unsteady, her face blank, Naomi looked as if she'd pass out any minute. Easton and Ruth helped her into a squad car waiting to drive her and Ruth to the Second precinct to give statements.

"I'll be there soon," he promised Ruth. "I need to question your neighbors . . . while things are still fresh in their minds."

Ruth nodded.

The squad car drove off.

# Chapter 13

Ira emerged from Taylor's Funeral Home and ran toward Easton. "We've got a robbery in progress in Northeast. I got to go."

Easton ran alongside Ira. "Who's in charge of this case?"

Ira shrugged. "Nobody yet."

Easton didn't try to hide his anger. "What's the chief waiting for, the killer to pack up and leave town?"

Ira sensed Easton's frustration. "As soon as I hear, I'll call you."

"Stop fooling yourself, Ira. The chief doesn't give a shit that Taylor's dead, and you know it," Easton said. "Look around . . . A Negro is murdered, and all I see is your boys standing around profiling. Have they even questioned people in the crowd?"

"Doubt it . . . have you?" Ira drove off.

Easton lit a cigarette and perused the crowd. A few people lingered outside the yellow tape as if they were waiting for something else to happen. Not one cop questioning anybody. He put out his cigarette and approached two women chatting on the sidewalk.

"Excuse me, ma'am," he said, tipping his cap. "I'm Easton Priest, a reporter for the ***Negro News.*** Do either of you know what happened to Mr. Taylor?"

"I don't no nuthin'," the first woman said. She shuffled up the sidewalk toward the corner. The other crossed the street and scurried into a house.

Startled by a loud bang, Easton whirled around and looked anxiously up and down Sixth Street. The once vast crowd had dwindled away, and while he didn't notice anyone wheeling a gun, he figured someone had banged a door shut so hard it sounded like a gunshot. He breathed a heavy sigh of relief and relaxed his shoulders. He didn't realize how tight he'd become, and for a moment he hesitated, not quite sure what to do next, his head still reeling from all the bourbon he'd consumed and the shock of Taylor's death. He straightened up, lit another cigarette, and started walking toward a group of people who'd made their way to the next block. Before he reached the corner, he passed by the first woman he spoke to, the one who said she didn't know "nothing." He stopped abruptly and turned to face her.

"Ma'am, I know you said you don't know what happened to Mr. Taylor. Can you tell me what you do know about him?" Easton asked.

She glared at Easton. "I tol' you, I don't no nuthin'. What makes you think I'd tell you anythin', evin if I knowed somethin'?"

"Ma'am, William Taylor helped a lot of people in this city, including people on this street . . . your street," Easton replied, as he pointed to the houses behind her. "I just want to know what happened to him. Did you hear or see something out of the ordinary?"

"What happind? The man is dead, that's what happind. I'd say that's out thu ord'nary."

"Did he have any enemies in the neighborhood?" Easton asked.

The woman stepped a few feet into the yard of a house.

"Now . . . this is far as you goin'. Don't come in my yard." She grabbed the arm of a little boy rolling around in a pile of leaves and yanked him up on the porch. "Cora, open the door!" A girl opened the door, and the woman disappeared into the house with the boy.

Easton headed toward the next block, where earlier he'd seen a group of people congregating. They had gone. A boy not much older than fifteen sat on the front steps of a house a few doors from Taylor's house. Easton hadn't noticed him earlier. Before he opened his mouth, the teenager spoke. "My mama don't want to be bothered, mistah."

"Well, maybe you can help me, son. What's your name?" Easton asked.

"Jeremiah Bailey."

"Jeremiah . . . that's a Bible name. I bet your grandmother named you," Easton said.

"Yes, sir."

"How long have you lived on Sixth Street?" Easton asked.

"Since I was five years old," Jeremiah replied.

"How well did you know William Taylor?" Easton asked.

"Kept his yard, washed his cars, cleaned gutters, stuff like that." Jeremiah picked at a bandage on his hand.

"He treated you okay, paid you when he promised?" Easton asked.

"Yes, sir," Jeremiah answered, still picking at the bandage.

"How did you hurt your hand?" Easton asked.

"Fell off my bike," he replied.

"Tell me what you know about last night," Easton said.

"Nothin'." All of a sudden, the boy looked wary.

"When did you see Mr. Taylor last?" Easton asked.

"Yesterday."

"With who?"

"Nobody."

Easton didn't let on that he'd seen Jeremiah cutting grass in Taylor's backyard a couple of times. He figured if he knew something about the murder, he'd tell

Ruth or Naomi. Easton wrote his name and phone number on a piece of paper and gave it to the boy anyway.

"Okay, son, call me if you remember anything." The boy put the paper in his coat pocket and went into the house. Easton made a mental note to ask Ruth and Naomi about Jeremiah's relationship with Taylor.

Easton hadn't learned any more about Taylor's murder than the man in the moon had. He rubbed his weary eyes, not wanting to believe that his hero had died . . . a violent death at that. He opened his notepad and stared at a blank page, as if he were waiting for his pen to scribble the killer's name across the page. He understood folks' reluctance to confer about a murder, especially if it went down in their neighborhood. Nobody wanted to be involved. Most people were afraid the killer might go after them, and sometimes they did. It was not uncommon to learn of a witness missing or found dead before the perpetrator's trial or hearing. Besides that, Negroes by and large weren't trusting people anyway. They'd tell you in a minute, "I don't trust you as far as I see you." Easton didn't blame them.

* * *

The dark night sky gave way to the dim light now covering the city. Through it, Easton spotted a taxi coasting down the middle of the street. It stopped and parked alongside a police car across the street from Taylor's house. The cops had closed off Sixth Street, so they must have made an exception for the driver, who guided an old woman wearing dark glasses and using a cane down steps. ***A blind person wouldn't have seen anything, maybe she heard something. I wonder where she's going this time of morning.*** He approached the two.

"Good morning, sir, ma'am," Easton said. The driver returned the greeting. The woman said nothing. She acted like he was invisible. He kept walking, having decided in all probability that she was deaf. The two got in the cab. The driver cruised up the street and made a U-turn in the alley. As it drove by, Easton's eyes shot to the rear window. The woman had taken the dark glasses off. ***Odd,*** he thought.

Easton schlepped along the sidewalk, weighed down by the horror that held Sixth Street captive. Contrary to the bloody and gross desecration of Taylor, Sixth Street appeared to be a clean, tidy block of detached row houses, between N Street to the south and O Street to the north. Even the alley stayed free of broken glass, empty beer cans, old tires, cars rusting in backyards, and paper strewn about. Several cats roamed the street. He guessed they were let loose to keep mice and rats off the block.

Easton turned into the alley, not looking for anything in particular. He walked past the backyards, some fenced in with swing sets, dogs barking, and clothes hanging on the line. He stopped and approached two policemen standing in front of Taylor's backyard. Easton flashed his press pass.

"Any sign the killer broke in through the pantry or the morgue?" Easton asked the cops.

"Keep moving, boy. We're not answering your questions," the older cop said.

"Yes, sir . . . I'll keep moving. Maybe I'll find a clue to Mr. Taylor's murder. I may miss it if I stay here talking to you," Easton said, and headed back around front. Before he reached the sidewalk . . .

"***Rags***, any ***rags***," the ragman called out, walking toward Easton with his pushcart. Easton had never seen a ragman before moving to DC. They'd sometimes appear before the crack of dawn like clockwork. Easton stopped and waited for him to get closer. His dark hair had grown as long as his beard. Sleep crusted in the corner of his eyes, and his breath smelled minty, like mouthwash. And although his clothes were not tattered or torn, they looked like he had been rolling in dirt.

"Good morning, sir," Easton said. "Did you know William Taylor?"

"My friend." The ragman squeezed his eyes shut and grimaced as if in pain.

"I'm sorry you lost your friend," Easton responded. "Do you know of anyone who wanted to hurt your friend?"

"Who are you?" the ragman asked.

"A reporter for the ***Negro News*** and Mr. Taylor's friend too," Easton replied.

I've got nothing to say." The ragman started walking away.

"Sir, please tell me what you know about Mr. Taylor," Easton pleaded.

"Nothing."

Easton watched the ragman cut across the grassy strip to the other side of the alley. As the ragman passed by the backyards, he'd empty brown bags stuffed with rags into his cart and trudge on, shouting, "***Rags***, any ***rags***."

Easton thought ragmen were lost souls, until his cousin set him straight. "The brother has more moola than you right now, from selling dirty rags to the paper mills. Did you know the paper mills convert that filthy stuff into fabric and paper?"

* * *

Easton plodded back to Sixth Street. The police had opened the street for the locals to come and go and the milkman too. He watched him scamper from door to door, leaving bottles of homogenized white and chocolate milk in metal containers on the front porches. No sooner than he left the milk, the front door opened and someone snatched up the bottles.

Like most of the row houses in DC, the ones on Taylor's block were all the same red brick and they all had the same windows, doors, and porches. When Easton first arrived in the city, he'd look twice to see where one house began and another ended. The one thing that helped was the different-color metal awnings that shaded the windows and doors. Easton wondered if Taylor's house had been mistaken for somebody else's. It crossed his mind that a burglar might have broken into the house and, when discovered by Taylor, panicked and murdered him. One thing certain, whoever killed Taylor didn't want his wife dead. Naomi was still kicking, barely though.

He yawned, his mouth stretched open so wide his jaws hurt. The fact is, Easton had been awake all night, and even though his adrenaline no longer pumped at the same speed, his mind raced at ninety miles an hour. He eased down on the front steps of the house next door to Taylor's and smoked a cigarette, while waiting for people to go outside to interview them. He watched cops carry boxes out of Taylor's house and others stroll up and down Sixth Street, stopping every now and again to look in somebody's yard or peep in a car. Easton rose from the stoop and approached one of the cops.

"Any evidence yet?" Easton asked.

"We're still examining the crime scene," the officer responded, with a puzzled look on his face.

"You talk to his neighbors yet?" Easton asked.

"Are you a relative or a reporter?" the cop replied.

"Reporter," Easton replied.

"It figures. Stay out of our way, or I'll have you banned from this street," the cop said, and walked away.

Easton ignored the cop's warning and canvassed both sides of the street, knocking on doors, inquiring about Taylor. ***I guess I have to do my job and theirs too.*** He'd gone without food for hours. Hunger gnawed at him, and each time a door opened, his mouth watered at the smell of fresh coffee, bacon frying, and homemade biscuits. Only a few people listened to him. Most sent him away without offering him either information or food.

"Good morning, I'm Easton Priest, a reporter for the ***Negro News***—"

"Son, I don't know anything, about anything." The woman who'd answered the door shut it in his face.

He jumped over the banister to the next porch. "Good morning. My name is Easton Priest and I'm—"

"Can't help you." The door closed.

Next door . . ."Good morning, sir, my name is Easton Priest and I'm a reporter for the ***Negro News***—"

"Can't talk now. I gotta a job to get to." The man ran past Easton to his car.

"Can I come by later?" Easton called out. The man drove off.

No one on Sixth Street wanted to interview with Easton. ***Scared to death,*** he guessed. He glanced at his pocketwatch—almost seven o'clock in the morning. From what he knew about giving statements to the police, he expected Ruth and Naomi to be at the precinct at least another hour. He walked up O Street to the market. It would be filling with people right now. ***Maybe I'll have better luck there.***

# Chapter 14

Easton smelled the fresh meat, fish, and aroma of coffee long before he reached the market, the smell of coffee so strong, it woke him. Even when the doors and windows of the market were closed, and they were open today, the smells drifted through the neighborhood and lingered for days at a time. He rushed into the building, bustling with activity. People whistled and hummed to the jazz melodies blaring from huge speakers, which had even the mundane nodding and tapping to the beat. He saw small clusters of women talking while children played at their feet. Men smoked cigars and cigarettes and sat on stools, reading the morning paper and drinking coffee while waiting for their wives or lovers to finish shopping.

He wound his way through the narrow aisles. Vendors were all over the place. Some lined the walls with refrigerated cases and coolers filled with meat, fish, and dairy, while others positioned their stands in the center of the market stacked so high with fruits and vegetables, if you picked one, two or three might roll onto the table or the cemented floor.

Mostly residents living in the Shaw neighborhood frequented the place, although black, white, and a person of every other color in the rainbow crammed into the market to barter for food, clothing, baskets, housewares, and knick-knacks from Africa—called the motherland by some Negroes—and the Caribbean. You name it, people sold it.

"How much for the tablecloth?" one woman asked.

"Give me three dollars. It's handmade. See the stitching?" The vendor pointed to the embroidered flowers and trim around the hem of the tablecloth. "Three dollars for it, that's it."

"Two dollars and I'll buy it," the woman said.

"It's handmade, lady. Two fifty, it's yours," the vendor retorted. "You can't get it nowhere for this price. It's one of a kind."

The woman handed her two dollars and fifty cents.

Prices on other items, such as vegetables, fruit, milk, bread, butter, and eggs, varied from one stand to another by a penny or two.

German immigrants were first to sell their goods in the market. While Negroes worked most of the stands now, a few Germans still sold there. Because a small number of vendors were from Tennessee, Easton often dropped in to shoot the breeze with them. In fact, the market was ***the*** place to socialize and gossip, second only to the beauty and barbershops, and the topic this morning—William Taylor's murder.

Easton wandered through the crowded aisles, watching shoppers decide on the "perfect cut of meat." He watched a vendor hold a slab of meat high above the counter as if it were a precious gemstone.

"Looks almost as good as my Tennessee prime rib," Easton yelled to him. Easton's family had raised beef cattle on his family's farm in Tennessee ever since his great-great-grandparents were given the land as freed slaves. Easton prided himself in knowing a good cut of meat when he saw it.

The vendor laughed. "Go on, boy! You keep braggin' on it. I ain't seen nothin' yet. Tell your old man I'm waitin'."

"Were you at William Taylor's house this morning?" Easton asked him.

"Wasn't that somethin'," the meatcutter said. "Taylor's dead. He'd be standin' right where you is now talkin' about somethin' if he weren't dead."

"Do you know anyone who had a beef with him?" Easton asked.

"Wish I knew," the vendor replied, swinging a shiny eight-inch breaking knife in the air. He limped to the end of the counter to wait on a customer.

The cheesemongers were situated at the far end of the market. He paused at the first one he went to. Rolls and blocks of different flavored cheeses were displayed in the refrigerated cases. Samples of the cheeses cut straight off the round sat on top of the case. He helped himself to a few chunks then moved on to the next vendor.

"You hear about Mr. Taylor?" Easton asked a cheesemonger.

"A sad thing. Folks around here talking about stringing up the killer, if they find him."

"They know who did it?" Easton asked.

"Some hooligan."

"You got a name?" Easton asked.

"No . . . and if I did, he'd be dead by now."

"Sir, be careful now . . . you don't want to take the law into your own hands," Easton said. "You have kids?"

"Yeah, I have a couple," the cheesemonger replied.

"I'm sure they don't want to see their daddy in jail," Easton said.

"Did I say something?" the cheesemonger said, with a puzzled look on his face. He cut a piece of sharp cheddar cheese off the round and handed it to Easton.

Easton grinned and took a bite. "This is real tasty. I'll have to come back and buy a few slices."

At another stand, he sampled homemade apple butter smothered on warm bread. It melted in his mouth like ice cream. "Oh, soooo good," he sang to the Bean Master, who poured him a fresh-brewed cup of coffee to wash it all down. With the coffee, cheese samples, and bread, it would be just enough to keep him going a little longer.

The Bean Master sold coffee beans, hence his nickname, for more than twenty years at the market. A short, stout man, he was the color of the beans he sold. No one knew coffee in the city better than he did. He'd look at a bean or smell brewed coffee and tell you its name.

"Tell me what you know about William Taylor," Easton said to him.

"You an undercover cop now?" the Bean Master asked.

Easton extended his hand to the man, smiling. "No, sir, I'm still a reporter for the ***Negro News***. I'm investigating William Taylor's murder for the paper."

"Just thought I'd ask. You sound like a policeman. I guess that goes along with the territory—questioning people," the Bean Master said, shaking Easton's hand. "Taylor's sister is married to my brother-in-law's cousin in Baltimore. They said after she got the call from Ruth this morning, she fell out. They took her away in an ambulance. I haven't heard no more about it."

Easton hesitated. He remembered calling Ruth, how it brought tears to his eyes. "How often did Mr. Taylor come to the market?"

"Every week, sometimes with Naomi, sometimes by hisself," the Bean Master replied.

"When did you last see him?"

"Last week. We talked for a long while. When you're in business for yourself like us, some fool is always trying to cheat you or use you, and Taylor said he'd been bilked out of a lot of money these last few months. He took on the no-good sharks. Odds are they killed him."

Easton recalled his conversation with Taylor about a meeting he'd attended with the Funeral Directors and Morticians Association, an organization Taylor had cofounded. Five other undertakers had told the same story—their clients' life insurance policies were canceled by Family Life without their knowledge. One thing certain, none of the five undertakers had confronted Family Life about what looked and smelled of fraud. Taylor did. Now he's dead.

"You think Family Life is responsible for his murder?" Easton asked.

The Bean Master chuckled. "That's right . . . you wrote that article about Family Life, didn't you?"

"Yes, sir," Easton replied.

The Bean Master stopped filling bags with coffee beans and looked up at Easton. "I'm not saying one way or another. What I've heard, and it's hearsay, mind you, the firm made a bundle last year, more than any other Negro-owned company in the city."

"How?" Easton asked.

"We asked the same question at the Negroes in Business meeting in March. Rutherford Daniels, the company president, ignored us. So Taylor stood up in front of everybody and accused the man of stealing money from their clients."

"What did Daniels do?" Easton asked.

"Accused Taylor of making false statements. Threatened to sue him for libel. When the other undertakers jumped up shouting at Daniels, the chairperson ended the meeting. He didn't want a riot."

"Does Daniels shop here?" Easton asked.

"Everybody and his mama shops here," replied the Bean Master. "I saw him here yesterday with his wife and kids, though, I didn't see too many people talking to him. After I read your article, I decided to stop doing business with Family Life and bought insurance from Metropolis. I know all those families they stole from, so you don't have to prove nothing to me. They're good, hardworking people. They ain't lying."

"Who did Taylor talk to when he shopped here?" Easton asked.

"Everybody," the Bean Master laughed. "He always made the rounds. Try Leslie Ann Penny. She comes in early when she's here. She sells hats near the north entrance. Daniels liked talking to her too." The Bean Master winked as he said it.

Easton bought a pound of coffee beans for Ruth and his landlord. He thanked the Bean Master and turned his attention to finding the hat lady.

* * *

A young woman sat behind a table covered with hats. Easton stopped and stared at her. She looked stunning wearing a mauve silk beret slanted to the side, underneath it, dark brown hair styled in a Marcel wave. She had rather broad shoulders, big brown eyes, mocha-colored skin, and she wore an orange shade of lipstick on her full lips. When she smiled, the dimples in her cheeks were more pronounced. As he moved closer, she smelled good too, the fragrance of her perfume a sweet scent Easton had never inhaled. Fur hats, feathered hats, turbans, berets, and toques of different colors were arranged on a red velvet cloth in front of her. Ruth wore fashionable hats like these. He remembered her saying she'd bought most of her hats at the market.

"Good morning, and what can I interest you in today?" the woman asked, smiling.

"Good morning, are you Ms. Leslie Ann Penny?" Easton inquired.

"It's me, in the flesh," she replied. "Of course, I've been known to answer to Leslie."

"I'm Easton Priest, and I work for the ***Negro News***. I'm writing a story about William Taylor, and I understand you two talked a lot when he shopped here."

Her smile quickly disappeared as she spoke, almost in a whisper. "Ah yes . . . yes, we did. A wonderful man. I was devastated to hear what happened to him."

"How long did you know him?" Easton asked.

"Uhm . . . about five years. I had just set up shop here, when I met him." She observed Easton carefully.

"Five years? You knew him pretty well," Easton said.

"Yes, I suppose I did."

"Had he been upset about anything of late?"

"Are you going to print everything I say?" she asked.

"Not if you don't want me to," Easton replied.

"I don't."

"Yes, ma'am . . . I won't," Easton said, looking straight into her eyes.

He must have made Leslie uncomfortable, for she turned away before she spoke. "Family Life Insurance Company, his number one enemy. Boy, did they get his goat." Her voice had started to rise with emotion. She ended in almost a murmur as if afraid someone overheard her.

"Anyone in particular?" Easton asked.

"No," she hesitated. "He didn't say. I'd try to change the subject. It didn't matter. He always came back to Family Life, even when we . . ." She salvaged used tissue from her purse and dabbed at her eyes.

"You talk with Rutherford Daniels too?" Easton asked.

She stood up, clasped her hands together, and stared at Easton as though he'd discovered a secret. She answered, "Yes—yes. His company insures my hats."

"Hats!" Easton said, surprised. "I didn't know they insured material goods." ***Have to check into that,*** he thought to himself. "Do you know who may have wanted Taylor dead?"

She sat back down. Her shoulders went limp. She lowered her head and planted her hands on the table. "No." She diddled with what looked like a sapphire ring surrounded by diamonds. "He didn't deserve to die. I can't believe he's gone."

"That's a nice-looking gem you're wearing," Easton said.

"Oh, uh, thanks. It's not real," she said, sliding her hands off the table.

"Well, it's a pretty decent imitation," Easton said.

She glanced past Easton, ignoring his comment, her mouth quivering. "It's hard losing a friend."

"It's even harder if it's someone you're fond of," Easton said.

Easton didn't know if he said the wrong thing or not. Leslie's jaw tightened; she sat rigid and stared straight ahead. She didn't say another word.

"Thank you for your time, Leslie," Easton said.

She nodded.

A woman approached the stand, and like magic, Leslie put on a new face.

* * *

Easton proceeded to talk with every vendor who'd talk to him about Taylor. The last one he interviewed kept pausing and looking around while he talked. Easton believed he wanted people to think that whatever information he got, it had come from somebody else, not him. The merchant grumbled a few words of contempt toward Taylor's killer then hurried to wait on a customer. Easton decided to move on too. He'd been at the market long enough. He had another stop to make before picking up Ruth and Naomi. He proceeded through the exit door and into the early morning light.

# CHAPTER 15

The red, white, and blue barber pole spun around outside Keith's Barbershop on Seventh Street, where Easton drove every two weeks for a cut and hot shave and where he first met Taylor. A student at Howard at that time, it always amazed him that no one ever interrupted or challenged Taylor when he spoke, especially if the topic centered on business or black people's struggles, and he'd always learn something new before he left the shop. When Ruth introduced him as her dad, he almost peed on himself. For a year he worried that he might not live up to Taylor's expectations. Ruth had sensed his apprehension and told him, "My dad is bothered by idle minds, wasteful spending, and the mistreatment of the Negro race. Other than that, he loves sports, a good conversation, and apple cobbler. You'll be fine."

Because the place stayed packed all day on Saturdays, the wait for a cut might be an hour or more. For that reason, Easton normally didn't go to the shop on Saturdays. Given Taylor's tragic death, he figured the old heads might be telling tales about him right about now, and maybe they'd give him something to nibble on. This is not to say that all the men in the shop were old. In fact, they were at various places along life's journey—retired, working, in college, married, single, divorced, some with children and grandchildren.

Inside the one-room shop, the cool smell of shaving cream and the jarring scent of ammonia-based lye cream used to process hair swept up Easton's nose. He grimaced. He believed if the brothas knew that the chemicals used to make lye cream were stronger than drain cleaners, they'd run the other way. If the cream burned their scalp, they'd run to the sink and put their whole head underwater.

The toned-down chatter in the room gave way to the jazz music playing on the radio, generally the other way around. Barbershops were the hub of activity for men in the city, black or white. A place to socialize, discuss commentary on current affairs, quibble over every sport you can think of, including fishing, and learn about local happenings—who hit the number, who'd been down south recently, who got caught cheating, Negroes evicted from their homes, and murder.

Easton walked toward Keith, who had draped a red, white, and blue striped towel around the neck of a brotha who'd just climbed into one of the four worn-out brown leather chairs. Dingy white webbing used to stuff the chairs poked out through cracks in the leather, and the razor strop had frayed in places. Oval-shaped mirrors hung on the plastered white wall above small tables positioned behind each chair. A circlet of shorn hair beads clumped on the floor around the chair, like a garland you'd place on a grave or hang up for decoration. Most, if not all, barbers in the city were self-employed and rented a chair from the owner. That was true of three of these chairs.

"Here he is, Sherlock himself. Isn't that what Jimmy calls you?" Keith asked Easton. They shook hands.

"You got me, man. Where is everybody?" Easton asked. The barber chairs were occupied, yet only four men were waiting. Normally there would be a line of men pouring out the door.

"Hung over," Keith said.

Everybody laughed.

"How you'll doing?" Easton asked, stepping from one customer to another shaking their hands.

Older man: "Okay, son."

Man in blue plaid shirt: "Fine and you?"

Bald-headed man: "No complaints."

Stout man: "I've seen better days."

"I guess you all know someone killed William Taylor this morning," Easton said, gazing around the room, which grew even quieter, except for the steady humming of the barber shears and clippers cutting and trimming hair.

"You here for a cut or to question my customers?" Keith asked.

"I've got one question," Easton replied. "Who killed Taylor?"

Older man: "If I knew, the jackass would be imprisoned by now."

Man in blue plaid shirt: "Hush yo mouf, you mean under the prison."

Bald-headed man: "Even if I knowed who did it, the police ain't going after him."

Stout man: "Taylor didn't bury the white and wealthy, only dirt-poor folks like me. You probably the only person running around trying to find out who killed him. I bet the police aren't." The man took out a handkerchief and wiped his eyes. "Don't get me wrong, son, I don't fault you. I hope you do find him. We were lodge brothers, a good man."

"Cops don't give a damn about Negroes dying," Keith said, "so don't hold your breath waiting for them to find the killer. Boy, you'll keel over and die." The others chuckled, echoing his sentiment.

"That's exactly why I'm here," Easton said, "to find Taylor's killer."

Older man: "I didn't kill Taylor. Anybody in here kill Taylor?"

The four men perched on seats along the wall looked at one another. The men in the barber chairs didn't move, a straight razor sliding across the neck of one man.

"Wait a minute, now," Easton responded, realizing they had misinterpreted what he said. "I'm here for information, not to finger one of you for his murder."

Man in blue plaid shirt: "Go to the zoo, he's probably in there sleeping with the gorillas, the sick MF." He made everybody laugh, including Easton.

Stout man: "Try the YMCA. They got more men hiding in there than they do at the monastery."

Bald-headed man: "Now, y'all oughta stop it, dis is serous bidness, Taylor's dead."

The chuckling slowly faded to a murmur.

"The killer stabbed Taylor to death. Anybody know a knife-wielding thug?" Easton asked.

Older man: "Not me. But I can tell you this, if he caught Taylor by surprise, Taylor didn't stand a chance. A knife fighter who sneaks up on you with a knife already drawn will shank you before you know it. No question. I've seen it with my own eyes."

Man in blue plaid shirt: "You're right. Even though I didn't see combat in the army, I learned how to use a blade. All of us did. That's probably what happened to Taylor. Somebody caught him off guard and attacked him."

Bald-headed man: "I got knife trainin' on the corna to protec myself from thu Klan. I had to. They'd come outta no where an' drag yo' ass away, if you weren't carefu'."

Easton checked his watch. "Well, it's been good talking to you all. If you hear anything, call me at the ***Negro News***. I need to move on and find me a killer," Easton said.

"Boy, be careful out there. You don't know who you dealing with," Keith said. "You're young. You got a whole lot of life ahead of you. And you're not the police."

Easton watched the brotha swing around in Keith's chair and inspect his hair in the mirror, turning right then left. When he nodded, Keith untied and removed the floor-length barber bib covering his clothes.

"No, I'm not the police. I'm a reporter doing what the police are supposed to be doing. Like you said, the cops don't give a damn about Negroes," Easton responded. "I'll need a cut before the funeral. I'll see you later." After he shook Keith's hand, he went out into the street.

* * *

Easton scanned both sides of the street, feverishly drawing on his cigarette. The sunshine flirted with clouds gliding across the sky. He didn't want it to rain, not today. He had too much driving around to do. It seemed his car didn't like rain. Sometimes it'd stall without warning, in the middle of the street, leaving Easton stranded for hours. He wandered into the alley behind the barbershop and spotted a group of men crouched down next to a building. As he got closer, two of the men stood in the middle of the alley, posturing. Easton continued to walk toward them. "Nothing but a partay," Easton said when he reached them. After a couple of high fives, the men went back to shooting craps.

Bets had already been waged. Easton watched the shooter roll out seven. The two dice toppled around on the ground. When they stopped, "three crap three."

No one had passed, so the shooter picked up the coins, laughing. Easton peered at the street-smart hustler he'd come to rely on for information about people and events going on in the city. He had no legitimate job that Easton knew of, yet when he cleaned up, he looked like he belonged on the cover of ***Esquire*** magazine. "Taylor's murder . . . what's the word on the street?" Easton asked him.

"Easton Priest, I haven't seen you in a while," the shooter said. "Where you been hiding?"

"Work," Easton replied. "Any word on Taylor's killer?"

"Nah, man, maybe lata."

"Later may be too late," Easton said. "The killer may be gone, lata'."

"Whatcha want me to do, brotha? That's all I got."

"You know how to reach me," Easton said. "If I had more time, I'd stay and take all your money."

The men laughed as Easton walked away.

* * *

The closer Easton got to the precinct, the worse the traffic; cars had backed up at least two blocks on the road leading to the precinct. Car horns made a racket, passing him by, then he saw the reason. A wedding had ended at a church around the corner. Easton and Ruth had agreed to a small wedding even though the House of Worship, Ruth's church, occupied half a block on a busy corner; it had its own parking lot, so Easton didn't expect this kind of gridlock at the intersection. He had to sit through three light changes and then inch along the road until he found a parking space four blocks from the precinct.

Easton walked briskly along the street, Taylor's death still haunting him, his head reeling like a spinning top, his mind a blur from no sleep. He bumped into a young woman who'd stepped from her yard. "Sorry, ma'am, I wasn't paying attention."

"Apology accepted." She smiled, straightened her black turban, and strutted off.

The woman's hat made him think of Leslie, the hat lady. He'd forgotten to ask the crap shooter about her. He stopped off at a pay phone to call Odean, his other contact on the street. Leslie had not only cried for Taylor, she also knew about his troubles with Family Life, unlike other women Easton had spoken to, which seemed to take their friendship to another level. He wanted to know more about her.

"Odean, Easton here. Leslie Ann Penny from the market, you know her?"

"Yeah," Odean answered.

"Who's she going with?" Easton asked.

"Quentin King. He sells washing machines, dryers, refrigerators at Boone's Appliances on Q Street," Odean said.

"Find out how tight Family Life's president, Rutherford Daniels, and Taylor were with Leslie," Easton said.

"Come again," Odean said.

"You heard me," Easton responded.

"I'll see about it," Odean said, laughing.

Easton didn't want to acknowledge that Taylor may have stepped out on Naomi. Carousing with other women had been part of his past—at least that's what Taylor had told him. He expected the truth would surface in due time.

# CHAPTER 16

Easton hurried into the precinct. He approached the counter in the lobby, where a policeman directed him to a room down the corridor to the sergeant's desk. The sergeant had a mean, cold, hard look etched on his pale face; the tone of his voice matched his face. "What do you want?"

"I'm here to pick up Ms. Johnson and Mrs. Naomi Taylor," Easton replied. "They're here giving a police report. Somebody murdered Mrs. Taylor's husband this morning. Where are they?"

The cop used a pen and skimmed a roster for Naomi's and Ruth's name. He paused and then looked toward the waiting area. "Mrs. Taylor is sitting over there."

Easton hadn't bothered to look toward the waiting area when he went in. He believed Naomi and Ruth were still holed up in a room somewhere. He spotted Naomi talking to a woman he didn't recognize. Actually, the woman talked. Naomi didn't even appear to be listening.

"They said I killed Taylor," Naomi blurted, as Easton moved toward her. She sat glassy-eyed as if death were staring her in the face. "They took our fingerprints and questioned us in separate rooms, treated us like criminals. My lawyer is with Ruth."

Easton knelt beside her and held her hand. "Are you okay?"

Naomi slumped over and rested her head on Easton's chest, crying. "They didn't want my lawyer with me. I told them to put me in jail, because I refused to say shit if he couldn't represent me."

Easton didn't know what troubled him more, Naomi cursing because he'd never heard her say a bad word, or the police handling her as a suspect. In his mind, he knew cops looked at spouses first if their better half went missing or succumbed to a suspicious death. It was not a rule of law; it simply was. Yet in his heart he knew Naomi didn't murder Taylor. The police were wrong; they'd made a mistake. ***They need to get off their ass and look at somebody else,*** Easton wanted to say out loud, but he didn't. "Where did they question you?"

"In a dirty room . . . no windows. They made me sit in a chair with a broken arm. Then a detective came in and asked me what happened."

Naomi wept as she sputtered through the events leading up to Taylor's death during what indeed sounded like an interrogation rather than Naomi giving a statement. "I told him about the Family Life investigation and the dinner party. He already had a copy of the *Negro News* with your report in it. I suggested he read the damn thing. He asked me what we did at the party and where Ruth had gone."

Easton wanted to know where Ruth had gone too, until three o'clock in the morning. "What time did the bridal shower end?"

Naomi didn't answer. She appeared to be deep in thought.

Easton waved his hand in front of Naomi. "Mrs. Taylor . . . Mrs. Taylor."

Naomi roused, a blank expression on her face. "I don't know," Naomi answered. "I left Taylor to lock up the house. Took a bath and fell asleep waiting for him."

"He never made it to bed?" Easton asked.

"He never made it to bed. I found him in the kitchen, blood everywhere. Oh lord! Oh lord! Why?" She grabbed Easton's arm and held on to it, her sobs deafening. Women listening nearby cried too. Others sat quietly watching her show of grief.

"Was he alive when you found him?" Easton asked.

"No." She raised her head.

"Mrs. Taylor, I'm so sorry. You know how much I respected Mr. Taylor. I'm going to miss him," Easton said, fighting back tears.

"Thank you," Naomi said, patting Easton on his face.

Easton attempted to dispel any notion that she might be a suspect, which had angered him earlier. "It's not unusual for the police to treat a spouse as a suspect. You and I both know you didn't kill your husband. You'll be okay," Easton said.

"You don't understand. The detective tried to say Taylor had an affair and I found out about it and killed him," Naomi said. "I was so mad I threw water in his face. I didn't care who he was. How dare he accuse me of killing my husband."

Easton sighed. "What did he do?"

"Wiped his face," Naomi said. "I told him to stop insulting me and find my husband's killer. I'm not taking bullshit from anyone, I don't care who it is!"

* * *

Thirty minutes later, Ruth appeared in the lobby with Naomi's lawyer, Collin Dewitt Unger, now her lawyer too. Easton scuttled through chairs filled with people, to reach her. Naomi stayed seated.

"You all right?" Easton enfolded Ruth in his arms.

"Yes," Ruth answered. "How's Mom?"

"Sad . . . angry," Easton replied.

They walked over to Naomi, and Ruth hugged her.

"What did they ask you?" Naomi asked Ruth.

"If you and Dad had marital problems, if you had a mental illness. Can you believe it?"

Naomi shook her head.

"It's not unusual for police to ask Negroes questions like that," the lawyer said. "I hear it all the time."

"Then they had the nerve to ask me why I wasn't home, where I had been. I told them, I'm not a biddy. I can stay out all night if I want to. I had to write it all down and sign it," Ruth complained.

That settled it for Easton. He had no intention of questioning Ruth about the bridal shower or anywhere else she might have gone. He'd always trusted her, so he didn't know why or how his doubt came about in the first place. ***Maybe fear.*** Riding around the city at three o'clock in the morning, Ruth had definitely been vulnerable. The fact of the matter is, Taylor had been murdered in his home, where Ruth also lived.

"I want to go now," Naomi pleaded.

"You can leave now, you just can't leave DC unless you call the detective first in case they want to question you again," Naomi's lawyer told her.

"You mean accuse me of killing Taylor again," Naomi said. "They know where to find me. I told them we're staying at the Jenkinses' until they finish in the house."

"There's no suspect yet, so they may pick on you for a while," her lawyer said. "No one's come forward with information about the murder and, no one's been assigned to lead the investigation yet."

Easton excused himself to bring his car around to the front of the building, his size 11 shoes pounding the floor as he left. He fired up a cigarette while he waited with his ride to deter any chance of being ticketed for "standing." A few minutes later, Ruth and Naomi came through the station door. He rushed to assist Naomi, slow-moving, down the steps and into the backseat of his car. Ruth sat beside her. As he drove off, he heard their sobs over the Platters singing "Earth Angel" and "Only You" and Fats Domino's "Ain't That a Shame" and "Blueberry Hill" playing on the radio. He wanted to turn the music up louder, except he didn't want to appear numb to their sorrow. He kept it low and listened to his own pain.

* * *

When they arrived at the Jenkinses', Easton waited in the foyer while Ruth and Mildred helped Naomi upstairs. When Ruth returned, he collected her in his arms.

"I talked to people all morning, trying to find out who murdered your father and why," Easton said.

"What did they say?" Ruth asked.

"He almost came to blows with the president of Family Life in March. Your father accused him of fraud."

"Did he threaten Dad?"

"For libel."

"Do you think he killed him?"

"It's possible. Even though we didn't prove fraud, he knew we were going to continue the investigation and that the insurance board was going to conduct an audit of their company, so they weren't off the hook. And I know at least one person who canceled his policy with the company after he read the report because he doesn't trust them anymore, and there may be others."

Ruth whimpered. Easton pressed her closer. "I love you so much. It hurts to see you suffer like this."

"I'm exhausted," Ruth said.

"Get some rest, baby. I'll call you later," Easton said.

"Promise?"

"Promise," Easton said, brushing away her tears. "Sweet dreams, baby."

# Chapter 17

Easton was tired too and hungry. The Jenkins lived less than a mile from Jimmy's Grille on Ninth and Florida Avenue Northwest. The cheese and apple-buttered bread Easton had eaten at the market were mere appetizers compared to what he'd feast on next. He parked his Buick on a side street, took the last puff off a cigarette, and stepped out of the car, the smell of greasy food stagnant in the air.

Jimmy, Easton's cousin twice removed on the Priest side of the family, had opened the Grille with his brother fifteen years ago. He looked nothing like the Priest side of the family. Medium height with sandy-brown hair and green eyes, his mustache, trimmed above thick lips, curled at the ends. A lively and boisterous thirty-eight-year-old, he'd stayed single, leaving some family members believing he was light in the loafers.

While a student at Howard, Easton had worked and earned his meals at the Grille. Oftentimes when the last customer left, Jimmy would lock the door and, for the rest of the night, preach about the amount of food people wasted and about the poor people who had none.

"Will you look at this? There's a child starving to death somewhere, and we're throwing food away. Oooh, it don't make sense wasting food like this. It's got to stop," he'd say. It never did.

It had taken Easton almost a year to get used to all the chaos behind the scenes of what he considered a big city restaurant, most of it brought on by Jimmy's gregarious personality. Working on the farm, backbreaking, yes, and thinking back, a lot less noise and commotion, except when the dogs chased the chickens through the yard. He took on all kinds of odd jobs in the restaurant. Once when Jimmy decided to change the menu, he asked Easton to help him. Jimmy liked his suggestions, how he worded the menu. He gave him extra cash that week. Other times, when Easton finished his chores, he'd head for the door, and before he opened it, Jimmy would slip him a few extra bills and say "I know your parents give you money too. Granny told me. Be wise about your spending." Now Jimmy treated Easton as a full-fledged adult.

"Bring on the Easton special!" Jimmy yelled to the kitchen as Easton went through the door. "Cuz, how's the little woman holding up?"

"She's a wreck," Easton said.

"Why aren't you with her?" Jimmy asked, his hands on both hips.

"The police questioned her and Naomi Taylor at the Second precinct, then I drove them to the Jenkinses'. They're staying there while the cops process the funeral home," Easton explained. "They were both tired and wanted to rest."

"Prepare yourself, Sherlock. They're gonna need beaucoup help recovering from this," Jimmy said. "So they're staying with the Jenkins?"

"Yeah, close friends of the Taylors," Easton replied.

"Good people. I bought most of my furniture from their store. I love it. They have reproductions no one else sells, and it's reasonably priced," Jimmy said.

"You hear anything?" Easton asked.

"Not a nary thing. It's been real quiet," Jimmy replied. "I opened late. Fighting that crowd this morning wore me out. Some of those people I didn't mind being close to. I'm gonna pray for the others. Smelled like they'd been sifting through garbage. Downright nasty."

"Here you go, baby." The waitress put a large orange juice and a generous serving of eggs, grits, ham, and biscuits in front of Easton.

"Thank you, beautiful," Easton said, grinning. He hadn't spent much time at Jimmy's lately. He'd been busy writing the series on segregation and then conducting the Family Life investigation. While he ate, they caught up on all the happenings.

"I'm asking Ruth to marry me Christmas Day," Easton said between bites of food.

"I knew it. That's the only way you'll get a piece of that," Jimmy said, laughing. "Your nose is so wide open I can see your brain sometimes. When's the big day, lover boy?"

"May. We started going together in May two years ago," Easton said. "Taylor's death may put things on hold. I'll leave it up to Ruth."

"Boy, I wish I was a fly on the wall, an ant, a roach, whatever . . . in that bedroom on your honeymoon." They both laughed.

Easton went on to tell Jimmy how Taylor had gone to him with Family Life's story of corruption.

Jimmy leaned toward him and whispered, "You think the SOBs put a hit on Taylor?"

"I wouldn't put it past them. They're the only folks he had a beef with that we know about. And they lost at least one client. Some people don't need proof when it comes to their money. Just a hint of doubt, they're off and running," Easton responded.

"Well, I canceled my insurance with those thieves for that very reason, so that makes two of us. They had the nerve to tell me some payments weren't recorded right and that's why those people's policies were canceled. I told them to kiss my canceled ass, because I didn't believe a word they said," Jimmy exclaimed.

Easton laughed. Jimmy never hesitated to say what popped into his mind. He finished the hearty meal and leaned back in his chair.

"That hit the spot, cuz. I need to go earn my pay and check on Ruth and her mother. Here you go." Easton handed Jimmy a couple of bills and some change. "Put a nickel on 270 for me, I'll call you later."

Easton's number had come up in combination three months earlier. He'd parlayed some of his winnings on the horse races and had lost it all. He wanted his number to come out again, yet he didn't. Since Taylor's murder, he'd been preoccupied with his own fate; even playing the numbers had him worrying about dying. He recalled an old saying that when your number comes up, it's your time to die. He wanted to go back and get his nickel. He didn't want to be so lucky.

# Chapter 18

Easton climbed into his car, almost eight hours after Taylor's murder. His temples began to throb, and he struggled to keep his eyes open. He wanted to go home and sleep. Instead, he shut his eyes and leaned back on the cool leather seat. The image of Taylor's blood, pooled into a brownish-red mess on the kitchen floor, popped into his mind. He recalled standing at the kitchen door, overtaken by what looked like several gallons of blood spread motionless on the floor. The sight and smell of it had almost made Easton sick. Now it made him angry. ***Taylor didn't deserve to die so violently***, he said to himself. ***No one does.***

He sat up and cranked the engine. It didn't start. "Oh shit, not today!" he said, hitting the console. He tried again. This time the engine turned over. "I'm trading you in. I can't have Ruth stranded out here fooling with you. It's not even raining and you're trying to conk out."

A block before reaching his house, Easton pulled to the curb. It dawned on him that he hadn't talked to Doc Nelson, Taylor's best friend. Besides Naomi, no one knew Taylor better than Doc Nelson did, at least that's what Taylor had said. He made a U-turn and sped to Doc Nelson's house, jerked to a screeching stop, jumped out the car, sprinted up steps to the front door, and rang the doorbell a couple of times—no answer. He climbed over the banister and jogged toward the rear of the house. Halted by two German shepherds barking and pawing at a fence taller than him, Easton bolted back around the front like a runaway horse spooked by a rattlesnake to the sidewalk.

"They ain't home." He stood face-to-face with a girl carrying grocery bags.

"Oh! Okay," Easton said, still trembling from the sight of the dogs clawing the chain fence, mouths curled back, saliva drooling around huge incisors sharp enough to rip out his heart. He jumped into his car and clutched the steering wheel. He hadn't been this afraid of the wolves in Tennessee when they went out of the woods, searching for food, and he didn't know the Nelsons owned dogs. He had thought the barking came from the yard next door, where the girl carrying groceries had gone inside.

Before he pulled off, a black Desoto coasting down the street turned into the Nelsons' driveway, Doc Nelson behind the wheel. While the engine was still running, Dorothy Nelson and Thomas got out of the car and went inside. Doc backed down the driveway and drove off. ***Maybe to the pharmacy he owns***, Easton assumed. The dogs, still agitated, growled even louder as Easton tiptoed back up the steps. His clothes were drenched with sweat. Perspiration trickled from his armpits down the sides of his body, like water trickling from a broken water spout. He felt like he'd taken a shower and hadn't dried off. Glad he had a jacket on, he hoped he didn't smell too ripe. He rang the doorbell. While he waited, he expected the ferocious-acting dogs to plow around the front any minute and attack him. Dorothy Nelson answered the door directly. Easton's fear turned to relief.

"Easton," she said. "Didn't I see you this morning?"

"Yes, you did, at Taylor's funeral home this morning," Easton replied, shaking his head. "May I have a few minutes of your time to talk about Mr. Taylor?"

"For what?" she asked.

"I'm writing his story for the newspaper. I want to know about the man, his life, friends, enemies, anyone who may have wanted him dead," Easton replied.

"Does Naomi know you're writing this story?" she asked.

"Yes, ma'am," he lied.

"Well . . . okay. I'm just not in the mood for a whole lot of questions," she replied. "Besides, I don't know a soul who wanted him dead."

Easton stepped inside.

She took his hat and hung it on a hook by the door. "In here." She motioned him to a room off the foyer. A plump, shapely woman of medium height, her thick black eyebrows were arched over clear yellow eyes that looked like the glass marble balls he used to play with in the dirt. She wore her black hair short and tapered at the neck, and although a mulatto like Naomi, Dorothy had darker skin—a copper-tone color.

Easton eased into a large overstuffed wing chair next to the fireplace and planted his feet on an oriental rug. He immediately began to sneeze, and his eyes watered. He suspected pollen, from the fresh bouquet of flowers on the coffee table, had been released into the air. "Excuse me," he said, wiping his eyes. "I think I'm allergic to your flowers."

"God bless you, son." Dorothy took the flowers to the kitchen. When she returned, she said, "Here, take this tablet, it'll clear up your head real fast."

Easton hesitated. He didn't like taking medicine, except he kept sneezing. "Thank you." He swallowed the tablet with a glass of water Dorothy handed him.

"Sit tight, I'll be right back," Dorothy said.

Easton gazed around the room. The Nelsons' wedding picture sat on a beige granite mantelpiece. That's when he realized that the Taylors, including Thomas, were important to the Nelsons. Their pictures were on the mantel too. Pictures of other people he didn't know were placed throughout the room, and photos of a boy at different ages were displayed on a sofa table. Dorothy walked back in the room, carrying a large black leather binder.

"Is that Thomas?" Easton asked, pointing to the pictures of the boy.

"That's him. Cute as a button," Dorothy replied, smiling. She stood beside Easton. "He's a handsome young man now. He's upstairs sleeping, the poor thing. He's taking his father's death very hard."

Easton became distracted by the large velvet tapestry centered on the wall behind the settee. Woven in brown tones with a hint of gold scattered throughout, two deer, one with antlers keeping vigil over a sleeping doe, were etched in thin black lines on the fabric, along with the grass, trees, and bushes. ***A peaceful, tranquil setting,*** Easton thought. He recalled a tapestry hanging in the viewing room at Taylor's home, one with a different scene, brighter colors, peaceful nonetheless. He turned his attention back to Dorothy. "I want to record Mr. Taylor's life journey. What can you tell me about him?"

"You should be talking to Doc," Dorothy said. "He knew the man inside and out."

"So I've heard," Easton replied.

"Well, since you're here . . . Naomi is my first cousin, on my father's side. Our families farmed in Virginia. That's how we survived, off the land. I left there before Naomi to study at Miner Teachers College. My second year, I met Doc. He'd already received his pharmacy degree. When he asked me to marry him, I left school and never looked back." She beamed. "Now, Taylor and Doc are native Washingtonians. Born and raised here." She opened the binder and handed it to Easton, pointing to pictures as she spoke. "This is the two of them in grade school, at their high school graduation, and their college graduation."

Easton grinned. Doc Nelson loomed over Taylor even as a young boy. The two of them reminded him of Mutt and Jeff. "They were fine young boys, if I must say so myself. If I include pictures with my story, I may want to print one of these."

"Let me know," Dorothy said, as she moved to the settee to sit down. "What gets me . . . we were just at Taylor's for dinner last night and had a ball. Lord have mercy, I don't know what happened when we left." Tears dribbled from under the rim of her glasses.

"I understand Mr. Taylor didn't mince words about Family Life. Did he talk about the company last night?" Easton asked.

"'Deed, he did."

"What did he say?" Easton asked.

"He thanked you and the ***Negro News*** for investigating the company then talked about how corrupt they are," she answered. "After we started eating, he didn't say much more." Dorothy began to sob. "I'm sorry I can't talk anymore, not right now."

Easton apologized for imposing upon her and got up to leave. ***It's going to be hard getting people close to Taylor to talk about him, they're all grieving,*** Easton concluded. Dorothy sobbed louder as she closed the door behind him.

* * *

Finally, Easton drove home to a boarding house on H Street where he'd rented a furnished room on the third floor of the four-story house his freshman year at Howard University, seven years ago. The cost of room and board in

Howard's dormitories had been too expensive for him to stay on campus. On the other hand, a rooming house off campus cost far less.

What he loved about his room, aside from the washroom on the same floor, and what sold him on it was that he shared the floor with only one other man. Two other dudes rented on the second floor: a homosexual, who aspired to be a singer, his processed hair never out of place, and the other taught eighth grade in a DC public school. At the YMCA, where he had first inquired about a place to live, he'd be living with twenty or thirty other men, and it smelled bad, worse than the boys' locker room at his old high school.

Easton earned enough to rent an apartment now. Then again, by boarding, he'd saved a lot of cash. And for an additional small price, he ate some of the best soul food in DC. Mrs. Kelly, the owner, cooked all day on Saturday for dinner on Sunday, always enough food for the whole week. And unlike some folks, Easton didn't mind leftovers.

During a visit from his parents four months earlier, Easton had been told by his father to move. "Easton, you need your own place. Buy yourself a house, or come home and buy some land. You need to invest your money. Where do you keep it, in a sock?" his pops had asked.

Easton had laughed. "Pops, you're not giving me much credit. I have a nice little bankroll. In fact, Ruth and I are buying a house right before we get married."

"Well, thank goodness for that," Pops had said. "I thought you were bringing her here."

Mr. and Mrs. Kelly lived on the first floor of the boarding house. Mrs. Kelly had made it clear. "I'm not putting up with women coming and going except mothers, grandmothers, aunts, or sisters. And the sister has to prove she's your sister." Because of that, Easton seldom invited Ruth over.

He skipped steps to his room. It screamed for new wallpaper and a new sofa bed. Beige paper with peach-colored flowers had turned yellow from the sticky dried tar affixed to it, after years of cigarette smoke lingering in the room. In some places where the wallpaper had peeled off, spots of pale green paint had shown through, which reminded Easton of his room on the farm painted a light green too. A venetian blind with slats that had turned gray from aging shaded the one window overlooking the alley, under it a small console television. What bothered him most was every Saturday morning, around seven o'clock, dogs barked at men dropping trash cans on the pavement in the alley and woke him. Sometimes he couldn't go back to sleep. He'd curse every dog in the neighborhood, the trashmen too. It was bad enough he slept on a mattress so thin he'd wake up with dents on his arm from the metal frame holding it together. He did have a choice in the matter though—to buy a new one or to sleep on the floor.

Easton had no problem taking work home. Sometimes he'd stop in the kitchen for a plate of food and take it to his room. He'd sit at a small table next to the door where he also kept his typewriter, a telephone, and a lamp.

"Don't forget to bring your plate and garbage down when you finish," Mrs. Kelly said every time. "I don't want roaches crawling all over the place."

"Yes, ma'am, as soon as I finish," he'd respond.

Against the lamp he'd propped a picture of him and Ruth at Sandy Point Beach the first summer they dated. She'd worn a yellow halter-top bathing suit with a belt that tied around her small waist.

"Would you rub some lotion on my back?" she'd asked him. Her back felt soft like cotton, and not a pimple or blemish in sight. He'd used every bit of control not to throw her down on the sand and make love to her. What he'd planned as a fun outing turned out to be a tough day on the beach for him. A framed photo of their graduation pictures from college and one of his family sat on a bureau along with a bottle of Old Spice, Royal Crown hair grease, comb, brush, toothpaste, soap, a small bottle of aspirin, and a radio.

The eight-by-ten room had one small closet. What it didn't hold, he stored behind the sofa. Since he didn't have a shelf, he arranged his books on the floor next to a wall. Easton tossed his jacket on the sofa. He surveyed the cluttered room. Newspapers were scattered everywhere, and carbon dust covered his desk. The odor of dirty clothes and cigarette smoke smelled so foul, he popped open the window to air out the place.

"What a mess," he said, disgusted. For the past two months, he'd spent most evenings working on his series of articles about Negroes' challenges with integration in DC. No matter the dirty room, the articles were more important than cleaning. He gathered newspapers and wads of typing and carbon paper that he'd thrown on the floor and emptied his ashtray overflowing with cigarette butts. Afterward he turned on the radio to the sound of Nat King Cole singing "Nature Boy."

Easton lay down and tried to sleep, except the bloody scene in Taylor's kitchen, now fixed in his memory, kept creeping to the surface. The throbbing in his head got worse, causing him to grab a hold of his head with both hands. He took in a long, deep breath, sat up, and lit a cigarette. He pondered over his report on Family Life, in particular the quotes from Taylor that questioned the company's business practices that may have set him up as a target of contempt. He had silently wrestled with the notion that he'd killed Taylor with his words. Too late now; he couldn't unpublish the report even if he wanted to. He jumped from the sofa and ran to the open window. "God, please forgive me," he spoke through the screen, his shoulders shaking, his tears dripping onto the windowsill.

After he had a good cry, he toddled over to the dresser, grabbed the bottle of aspirin, and washed down four of them with a half-empty bottle of soda. He lay back on the sofa, speculating about the people on Sixth Street who'd refused to interview with him. He believed paying reverence to fear was sanctimonious because he'd been taught to fear God, not man. Notwithstanding Taylor's horrifying death, he realized that some people needed time to deal with a tragic situation. Sooner or later they'd start talking, unless, of course, one of them killed him.

Easton breathed in the hot smell of fried chicken rising from the kitchen. It brought a faint smile to his face. He'd make sure he got a few pieces before the other tenants went in from work. The old clock on the mantel in the front room downstairs chimed. The hour strike came right after noon, and it had already been a long day. He plummeted into a deep sleep.

* * *

The jingling of his telephone awakened Easton hours later.

"Hello."

"Easton, Dorothy Nelson's at the Second precinct," Odean said.

"What? Why?" Easton asked, his voice slow and lethargic.

"Don't know, brother. I'll talk back to you." Odean hung up.

Easton dragged himself off the sofa and grabbed his jacket and briefcase. He didn't know of any reason why Dorothy Nelson might be there, except for Taylor's murder. And he did not what was worse, knowing or not knowing why. He almost ran down a car speeding to the precinct.

# Chapter 19

A different cop sat behind the sign-in desk at the police station. This time Easton didn't have to bang on the window for service.

"Is Mrs. Dorothy Nelson ready to leave?" Easton asked.

"Who are you?" the cop asked.

"A friend of the family," Easton replied. "Dr. Nelson, her husband, asked me to pick her up." Easton lied through his teeth.

"She'll be out soon," the officer said.

Easton resorted to waiting in the uncomfortable metal chairs in the waiting room. He observed the young cop shuffle through papers on his desk. When his phone rang, he picked up the receiver and swiveled around in his chair, his back now turned toward Easton. Easton jumped from his seat and bounded the short distance to the squad room and peeped through the open door. He didn't see Dorothy Nelson or any other familiar face. Right when he returned to the waiting area, the cop hung up the phone.

After a few minutes, a sudden, shrill sound coming from the squad room jolted him from his seat. The cop on the phone heard it too. His phone started buzzing, and within seconds, policemen emerged from every crack and crevice in the building, like cockroaches let loose at night, and ran past Easton, hands on their guns. He followed them. When he reached the doorway, a cop pushed him back so hard, he fell and hit his head on the wall, his briefcase flung from his grip.

"You don't belong in here, Sambo." The officer darted in the squad room, laughing.

"Asshole," Easton said. He scrambled to retrieve his briefcase and vowed to get even with the officer. He rubbed his sore head, a knot rising on it already. Dazed and angry, he watched policemen escort people from the squad room and out of the building. ***Dorothy Nelson must be still in there or had he missed her?*** Several black men handcuffed to one another were pushed and prodded by cops to another part of the building.

"Move it, you coons," one of the cops called them.

Easton didn't know what wrong they'd done. What he did know, no mother or father would name their child coon. He didn't want to think about how they'd be treated in police custody. From what ex-cons had told him, they endured the same oppression and humiliation as slaves did at the master's hand. He figured at least one of the black men would fight back and wind up dead in jail.

A policeman approached Easton. "Leave now."

Easton didn't move. He glared at him.

"Now, unless you want to sleep here tonight," the policeman said.

Easton reluctantly left, still dazed from his head hitting the wall. The policeman slammed the double door behind him, which jarred his head even more. Once outside, he saw people milling about in constant chatter. He noticed a young pregnant girl standing on the treed lawn, wiping her eyes.

"Miss, are you all right?" he asked, walking toward her.

She massaged her stomach while she spoke. "I'm just nervous."

"Were you in the squad room?" Easton asked.

She nodded. "My cousin . . . got caught shoplifting. The police was questioning her."

"What happened in there?" asked Easton.

"A man stabbed a woman," she screeched, and began to cry.

An ambulance, its sirens blaring, came around the corner and stopped in front of the station. Easton turned away from the girl and observed the paramedics dash into the building with a gurney. He turned back to the girl. She'd gotten in a cab.

"Damn," he said.

"Mrs. Taylor!" shouted a voice in the crowd.

Ruth and Naomi stepped through the station door. Easton had no idea they were in the precinct. He met them halfway on the landing.

"You killed my husband!" Naomi screamed at Easton. She ran from him. Ruth, stunned, ran after her.

Easton stood petrified, his mouth opened in disbelief. He believed his report and Taylor's murder might be connected, and though he'd blamed himself, he didn't expect anyone else to. He regained his composure and raced toward the Packard. Ruth drove off before he reached her. He paced the sidewalk, Naomi's words shooting through his head like a round of bullets, finally ricocheting off into her darkness. What he believed in his mind, he spoke from his broken heart. "I did it. I put the knife in the killer's hand," he said, his head bowed. "God help me!"

He stood stock-still until an ambulance crew passed by, rolling Dorothy Nelson on a gurney, her eyes closed.

"Lawd a mercy . . . stabbed by that boy," someone said in the crowd.

"Who stabbed her?" Easton asked.

"Taylor's boy, high on somethin'," the person answered.

"Thomas?" ***Can there be any more surprises today***, Easton pondered.

"I saw it. He yell'd somethin' 'bout his father. Swung a blade aroun'. Caught her. It took four police to put'm down."

In spite of this new revelation, Easton focused on Naomi, and what she had said, rather than the altercation between Dorothy and Thomas. He needed to find out from Ruth what brought on Naomi's outburst. He'd call Aaron first.

* * *

"Easton, the investigation is over for you. You're too close to it," Aaron said, after hearing Easton whine about what Naomi had said to him.

"No, Aaron, don't do this. Please don't," Easton pleaded. "I got this. I'll be just fine."

"Then why did you call me?" Aaron asked.

"I guess I just needed to talk to somebody," Easton replied.

"Easton, don't take Naomi Taylor's comments personal, even if they're meant to be. She needs someone to blame for her husband's murder. The police haven't arrested anyone. They don't even have a suspect. She's lashing out, and I can't blame her," Aaron said. "Go back to Sixth Street. The cops aren't coming to you with anything. And find out what happened to Dorothy Nelson. This is a big story too." Aaron hung up the phone.

Easton expected at least a little empathy from Aaron. As it were, Naomi Taylor had accused him of murdering her husband, his hero, no less, and now Taylor's only son, Thomas, sat in jail after stabbing his godmother, Dorothy Nelson. It all seemed like a bad dream Easton wanted to awake from. Whatever else he did this day, he vowed not to call Aaron again. He didn't want to be yanked off the investigation no matter how crazy or personal things became.

# CHAPTER 20

Easton inched into a parking space on Sixth Street, surprised to find one with so many black-and-whites still on the block. He paused to watch the sun go down behind the trees. It was like God had flicked a switch and instantly covered the city with a veil of darkness.

Lit up like a Christmas tree, it appeared as if every light in the funeral home had been turned on. Easton left his car and approached two cops on the sidewalk. One was Ira.

"Find anything?" Easton asked.

"You back again?" Ira answered.

"Are you leading the case?" Easton asked.

"Right now I'm not," Ira replied.

"You here all night?" Easton wanted to know who'd be around later. He wanted to take pictures of the crime scene and snoop around. A few months ago, Ruth had shown him where to find the spare key, after she'd left hers at work. He wondered if the cops knew about the key. As long as they remained in the funeral home, he'd have to wait to take pictures anyway.

"We're here 24-7, until we're done," Ira responded.

"Can I print that?" Easton asked.

"Don't quote me," Ira replied.

"Not a problem, brotha," Easton said. "By the way, an officer almost knocked me cold at the precinct. I'm standing at the squad room door after Thomas stabbed Dorothy Nelson, and he jammed me up against the wall. My head still hurts. How much time will I get for kicking a cop's ass?"

Ira laughed. "Let me put it this way. You'd be too old to father any children when they let you out."

"I'm not spending the rest of my life in jail because of his ass. I'm putting you on notice, if he lays a finger on me again, I'm suing for police brutality," Easton said. "Oh, I almost forgot. Have you all been questioning people you've arrested today about Taylor's murder?"

"I haven't arrested anybody today. I can't speak for the others," Ira replied.

"It might be worthwhile to ask people for information about the murder, maybe you'd offer them a lighter sentence or something," Easton said.

"Now you want to tell me how to do my job," Ira said.

"No, brotha, I just want to find Taylor's killer," Easton replied, and left.

* * *

Mrs. Kelly opened the door before Easton put his key into the lock. The concerned expression on her face told him she'd been waiting for him.

"What's wrong?" Easton asked her.

"Your mother called. She said call her no matter what time you get in. She's on pins and needles, worrying about you. She thinks Mr. Taylor's killer will come after you next because you exposed that company," Mrs. Kelly said. "Your father's cousin told her about Mr. Taylor."

"Thanks, I'll call her."

Up until now, Easton hadn't considered himself a target. On account of Naomi's accusations and, now, his mother's concern, he began to question his vulnerability. His report had fulfilled its purpose—to investigate Family Life's alleged fraudulent activities. Since he hadn't found any serious evidence, he didn't anticipate problems beyond its original intent, much less Taylor's murder or a threat to his own life. It's the last thing he'd considered. ***A "fluff" piece, how can it possibly be connected to Taylor's murder?*** Easton asked himself.

* * *

"Stop worrying, Ma. I'll be fine. They'd come for me by now, if they wanted me. Put Pops on the phone," Easton said. He heard her calling his father. He imagined him lumbering to the phone in the bedroom, while she stayed on the one in the dining room.

"Hey, Easton, what happened up there?" Pops asked.

"Somebody murdered Mr. Taylor in his kitchen," Easton answered. "Ruth and Mrs. Taylor are taking it real hard."

Pops heard the strain in Easton's voice. "Jesus Christ, where are they?"

"The Jenkinses—you know, the couple who owns the furniture store—until the police finish going through the house. Are you coming for the funeral?"

"We'll be there. I've already arranged to stay with cousin Bessie whenever it is," Pops answered.

"Good, I appreciate you coming. I don't know if this is the right time to tell you, I bought Ruth a ring. I'm asking her to marry me Christmas Day," Easton said.

"Oh, Easton, I'm so happy for you. You know we adore Ruth," his mother exclaimed.

"I'm glad you're settling down," Pops said.

"Have you heard from Thelma Junior?" Easton asked. Thelma Junior, Easton's sister who lived in Germany, had the same name as their mother.

"We got a letter yesterday. She's just fine," Easton's mother replied. Pops didn't comment on the letter.

"Good," Easton said. "Well, I've got to go. I need to call Ruth. I'll ring you with details of the funeral when everything's final. Holler at you later."

Easton puffed on a cigarette and gazed out the open window. The temperature had dropped, and cold air rushed in, whirling smoke around in the room. About to shut the window, he saw a form standing at the end of the alley under the dimly lit lamppost. Grayboy, the Kellys' doberman, noticed it too. Barking and growling, he ran back and forth along the fence separating the backyard from the alley.

Easton ran downstairs and out the back door to the fence. The person had gone. Grayboy had stopped barking and pacing. He trotted back to his corner under the back porch. Easton stared down the alley for a few more minutes to see if the person reappeared—nothing. He returned to his room, closed the window, and phoned Ruth.

"Hello, this is the Jenkinses' residence."

"Ruth, please," Easton said.

"Easton . . . do I sound like some other woman to you?" Ruth asked, annoyed that Easton didn't recognize her voice.

"Yes, your mother. It's in your genes, I guess."

"So you say. I thought you were coming over this evening."

"I didn't know if I was welcome after what your mother said at the station."

"Mom didn't mean what she said, Easton. She can't take much more," Ruth exclaimed. "With Dad killed, Aunt Dorothy stabbed, Thomas in jail, it pushed her over the edge. I'm scared for her."

"How's she doing?"

"She's been in bed since we got back. Mrs. Jenkins got her to eat a little chicken soup."

"What about you, did you get some rest?" Easton asked.

"I slept three hours. Most of the time I dreamed about you," she replied.

"Other times?" Easton asked.

"Dreamed about you." They both chuckled.

"Why did you go back to the precinct?" Easton asked.

"The police found Thomas in the street, acting erratic. They called Aunt Dorothy because his mother had gone to Baltimore to Dad's sister's house, and he didn't know her phone number. The police were taking him to Saint Elizabeth's Hospital for observation, so she asked me to bring clothes for Thomas. He keeps some in his old room. Mom decided to ride with me," Ruth responded.

"Jesus," Easton said.

"All of a sudden, Thomas pulled out a knife. Aunt Dorothy tried to take it from him, and that's when he stabbed her. He didn't realize what he'd done until after the police tackled him and took the knife. He cried like a baby. Mom almost passed out."

"Damn," Easton said. "I'm glad you all are all right. Will I see you at church tomorrow?"

"I don't know. I'm afraid to leave Mom by herself too long. She's not eating or sleeping and won't talk unless you say something to her," Ruth replied.

Ruth went on to chat about her mother and Taylor at length. Every now and again she'd laugh about one of their embarrassing moments. Easton wanted to hear her laugh more. He waited until she finished telling one of her stories, and then started singing "The Great Pretender."

"Easton, love, you can't sing," Ruth said, giggling. "Please, please stop trying, and keep writing. You're much better at it."

* * *

After Easton finished talking with Ruth, he called Toast. He needed to talk to somebody about the gut-wrenching pain tearing him apart inside, somebody to soothe the sting of Taylor's murder, Ruth's broken heart and Naomi's accusation that he killed Taylor. Besides, at nine o'clock in the evening, he'd just be getting started and his eyes were wide open. "Man . . . I'm barely holding on. I feel like I've been run over by a bulldozer and about to be ripped to shreds."

"What . . . don't tell me somebody's after ***you*** now?" Toast asked, in a concerned voice.

"No, I'm not that important," Easton replied. "No hired guns that I know of. I just can't believe Taylor's dead. He's gone, man, gone."

"Easton . . . brotha, it'll be okay. Stop running yourself ragged, get some rest," Toast said.

"I can't, I have a story to write and a killer to find," Easton responded.

"You're not the police, and you best remember that. Ruth and her mother need you," Toast said. "Stay cool, man."

"You're right, as always," Easton said. "God must be testing me. One day everything is copasetic. The next day, all hell breaks loose."

"And this too shall pass," Toast said.

Easton hung up and turned on the TV. Patti Austin, a pint-sized colored girl, was singing to the top of her lungs. He smiled. ***And she's just getting started.***

# CHAPTER 21

The next morning, Sunday, October 14, Easton set out for the House of Worship, looking for Ruth. The service started; she didn't show. He slipped out and drove to the Jenkinses. Ruth stood as he climbed steps to the porch. Smiling, she put down the magazine she'd been reading and reached up to hug him.

"Hey, baby," he said. "I went to your church, looking for you." Easton touched her lips, her eyes, and stroked her cheek. Her body collapsed into him, and he held her close.

"Mom had a bad morning," Ruth sobbed. "I don't know how to help her."

Easton kissed her lips. "Ruth, you're grieving too. Be your mother's daughter, not her nurse. A Band-Aid ain't going to fix her broken heart."

"I don't want to lose her too." Ruth cried. Her face turned red, and she gasped, trying to catch her breath.

"Hey . . . your mom has to grieve her way, you know that," Easton said. "Be there when she needs you. She'll be okay and so will you."

Ruth told him how overwhelmed she felt with all the responsibility for the funeral home business falling on her. "Since Mom is in no condition to conduct business, I've got to do it."

"I'm here," Easton said. "Leroy can help too."

"He's in the dining room," Ruth responded.

"Let's talk to him."

* * *

They entered the dining room, where Naomi, Leroy, and the Jenkinses were having brunch. Naomi's eyes were red and swollen, her face white as a ghost, her hair combed back in a ponytail. She appeared ten years older. Eyeing Easton, she neither frowned nor smiled.

"Good afternoon, Mrs. Taylor, Mr. and Mrs. Jenkins, Leroy. Please let me know if I can help with anything," Easton offered.

"Why, thank you, Easton," Mrs. Jenkins said. "We may have to call you at some point. Are you hungry? We have plenty of food. You don't have to eat in here with us old folk. You two can sit in the kitchen."

"Old folk?" Leroy said. "I'm younger than Easton."

They all laughed, except Naomi.

"Thank you, Mrs. Jenkins. We'll eat in the kitchen," Ruth said. "Leroy, we need to talk. Can you come with us, please?"

"I'll return soon, Etsi," Leroy said to Naomi, using the Iroquois word for ***mother***. Leroy, an Iroquois and Negro mix, had lived on a farm next to Naomi's family's farm in Virginia. When his parents and two brothers died from tuberculosis, Naomi's parents adopted the seven-year-old orphan. Since he was only two years older than Ruth at that time, he claimed Naomi as his mother rather than his adopted sister. Between munching on fried chicken, turnip greens, rice pudding, and drinking iced tea, Easton, Ruth, and Leroy developed a plan to deal with the business.

"I'll review the ledgers to see what bills need to be paid," Leroy said.

"Mom hid the current ledger and gave the police the old ones. She said they didn't even look at the dates. She won't tell me where she hid the ledger, before she slipped it in her case."

"Why didn't she give them the current ledgers?" Easton asked.

"She said it was none of their business," Ruth replied.

They talked about other things that needed taking care of, and when they finished . . .

"Want to ride to Hains Point?" Easton asked Ruth.

Ruth's eyes brightened, then she hesitated. "Maybe I should stay here with Mom."

"She'll be fine here with the Jenkinses. Come on, go with me," Easton begged.

"Okay, I'll go," Ruth replied

"You can't go," Easton said, turning to Leroy.

Leroy laughed. "I don't need to watch you two get down. I've got my own thing going."

"Who?" Ruth asked, surprised.

"Me no speak," Leroy answered. He waltzed back to the dining room.

* * *

"When was the last time you and I went on a date?" Easton asked.

"***Carmen Jones***," Ruth answered. "My god, what have we been doing?"

"I've been investigating Family Life, and you've been working overtime almost every day," Easton answered. "How much material do you need for a wedding dress?"

Ruth laughed. "It's not just the dress. It's the food, decorations, music, all that stuff," she answered.

"I thought we agreed to a small wedding."

"We did, love. I still have to pay for it," Ruth said.

Hains Point, located where the Anacostia River and Potomac River converged in Southwest DC, evolved into a favorite spot for bikers during the day and for lovers after sundown. The peninsula of land offered great views of the Washington Monument and the Capitol Building, two popular tourist attractions. Easton and Ruth cuddled on a bench, watching the water ripple from boats skirting its surface and enjoyed the cross breeze blowing from one side of the peninsula to the other bathing their face.

Ruth cast her eyes toward a jet plane approaching the city, while another soared to some faraway place. "I needed this," she said. "What happened to Dad, seeing Mom suffer, it hurts so bad I want to just fly away on one of those planes."

"And leave me? You can't do that." Easton held her face in his hands. "I won't let you leave me. It'll get better. Please don't give up, Ruth. Remember you're supposed to marry me." He soaked up her tears with his lips, kissed her hard, and felt her relax in his arms; the tension in her body dissipated. How long it would last, he didn't know.

# CHAPTER 22

Monday morning came too soon for Easton. The loud beeping from his alarm clock jolted him from sleep to a ray of sunlight peeking under the bottom of the venetian blind. The aura of death had summoned his dead grandparents to consciousness, and he had lain awake for several hours during the night, remembering. They'd died a year apart, joining their Maker and each other in that place where supposedly there's no pain, sickness, sorrow, or people killing one another, where everybody binds together in peace. He'd come to realize as the years went by that the pain of losing a loved one never goes away. Like the common cold, there was no real cure for sorrow, though it seemed to lessen with time. What hurt Easton most—they didn't live long enough to see him graduate from college.

He felt cold and pulled the covers up around his face. The thought of Ruth wanting to escape from the tragedy that unraveled her scared him. He'd watched her spirit break a little each minute. Taylor's death had thrown her into bouts of hopelessness, and it hurt Easton to see her suffer. His heart felt heavy, and he wondered if he'd taken on her pain. ***Maybe this is what loving a person means,*** he thought. After they'd left Hains Point, he'd made her promise to call him anytime, if she needed to talk, about anything.

* * *

"Good morning, Easton. How are the Taylor women doing?" Mrs. Kelly asked as he entered the kitchen.

"Not so good," Easton responded, pouring a cup of coffee. He sat at the Formica table, and Mrs. Kelly served him a plate of waffles, eggs, and sausage.

"Pray, Easton, pray. Mr. Taylor is not coming back, so everybody has to learn to live without him," Mrs. Kelly said, patting him on the back.

"Oh, so we all just pray and forget about Taylor? Forget that he was somebody's husband, somebody's father, somebody's friend," Easton said, the tension in his voice rising. "What prayer do I say?"

"Easton, the Lord's Prayer will do just fine," she answered, and marched out of the kitchen.

Anger had festered inside Easton, and coupled with sleep deprivation, the perilous combination had made him weary and he'd taken it out on Mrs.

Kelly. After he picked over his food, he went in search of her. He found her in the basement, washing clothes, and apologized for being rude. She accepted his apology and sent him on his way—to Family Life. Rumor had it that Daniels was out for blood. He believed the ***Negro News*** had tarnished his reputation and painted him as a criminal, even though Easton's report stated all allegations were just that, allegations. Every day Daniels's clients, who were also clients of Taylor's and friends to some of the victims of Family Life's alleged crime, bailed out and went to other companies for life insurance. It didn't surprise Easton. Black folks were funny about their money. For most, it didn't come easy. With any inkling of doubt, they'd take what they had and go somewhere else with it. It had only been a couple of days since Taylor's murder and from what Easton had heard, Family Life had already lost a small fortune. Easton wanted to take him on.

* * *

Rutherford Daniels refused to see Easton.

"I'm sorry, sir. Mr. Daniels wants you to leave and not come back here," the receptionist said as she hung up the phone.

Easton had been shunned by suspected criminals before. Most of them sought legal counsel; none were stupid. Yet one, usually living high off the hog, would rattle off at the mouth and give the paper fuel to print and prosecutors enough to convict their ass. Easton hoped Daniels had a loud mouth. He looked down at the receptionist desk for something to hurl through the window behind her since he couldn't hurl anything at Daniels, who cowered behind closed doors; at least that's how Easton rationalized his snub.

"I'm very sorry, sir," the receptionist said, and slipped Easton a note, "Meet me at Central Library, 5:30 pm. in the Back Room. Louise Palmer." The same name was printed on the wooden nameplate centered on her desk. Easton gripped the note in his hand. He opened his mouth to speak. She quickly placed a finger on her lips, a signal for him to keep quiet. He left. ***Maybe she has the evidence we need.*** Because Family Life had threatened to fire employees who talked with the media, he'd never met Louise or interviewed any employees working for the company, not for a lack of trying. He'd drive by the building at least two or three times in a day, hoping to catch an employee leaving the building. When he did, they'd refused to talk to him. They wouldn't even take his money. They were a scared bunch of Negroes.

Easton leaned against his car, frowning, thinking about Daniels's rejection. The morning hadn't started off worth a damn, and it seemed as if things were going downhill fast. His eyes followed low gray clouds gliding across the sky, and he wanted to go home and wait for the rain. It had a hypnotic effect on both him and his car; they'd both fall asleep at the first drop on the windowpane. ***Not now,*** he said to himself. He hadn't talked to Doc Nelson yet. He glanced at his watch. He had plenty of time to interview him before meeting with Louise.

* * *

Doc Nelson's clerk buzzed him from the back of the Pharmacie. Easton struggled to keep from laughing at him. He appeared in a white lab coat, his arms so long, the sleeves stopped way above his wrists. He looked as if he'd borrowed one of Ruth's lab coats. He took off his hound's-tooth-framed glasses, and Easton shook his hand, which had a slight jerk to it. He'd have to ask Ruth about it.

"Dr. Nelson, how is Mrs. Nelson?" Easton asked.

"She's home and doing just fine," Doc Nelson replied. "Thank you for asking."

"I'm writing a story about William Taylor for the paper. I'd like to hear your thoughts about him," Easton said.

"Be glad to give some to you."

Easton followed the doctor to a room stretched across the rear of the store. The smell of antiseptics, ammonia, and rubbing alcohol cooled his nostrils. A partition separated office space from boxes piled to the ceiling. He wondered what Doc kept back there. He heard something dripping. ***Maybe a leaking faucet,*** he thought. He perused the title of books arranged on shelves built in the wall above the doctor's desk. Nothing looked familiar. Bottles, tubes, and jars of medicine sat in bins around the room. He saw other medicinal preparations, mostly pink, orange, and yellow-colored liquids, through the glass door of a large refrigerator-freezer that sat in a corner next to an open window.

Doc Nelson turned down his radio and sat at his desk, hands folded in his lap. He spoke in a pleasant voice.

"Young man, I have to say, you more than impressed Taylor. He wanted to see you and Ruth get married. I told him to leave you two alone to make that decision, to mind his own business."

"Mr. Taylor didn't strike me as an easy man to impress. I'm pleased to hear he thought well of me. Ruth and I are getting married next year, and of course, you and Mrs. Nelson are invited," Easton said. "Thanks for taking time to see me, Dr. Nelson. Mr. Taylor's sudden death upset a lot of us. Nevertheless, it must be devastating—your best friend murdered, your wife stabbed by his son."

With a pitiful sigh, Doc Nelson slouched forward. "It's been a roller coaster, for sure. Dorothy's okay now, I'm not sure about Thomas. He's my godson." He shook his head, his face reflecting concern. "You know he's at Saint Elizabeth's."

Easton nodded. "Ruth told me, she plans to visit him this week." Ruth had told Easton that she'd called the hospital and Thomas had agreed to see her and Naomi.

"Taylor and I had been friends since kindergarten," Doc said, chuckling. "We lived on the same street and played at each other's house almost every day. We made up our own games because we didn't have toys. Our families were poor, struggling through the Depression, that aside, Taylor and I were determined to attend college. We made money delivering newspapers and cut grass all over

Shaw. When we got older, we'd get jobs busing dishes and cleaning bathrooms. We saved just about every penny we made, it helped too. I went to pharmacy school at Howard, and he majored in business." He paused. "When the opportunity to own houses opened up for Negroes, we both jumped at the chance and bought one. And Taylor partied for days when they laid new streetcar tracks on Seventh Street for people to travel downtown and uptown to the Maryland/DC line. 'I'll be a rich man soon,' Taylor had said. He put a sign at the streetcar stop advertising the funeral home so people knew where to find him. And they did."

"Did he get rich?" Easton asked.

"None of us are rich, though some of us learned how to stretch a dollar and save," Doc Nelson replied. "Truth told, he made a lot of money. Now how much of it he spent burying people free, I don't know."

"Do you think someone in Family Life killed Mr. Taylor?" Easton asked.

"I don't know that either," Doc Nelson replied, staring down at the floor, rubbing his forehead. Without any prompting, he said, "We were best men at each other's wedding." He looked up at Easton. "I stood by him at both of his."

"Speaking of Mr. Taylor's marriages, how did he get along with his first wife after they divorced, and her husband?" Easton asked.

"Boy, did Elaine hate Taylor for cheating on her. After they divorced, she'd find every excuse in the world to keep Thomas away from him, even though they had joint custody. So when she left Thomas with me and Dorothy, I'd call Taylor. He'd come right over. When we took Thomas to Sandy Point Beach, I'd call Taylor and he'd spend a few days with him at the beach. He loved that boy," Doc Nelson said, unfolding his hands. "After Elaine remarried, Thomas stayed with Taylor more often. I guess she wanted extra time with her new husband. Things seemed to get better between the two of them. Don't put any of this in the paper, it's personal. I don't want to embarrass Elaine or upset Thomas."

"I won't," Easton said. "Any idea who killed Mr. Taylor?"

The fine lines around Doc Nelson's eyes deepened. "No," he answered, watching over his shoulder as if expecting someone to come through the back door. Easton noticed Doc's right hand jerk again.

"Do you think Thomas killed him?" Easton asked.

Doc Nelson acted surprised. "Thomas? For Christ's sake, no! He loved the ground Taylor walked on. He'd kill himself, before he'd kill his father."

"Thomas stabbed your wife, an accident, I hear. Was he on drugs?"

Doc Nelson nodded. Easton noticed his speckled gray hair had thinned at the top. "The police said so. Dorothy hit the ceiling. She says every time a Negro man has a problem, the police points to drugs or alcohol. Thomas told us his daddy died and he just lost his mind . . . that he wasn't on drugs when they took him in."

"Can he lift drugs here without you knowing about it?" Easton asked.

"Prescription drugs, no. They're all locked up. Drugs off the counter, yes. No matter how attentive we are, we lose some off the counter every day. People come in here with a plan to steal, they're professionals. So I can't say with certainty that Thomas took anything, if we conduct an inventory and come up short," Doc Nelson explained.

"Which drugs on the counter can he get high on?" Easton asked.

"I thought you wanted to talk about Taylor," Doc Nelson said, crossing his arms.

"From what I've been told, Thomas was important to Mr. Taylor. Even you said so," Easton replied. "I want to know how they got along, given his rumored drug use."

Doc Nelson stood up, his tone sterner. "Thomas doesn't get his drugs here, if he is using. Now, I have to get back to work. I have prescriptions to fill."

"One more question," Easton said, standing in the doorway. "Who on Sixth Street disliked Taylor?"

"No one that I know of," Doc Nelson replied.

"Thank you again for your time, Dr. Nelson. By the way, your wife said you all had a ball at the Taylors' dinner party."

Doc Nelson hesitated. "Yes, we did. Now if you'll excuse me."

Easton had difficulty reading Doc Nelson. He hadn't shed one tear talking about his best friend's vicious murder. His tone seemed more matter-of-fact, except for a few solemn moments, not what you'd expect from someone who'd lost a lifelong friend.

* * *

Easton traveled the short distance from the Pharmacie to the jewelry store where he'd bought Ruth's engagement ring, where Taylor had suggested he go. He'd ordered a pair of yellow topaz earrings that he needed to pick up for Ruth's birthday in November. He wanted her day to be special, not just her gift. Then again death had a way of turning a person's world upside down. That's what happened to Easton's grandmother when his grandfather died. She never got over his death, and she died in her sleep one night. Easton hoped his love would sustain Ruth enough to celebrate her day.

While he waited for the earrings to be wrapped, Easton browsed at the jewelry displays. He eyed a gold necklace, a round locket hanging from it with a pink rose carved on it. He bought it for Naomi—a Christmas present—thinking she might put Taylor's picture in it. Last year he'd given the Taylors a bottle of wine and a year's subscription to the ***Negro News. It's strange how death transforms the way holidays are celebrated and the gifts you give,*** he thought.

"Thank you, Buford. I can go broke in here buying for the women in my life. You have some nice pieces," Easton said, flashing a smile. He picked up the bag with his wrapped gifts. "Any talk about Mr. Taylor's murder?"

"More talk about Family Life than the murder, although most believe one has to do with the other," Buford responded.

"How so?" Easton said.

"Family Life crossed the line when they started messing with people's life insurance. Negroes aren't stupid and aren't buying this whole 'didn't receive the payment' crap," Buford said. "They're people just like you and me, working every day, trying to take care of their families. I know damn well if Taylor hadn't raised hell, he'd still be alive."

"It's still speculation," Easton reminded him. "After the insurance board audits the company, we'll know for sure if they stole money and who they stole from. Right now it's the company's word against the families'."

The veins popping out on each side of Buford's forehead looked like uneven roads winding down behind his ears into a forest of silver-gray hair. He spoke, his voice sounding agitated, "I don't care if it is speculation. I believe Taylor was collateral damage. Family Life didn't count on him or any other undertaker caring about those poor people. He died right after you published that story. Coincidence, Lord, I don't know. It's upset me so much I can't halfway sleep."

"Have the cops talked to you or others on the block Taylor did business with?" Easton asked.

"No, son, I haven't seen a policeman around here in days, not one."

"I'm not surprised," Easton said. "I doubt if they asked Naomi Taylor who he did business with. Give me a call if you hear anything."

"Sure thing," Buford said.

* * *

Easton stopped at the newspaper stand nearby and bought the ***Washington Star***, a local paper. He wanted to know what they'd written about Taylor, if anything. There on the last page of section A, the whereabouts of Taylor's killer, "Still at Large." He drew on his cigarette. At the sound of boisterous laughing and clapping, he turned to see the crap shooter with his entourage standing in front of the corner deli. He rolled the newspaper and stuck it in his pocket then joined the four men and one woman, Leslie Ann Penny, the hat lady. Standing, she seemed taller than she had appeared sitting behind the table at the market. She wore a green beret this time and a black tweed blazer over a green sweater dress that stopped at the knees, her black stilettos showing off perfectly shaped legs. Easton eyed her, thinking how fine she looked, still no match for Ruth; a natural beauty and more refined. Easton would never have to worry about Ruth hanging on the corner with the hustlers.

"Why, do tell," Easton said. "Just the Negroes I need to talk to."

"Easton Priest . . . any news about Taylor's killer?" Leslie asked, smiling.

"I was about to ask you the same thing," Easton replied.

"Is it true, Mrs. Taylor slept through the murder?" Leslie asked.

"Who told you?" Easton asked.

"Sorry, I can't divulge my sources. I promised," she answered.

"It's true," Easton said. "Anything else?"

"Nada," she replied.

"What about you, brotha man, whatcha got?" Easton asked the crap shooter. "A knife-wielding lunatic?"

"Family Life, I . . . N . . . C," the shooter replied.

"That's it?" Easton asked.

"That's all I got," the crap shooter responded. "If the bitch is underground, it might take a few to flush his ass out."

"Today is a perfect day to flush out a killer," Easton said, and the two slapped palms. Easton faced Leslie and tipped his hat. "And good day to you, Leslie."

Leslie blew him a kiss.

The men hollered as Easton grinned from ear to ear. Easton walked away, feeling a bit exposed. Something about Leslie Penny had appealed to him. ***Her free spirit,*** he guessed. Because Taylor's murder had taken such an emotional toll on him, he felt vulnerable. He'd have to check in with Ruth more often. He had expected the killer to be arrested by now. Only one person appeared suspect, and only because of his company's alleged practices, Rutherford Daniels, and his arrogant ass wasn't hiding. ***Maybe I'd learn something from my meeting with Louise.***

With time to spare, he drove to the ***News*** room and called the insurance board, which confirmed that Family Life not only provided life insurance, they also insured material goods as well. ***Leslie had told the truth.*** He then met with Lloyd to discuss the topic for his next column. He decided to wait until after his meeting with Louise, in case she gave him some compelling news.

* * *

Easton arrived at Central Library right on time. He walked quietly to the back room. Louise saw him coming. She pointed toward an exit door. He followed as her high heels clicked on wooden steps leading down to a room full of books. A few inches taller than Ruth, slim, and well formed, she wore a pink sweater and a full black skirt.

"You're not supposed to be down here, so we have to talk softly," she said, turning around to face him, her hands on both hips. Heavy makeup outlined round eyes. She'd painted her pouted lips with a dull shade of red. Her long fingernails polished the same color. "I work here part-time sorting books to make money so I can finish college. I have two more semesters at Miners Teachers College, thank you, Jesus! I'll have my degree in education. I want to teach elementary school. I so love being around little crumb snatchers." Louise sat on a box, giggling.

"My mother taught elementary school," Easton said, amused at her excitement about teaching. "She loved every minute of it."

"I can't wait," Louise said, with a gleam in her eyes. "You know, I really wanted to talk to you sooner, but after Mr. Daniels threatened to fire anybody who talked to the media, I decided not to."

Easton sat on a box next to her. "What changed your mind?"

Louise's tone became more serious. "I have to tell somebody what I know. I just can't keep it to myself anymore. After I read your article, I figured you were trustworthy. Do not use my name in anything you write, or I'll deny every word I say to you. I can't afford to lose my job."

"I don't reveal my sources, unless I'm given permission," Easton said. "I won't mention your name."

"Well, Thomas Taylor, Dr. Nelson, and Mr. Daniels used to meet at Family Life once a month, now they meet almost every week. About what, I don't know. Thomas can't seem to keep still. He's all over the place. Half the time, his speech is so slurred, I can't understand a word he's saying. He's high on something. It's not alcohol either, because I don't smell it. He acts like my brother when he's high off cocaine." She frowned and shook her head in disgust. "The three of them go into Mr. Daniels's office for an hour or so, then Thomas comes out first. Dr. Nelson and Mr. Daniels, they come out about ten minutes later. Whatever they're involved in, the rest of the staff is not included."

"Thomas, Doc Nelson, and Mr. Daniels—what a surprise," Easton said.

"What surprises me is why Thomas still meets with Mr. Daniels," Louise said.

"What do you mean?" Easton asked.

"He had to know his father lost money burying people for free after Mr. Daniels canceled those policies," Louise said. "It didn't seem right that he'd still meet with the man. Like I said, he's always high when he's here. Maybe he didn't care about his father."

"Is Mr. Daniels still canceling policies?" Easton asked.

"It's still going on."

"Can you get me copies of the policies or names of the families?" Easton asked.

"I doubt it. They're in files in an office I never go into. The girl who told me about it resigned the day after your article hit the paper," Louise said. "It'd look strange if all of a sudden I started hanging around in there."

"What's her name?" Easton asked.

"I can't tell you. I promised not to tell anybody what she told me," Louise said.

"Louise, she may be the key to proving fraud in Family Life and solving Taylor's murder," Easton exclaimed. "Please . . . you have to tell me her name."

Louise stood up. "No! I promised her."

Easton's first thought was to shake some sense into her naive young head; shake you till your teeth rattled, that's what his mother used to say to him when he didn't listen to her. He looked up at Louise, who had had turned away, arms crossed, tapping her foot so fast, her high heels started sliding from side to side and skidded on the linoleum floor. She lost her balance and fell back toward Easton. He caught her before she landed on top of him.

"Oh god, I'm so sorry," Louise said, straightening her skirt.

"It's okay, I upset you," Easton said. "Louise, your friend can help us prove Family Life is corrupt and may have been involved in Taylor's murder. Since you can't give me her name, please ask her to call me." Easton handed Louise his business card.

"Sure, I'll ask her," Louise said, still sounding apologetic.

"Do you remember the last time Doc Nelson, Daniels, and Thomas met?" Easton asked.

"They didn't meet all together this last time. Thomas came two days before his father died. Dr. Nelson came yesterday," Louise said. "Anyway, Mr. Daniels is closing the office so we can all attend Mr. Taylor's funeral. He's going, even though he's received hate mail since you wrote that story."

"Hate mail, from whom? Do the police know about it?" Easton asked, baffled.

"I don't know where it came from, Mr. Daniels never said. The police were here three times. Scared me to death." She gripped Easton's arm.

"Did they threaten to kill him?" Easton asked, completely thrown by this disclosure.

"Don't know."

"Where are the letters?" Easton asked.

"The police took them."

"Were they Negro police?" Easton wondered if any of the Negro cops were involved. He'd call them if they were.

"No, they were white as snow."

"Did you hear Doc Nelson or Daniels talk about Taylor?"

"Not a word."

"Anything else you can tell me?" Easton asked her.

"Let's see," she said, fluttering her fake lashes, thinking to herself. "Yes . . . about a month ago, Mr. Daniels came running from his office, cursing and carrying on about a package from New York City lost in the mail. He had me calling all over the place. When I tracked it down, he and Dr. Nelson stood at my desk until the mailman delivered it. Mr. Daniels had never waited at my desk before, not for anything."

"What was in it?" Easton asked.

"No clue. I figured it had nothing to do with the business, since he didn't ask me to open it and note the contents in our mail log," she replied.

"Where do you put empty boxes?" Easton asked.

"In the trash bin in the alley, unless someone in the office wants them," she said.

"Thanks, Louise. I'm not sure what to make of all this right now. Can I call you if I have more questions?" Easton asked. He removed her hand from his arm.

"Not at Family Life." Louise wrote her home phone number on a piece of paper and gave it to Easton. Holding on to his arm, she walked him to the steps they went down on.

Two years ago, Easton would've pursued Louise. Young, attractive, a nice lay. It crossed his mind, then he promptly dismissed it. ***Get a grip, Easton,*** he thought. He loved Ruth and didn't want to risk losing her for a one-night stand. He rushed to the alley, hoping to find the empty box from New York. After one month, it was a long shot, still he needed to try.

The stench from the trash and garbage in the alley smelled like stinking goosefoot weed. Easton covered his nose and his mouth. He froze when a rat the size of a tomcat skittered up the side of a trash can, and unable to pry the lid off, it jumped down and squeezed through a hole in a building. Easton chuckled. Watching the rat reminded him of how he had to pry information from people who were reluctant to open up during interviews. He stood on a trash can to see over the large black receptacle. He saw remnants of dirty paper stuck at the bottom with other matter that wasn't discernable. No boxes, though.

* * *

When he returned to the ***News*** room, he called Lloyd over to his desk, told him about the interviews he'd conducted, and condemned the police department for not conducting a thorough investigation into Taylor's murder.

"They've put forth more effort searching for lost dogs of the wealthy whites than they have finding Taylor's killer," Easton said.

"Have they questioned Taylor's business associates or friends?" Lloyd asked.

"Not on the block where Buford's Jewelry Store is. I know because I shopped there today. They haven't even questioned me, and I'm at the funeral home more than most people," Easton replied. "We better get moving on this article. Remember, Aaron moved up the deadline for everything. We need to have a draft ready by noon tomorrow."

The two men quickly drafted an article for the column: "No Arrest in Murder of Undertaker." It drew attention to the police department's halfhearted efforts to investigate Taylor's murder "He's one less Negro to deal with," the article said of the police department's attitude about Taylor. It also alluded to a person of interest with information that might help solve Taylor's murder. Aaron arrived at nine thirty that evening and made a few edits.

Easton asked Aaron about promoting Lloyd to a full-time investigative reporter. "He's good, Aaron. He knows the job and does it well."

"What about his working in the field? Do you think he can handle it?" Aaron asked.

"I found him in the street. He'll figure out a way," Easton replied.

"All right, I'll talk to him tomorrow," Aaron said.

Lloyd and Easton had taken classes together at Howard University and graduated the same year, though they hadn't stayed in touch. One Friday night, Easton stopped at a steak and cheese carryout for a late night snack. Lloyd sat in front of the carryout in a wheelchair. The Lloyd he'd known had two legs. This man only had one leg. Easton almost passed by him. When Lloyd thrust his beggar's cup toward him, there was no getting around the distinct red blemish covering the entire right side of his face. "Lloyd!" Easton had called his name.

Lloyd shook his head. "No," he'd said, and started to roll away. Easton grabbed the arm of the wheelchair and demanded to know what happened to him. Lloyd reluctantly acknowledged Easton and told him that he'd been drinking too much one night and crashed his car into a tree in Rock Creek Park, his leg mangled so badly, the doctors had to cut it off to save him. Disability didn't cover everything he needed, and he'd refused help from his family. He didn't want their pity, so he begged for money. Easton had promised to help Lloyd, and he did. He'd convinced Aaron to hire Lloyd to help him with his investigations, his column and to help Lloyd get his life back.

* * *

Before he left for home, Easton packed notes and a carbon copy of the article in his briefcase. He expected some backlash once it was published; after all, the article berated the police department for dragging their feet in a very public way—in the newspaper. He worried about Ira and the other Negro cops on the police force who were bound to take heat for the article. He imagined the unimaginable, that they'd wake up one morning before the sun, with a fiery cross ablaze in their yard. He shook his head, grabbed his briefcase and left for home.

# Chapter 23

Later the next day, Tuesday October 16th, neither Easton nor Aaron had received any calls about Easton's column. He expected that the chief of police and others in the department would read the article and get pissed off and thus he'd achieve his goal—to get their attention. It was more than a notion to expect Louise's friend to come forward. It would be a miracle if she did.

"Has the chief called you in his office yet?" Easton called and asked Ira.

"Now why would he do that?" Ira asked.

"The article in my column, brotha," Easton replied. "I thought he might mess with you and the other Negro cops since I took it to him."

"I read it, but no, nothing from the chief, a few snubs from some other rednecks," Ira replied.

"Well now, I guess I don't have to worry about a cross burning in my yard or yours," Easton said.

"Watch your back anyway," Ira said. "So far, only four cops think your article read true, and you know who they are. If you get squeezed by one of the others, let me know. I'll try to keep you from getting jammed up."

"Thanks, brotha, I'll do that," Easton said.

* * *

Since Taylor's murder, Easton had spent most days driving all over town, interviewing people and following leads that led to nowhere. Even so, he welcomed the chance to talk with people of Shaw and other districts, each time believing somebody might reveal a killer or lead him to somebody who knew. Today was no different. He journeyed to Fourteenth Street, parked a block down from the Car Barn, a boxed red brick building where streetcars rolled in and out to connect and transfer passengers to other lines. He walked north to the ***Tourist House***, a three-story building, also known as the Knock, Knock House by some of its patrons. Easton felt so stupid when he learned that no tourists stayed at the place, only locals who went to be with their lovers or mistresses. The nickname Knock, Knock House came about from patrons knocking on doors all night long: "It's me, Tony"; "Open up, it's Jewell"; "Hurry up, baby, let me in."

Easton walked to the side entrance where the tourists checked in. No stranger to the place, he'd take his women there since they weren't allowed at the boarding house. Mrs. Kelly would kick his behind out if he got caught with a woman in his room. So this was the next best place. As the place was cheaper than a motel, for five dollars he'd often stay all night. He grinned. If only the walls of this place could talk, people would be shocked and amused at the stories it might tell.

Easton remembered the rooms he'd occupied. Sometimes he'd luck up and get one with a sink and a chair. Pictures of colorful flowers and landscapes cut from magazines were taped on plastered walls. Plaid and printed curtains you'd normally see in a kitchen covered the windows. The mattresses were old with broken springs and the pillows flat as a pancake. The first time he went there, he didn't know to take his own toilet paper, soap, towel, and washcloth. He smiled thinking about how he'd knocked on doors, borrowing what he needed to get back to work in time for a meeting. During his last visit, right before he met Ruth, the owner had plodded up and down the hall, fussing about watermelon rinds left in a room and a sink stopped up in the only bathroom on the floor. He remembered her buxom body laboring down the hall, threatening to put everybody out, butt naked. Easton had laughed till his side hurt. His date didn't.

"Ms. Ann, how you doing?" Easton asked, hugging the owner.

"I haven't missed a damn thing, so don't call me miss," she replied, smiling. "And where have you been, sleeping around somewhere else?"

"If I wanted to sleep around, I'd come back here," Easton replied, laughing. "I've changed my ways. I'm marrying Ruth Johnson next year, if she says yes."

"Well, I'll be damned, Taylor's daughter." Her smile faded. "Taylor didn't deserve to go like that." She pulled a handkerchief from her dress pocket and dabbed at her eyes. "I loved that man. He was a pistol though. He'd bring women up in here three, four times a week. For a while I think he slept here more than he slept in his own bed. I have to admit, I made a lot of money off of him."

"Had he been here recently?"

"No, sirree. After he met and married Naomi, he straightened up. Came by and told me he'd fallen in love with an angel. Not to look for him anymore, at least not here."

"Have you heard any rumblings about who might have killed him?"

"He trampled over a lot of women. True enough, some were married. That was so long ago, I can't imagine any of them or their husbands coming for him now."

"What are your visitors saying about the murder?" Easton asked.

"Funny thing, don't have any checked in right now. Taylor's murder must have scared them off."

"Don't worry, they'll be back. They'll want to feel that ***fever in the morning, fever all through the night***," Easton sang.

Ms. Ann laughed. "You something else, boy."

"Call me at the paper if you get a confession from somebody," Easton said.

* * *

When Easton arrived back at his office, he checked his messages—no call from Louise, her former colleague, or anyone else from Family Life. ***What if the girl doesn't come forward or Louise doesn't give me her name?*** he mused. He took a drag off his cigarette and called Odean.

"Odean," Easton here. "Do you know anyone working at Family Life?"

"Yeah, the janitor and one of the file clerks," Odean replied.

"I need the name of a girl who quit working there the day after we published the Family Life report," Easton explained. "Don't tell anyone it's for me. It might scare them off."

"Give me a day or so. I'm off to my cousin's funeral in Virginia," Odean said. "He died from lung cancer. Only forty-two years old."

"I'm sorry to hear that," Easton said. "Was he a smoker?" Easton asked.

"Two packs a day," Odean replied.

"Call me when you get back," Easton said.

"Will do," Odean said.

Easton hung up the phone and stared at the cigarette clasped between his two fingers, smoke rising from it. Ruth had told him to quit smoking after research had linked smoking to lung cancer. He said he would, one day. He crushed the cigarette.

# Chapter 24

By noon on Wednesday, neither Odean nor Louise had contacted Easton. He called Odean. He didn't answer. He called Louise. She didn't answer her phone either. He'd grown impatient and wanted answers. "Shit, where is everybody?" He slammed down the receiver. "God, give me somebody who will drop a dime on Taylor's killer . . . please," he blared aloud. When he realized every eye in the office had turned toward him, he straightened his back from a slouched position, lit a cigarette, and waved Lloyd over to his desk.

"I have an interview to conduct, and if it leads to something else, I may be gone most of the afternoon," Easton said.

"You want me to start drafting the column?" Lloyd asked.

Easton laughed. "We have plenty of time . . . you must be bored. What did you have in mind?"

"The police department didn't respond to the last column, so we can invoke their lack of response as not giving a damn about Negroes, reiterating what we've said all along, and publish another plea for help in solving Mr. Taylor's murder," Lloyd replied.

"I like it," Easton said. "Do it."

* * *

Easton cruised past Edith's Beauty Shop, looking for a parking space, and saw the door sitting wide open. ***It must be hot in there,*** he thought. There had been times when he'd visit the one-room shop, no matter the day or season, and he'd leave, sweat dripping from his brow and armpits like a leaky faucet from the sweltering heat inside. Brought on by a constant surge of steam and smoke billowing from strands of hair greased and straightened with hot combs to make it smooth and shiny, there was no thermostat to regulate this kind of heat. After he parked, he took off his suit jacket, hung it over the front seat of his car, and walked the short distance to the shop. There in front of the Pharmacie, which happened to be next door to Edith's Beauty shop, stood Doc Nelson. Easton greeted him.

"Good morning, Dr. Nelson," Easton said, shaking his hand.

"Good morning," Doc Nelson replied. "I'm sorry we can't talk this morning. I'm about to leave."

"I'm actually here to talk with Ms. Edith," Easton said, pointing toward the beauty shop.

Doc Nelson snickered. "You came to the right place. Edith loves to talk. As a matter of fact, every woman that goes in there likes to talk, so be prepared to listen to more than you ask for. You know how it is. All our women have an opinion about something, including my wife, and if they don't like your attitude, what you say, or how you say it, they will gang up on you in a minute and rip your ass apart, so good luck, son."

Easton smiled as he entered the beauty shop. Yes, he knew how it was. He had been a victim of the women's wrath all too often, though he'd take it in stride because he always got what he needed—valuable information. Women of all ages and all walks of life—homemakers, nurses, teachers, housekeepers, file clerks, seamstress, government employees, students—you name it, they all spent time at the beauty shop, if not Edith's, somebody else's. The shop had one large room sectioned off for the shampoo bowls, the dryers, the beautician's chairs, and the waiting area. They were all occupied. The scent of paint from the freshly coated yellow walls mingled with the smell of burned hair and smoke. Houseplants were positioned throughout, and large posters of beautiful black women with bouffants, waves, and curls were taped on the walls.

Edith's high forehead glistened from the sweat seeping from her brow each time a wave of steam and smoke from the hot comb engulfed her face. An attractive middle-aged woman with milk chocolate skin, she stood about five foot seven, slender, with dyed red hair streaked blond styled in a french roll. Her eyebrows were plucked so thin, they looked as if they were penciled on her face. When she smiled, the lines under her eyes and around her mouth disappeared and she looked younger, her pale peach lipstick adding softness to her face. Edith owned the shop, and like the barbershops, she rented chairs to three other beauticians. And like the barbershops, Edith's shop didn't lend itself to private conversations, so he expected every woman in the place to eavesdrop when he spoke.

"Ms. Edith, how you doing?" Easton asked her.

"I'm fine and busy," Ms. Edith replied.

"I won't keep you too long," Easton said.

"You can keep me as long as you want," one of the women said, lifting the lid of the dryer she sat under, her head covered with pink plastic rollers, a smile spread wide across her face.

"Jennifer, get back under that dryer," Edith said. "He doesn't want anybody as old as you."

Everybody in the shop rolled over laughing.

"Honey, don't pay no attention to Edith. If you want a lesson in love, I'm the one to teach you," Jennifer said.

Easton laughed along with the women in the shop and politely said, "Thank you, Ms. Jennifer, but I'm getting married soon."

"You're not married yet," Jennifer said. "Call me if you change your mind." She handed him a card. Jennifer worked in a massage parlor on Fourteenth Street.

"Thank you," Easton said, and put the card in his shirt pocket.

Easton turned back to Edith. "Ms. Edith, I'm writing Mr. Taylor's story for the newspaper. Taylor's killer is still on the loose, so I don't have an ending for my story. What are you hearing?"

"Easton, you know I don't gossip, but I will say this, it's most likely somebody he knew," Edith responded. "How else can a person get into your kitchen, no evidence of forced entry, and kill you?"

"Where did you hear that?" Easton asked.

"A reliable source," she replied.

"Okay . . . anything else?" Easton asked.

"Naomi came in a couple of weeks ago for a trim and said everything was fine. Of course, Naomi never talks about her personal business," Edith said. "Except, she did mention they'd had a string of families without life insurance and no money to pay for the funerals. She said she might have to rent a chair from me and do hair part-time to pay her bills. We laughed about it, and then she left."

"Any rumors of another woman?" Easton asked.

"Now, where did that come from?" Edith asked, surprised.

The chatter in the room quieted, and all ears leaned toward Easton.

***Here we go***, Easton thought. "Just covering all angles."

"I be damned," the woman in Edith's chair screeched.

"Uh-huh," said the woman in the chair next to Edith's. "Blame it on a woman, that's right, just blame Taylor's murder on a woman. If the man did have another woman and got caught, serves him right. Did he still have a penis when he died?"

Every woman in the shop hollered. Easton didn't; he just smiled and answered her. "That's privileged information."

"Privileged, my ass," the woman said. "You don't know, do you?"

Easton visualized all the blood pooled in Taylor's kitchen. He believed it all came from Taylor, though it never crossed his mind that he might have been castrated. "No, I don't know," Easton replied.

A woman squeezed by Easton, heading for the shampoo bowl, and said, "If he had another woman, she must have been really pissed off with him. Some women love so hard, they don't want to let go. They'd rather risk going to jail than to see their man with somebody else."

"Not me," Edith said. "I'm not going to jail for no damn man. There's always somebody else."

"Has anyone heard anything that might help with the investigation?" Easton asked, glancing around the room.

"Money . . . now that's a motive for murder," said a woman in the waiting area. "People don't kill each other over simple stuff like he said—she said but mess with their money; you'll end up on a hit list, a shit list, and your ass is mine list. I have a list, I'm slowly whittling down."

"Child, you know that's right. You call yourself helping somebody, and all they want to do is use you. I've had to kick some ass myself," another woman said.

A chorus of amens sang throughout. ***They're on a roll,*** Easton thought, and from what he'd learned, money or perhaps greed may have been a motive for Taylor's murder. He'd go back to his office and reread his notes.

"Well, I best be going," Easton said. "Thank you all for your input, and if you need a subscription to the ***Negro News***, call the paper and ask for Easton Priest. I'll take care of you."

"I'm calling you right now," Jennifer said, and jumped out from under the dryer chair and ran to the telephone. She turned to Easton. "I'll call and leave a message." The room erupted in laughter.

* * *

After leaving Edith's, Easton went back to his office and called Ira. It had been five days since Taylor's murder, and the police hadn't made any arrests, didn't have a drop of evidence, and no suspects. The killer apparently left no clues. "Tell me something good," he said to Ira.

"We're still trying to match fingerprints from people in Taylor's files with those we collected at the crime scene," Ira replied. "We matched a few from the viewing room and his office, and they all had alibis. So far, no matches from the kitchen. We still have a few more people to bring in."

"Any cops on the street looking for his killer?" Easton asked.

"They go out on the street for hours and don't come back with anything," Ira replied. "It's still early in the investigation though, so be patient."

"You know, the longer the killer remains free, the harder it will be to find him," Easton said. "He probably already left DC."

"I hope not," Ira said, and hung up.

Easton knew he'd accomplish nothing spewing unnecessary pressure on Ira. The truth being Ira had no clout in the police department, and with no motive for the murder, no one in the department would listen to him. Still, the police had not yet interviewed Taylor's friends or acquaintances, not even those who attended the dinner party. Easton grimaced in disgust. ***The police don't give a damn. If Taylor had been white, the killer might be tried and convicted by now.***

The telephone rang. It turned out to be a wrong number. Easton had hoped to hear Odean or Louise on the other end. ***Maybe they forgot about me,*** he thought. The usual buzz in the office had died down. His eyes had glazed over from reading, writing, and the daily haze of smoke occupying the office, although there was no mistaking what he saw—the DC chief of police walking into the ***Negro News*** room. Easton stood with others in the room, not out of respect for the man; on the contrary, they wanted to know why he'd come.

The receptionist escorted the chief to Aaron's office, his deputy beside him. Easton moseyed over to the water cooler near Aaron's office. The door slightly ajar, Easton could hear the chief grunting and complaining about the article Easton and Lloyd had written for his column last week, "No Arrest in Murder of Undertaker." The article had lambasted the police department for their lackluster efforts to find Taylor's killer. The chief insisted that Aaron print a rebuttal.

"What do you expect me to say?" Aaron asked.

"We're doing our job," the chief responded. "I've got men on the street trying to interrogate people. It's not our fault they won't talk to us."

"Maybe you're talking to the wrong people," Aaron said. "Mr. Taylor didn't live in the street. He didn't hustle with the drug dealers and pimps you're questioning. He was a respectable businessman. Maybe you need to talk to people he did business with. Learn more about the man." Aaron flat out refused to print a rebuttal.

"Then I suggest you watch your back," the chief said, walking out the door.

"Are you threatening me?" Aaron asked.

"I'm the chief of police. I don't need to threaten your black ass."

Easton, along with everyone else in the office, watched the chief storm out of the door, fuming at the mouth. Easton shook his head. "Negroes go through this every day in the South—intimidation, harassment, just outright hatefulness," he said to Aaron.

* * *

Thursday morning, an excited Ruth called Easton to say she and Naomi were allowed to go home. "Mom just got word, we can go home day after tomorrow. I get to sleep in my own bed again, thank goodness."

"Good news, baby. Who's cleaning the house?" Easton asked.

"Ira gave Mom a list of companies that clean up after . . . homicides. I hope one can come tomorrow," Ruth replied.

"If you need help, I'm here," Easton offered. "I love you."

"I love you more," Ruth said.

Easton hung up and called Ira. "I just talked to Ruth. She and Naomi can go home?"

"Yeah," Ira replied. "Forensics didn't find jack shit, so the chief had me call Naomi to tell her she could go home, since I know her."

"You mean since you're a Negro too," Easton said.

"Probably so," Ira responded. "I asked the chief what to say if Naomi asked me about the investigation. I didn't know whether to duck down or pump up, the way he leaned into me. Told me to tell her the truth . . . we're still investigating her husband's murder."

"He wouldn't know the truth, if it smacked him in the face," Easton said. "Did Naomi ask you about the investigation?"

"Yes, and I told her exactly what the chief said, and she thanked me."

"What else can you say?" Easton asked. "The killer is still out there."

"And I'm in no position to tell Homicide to get up off their ass and go find him," Ira responded.

"I know, Ira," Easton said. "Do what you can, I'll check back with you."

Since Easton wanted pictures of the bloody crime scene for the paper, it had to be tonight. The crime scene might be gone tomorrow, if Ruth found a company to clean the place. He called Leroy, who had agreed to go in with him at the first opportunity. "We're on tonight. We'll use the spare key. See you at eleven."

* * *

Easton changed into dungarees and a black jacket and met Leroy in the ***Negro News*** parking lot at eleven o'clock sharp. He drove to Sixth Street and stopped on the corner. The porch light lit up the outside of the funeral home like daylight. He strained to look up and down the block for obvious signs of police presence. He didn't see any black-and-whites visible on the street. He crossed over Sixth Street and turned into the pitch-black alley behind Taylor's house, where the lightbulb had blown out in the lamppost. He eased alongside the garage next door to Taylor's house, almost scraping his car, turned off the headlights, cut the engine, and rolled down his window. Huge branches dangled from a cypress tree, shrouding most of the garage door. A blustery wind shook leaves from the tree and carried the colorful foliage bouncing through the alleyway and into the street. Easton hung his camera around his neck and tucked it under his jacket. "Let's go."

They crouched down alongside the garage and moved on toward Taylor's backyard, acorns and small pebbles crunching under their feet. When they reached the yard, Easton peered up at the house. His eyes watered from a blast of wind, blurring his vision, though he saw light peeking through the blinds in an upstairs bedroom, no light visible from the morgue. He opened the metal gate, and Leroy slivered through the grass like a boa constrictor winding its way to its prey. Easton crawled behind him. When Leroy stopped, he stopped. They lay quiet for a moment. ***The cops must be gone, or we would never have gotten this close to the house,*** Easton thought. When they finally reached the rock garden on the side of the house, Easton pulled up one red brick after another until he felt the key. He crawled a few feet to the door and fussed with the lock until the door opened into the pantry. The two men went inside on their knees.

Easton opened the kitchen door to the pungent odor of sour blood. They quickly covered their nose and their mouth. The house was still, except for the hissing sound coming from steam circulating in the radiator in the hallway. Leroy turned on his flashlight long enough to get his bearings and close the curtains over the sink. The two men tiptoed around the massive collection of Taylor's dried blood crusted on the floor like a huge scab.

"Three seconds for a picture," Leroy whispered to Easton. "Ready."

Easton turned on the camera's flash. "Ready."

Leroy clicked on the ceiling light and counted, "One . . . . two . . . three." The light went off.

Easton let out a loud sigh. He'd finally gotten what he wanted, a picture of the crime scene, although seeing Taylor's lifeless blood again angered him. Leroy sensed a problem and nudged him quietly out of the kitchen and into Taylor's office, where he eased himself behind the desk and into a chair.

Leroy peered between slats in the closed blinds onto the street. He signaled Easton over to the window and pointed to a dark blue sedan parked in front of the house next door. Easton shook his head, not recognizing the car. From his angle, no one appeared to be in it. He stepped soft footed into the parlor, where the drapes were open. He bent down, crawled over to the window, and peeked behind the tied-back drapes, still too dark to make out anyone in the car. He scurried back on his knees to the office and thumbed through Taylor's desk. He knew the police had already taken anything that might be used as evidence. He thought, ***Maybe they missed something.*** He perused the bookshelf. On the bottom sat Taylor's senior high school year book. Easton clutched it under his arm. About to leave, he heard a noise coming from upstairs. Leroy heard it too. They locked eyes.

When the sound of voices became more distinct, they hustled into the kitchen. Easton stood over Leroy, who had stooped behind the kitchen door. They peeped through the gap between the doorframe and the door. Laughter and footsteps descended the stairs, and the hall light came on. Easton and Leroy held their breath as they eyeballed the couple.

Easton, both furious and surprised, watched the officer who called him a nigga kiss and paw on a woman half his age. He smiled. ***I must be living right. I doubt that's his wife.*** He waited for an outburst of laughter and turned off the camera's flash. When they laughed again, he snapped a picture through the crack in the door. He prayed it would come out.

The officer buttoned the front of the woman's dress and kissed her on the mouth for what seemed like forever. When they came up for air, he opened the front door and she stepped outside. He turned off the hall light and joined her, locking the door behind him.

Easton and Leroy flew into the parlor and peeped behind the drapes to eye the couple. The officer opened the sedan door for the woman then walked to the driver's side, got in the car, and drove off. Easton and Leroy moved with top speed through the rest of the house. The pair had rolled around in Thomas's bed and did a half-ass job making it up.

"Thank God they weren't in Ruth's bed. She'd have a fit," Easton said. "We'd have to bail her out of jail for threatening to take out the police."

"'Who's been sleeping in my bed?' asked the baby bear," Leroy said in a high-pitched voice. The two men laughed.

"The cleaning company will take care of this room," Easton said. "We're outta here."

* * *

"The first time I saw Taylor's blood on the floor, it made me sick," Easton confessed, as he drove Leroy back to the ***Negro News*** office for his car. "I didn't choke tonight. I must be getting used to the sight and smell of blood."

"What do you mean . . . you almost passed out in there," Leroy said.

"When Ruth told me Taylor had been murdered, my whole body hurt, and yeah . . . I almost passed out, I almost puked too," Easton said.

Taylor's blood had since dried into thin flat pieces, no different from red paint dropped on the floor and left to dry.

# Chapter 25

Early Friday morning, October 19, Easton pulled alongside the curb in front of the funeral home. The place had been cleaned the day before, and he came to help Ruth and Naomi settle in. Ruth had just stepped out of the Packard, when she ran to him and jumped in his arms. He kissed her like he hadn't seen her in a year, yet it had only been a few days.

"Don't forget the suitcases," Naomi said, smiling at the two. She went into the funeral home.

The lovers retrieved the suitcases and joined Naomi inside.

"It feels awfully close in here," Naomi said, standing in the hallway.

Easton dropped the suitcases and ran to open windows in the parlor, in Taylor's office, and in the viewing room. Naomi didn't ask him to open the kitchen window, nor did she go anywhere near the kitchen, neither did he. Instead, Naomi followed Ruth upstairs. Easton followed Naomi. He left her suitcase on her bed and then took Ruth's suitcase to her room. Ruth sat on her bed, going through her jewelry box.

"Is it all there?" Easton asked.

"Yeah, it's all here," Ruth replied, smiling. "I'll be down in a minute."

Easton took it to mean she wanted privacy, so he went downstairs and out on the front porch to smoke a cigarette. Looking around, he wondered who had been so bold as to enter the funeral home in the wee hours of the morning and kill Taylor. Easton had returned to Sixth Street and interviewed Taylor's neighbors, who refused to talk to him the morning of the murder. None of them heard anything unusual the morning of the murder. All of them were sound asleep until the sirens frightened them awake.

He took the last puff from his cigarette and went back inside. He wandered through the house, surprised to stumble upon Naomi in the kitchen, making coffee. He stopped at the door, remembering the dried blood, expecting to see it again. He looked down at the floor. Not a drop in sight. "May I sit down?" Easton asked Naomi.

Naomi nodded.

Easton sat at the table and gazed around the room. A waft of blood mixed with bleach floated in the air. He felt dizzy, thinking it might be from the toxic vapors, then he remembered he hadn't eaten breakfast. Naomi set a cup of coffee in front of him. He watched her drink hers as she stared out the open window.

“I’m waiting for help God promised to send me,” she whimpered, her face pale and drawn. She slid into a chair at the table and fixed her eyes on the place where Taylor had sat every morning, where Easton sat now. Suddenly she grabbed her chest.

“What’s wrong?” Easton asked her.

“My chest . . . pain,” she replied.

Easton watched drops of sweat trickle from her head down her face. He jumped up. “I’ll get Ruth.”

“No,” Naomi snapped at him. “Sit down. No one can help this pain.” She pressed a hand firm against her bosom, lay her head on the table, and sobbed. “Maybe when I bury him . . . the pain will go away.”

Easton sat down, not knowing what to do or say.

The sudden ringing of the phone startled Naomi. She raised her head and reached for the wall phone.

“Naomi, is that you?” the voice on the other end asked.

“Yes, yes, it’s me, Mildred,” Naomi replied, looking at Easton, his cue to leave.

* * *

Easton skipped steps upstairs to Ruth’s bedroom. She had just finished unpacking her mother’s suitcase.

“Your mom is having chest pains,” Easton said.

Ruth started out of the room. Easton grasped her arm. “She didn’t want me to come get you—she said no one can help her pain.”

“I don’t care what she said!” Ruth pulled away from Easton and sprinted down the steps to the kitchen.

Naomi, still on the phone, looked at Ruth and Easton, who were staring at her. She finally said, “I’ll be off the phone in a minute.”

Easton grabbed Ruth’s hand, and they went into the parlor. “I told you what she said,” Easton reminded Ruth.

“I heard you,” Ruth responded. “I wanted to make sure my mother wasn’t having a heart attack.”

“She will heal in time,” Easton said, hugging Ruth.

“Did you want me for something?” Naomi asked, standing at the parlor door.

“Mom, are you all right?” Ruth asked.

“Yes, I’m all right, Ruth. Please stop worrying about me,” Naomi said, and went upstairs.

A few minutes later the phone rang again. Ruth ran to the telephone chair table in the hallway and answered it. She talked for a few minutes then returned to the parlor. “The coroner. I need to talk to Mom.” She moved swiftly up the steps.

* * *

Easton called Odean. "Whatcha got for me?"

"Georgia Reed, the girl who quit Family Life, moved to South Carolina the day after she quit," Odean said. "Her family won't give me a number. I even offered them a little change, knowing you'd pay me back . . . They ain't budging."

"She must know something," Easton said. "Where in South Carolina?"

"I asked, they won't tell me shit," Odean replied.

"Maybe Louise knows, but she won't return my calls," Easton said. "Somebody knows who killed Taylor and where Georgia Reed is. DC is not a big city. Stay on it."

"Will do," Odean responded. "People at my cousin's funeral asked about Taylor's murder, and all I said . . . he's dead and nobody knows who killed him or why," Odean said. "One dude said to look close to home."

"You mean Naomi . . . Thomas . . . Ruth?" Easton asked.

"I don't know about you, brotha, but I ain't looking that close," Odean replied.

"Me neither," Easton said. He heard clicking on the stairs. He turned around to see Ruth descending the staircase. "I got to go, brotha, I'll call you later."

"The coroner released Dad's body. Leroy is picking him up at four o'clock," Ruth said to Easton as she reached the bottom.

Easton glanced at his watch. "I have work waiting for me, so I'll come back around four o'clock."

"Mom's going to embalm Dad herself," Ruth said.

"What!" Easton shouted.

"That's what she said. I tried to talk her out of it, but she said the hospital already cut him up during the autopsy and she's not letting anyone else touch him."

"What are you going to do?" Easton asked, perplexed.

"Help her," Ruth replied, as she walked into the parlor. She opened the record player. "I wonder if these are the records they played at the dinner party." She started to cry and turned on the record player. A 45 dropped, "Sentimental Reasons." Ruth fell into Easton's arms. "Let's dance."

Halfway through the song, Easton stopped dancing. "Mrs. Taylor, are you okay?"

Naomi stood at the parlor door, smiling. "I'm fine, keep dancing." She went back upstairs.

# Chapter 26

When Easton reached his office, he sat at his desk, not knowing what to think. He had learned more about death and despair than he'd wanted to. After his grandparents had died, he thought he knew it all. Yet he knew of nothing to compare this tragic love story of Naomi and the death of her Taylor to not even one of Shakespeare's tragedies.

"Georgia Reed, the girl who quit Family Life after my report was published," he said as Aaron approached his desk. "She moved to South Carolina. Her family won't say where in South Carolina."

"She knows something," Aaron said.

"That's what I said," Easton replied.

"I don't know any Reeds in the city. Let me ask around; I'll get back to you," Aaron said, and left the office.

Easton called Ira. "Do you know any Reeds?" Easton asked.

"No . . . should I?" Ira replied.

"Georgia Reed quit her job at Family Life the day after my report was published, and moved to South Carolina."

"Holy smokes," Ira said. "You got a phone number, address?"

"Nothing," Easton replied. "Her family won't share. Odean tried."

"Where does her family live?" Ira asked.

"Odean knows," Easton said

"I'll call him then pay the family a visit," Ira said.

"She may be the one person to bring Family Life to its knees," Easton said.

"That's a lot to put on a young girl," Ira said.

"Taylor's dead. She has her whole life ahead of her," Easton said. "She'll survive."

For the next few hours, Easton reread all his notes from the investigation, wondering what he had missed. He'd expected Taylor's killer to be behind bars by now. With the presidential election fast approaching, Aaron had already assigned three other reporters to cover the candidates running for office. If it weren't for the investigation, he'd be running with the candidates too.

* * *

Easton made his way back to the funeral home before four o'clock. Mildred Jenkins, Doc Nelson's wife, and Reverend Ford, the Taylors' minister, were in the kitchen with Ruth and Naomi, eating the food Mildred had taken to the house. Naomi opened a brown binder and began to speak.

"Taylor's lodge brothers want a private viewing Sunday evening, October 21. I want the public wake Monday evening at six o'clock. The funeral, the next morning at eleven thirty." Naomi drew a deep breath. She pulled some papers from the binder and handed them to Reverend Ford. "Please offer the eulogy and give these songs to the choir director and give Taylor's picture and obituary to the secretary." She turned toward Mildred. "Please sing the twenty-third psalm. Taylor loved hearing you sing it."

"Whatever you want, I'll sing," Mildred said.

"Thank you." Naomi sounded anxious. "Ruth, please order a spray for the casket and speak for the family. Doc Nelson said he'd talk about Taylor too. Taylor's lodge brothers want to be pallbearers, which means we'll need three cars, one for them and two for the family." She turned to Reverend Ford. "And I don't want a three-hour service." Naomi stopped talking at the sound of the hearse coming up the driveway.

"He's here," Naomi said.

"Mom, I'll help Leroy bring him in. You stay here," Ruth said.

Easton watched Ruth dash through the pantry door. He didn't know whether to follow her or to stay in the kitchen. The room fell silent, except for Naomi, a pitiful sight, as she cried out to her maker.

"Oh, God, help me," she pleaded, tears plummeting down her face.

The reverend stopped eating, moved his chair closer to Naomi, and held both her hands.

"Naomi, God will give you strength to get through this difficult time." He prayed with her.

* * *

Fifteen minutes later, Ruth returned to the kitchen with Leroy. Easton watched Naomi jump up and feverishly dish out food for them. No one spoke. Reverend Ford eventually broke the silence.

"Naomi, do you want me to preach a sermon or just read the scriptures and give a eulogy?"

"The scriptures and eulogy is enough," Naomi replied. "Taylor didn't like long-drawn-out funerals. He always said if you can't say something decent about somebody in a few words, then don't say anything at all."

"So we need to keep it short and sweet," Ruth murmured.

"Yes," Naomi said.

The doorbell rang. "I'll get it," Ruth said.

This time Easton followed Ruth down the hallway to the front door. One of the neighbors had prepared food, a gesture of kindness for the grieving family.

Eventually, other neighbors and friends trickled in as word got out that Naomi had returned home. She directed everyone to the parlor because the kitchen had gotten too crowded. ***Where did they all come from?*** Easton asked himself.

After the visitors left, Easton and Ruth cleaned up the kitchen and joined Naomi in the parlor. She sat at the piano and played one song after another. She kept playing even through her tears that dripped onto the piano keys. After playing "Sentimental Reasons," she left the parlor without closing the key lid, without speaking.

"Where is she going?" Easton asked.

"To the morgue," Ruth replied.

Easton and Ruth trailed behind Naomi to the morgue.

"How did you know?" Easton asked.

"The songs . . . remember they danced to those songs the night Dad died," Ruth replied. "She wants to be with him."

As many times as Easton had visited Ruth, he had never gone into the morgue. He didn't want to. A square-shaped room encased with cement walls, the place smelled of blood and body. A brilliant light from a large unshaded bulb hung over a horizontal metal table where Taylor lay, beneath it a sewage drain. At the foot of the table sat a wood stove used to heat the room. Exposed gray piping with a pump handle and a clear hose at the end hung from ceiling to floor behind a double-sided water basin, two pairs of black rubber gloves draped over the side. On one wall, rubber aprons dangled on hooks nailed to a wooden plank, next to it a large diagram of the human body and a framed picture of Jesus Christ on the cross, blood dripping from the holes in his head, hands, and feet. Taylor lay on the table, covered up to his neck with a white sheet.

Easton watched Naomi caress Taylor's face, kiss him on the forehead, and then lie across his chest.

"God, oh, God, where are you? Please help me!" Tears flowed from Naomi's eyes so plenteous, she wet the sheet that covered Taylor. She walked toward the door where Easton and Ruth waited, her body trembling. She fell in their arms.

# Chapter 27

At the crack of dawn Saturday morning, October 20, Easton stood on the sidewalk in front of Taylor's house, smoking a cigarette, thinking, ***What the hell am I doing here?*** On the front door of the funeral home, a large black funeral wreath swayed in the cool breeze. A scrawny black squirrel bounded across the front yard and scampered up the tall oak next door. He stared at the rare sighting of the black rodent perched on a branch high up in the tree. ***I guess we're going to have a bad winter,*** he thought. He tried to picture Naomi embalming her husband, even though he'd never seen it done before. He didn't figure on much blood oozing from Taylor's body since most, if not all had seeped onto the kitchen floor. Still, he didn't want to witness any of it. Ruth had asked him to be present, just in case. He wanted to say no because he didn't want to see his hero poked and prodded like a carcass, nonetheless he'd promised to be there for her. He pocketed an extra pack of cigarettes to help him get through it.

Just when he'd started up the front steps, he heard a door slam. The woman with dark glasses he'd seen the morning of Taylor's murder had come out of her house and plopped down on the glider, a newspaper under her arm. She took off her glasses and peered at Easton. ***She's not blind.*** He hadn't bothered to interview her because he believed she might be deaf and blind. He crossed over to her.

"Good morning, ma'am. I'm Easton Priest, a reporter for—"

"I know who you are. You're the Priests' boy. Have mercy, you sure do resemble your mother. She'd bring your grandmother over whenever they came to town. We all grew up together in Harrington. Everybody knew your grandfather would never leave there. The rest of us did. When you came to Howard, I felt so sorry my rooms were full. Anyway, you made it. It's good to see you turned out to be somebody. That's not why you came over here. What do you want to ask me, son?"

Easton hesitated, surprised she knew his family. He wondered why she hadn't spoken to him the morning Taylor died. "I'm writing Mr. Taylor's life story for the ***Negro News***. Can you tell me anything about him?"

"Yes indeedy . . . I can tell you a whole lot. But how do I know you won't turn my words around and say what you want instead of the truth?" she asked.

"I'm sorry, I didn't get your name," Easton said.

"Mrs. Vertie Young," she replied.

"Mrs. Young, I only report the facts," Easton replied. "People draw their own conclusions and believe what they want. I can't stop them."

"I know, son, that's why I don't want everything I say in the paper. It may be embarrassing for the families and Shaw."

"I have a lot of respect for Mr. Taylor and his family. I don't intend to slander his name in anyway," Easton said.

"Well then . . . I've lived on Sixth Street longer than Taylor. I've seen it all. Lawd have mercy, he was one handsome son of a gun, a real pistol. He'd crawl into the house drunk many a night. As soon as Elaine, his first wife, walked out the front door, some woman would sneak in the back door. When he'd leave the house, Elaine had some man over there. What a mess. Now Naomi, she's one classy lady. She helped him build that business. They had more customers than you can count after he married her and she got her undertaker's license."

"Was he still running around?" Easton asked.

"If he was, he didn't bring it home," Mrs. Young replied. "At least, I didn't see it, and I see 'most everything on this block."

"Did you see who killed Taylor?" Easton asked.

"I didn't see him, but I heard his car," she replied.

"You heard him?" Easton asked.

She chuckled. "Most people don't bother asking me nothing. I'm too old, blind, and don't have any sense. At least that's how some people think of me. My bedroom faces Taylor's front door. You'd think the police would come talk to me . . . never did. Yes, I heard him race off. I didn't leave my bed until I heard the sirens, so I didn't see a thing."

Mrs. Young had given Easton something—a car racing off, which was more than he'd gotten in a week of investigation. "Is it unusual to hear a car racing on Sixth Street that early in the morning?"

"Only two people on the block leave out of here before dawn on Saturday mornings, not at three or four o'clock though, and they're not speeding off the block. Both are nurses—Ruth and a girl up the street."

"Anything else you can tell me about Taylor or that night?" Easton asked.

"Taylor had a good soul. Treated people with the utmost respect, I know because I sent a lot of customers to him," she replied. "And he loved his boy, Thomas. Shoot . . . he wanted him to take over the business one day. Taylor was crushed when that boy told him he didn't want a thing to do with it. Naomi told him to let Thomas do what he wanted."

"How often did you talk to Mr. Taylor?" Easton asked.

"Almost every day," she replied. "He'd come by to see if I needed anything. I don't have children, just my sister, and she's just as old as I am."

Easton checked his watch. "Thank you, Mrs. Young, for talking to me. I really appreciate it."

"You're welcome, son. Have a good day," she said.

"By the way, why didn't you speak to me the morning Taylor died, when the cabdriver helped you down the steps?" Easton asked.

She shrugged. "I didn't want to talk to nobody. It hurt my heart when I learned what happened to Taylor. I told the cab company I was blind and had to get to my sister's house because she had come down sick in the night. The cabdriver told the police, and they let him through." She raised her head toward the sky. "Forgive me, Lord, for lying. I just wanted to leave Sixth Street." A sudden gust of wind came up. She wrapped her shawl tighter around her body.

"I understand," Easton said.

"Can you tell me what my face is saying right now?" she said.

Easton stepped back to get a full view of her face. Her blue-gray hair, combed in a french braid, framed a square face the color of oak. Lines of wrinkles on her forehead and around her eyes told of years gone by. Even her brown lips, probably plump at one time, were shriveled. Her large oval-shaped eyes stared back at him. He didn't know how to answer her.

"You see, you need to learn to read people's faces. Don't always trust what they say. You probably already talked to the killer and don't even know it," she said. "You went to Sunday school when you were a boy, do you remember what you learned about sin?"

It had been drilled in his head from day one. "We're all sinners," he replied.

"That's right! That's right! We're all sinners. Anybody can be a killer. It don't have to be a criminal or a thug. You'd be surprised what good people do when the devil gets hold of them. They act like jackasses. Some end up in prison. Be careful out here. The devil might come after you next," she said. "I'll be praying for you."

"Thank you," Easton said. "I need all the prayers I can get." Crossing the street, he wondered what she read in his face, why she said the devil might come after him. He'd ask his parents about her the next time he talked to them.

* * *

***Naomi must be out of her mind,*** Easton said to himself, as he waited for Ruth to answer the door, his stomach as tight as a slipknot used to catch cattle.

"Morning, love," Easton said, kissing Ruth on the lips. He followed her to the kitchen, where she and Leroy had been waiting for Naomi to summon them to the morgue to help her or to rescue her, whichever the case might be.

"Good morning," Leroy said, and went back to reading the ***Negro*** newspaper.

"Morning," Easton said. He looked around. Despite the well-lit room, a sense of darkness loomed about, and he wanted to turn around and leave. Instead, he sat next to Ruth and sipped on the coffee she'd poured for him. No one spoke. Through the open window, Easton heard dogs growling and barking, making an awful racket, as a trash truck clamored through the alley. The ruckus ended just as Naomi strolled into the kitchen. The sense of darkness Easton had felt seemed to fade.

"Did you two stay here last night?" Naomi asked Easton and Leroy.

The two men stood to greet her.

"I did," Leroy answered.

She looked at Easton.

"I just got here," Easton replied.

"I guess you didn't want to miss the show," Naomi said.

Ruth sensed Naomi's anxiety. "Coffee, Mom?"

"No, when I'm done." She turned stiffly and went through the pantry to the morgue. "Let's get this over with."

* * *

Easton watched with one eye open from the corner of the morgue. Ruth and Leroy stood on opposite sides of the table where Taylor lay. Naomi started removing stitches the coroner had used to sew him together after the autopsy. A yellow fluid oozed from the incision. She hesitated. Sweat dripped from her brow.

"I can't," Naomi gasped. Without warning, tears gushed from her eyes. She stopped, stripped off her apron, the rubbers covering her shoes, and ran out the morgue. Easton, Leroy, and Ruth ran after her. Naomi slipped on the rug in front of the pantry door. They caught her before she fell, and eased her down on the floor.

"Mom!" Ruth pushed Naomi's hair away from her face. Her lips were without color like her face.

"Etsi, Etsi," Leroy yelled, shaking her.

"Leroy, wet the dish towel with cold water. Hurry up!" Ruth yelled.

Easton kneeled beside Ruth. "Should I call an ambulance?"

Ruth didn't respond right away. She wiped her mother's face with the cold, wet towel. Seconds later, Naomi opened her eyes to the three of them staring down at her. Ruth answered Easton, "No."

"What happened?" Naomi asked.

"You fainted," Ruth said, and continued to cool Naomi's face with the wet towel. When she finished, she said, "Let's get her up."

The two men lifted Naomi into a chair and stayed with her while Ruth called her doctor.

"Here, Etsi, drink this." Leroy handed Naomi a glass of water, and she took a few sips. The color in her cheeks gradually returned, eventually evening out the rest of her face.

Ruth directed Easton and Leroy to help Naomi upstairs. Though she still acted feeble, she made it upstairs without fainting again.

Once in bed, Naomi ordered Leroy to call Murphy's Funeral Home and ask him to finish what she'd started. "Send Taylor's black double-breasted suit, white shirt, and red and black striped tie to Murphy's. His shoes are in the corner by the window, socks and underwear in the chest of drawers." She kicked off her shoes, yanked the covers over her head, and prayed to God for help.

Ruth sat with Naomi until the doctor arrived. Easton and Leroy waited outside Naomi's door. The doctor arrived in short order, and after examining Naomi, he attributed the fainting spell to lack of food, sleep, and heartache. He gave her a Valium, and she soon fell asleep.

* * *

An hour later, around ten o'clock in the morning, Easton sat in his office, editing manuscripts Aaron had left on his desk yesterday. There weren't as many people in the office on Saturday, just enough to wrap up unfinished business from the week. Easton actually appreciated the break from the investigation. It had begun to take a toll on him. Some nights he'd wake in a cold sweat, visions of Taylor's blood pooled on the kitchen floor, Ruth bent over in tears. He'd chain-smoke and throw down two or three shots of bourbon before he'd settle down and fall asleep again. When he finished editing the last manuscript, he called Ira.

"Did you see Patti Austin on TV the other night?" Easton asked Ira, "A heartbreaker on the rise."

"Yeah, I watched her with my daughter," Ira replied. "Seven years old, singing and dancing like a pro. When do you have time to watch TV?"

"When I'm home or over Ruth's," Easton replied.

"Okay, that's not why you called me," Ira said. "What's on your mind?"

"Who's the best psychic medium in town?" Easton asked. "We need to ask Taylor who killed him, since nobody living seems to know."

Ira chuckled. "I didn't know you believed in that stuff."

"I'm desperate," Easton replied.

Easton remembered the very first time he'd heard about a psychic medium, a young boy at the time; his grandmother had called on one to find out who had put a spell on her brother, Juniper, who had stopped talking one day. He'd wanted to talk, but not one sound came out of his mouth and nobody knew why, not his doctors, not his preacher, no one. For almost a year this went on. As Easton remembered, it was one Sunday morning during church services that folks were shouting and clapping, when Juniper suddenly jumped from his pew and started singing and dancing and praising the Lord. For the first time Easton saw his grandmother cry; the last time, when his grandfather died. Juniper talked all the time after that, though he never said why he had stopped talking in the first place. Easton's grandmother believed the good Lord had more to do with him talking again than the psychic had.

"One of Taylor's neighbors heard a car race off around the time of the murder. She thought it was unusual, but didn't get out of bed to look."

"He's probably not a neighbor, if he raced off the block," Ira said.

"Did you talk to Georgia Reed's family?" Easton asked.

"They gave me the blues. Wouldn't let me in the house or tell me anything. They're scared to death," Ira said. "I told them we will subpoena her when we find her."

"We don't even know what part of South Carolina she fled to," Easton said.

"No, we don't," Ira said. "We'd have to call every jurisdiction and ask for help finding her. Mind you, we're talking about one racist state. They'd probably tell us to go to hell."

After Easton hung up the phone, he walked over to Lloyd's desk. "If we don't get a lead or a suspect soon, Aaron will make us put the investigation on hold until after the election. We . . . the police should have somebody in custody by now. Something's not right."

"I'm with you," Lloyd said. "A week ago, I would have bet my whole salary on finding Taylor's killer, not today."

"I'm a gambling man too, but the odds on this one ain't too good," Easton responded. "I'm going back to the funeral home. We need something for the column. Maybe a thought will come to me."

* * *

"Mrs. Taylor, you're up," Easton said, surprised. "I told Ruth I'd be back. I had a few things to do at the office. Is she here?"

"Easton, come in," Naomi said. "I thought I heard the doorbell when my teapot whistled."

He walked behind her to the kitchen. The door to the viewing room, usually closed, was open. He stopped to look at the velvet tapestry hung on the wall next to an extraordinary brass pipe organ that Naomi played during funeral services, Ruth had told him. When he'd opened the windows, the day before, he'd noticed the tapestry on the wall. It depicted the three wise men bearing gifts for the Christ Child, the Star of David hovering over them. Their raised images, sewn in muted shades of beige, were clothed in blue and red garments. They wore embellished gold crowns like kings in ancient times.

"You like that tapestry?" Naomi asked.

"A lot of work went into it," Easton replied.

"Yes, it did," Naomi replied, and continued on to the kitchen. "I'm glad you're here, Easton. I'm sorry for what I said at the precinct. I apologized to Ruth, now I'm apologizing to you. I know it's late coming, but someone killed my husband, and when Thomas stabbed Dorothy, my poor heart couldn't take any more," Naomi said. "I know you had nothing to do with Taylor's death. He didn't do anything he didn't want to do. Ruth loves you, and I don't want to be the reason you two break up. She's out running errands. Would you like a cup of tea?"

"Yes, thank you." He sat at the table. "Mrs. Taylor, you don't need to apologize. Ruth and I are fine. I want to ask her to marry me Christmas Day, if that's all right with you."

Naomi smiled and set a steaming cup of tea in front of Easton. "I know my daughter loves you, and if you two want to marry, you have my blessing."

The response he had hoped for. "Thank you," Easton said. "I've been asking around about Mr. Taylor's murder. People in Shaw are shocked. They can't believe he's gone. Some say Taylor knew his killer. What do you think?"

"Taylor wouldn't let anybody he didn't know in this house . . . in the middle of the night. I know that," Naomi replied. "The police claim there was no forced entry."

"Besides you and Ruth, who else has a key to the house?" Easton asked.

"Thomas, Leroy," Naomi replied, "and we keep one in the rock garden. Ruth can't seem to keep up with her keys."

Easton rubbed his chin.

"I know what you're thinking," Naomi said. "Thomas didn't kill his father. He worshipped the ground he walked on, and Leroy doesn't have an evil bone in his body."

Easton paused before responding, trying to think of words that weren't accusatory. "Thomas stabbed Dorothy Nelson. His father was stabbed too."

"No, he didn't kill his father. Ask around . . . he was probably bedded down with some woman," Naomi said.

Because Naomi still seemed weary from her fainting spell, Easton wanted to move on before she tired of him. "I'm writing Mr. Taylor's life story for the ***Negro News***. He didn't flaunt his good deeds, so not everyone knows the magnitude of his generosity to the people in Shaw. I want everybody to know what all he did in his lifetime. Will you help me?"

"I've been questioned by the police and almost slapped the devil out of one of them. I believe Taylor or the Good Lord, one of the two, kept my hand from landing on the man's face," Naomi said. "And your reporter friends call here every day, and I tell them the same thing . . . no comment, but I like you, Easton. Besides, you're my daughter's lover. I'll give you Taylor's story, on one condition . . . I read it before it's published."

"Yes, ma'am, it won't go to print before you read it," Easton assured her.

Easton watched Naomi remove her glasses and clean them with a handkerchief she pulled from her dress pocket. He studied her face, not a wrinkle in sight, a young woman's face. He'd tried to guess her age once, throwing around a few numbers. Ruth laughed and refused to tell him.

Naomi scooted back in her chair and started talking. "Don't ask me about the night of the murder, the police don't want me to talk about it. I might compromise the case, they said."

"Yes, ma'am," Easton said, eager for her to begin.

Naomi hesitated. "I'd rather do this after the funeral." She fixed her eyes on the floor where she found Taylor. "Taylor, my Taylor. He worked hard and loved hard, and yes, he had a few slips along the way." She paused. "His grandmother delivered him and his sister in a house not far from here. He's the oldest. His family lived with his grandparents in the first funeral home they opened on First Street during the horse-and-buggy days. He said after a funeral, they'd load the body on a wagon and a horse pulled it to the cemetery. You know the Iroquois still do that in Virginia, where I'm from. Sometimes they use a pickup truck." Naomi laughed and sipped on her tea. "Goodness, this is still too hot to drink." She eased her cup onto the saucer.

"I remember watching the horse-drawn wagons passing by my house, carrying caskets to our church right down the road. I saw them all the time," Easton said.

"People tried to burn down the funeral home once. Broke windows, poured urine on the front porch. Taylor believed white undertakers did it, trying to force his grandfather to close down."

"Did anyone get hurt?" Easton asked.

"No, they were asleep upstairs. The noise woke his grandfather, and they all ran out the back door, afraid the vandals might set the place on fire. Taylor said they always did their dirt at night, while everyone slept, trying to catch them off guard, the cowards. Eventually, Taylor inherited the business and moved it here." She clenched her hands together and paused, her voice cracking. "He'd been in the business . . . for a long time."

Easton sensed her sadness but wanted to hear more. "I understand Doc Nelson and Mr. Taylor were very close."

"They've been friends since they were little boys, always together, so most people believed they were brothers," Naomi responded. "I first met Taylor at Doc Nelson's and Dorothy's wedding in Virginia. She's my first cousin. Taylor and Elaine were still married at the time. About five years later, after my first husband died, Ruth and I moved to DC and stayed with Doc Nelson and Dorothy. By then Taylor and Elaine had divorced. He'd come by to see Doc Nelson, and we'd chat sometimes. About a year after I got here, he asked me out. He had me by eight years, but it didn't matter. The next thing I knew, we were married. He talked me into learning the funeral business, I got my license, and we worked together ever since." A branch from the dogwood tree on the side of the house slapped against the windowpane. "Leroy needs to trim those branches before they crack a window."

Easton believed she wanted to stop remembering. She'd focused her attention elsewhere. He'd press on until she said ***enough***. "Has anyone from Family Life called you since Mr. Taylor died?"

"Yes, Rutherford Daniels, the president. He claimed they had nothing to do with Taylor's death. I told him I hoped not, because I'd make sure he'd never do business in this city again." Naomi got up and placed their empty cups in the sink.

"Easton, I have things I must get done today. I'll have more time to talk after the funeral."

"Thank you, Mrs. Taylor. Do you mind if I come?"

She laughed. "You'd come anyway, even if I did mind." She escorted him to the door. "I'll tell Ruth you came back looking for her."

# Chapter 28

Sunday morning, October 21, Easton rushed to the kitchen for breakfast. When he finished, he called Ruth.

"Are you all set for the wake?" Easton asked.

"I think so. Mom's getting calls from reporters asking if they can come to the wake and the funeral. She told them no, only one reporter is invited, Easton Priest."

"Does your Mom know any other reporters?" Easton asked.

"No." Ruth laughed.

"How is she doing?" Easton asked.

"She won't come out of her room," Ruth replied.

"I'll come early. I love you, baby," Easton said.

"Me too," Ruth said softly.

* * *

Easton arrived at Taylor's Funeral Home an hour before the wake. Naomi had stayed in her room all day. A half hour before the wake, Ruth grew worried. Easton stood by while she knocked on Naomi's bedroom door. When Naomi didn't answer, Ruth pushed open the door.

Naomi knelt on the floor, her head resting on the bed, her hands folded as if in prayer. She either felt their presence or heard the door squeak when it opened, because she looked toward them, hair tousled around her face, the rims around her eyes red as a beet against her pale skin, and her hair hung loose.

"I don't want to see him in a coffin!" Naomi screeched.

"Mom, please . . . at least for a few minutes. I'll sit with you," Ruth pleaded as she helped her mother from the floor.

Naomi shook her head, moaning, and walked past the couple to the bathroom.

* * *

Easton and Ruth waited for Naomi downstairs. Thirty minutes passed, and she still had not showed. The viewing room had already filled with people waiting to offer their condolences.

"Where's your mother?" Easton asked.

"I'll get her," Ruth replied.

Just as she started for the door, Naomi walked into the viewing room. Easton stood with all the other men and women as Naomi made her way to the coffin. The room grew quiet as all eyes were now focused on her. Rouge on her cheeks had added a bit of color to her washed-out skin. She'd covered her hair, twisted into a bun, with a black lace veil. She wore pearl earrings and a cameo brooch that added a touch of elegance to her black dress. Her black high heels made her stand taller than her five foot nine. She looked striking even in grief. Ruth rushed over to her. A warm smile appeared on Naomi's face as she stood before Taylor, not what Easton expected. After she sat down beside Taylor, she greeted her guests.

When Easton stepped backward to get a wide-angled picture of Naomi, he bumped into Doc Nelson and Dorothy, who had walked in with Thomas, and his mother, Elaine. Thomas took two steps toward the coffin and fell to the floor, wailing. Easton turned away, unable to watch the heart-wrenching display of anguish, fighting to keep his own pain from surfacing. Since Dorothy had refused to press charges against Thomas, the police had negotiated his temporary stay at Saint Elizabeth's. He'd just been released into the care of Doc Nelson to attend his father's wake and funeral.

After Doc Nelson and Leroy helped Thomas to his old room, Easton regained his poise and set about interviewing Taylor's lodge brothers and their wives too. To his disappointment, he learned nothing new pointing toward a motive or a murder suspect. Within two hours of the private viewing, over one hundred people had signed the memory book. They had honored Taylor with words and song and praised Naomi for the endearing love she'd shown for Taylor. Naomi, content with the evening, retired to her room, leaving the others to close up the house.

* * *

Ruth and Easton clung to each other, staring at Taylor in the coffin.

"He looks like he's sleeping," Easton said.

"He is," Ruth responded. "He's just not waking up this time."

# Chapter 29

Easton picked up his parents from National Airport early the next morning and took them to cousin Bessie's house, his father's first cousin. Afterward, he went to his office. With everything abuzz as usual, a gust of air blew through the open windows, carrying smoke, carbon dust, papers, and napkins throughout the room, landing on the floor. Easton planted an ashtray on top of his papers to keep them from floating away. He called Odean. "One of Taylor's neighbors heard a car race off around the time of the murder. Maybe somebody saw it speeding through the city. See what you can come up with. Anything on Leslie Ann Penny?"

"Tonight," Odean said. "Look here . . . Doc Nelson came in the Grille yesterday with a dude I'd never seen before."

"Did Jimmy know him?" Easton asked.

"I asked, he said no," Odean replied. "They were whooping it up like nobody's business. Now, if somebody murdered your best friend and his son stabbed your wife, would you be out having a jolly old time? I'm not saying he ought to roll over and die too, but at least pretend he's missing his friend."

"Anything special about him?" Easton asked.

"Your height. Brown skinned, maybe forty-five or fifty, bald headed, dressed real nice, a scar on his face," Odean replied.

"What kind of wheels?"

"Don't know. I left before him."

"Keep me posted, and thanks," Easton said.

After Easton hung up the phone, he mulled over what Mrs. Young had said, "Anybody can be a killer." In truth, he had fingered a thug for Taylor's murder, like most people in Shaw had, yet it may have been someone Taylor knew. He reflected on the people he'd interviewed. None came across as violent, let alone homicidal. Though his father used to say all the time "You don't really know anybody, because everybody and I mean everybody, has a secret," Easton didn't recall having any secrets. If he did, he must have blocked them out of his mind or wherever secrets are kept.

Easton and Lloyd proceeded to call the victims of Family Life's alleged scam. They wanted to know if the company had contacted them or reinstated their policies, in light of all the publicity and the impending audit by the insurance board. "No such thing," one victim said. The others echoed the same response. When the time came, everyone in the office left for Taylor's public wake.

* * *

Easton drove his parents and cousin Bessie to Taylor's funeral home to ride in the limo with Naomi. Naomi had insisted.

"When you and Ruth marry, we'll all be family."

The spacious chapel became very warm with the throng of people moving through it. Naomi's face turned pale. She jumped from her seat and covered her mouth. Leroy hustled her through a side door before she vomited, Ruth trailing close behind. When Naomi said she wanted to leave, Leroy took her home. Naomi's older brother left with them. Ruth and the rest of the Taylor family stayed.

When the wake ended, over two hundred mourners processed through the church. Some folks waited an hour to pay their respects and bid farewell to Taylor.

Leroy had driven Naomi home in the limo, and while her brother stayed with her, he'd returned to the church for Ruth and Easton and his family. A few of Taylor's neighbors were outside the funeral home when they arrived, expressing their sorrow to Ruth and offering to help her with anything, at any time. Ruth thanked her neighbors, and Easton escorted her inside.

On the drive to cousin Bessie's house, Pops asked, "Easton, do you think Naomi will make it through the funeral?"

Easton's mother answered before Easton parted his lips. "The wake is harder than the funeral. You see the body in the casket and there are no ifs, ands, or buts about it—the person is gone. May he rest in peace."

* * *

Tuesday, October 23, the morning of William Taylor's funeral, Easton sprang from his bed and opened the blinds. The sun seemed to shine brighter than it had the day before. It was indian summer in DC., with temperatures expected to peak around eighty degrees by noon. According to Ruth, indian summer had been Taylor's favorite time of year—no loud, cracking thunder or lightning ravaging in the sky, no hot, humid days, and no snow drifts or ice on the roads threatening to shut down the city—a simply calm and tranquil morning, so fitting for Taylor's transition from a violent death.

Over one hundred people congregated outside the church, the numbers beyond Easton's expectation. DC police stood among them in their dark blue uniforms and around the perimeter of the church. Leroy pulled up behind the hearse. Naomi's older brother escorted her inside. Naomi had invited Thomas to ride with her; instead, he rode with his mother and Taylor's sister in the second car.

Once inside, Easton saw Naomi's two sisters and younger brother, who'd crossed the line, sitting in the back pew. He had met them earlier that morning, when they went by the funeral home. He fretted, trying to understand why they gave up their Negro heritage for a so-called better life. They had to know that the blood in their body would always flow black, even if they were light skinned with hair and eyes the color of white people. They might in fact pretend to be white, nonetheless, they'd always be black. ***At least they were there supporting their sister,*** Easton thought.

Easton, along with other reporters and photographers, were positioned on the outside aisle and instructed not to move about during the invocation and prayers. The ***Negro News*** had sent a photographer; however, Easton brought his own camera. No one would take as many pictures of Ruth as he planned to. He perused the crowd. He recognized a few cops sitting in the pews, dressed in suits and ties. ***Looking to spot a killer,*** he surmised.

Rows of people stood singing "Shall We Gather at the River" as the Taylor family processed down the center aisle, escorted by church ushers. Ruth wore all black, her fedora tipped to the side, a french braid resting at the small of her back. When out together, she'd strut in her three-inch heels and hold her head high. Not today. She moved at her mother's pace, slow and deliberate. At the flash of the camera, she gazed over at Easton. He snapped her picture again.

The flash from the cameras didn't faze Naomi, not one bit. Whenever she entered a room, her presence alone demanded respect. Today she had a more majestic sense about her as she moved forward like a grande dame. Adorned in black from head to toe; the netted veil on her velvet hat shadowed her wire-rimmed glasses. The hat, garnished with small black roses or maybe carnations, Easton couldn't tell from a distance, sat forward on her head like a crown. Two strands of pearls collared her dress, which allowed a hint of her legs to show. Red peeked from toeless high-heel shoes that added two inches to her height.

The order of service proceeded as planned. When time came for Ruth to speak, Easton moved closer to the front.

"On behalf of William Thomas Taylor III, we ask you to take a moment and pray for the one who killed him." Mourners whispered and squirmed in their seat, perhaps uncomfortable with Ruth's request. "We thank all of you for your love and support throughout the years and especially this past week as we mourned the death of our father, uncle, brother, friend, and husband," she said, sorrow in her voice. "My father was a peaceful man. We don't know why someone murdered him, and so we're left confused and angry. Someone took away the heart of our family, a friend to the community, a partner in business. We know we can't dwell in this angry place for long. He'd want us to move forward, to serve others as he did. My father was the blessing in our lives, and we miss him. He's at rest now, or maybe he's up there dancing with the angels, that would be more like him." She paused. "Thank you again for loving him." She went back to her seat and wept.

Doc Nelson spoke next. "William Thomas Taylor, my friend, my brother. Taylor, that's what most people called him. He followed a path paved by his grandfather and father before him. I know because I walked with him. Who would have thought his journey would end the way it did?" he asked, his voice cracking. "A good man, Taylor despised deceit and relished respect. He comforted many of you in this church today, when you lost loved ones. He's here now comforting us while we mourn his passing. No words can describe the pain I've felt since he died, and he dealt with this kind of pain all the time. How did he do it? A gift of the spirit, I guess. Naomi, you were his prize. Thomas and Ruth, his future. I pray God will continue to protect you and have mercy on the soul who took him away. I'm so sorry." Doc, weakened with emotion, needed help back to his seat, next to Dorothy.

Two of Taylor's lodge brothers shared memories about him, and afterward, Dorothy sang the twenty-third psalm, bringing mourners to their feet, clapping and praising the Lord. Two women, who had been wailing and shouting, passed out and fell on the floor. Ushers, decked out in all white, ran with smelling salts in one hand, waving fans in the other. Others wept loudly. At the close of the service, the choir sang Taylor's favorite song, "In the Garden," as the family departed for the cemetery.

* * *

During the internment, a brilliant sun blazed through the tall pine trees lining the narrow road in the cemetery. A warm breeze shook the colorful leaves from the tall oaks and cypress trees, toppling them on tombstones throughout the graveyard. Easton watched Naomi clutch her chest as she watched Taylor's body lowered into the ground. She would say later that a piece of her heart had broken off and gone with him. She cried so hard, she almost fell from her seat. The reverend quickly concluded the graveside service, and Leroy and Naomi's brother helped her to the limo.

By the time the limo reached the church for the repast, Naomi had stopped crying and opened her eyes.

# CHAPTER 30

Easton glanced around the fellowship hall in the House of Worship, flooded with people for the repast. It smelled like Mrs. Kelly's house on a Sunday afternoon. Churchwomen rushed about servicing the Taylor family and others who'd gathered to eat fried chicken, ham, turkey, potato salad, greens, corn bread, rolls, and biscuits—a colored man's feast. Naomi had insisted there be enough food for anyone who came in off the street. The church had planned for the largest repast ever. Banquet-sized tables filled in no time. An overflowing crowd ate in classrooms used for Sunday school and Bible study. Easton's stomach growled so loud, he knew everyone at the table heard it.

"I take it you didn't eat breakfast," Ruth said, smiling.

"No, I didn't." Easton swallowed large mouthfuls of food. Ruth didn't touch her meal. "I take it you did since you're not eating."

"No appetite. I'll eat later." Ruth forked the food from her plate onto Easton's. "At least I know it won't go to waste."

"Thank you, baby, you take such good care of me," Easton said, washing down the food with a cold soda.

When he finished, he put his arm around Ruth's shoulder, and she moved in closer to him. The noise in the room seemed to fade as the sadness buried deep inside Easton threatened to surface again. ***No, not now.*** He still had work to do. Taylor's killer lurked somewhere out there or maybe in here.

"You look so much like your mother," Ruth said, glancing across the table at Thelma Priest. She saw where Easton had gotten his dark eyes. His mother's seemed darker. Her dyed, thin reddish-brown hair worn in a pageboy style with bangs framed an angular face. She had caramel-colored skin, a medium build, and her manicured nails were painted pink. Ruth glimpsed at her own nails. She hadn't polished hers since Taylor died.

"Folks at home say I'm the spitting image of Pops," Easton said. The same height as Easton, Pops had thick chocolate-brown skin, a receding hairline, and oval-shaped eyes. More beefy than Easton, he'd laid tracks on the railroad as a young man and, for the last twenty-five years, raised beef cattle.

Ruth studied Easton's face and smiled. "You got the best of both of them," she whispered in his ear. "We're going to have some beautiful babies."

"And I'm going to enjoy making them," Easton said, grinning. He kissed Ruth on the cheek. "I don't want to leave you, but I need to interview people before they run off."

Ruth sat up. "Don't work too hard."

* * *

Easton ambled between the banquet-sized tables, eavesdropping on the undertakers, businessmen, doctors, lawyers, nurses, tradesmen, and laborers, wondering if one of them may have sold out Taylor or did him in. He stood alongside the walls and scrutinized them all. A few eyeballed him and promptly turned away. He didn't make much of it. When it came to Negroes, "no eye contact" didn't always translate into guilt. Black Codes created after the emancipation in 1865 outlined how freed slaves were supposed to behave. One of the codes, ***no looking at white women twice***, had somehow expanded to include authority figures as well—parents, teachers, doctors, anybody who had power over someone else, black or white. Easton saw this behavior more so in Negro men who'd recently migrated from the South rather than in women, some of these men not so far removed from enslavement.

***Which of these folks did the devil get hold of and kill Taylor?*** he asked himself. He tried to read their faces like Mrs. Young had said. They didn't tell him nothing. Come to find out, she'd been a midwife in Tennessee and helped to deliver some of Easton's cousins. When she moved to DC, she'd worked as a nurse's aid at DC General Hospital, retiring five years ago. Easton's connections to home had grown, having run into people like Mrs. Young, merely doing his job. It seemed the longer he lived in DC, the smaller it became.

Off to the far corner of the room, a sudden flurry of activity quieted the mourners. Easton rushed over and saw Taylor's sister lying flat on her back, Ruth and Doc Nelson tending to her. Her eyes were partially open and her mouth moved, although no sounds came out except for the air she exhaled.

"What happened?" Easton asked.

"She fainted," Ruth said. An usher handed Ruth a wet towel. She gently wiped her aunt's face just as she'd wiped her mother's, when she fainted. Her aunt gradually came around and let out a piercing cry that split Easton's ear. ***She's going to live,*** he thought, and moved on among the somber gathering. Many of the people he knew, some he'd never seen before.

"Hello, my name is Easton Priest, a reporter for the ***Negro News***. Would you care to comment on how Mr. Taylor impacted your life?" Easton asked a young man sitting alone at the end of a table.

The man loosened his tie. "It's pretty warm in here." He gulped down a glass of water. "I used to work in the morgue at Freedman's Hospital. I met Mr. Taylor there. He wanted me to go into the undertaking business with him. I didn't see myself handling dead bodies the rest of my life, so he told me to go to college, I'd figure on a trade once I got there. I'd never considered college. I'm in medical school now." He pulled a handkerchief from his pants pocket and wiped his eyes. "I thank God every day for him caring about me. I don't know where I'd be otherwise."

"When did you see him last?" Easton asked.

"A few months ago. I didn't see him much after I quit the morgue."

"What's your name, son?" Easton asked.

"Jesse Bowen."

"Well, Jesse, its good you two crossed paths. Good luck in school," Easton said.

More folks were up and moving about the room. Easton cut through the mass of black and navy blue and ran into Ira. "You find Taylor's killer yet?" Easton asked him.

"No," Ira answered. "I know you don't want to hear this, but push comes to shove, the chief's going after Naomi Taylor, the one person in the house at the time of the murder. She had access and, maybe, motive."

Easton glared at Ira. "No shit. Do you realize what you're saying? According to Ruth, Naomi didn't put up with a lot of shit from him. That aside, she worshipped the ground Taylor walked on."

"That may be true," Ira said. "Answer me this, can you say for certain he didn't have a woman on the side? If Naomi Taylor got wind of it, she might've killed him in a jealous rage. You know for yourself, he's been on the prowl before."

Easton lit into Ira. "I see now. Your racist cop buddies even got you turning on your own. You know damn well Naomi Taylor didn't kill her husband. What the hell is wrong with you?"

"Come on, Easton, you know better than that." Ira shook his head. "I'm not accusing the woman of killing her husband. I'm telling you how it is."

Easton stalked off livid and went to the john. He finished his business, washed his hands, and splattered cold water on his face. He regretted what he'd said to Ira. He'd promised Aaron that his relationship with Ruth would not hinder his investigation, though Aaron had warned him that he'd have difficulty ignoring things he'd hear about the Taylor family, things that might not sit right with him. He reacted precisely the way Aaron predicted; he'd made it personal.

Over the two years he'd dated Ruth, Easton hadn't forged a real bond with Naomi; he knew her and he didn't. He had reason to worry. Once you probe deep into someone's personal life, just as sure as day turns to night, some reckless piece of information always surfaced. He'd talk to Naomi before the police got to her, though he worried about appearing disloyal to Ruth, intimating that her mother may have killed her father. He'd tell her what Ira had told him, except he'd be more gentle.

Easton surveyed the room. He'd never seen such an overwhelming show of devotion for a Negro who'd passed in the DC area, not even for the dead preachers who'd gone on to glory, as Mrs. Kelly said, after electrifying pulpits to massive Sunday morning crowds. He spotted Doc Nelson, Thomas, Daniels, and another man near the service entrance. Easton snapped a picture of the men.

"Thanks, gentlemen. I can't promise the picture will make the paper," Easton said. "I'll make copies for you, if you want me to." The men regarded each other.

"Sure, fine with me," Doc Nelson responded. The others nodded in agreement.

"We're in business, now." Easton turned to the man he didn't know. "Easton Priest, a reporter for the ***Negro News***." He shook the man's hand.

"Israel Bailey," said the man, smiling, a gold tooth gleaming like the sun.

Easton noticed a scar on the left side of Israel's face. It extended from behind his ear, across his cheek, to the corner of his mouth. It wrinkled when he smiled.

"How did you come to know Mr. Taylor?" Easton asked him.

"We played baseball together at Armstrong High School." Israel reared back, rubbed his chin, and stared at Easton.

"Wow, you two go way back. Where can I send your picture?" Easton asked.

Israel told Easton he lived in New York City. "Give mine to Doc here. He'll send it to me."

"Will do." Easton faced Thomas. "I talked to Ira. The police still don't know who killed your father. No one I've talked to knows anything either." He sighed, a twinge of frustration in his voice. "You got my word . . . I'm staying on the case until the prick is found. Call me if you want to talk or if you need anything."

Before Thomas answered, "I got it covered, son. He'll be fine," Doc Nelson said.

The men shook hands, and Easton left them huddled together. Before he reached the exit, Thomas whisked by him and out the door. He wondered what had provoked his sudden exodus.

Odean caught up with Easton. "Who's the brotha with Doc Nelson and company, the one with the scar on his face?" he asked.

"Israel Bailey," Easton answered.

"That's him . . . the one that I saw with Doc Nelson at Jimmy's, remember, the dude I told you about?" Odean exclaimed.

"Yeah." Easton remembered. "He played baseball with Taylor in high school. He lives in New York City now."

"But he was here when Taylor died," Odean said.

Israel Bailey had added a new face to the investigation.

"See if you can get a line on his whereabouts the night of the murder," Easton said. He caught a glimpse of Ira with a uniformed cop. "I need to talk with Ira before he leaves. I'll call you later."

Easton raced to catch Ira. "You got a minute?"

"A minute, that's it," Ira answered. He kept stepping as he spoke.

"Israel Bailey. Said he knew Taylor from high school. Can you run a sheet on him?" Easton asked.

"Israel Bailey. That name sounds familiar." Ira picked up his pace. "I got to go. We've got a bust a couple of blocks over. I'll run a rap sheet on him when I get back to the office."

Easton stretched his neck; the weight from his bulky camera draped around his collar caused it to ache. He wandered outside, lit a cigarette, and observed the small group of people loitering in front of the church. He saw Thomas with Louise, the receptionist from Family Life, on the corner, holding a powwow. Louise made an abrupt turn and started to run off. Thomas grabbed her arm. She tried to wrestle from his grip, averting her gaze everywhere, except at him. He kept talking to her. After a minute or so, he dropped her arm. She stayed put, this time giving him the glad eye. Whatever he said had calmed her.

Easton put out his cigarette and returned to the fellowship hall. Naomi and Ruth were walking toward the restrooms. He took hold of Ruth's hand. "How you holding up?" he asked her.

"I'm so tired. I've got to lie down before I pass out." Ruth kissed him on the cheek.

Easton smiled at her. "I've got work waiting for me at the office. I'll come by this evening, if it's all right with you."

"I can't wait." Ruth grinned.

At that instance, Easton's parents and cousin Bessie joined the couple. Naomi went out of the ladies' room seconds later, and they all headed to the limo.

"Ma, Pops, I'll call you later," Easton said, before closing the limo door. Since his parents were flying back to Tennessee the next morning, he planned to go by cousin Bessie's before going to Ruth's.

The limo drove off. Easton burned another cigarette. The crowd had dwindled, though some didn't go very far. Three brothas congregating in the gas station across the street were passing a small brown bag to one another. ***A pint of whiskey or gin,*** Easton surmised. ***They'll be drunk before the sun goes down.*** A black '52 Buick drove by. It dawned on him that he'd left his car at Ruth's. He ran back in the church.

"Odean," Easton hollered. "Can I hitch a ride with you? I left my car at Ruth's, and the limo's gone."

"You almost missed me. Come on, I'm parked behind the gas station," Odean said.

* * *

Driving down Seventh Street proved to be a disaster. Someone had sideswiped a car that had run out of gas in the middle of the street. Cars weren't moving in either direction. Odean, stuck in the middle, had no room to make a U-turn back toward the church. Angry drivers were leaning on car horns, cussing out their windows, and pacing in the street.

"Damn, why didn't I take Sixth Street? It ain't much traffic over there," Odean said, slapping the steering wheel.

The gridlock didn't bother Easton. "Who killed Taylor?" he asked, musing about possible suspects.

"I'd tell you, if I knew," Odean answered.

"Family Life had nothing to gain by killing him. Yes, they lost money and somebody in the company is going to jail for fraud, the corrupt SOBs. Killing Taylor, I don't know." Easton wavered a moment. "Doc Nelson said Thomas idolized his father. Naomi, Ruth, and Taylor's neighbor said the same thing. I'm inclined to give Thomas a pass, except his relationship with Doc Nelson and Daniels bothers me. I want to know more about those meetings at Family Life. Have your contacts come up with anything?"

"Not a damn thing," Odean replied. "What about Israel . . . what's his name?"

"Bailey . . . his last name is Bailey," Easton replied. "He's without a doubt someone of interest. By the way, anything on Leslie?"

"Almost forgot, again," Odean replied. "It seems she and Taylor talked a lot at the market. No one's seen them together anywhere else. She's supposed to marry Quentin King in January. Did you see him at the funeral?"

"Sitting with her and the Bean Master?" Easton said.

"That's him. He'll never make the best-dressed list with his plaid jacket and striped tie."

Easton laughed along with Odean. Doc Nelson, Thomas, Daniels, and Israel were dressed to the max for the funeral, donned in black silk suits, starched white shirts, gold cuff links and tiepins, monogrammed handkerchiefs peeking from their top pockets, and fedoras slanted to the side. Tall and short, young and handsome, it was not unimaginable to envision these men on the cover of ***Ebony*** or ***Jet*** magazine. Even so, their bonding at the repast bothered him.

"Something's not right about Doc Nelson and Thomas fraternizing with Daniels and Israel," Easton said. "Doc Nelson and Taylor were ace boon coons, but Taylor despised Daniels. I need to figure out how they all fit together."

"Easton, don't you think you're reaching a bit? Doc Nelson and Taylor were blood brothas," Odean said.

"They weren't real blood. How do we know trouble wasn't brewing between the two? Even friends argue at times. I tell you what . . . get the goods on the two brothas and I'll cross the good doctor off the list, if nothing is amiss," Easton said.

"Consider it done," Odean said.

Thirty minutes after leaving the repast, Odean stopped alongside Easton's car. Pops had left a note on his windshield. Leroy had taken them to cousin Bessie's. "Damn," he said. He forgot they weren't driving. He headed for the ***Negro News*** office.

# Chapter 31

Aaron raced past Easton's desk, barking out orders like a commander in chief directing his troops in battle. Apparently, Juno, one of the city's biggest number runners, had been arrested for operating a lottery in his home. Easton remembered seeing him at Taylor's funeral. The arrest must have happened soon after. ***The bust Ira ran off to,*** he thought.

Aside from church, playing the numbers ranked pretty high in matters of importance to the Negro community. For that reason, many in the city had a vested interest in Juno's future. He had their money. Easton had stopped at the barbershop before the funeral and put a nickel on 912, his birthday. Even if his number came out, he would not reap the rewards now that Juno sat in jail. Although the playing field had changed, there were others who'd take over Juno's territory, if needed, except they wouldn't pay out his client's winnings today.

"Easton, you have two columns for the funeral. Hurry and finish it. I need your help," Aaron said, sweeping past his desk.

"How much did you play this morning?" Easton asked Aaron. He'd never seen him in such a dither.

"Don't ask," Aaron replied. "Lloyd's at the precinct where they're holding Juno." Aaron disappeared into the copy room.

Easton conceded to writing about the funeral without Lloyd's input. As he wrote, his mind drifted to Taylor's yet unsolved murder. He believed Taylor knew his killer. Ira had told him that the locks on the funeral home doors and windows were intact. No forced entry. Naomi had said the same thing. Easton gazed around the smoke-filled room. It looked as if fog had set in. Aaron scrambled over to his desk through the haze.

"Your draft ready yet?" Aaron asked.

"Thirty minutes and it's yours," answered Easton. He didn't like seeing Aaron on edge and didn't want to make things worst. He refocused and quickly drafted the story. He decided to end it with a quote from Dr. Martin Luther King Jr., "We are impatient for justice but will protest with love." He selected an array of photos from proofs the ***Negro News*** photographer gave him, attached them to his article, and passed it on to Aaron.

"Here, read this while I review your piece." Aaron handed Easton a story written by one of his colleagues.

Editing someone else's work didn't require the same creativity as writing from scratch did. Easton welcomed the break. He reared back in his chair, propped his feet on his desk, and exhaled the smoke from his cig. Within the hour, a copyboy delivered his story from Aaron, a few marks scrawled on it. Easton made the changes and shouted for the copyboy. "It's a go." The boy grabbed the document, whirled around, and ran off. Easton smiled. The kid stirred up memories of his own internship at the paper, how he tried his damndest to impress Aaron. It worked. Easton finished editing his colleague's story, which talked about the possible reelection of President Eisenhower and how it might impact on the black community.

"This story is smoking," Easton exclaimed, handing it back to Aaron. "For sure, black folks are taking a huge risk voting Republican, but we got to do it. I hope when it's all over, both parties will understand that our votes can't be denied any longer."

Easton stayed around and helped Aaron edit more articles. Afterward, he gathered his belongings to leave. A single photo of Taylor fell from his notebook. He stared at his hero's face, trying to comprehend why someone wanted him dead. It happened so sudden, it lent credence to the old saying "Here today, gone tomorrow." He felt he'd let Taylor down, his killer still on the run, roaming around the city or maybe hiding under a rock, instead of in jail. He'd keep searching for the scum, even if it meant turning over every rock in the city.

* * *

Easton's mother embraced him the second he walked in the front room of cousin Bessie's house. He sat in a plastic-covered chair; his mother and Pops sat on a sofa across him. Cousin Bessie marched into the room with a tray of glasses filled with sweet tea.

"Child, it's been hot as Hades around here. I can't drink enough cold water or iced tea. Here, have some." She handed Easton a glass of tea.

"Are you all right?" Easton's mother asked Easton.

"It's nerve-racking investigating the murder of my fiancée's father," Easton answered. "The police are dragging their feet, and I don't have to tell you why."

"Easton, do what's right. You know the police don't care none about Negroes," Pops said. "Just because someone killed Taylor, isn't going to change their prejudice. You'll have a stroke worrying about what the police aren't doing."

What he heard next came as no surprise.

"Don't be shocked if family or a friend killed Taylor," cousin Bessie said.

Easton had heard others make similar remarks, and he wanted nothing better than to prove them all wrong, though he couldn't ignore the fact that whoever killed Taylor didn't break into his home; they were let in.

Easton's mother slid to the edge of the sofa and leaned toward her son, her eyes watering. "Be careful, Easton. I worry about you up here, and Ruth and Naomi too."

Easton moved to sit beside her. He gave her his handkerchief. "Ma, stop worrying." He put his arms around her as she wept. "I'm fine. Aaron needed me in the office. Otherwise, I would've spent more time with you."

"Easton, you're my son. Even though I know the Lord's watching over you, I can't help worrying," his mother exclaimed.

"I'll come by early tomorrow morning, and we'll go to Jimmy's for breakfast and then to the airport. Okay with you?" Easton asked.

"Sounds good to me," Pops replied.

His mother nodded. Easton didn't want to leave her upset, so he rambled on about his plans to marry Ruth and the engagement ring he'd bought her. "White gold with a pear-shaped diamond surrounded by smaller diamonds. I think Ruth will like it."

"If she don't, I'll wear it," cousin Bessie blurted. They all laughed.

"She will," Easton's mother said, smiling.

"I need to go check on her and Mrs. Taylor," Easton said, and kissed his mother and cousin Bessie good night. He hugged Pops. "Remember . . . breakfast at Jimmy's tomorrow."

"We'll be ready. Go do what you need to," Pops said.

* * *

Before going to Ruth's, Easton swung by the Second precinct, hoping Ira had received information on Israel Bailey. He called Ira from a pay phone, and a few minutes later, they met on the street. Ira got in Easton's car and handed him a rap sheet on Israel Bailey almost a mile long. Most were misdemeanors and felonies he'd acquired as a teenager. No armed burglaries, assaults, or murder charges.

"Does he have a sheet in New York?" Easton asked.

"I'm working on it," Ira replied. "After I read his sheet, I remembered my old man talking about how Israel kicked ass playing baseball in high school. Everybody thought he'd break the color barrier, he was that good. He got hung up with the wrong crowd his senior year and threw away a chance to play in the big league. It don't seem likely he'd escalate from minor offenses to murder. Then again, he's lived in New York for years. Who knows what he's been doing there."

"What's the story on Juno?" Easton asked.

"Out on bail. He left here with his lawyer about an hour ago. His hearing is Friday," Ira responded.

"I'm not playing a penny until this is over. Is the chief going after the others?" Easton asked.

"He's been after these cats since he got the chief's job five years ago. It took him this long to snag one. He's been smiling all day," Ira replied.

"It's Lloyd's story," Easton said. "Give the brotha some slack, he's good."

Ira laughed. "You say that about all your boys."

* * *

Halfway to the funeral home, the sky darkened and the streetlights came on. Thunder boomed in the distance. A sudden downpour of rain and hail the size of mothballs pounded Easton's windshield. He hadn't at first noticed the car tailing him. He turned off Georgia Avenue onto O Street, and so did the other car. That's when he became suspicious. Before he made the right onto Sixth Street, the car sped around him, blocking his turn. A man jumped from the car, his hands in the pockets of a black jacket, a baseball cap covering his head. He rushed toward Easton, motioning for him to put down his window. Easton struggled to see the man's face through the rain-drenched glass. It didn't help that the large square-framed eyeglasses the man wore obscured his face.

The man shouted at Easton to put the window down. Easton rolled it down an inch.

"How do I get to Freedman's Hospital?" the man asked in a high-pitched voice.

Easton let out a sigh, wound the window down a little more, and gave him directions. The man thanked him, ran back to his car, and drove off. ***What a strange voice,*** Easton thought. He wiped off the sweat dripping down his face, completed the turn onto Sixth Street, and parked in front of Taylor's house. ***I guess it's Mrs. Taylor's or Ruth's house now.*** He noticed a dark shadow moving down the driveway to the pool of illumination from the front porch light. Jeremiah, the boy he'd interviewed the morning of Taylor's murder, continued to shuffle down the driveway to the sidewalk.

Easton exited the car, threw on his raincoat, and approached him. "What were you doing back there?" he asked Jeremiah.

"Putting the trash out," Jeremiah answered. "Why?"

"Because Mr. Taylor is dead and anyone snooping around his house is a suspect, including you," Easton replied.

"I didn't kill Mr. Taylor and I wasn't snooping around. You can ask Ms. Ruth," he shouted over the sound of thunder.

"I plan to." Easton watched the boy run through the darkness to his house.

# Chapter 32

Easton reached the front porch, soaked and wet from the rain. He removed his hat and raincoat to shake off the water. A surge of rain flowed through the old gutters. He looked up toward the roof, expecting to see rain drip down on him. It didn't. He checked his watch. After seven o'clock. He hoped Ruth still wanted to see him. He rang the doorbell. She opened the door and smiled as Easton stepped inside. She grabbed his hat and coat, dripping wet, and hung it on the coat tree. When they embraced, Ruth's body flopped in Easton's arms like a Raggedy Ann doll.

"I missed you," Easton said. He held her head in both hands and kissed her lips.

They stumbled into the parlor, clinging to each other and sat so close, you'd need a sledgehammer to pry them apart.

"The boy from up the street came from the back of your house. Did you ask him to put out the trash?" Easton asked.

"I sure did," Ruth replied. "He's a good boy, Easton. You didn't scare him, did you?"

Easton chuckled. "He seemed more angry than scared. If he knew something about your father's murder, would he tell you or your mother?"

"Of course, he thought the world of Dad," Ruth replied. "Dad was the father he didn't have."

"I didn't know that," Easton said. "How's your mother?"

"She's been in bed since we got home. I don't think she's sleeping though," Ruth replied.

"Ruth, I have to ask your mother some hard questions. I want you to know that I don't believe she'd do anything to hurt your father, even though the police are looking at her for his mur—"

"No!" Ruth screamed, before he finished his sentence. She wrestled from his embrace. She pushed him backward, got up, and stood over him. The sledgehammer that pried the lovebirds apart—Easton accusing her mother of murdering her father. "How dare you! How dare you!"

Easton tried to get up. She pushed him backward again. She pounded at his chest, stuttering. "This . . . is . . . not . . . just . . . a story. My mother would never hurt Dad, never!" Ruth fell over on Easton, shattered at the suggestion that Naomi killed Taylor.

"I'm so sorry, Ruth, so sorry. Baby, please forgive me, I didn't mean to upset you," Easton pleaded, while holding her trembling body tighter. He pressed his face in her hair. She screamed as if she'd been stung by a swarm of bees. It frightened him so he didn't notice Naomi standing in the doorway of the parlor.

* * *

Naomi had heard Ruth shouting and screaming, and with all the energy she'd conjured up, she leapt from her bed and ran downstairs. She rushed to her daughter, motioned for Easton to loosen his grip, and rested Ruth's head on her shoulder. Easton opened his mouth to speak. Naomi held her hand up, signaling him to silence. She held Ruth until she quieted down.

"Ruth, what upset you?" Naomi asked her.

"The police think you killed Dad," Ruth replied, still sobbing.

"I killed Taylor?" a stunned Naomi asked, glancing at Easton.

Easton spoke before Ruth answered. "Mrs. Taylor, the police don't know who killed Mr. Taylor. They need a scapegoat—you." Easton took Ruth's hand in his. "I love you, Ruth, and would never do anything to hurt you or your family on purpose, but your mother must know that the she is a suspect so she can protect herself."

"Ruth, don't be angry at Easton, he's just doing his job. And, Easton, thanks for telling me. Now I know why Taylor's killer is not in jail. My lawyer needs to know too." Naomi stood up. "I'll go make tea, and when I come back, I want to know everything about the investigation, because the police haven't told me anything."

* * *

Naomi wept as she ambled to the kitchen, thinking about Taylor. Like the dead children that rattled him, he was not supposed to die this soon. She didn't kill Taylor, and the thought of answering to the police made her angry. She stood in front of the pantry door, where she'd found his body. "Who murdered you?" she spoke out loud, as if he were in the room. In a split second, the telephone rang. Naomi thought her heart had dropped to her stomach. She took a deep breath and picked up the receiver. "Hello, Taylor's Funeral Home."

"Naomi, this is Doc Nelson. Are you okay, do you need anything tonight?"

Naomi sighed. "I'm fine, Doc. I don't need a thing right now. I'm here with Ruth and her boyfriend. Tell Dorothy I'll call her tomorrow. Thanks for calling."

"I'll tell her. Good night, Naomi."

Naomi wiped beads of sweat off her face with a napkin. ***Taylor, you almost had me going there for a minute,*** she murmured to herself. She returned to the parlor with hot tea and slices of pound cake she'd warmed in the toaster. She sat and faced Ruth and Easton, who were now talking civilly to each other.

"Okay, Easton, what are the police doing to find my husband's killer?"

"To be honest, not much at all," Easton replied. "I know they've questioned people on the street in Shaw and Ira said they interrogated a couple of drifters, but both had tight alibis. No weapon has been found, and in spite of the two-thousand-dollar reward from the Funeral Directors and Morticians Association, no one has come forward with information about the murder." Easton ate a slice of cake and washed it down with the tea.

"Why me?" Naomi asked.

"No forced entry and you were the only person in the house at the time of the murder," Easton replied.

"That's what I get for drinking too much sherry . . . I slept through the worst of it," Naomi said. She wiped tears from her eyes with a napkin.

"Mrs. Taylor, please don't blame yourself. You were spared, and we're all thankful," Easton said. "Do you know a man named Israel Bailey? He said he played baseball with your husband in high school. He lives in New York City now."

Naomi stirred sugar in her tea. "I heard Doc Nelson and Taylor talk about an Israel. I never met him. How does he fit into all this?"

"Didn't he extend condolences to you at the repast?" Easton asked.

"I would have remembered if he did. Israel is not a common name," Naomi replied.

"I talked to him, Doc Nelson, Thomas, and Daniels," Easton said. "They were all together."

"Thomas is spending time with Daniels from Family Life?" Naomi asked, surprised.

"Yes," Easton replied. He told Naomi about Thomas's meetings with Mr. Daniels and Doc Nelson and about Thomas's drug use that Odean had confirmed from dealers in southeast DC.

"It makes sense now. How did I miss it?" Ruth broke in. "Thomas can't keep a job. He's always here asking Dad for money, he's jumpy, and he avoids me like the plague. He can't stand still long enough to carry on a decent conversation. He knew I'd figure it out and tell Dad. Even when we saw him at Saint Elizabeth's, he fidgeted in the room. He claimed the medicine the doctors gave him made him jumpy."

Naomi set her cup down so hard the saucer cracked. "Wait a minute. Are you saying that Thomas and Doc Nelson are involved in Taylor's murder?" Naomi asked, her stomach feeling queasy.

"No, I'm not saying that, Mrs. Taylor. The police questioned Mr. Daniels and Thomas. They haven't got to Doc Nelson or Israel yet. Ira asked the New York City Police Department to run a sheet on Israel," Easton replied. "I believe Mr. Taylor was right about Family Life stealing money from their clients. How the scam played into his murder, no one knows."

Naomi sat speechless, holding her stomach. It hadn't felt right since Taylor died. No matter what the doctor prescribed, it didn't help. She drank more tea and said, "Lord, today, I wondered if Dorothy knows anything."

"Mrs. Taylor, please don't ask Dorothy about anything I've told you," Easton begged. "We're not sure about Doc Nelson's involvement in Mr. Taylor's murder, and if you let on that he's someone of interest, Dorothy will tell him. If he's involved, he may destroy evidence the police can use against him."

The grandfather clock in the hall chimed the nine o'clock hour. Easton walked over to the window. "I have to leave now. I'm taking my parents to Jimmy's for breakfast in the morning and to the airport."

"They were very kind to me, Easton. Please thank them for coming," Naomi said.

"Yes, ma'am, I will," Easton responded. "Mrs. Taylor, the ***News*** team is working overtime investigating Mr. Taylor's murder. We're committed to seeing this through, and Ira and the other Negro cops are helping to the extent they can without getting in trouble. We're going to find Mr. Taylor's killer. Don't hesitate to call me if you think of something that might help us. Ruth has my office and home number."

Ruth helped Easton into his raincoat and waited at the door until he drove off. A car parked next door pulled off behind Easton. She closed the door.

# CHAPTER 33

Easton kept within the speed limit as he drove through the quiet streets. Wet leaves covered the roads, making for slippery conditions. He laughed at himself, reflecting on the man who cut him off on Sixth Street, though he didn't laugh at the time. Jimmy would get a kick out of hearing about it. He drove past his street and to the Grille.

Music blasting from the radio in the Grille competed with loud talk and even louder outbursts of laughter. Easton searched for a seat in the packed room. He squeezed into one at the counter next to the wall. Jimmy zoomed from the kitchen, mumbling under his breath.

"Jimmy, how's it going?" Easton asked.

Jimmy stopped abruptly and grinned at his cuz. "You need another job? These kids today want money, but they don't want to do shit to earn it. I'm sick of them. All they do is call in sick or quit after they get a couple of paychecks. Other than that, life is good. How are the Taylor women? They looked so sad yet so beautiful today."

"Grieving hard," Easton said.

"The good Lord will help them," said the woman sitting next to Easton.

"Thank you, ma'am," Easton said, remembering a similar comment from Mrs. Kelly.

"Whatcha having tonight?" Jimmy asked.

"Coffee."

Jimmy poured Easton a cup of coffee. Easton picked it up and pointed toward the kitchen. Jimmy did an about-face, and Easton followed him, as he'd done many times when they needed to talk in private.

Smoke swirled upward from a hot grill cooking steaks with mounds of onion sizzling on top. Cooks were scrambling and frying eggs in big black wrought-iron pans, flipping pancakes on the griddle, and dropping butter in a huge pot of hominy grits. Customers ordered breakfast food any time of the day or night at Jimmy's. Loaves of bread stacked on a table waited to be toasted, slapped with meat for sandwiches, or broken up into pieces to stuff pork chops, fry crab cakes, and make bread pudding. Waiters yelled out orders every few minutes, and dishwashers banged pots and pans on a steel counter, adding to the already noisy place. Easton restrained himself from lifting a triple-layered slice of chocolate cake off a plate, the same cake he ate every Thanksgiving and Christmas. Scrumptious didn't come close to describing how good it tasted, the recipe from Jimmy's mother, who happened to be Easton's fist cousin.

"Israel Bailey, what do you know about him?" Easton asked as they stepped out the back door.

"Israel Bailey. I haven't heard his name in a while. He lives in the Apple, if I'm not mistaken," Jimmy replied.

"He ate here with Doc right after Taylor died. Odean said you didn't know him."

"I'll be damned . . . Israel. I thought he looked familiar. I haven't seen him in ages. He's changed a lot. Skinnier than I remember and not as handsome . . . that ugly scar on his face. Jesus," Jimmy said. "When I moved here with Granny, I used to sneak over to Armstrong and watch him play baseball. He threw a mean pitch. His arm muscles were huge, and he looked good enough to eat. He made All-Met two years in a row, quit playing his senior year, and stayed in trouble after that. Granny believed something awful happened to him. That's all I know."

"He's got a rap sheet here—nothing violent on it though," Easton said. "Ira is checking to see what he's been up to in New York."

"Oh my lord, I hope I haven't had a killer holding court here," Jimmy exclaimed.

Easton went on to tell Jimmy about the man who cut him off on Sixth Street. "The sucker pulled in front of me and blocked my turn. I had nowhere to go."

"Did you cuss him out?" Jimmy asked, laughing.

"When he jumped out of his ride, shouting at me to put the window down, I felt trapped. After he left, I realized I could have backed up, given myself a little space, and then run over his ass."

"Easton, stop it," Jimmy said. "You know you don't have an evil bone in that body of yours."

They laughed together. Easton finished his coffee and handed Jimmy the cup. "It's been a long day, I'm turning in. I'll be here in the morning with Ma and Pops."

* * *

Easton didn't pussyfoot around in the dimly lit alleyway. He frowned at the tainted smell of garbage seeping from trash cans and large receptacles pushed up against dirty brick buildings. Muffled voices coming from open windows and doors were drowned out from the eerie cries of wildcats hiding in the dark corners of the alley. Easton picked up his pace. Halfway to the street, two men jumped from a space between buildings, the barrels of their guns raised to meet Easton's eyes. He drew back, hands in the air, his heart pounding so fast he thought it might explode any minute.

"My pocket!" Easton shouted.

"Shut up before I blow you away," one man said. He shoved the gun barrel into Easton's cheek. The other man frisked his pockets.

An explosive sound rocked the air. Easton fell to the cement. His head jolted and his eyes rolled around in their sockets. He believed he'd been shot. He groped his body, expecting to feel blood seeping from a hole somewhere. He quickly realized the bullet missed him. He veered his head toward the sound of his name.

"Easton, are you all right?" Jimmy asked, his voice sounding anxious. "Can you get up?"

Easton moved his arms and legs around. "Yeah."

Jimmy and one of his cooks helped Easton to the Grille. Jimmy examined Easton's head. "Thank goodness the skin just scraped off. My fault, cuz, I should've stopped you from going through the alley. Four couples have been robbed around here in the last three months. That's why I keep this under my apron." A small handgun stuck out from Jimmy's belt. "Something told me to watch you go down the alley. When I saw those two thugs come out of nowhere, I fired my pistol. They ran off like rabbits. I'll clean your head. The men in blue will be here sometime tonight."

Twenty minutes later, two white cops arrived. Other than their hands being black, Easton's description of his would-be robbers didn't amount to anything. They wore stocking caps over their faces. He remembered them jumping in his face, hearing a gunshot, and falling to the ground.

"I heard the gun too," Jimmy said. "When I saw my cuz stretched out on the cement, I thought he was gone, dead." Jimmy didn't want the police to know he fired the gun.

Easton listened to the cops promise to put more patrols on the block. A promise he'd often heard after a rash of burglaries or murders in Shaw. After drinking the coffee Jimmy had served them, the cops took off in search of the robbers, so they claimed. Easton left too.

* * *

Although he felt okay to drive, Easton crept along the roadways. Impatient motorists fingered him as they passed by. He downed two aspirins as soon as he got home, changed into his pajamas, and turned on the television. The news was on. Juno's attorney had accused the police of planting receipts and a logbook of numbers in his house. "More to come," the announcer said.

After the commercial, clips from Taylor's funeral and repast showed on the screen. Easton saw himself, Ruth, Naomi, and her brother getting into the limo, headed for the cemetery. Israel stood on the far side of the limo, his arm around Jeremiah's shoulder, the boy who put out the trash for Ruth. He grabbed the phone.

"Odean, you watching the news?" Easton asked.

"No, I'm about to turn in," Odean said.

"Does Israel Bailey have a nephew, son, brother, or cousin, living on Sixth Street?"

"Don't know. I'll ask around tomorrow," Odean said, and hung up.

Easton wanted to know what Israel and Jeremiah had in common besides Taylor. His head still hurt from being bounced around on the cement when he fell. He stopped thinking and turned off the TV.

# CHAPTER 34

The next morning, Easton woke from a restless slumber, his head throbbing. He eased from his bed, groaning, and swallowed two aspirins. Every muscle in his body ached as he wobbled on the cold wood floor to the bathroom. Steam from the hot tub of water coated the bathroom mirror and formed a huge cloud in the small space. He soaked in the water until it cooled. When he returned to his room, he crawled back in bed and lay facedown. He stayed that way until the throbbing in his head stopped. He replayed in his mind the failed robbery attempt. He'd never had a gun pointed at him and believed the sorry bastards would've killed him once they realized he only had two dollars in his pocket. It occurred to him that he owed Jimmy his life.

He stayed still not eager to leave his bed. He needed more time to get over his near death experience. Now he knew what people meant when they said their life passed by them in the face of death. He saw his race by like a cheetah going 70 miles an hour. He dragged himself out of bed and got dressed. He had no choice given that his parents would be waiting for him. He didn't want to disappoint them He peeled the Band-Aid off his head and put on a cap so as not to bring attention to his injury. He also called Jimmy and told him not to mention the robbery in front of his parents, since he'd told them not to worry about him, that no one was after him. He didn't want to give them any more reason to worry.

* * *

Jimmy had reserved a table by a window in the rear of the Grille, and in short order, hot coffee and biscuits were on the table.

"Right on time," Easton said, grabbing a biscuit.

"Easton, we haven't said grace," his mother exclaimed.

"I told him about that," Jimmy said, laughing.

Easton put the biscuit down, and Pops blessed the food.

Jimmy didn't half-step when family came to visit. He served enough food to feed a dozen people. Of course, he sat and ate too. They stuffed their faces and laughed for over an hour at Jimmy's incredulous stories. For a minute, Easton almost forgot why his parents had come to town.

When Jimmy laid the ***Negro News*** on the table, he said, "We have to be nice to Sherlock, you know he's going to be famous one day."

Easton picked up the special edition of the ***Negro News.*** On the front page was a picture of Taylor. Aaron had edited Easton's draft for his column and printed it on the front page. He stared at the picture. He didn't mention Taylor's name, and neither did anyone else. Although he appreciated what he had achieved in his short career, he didn't expect to reach the top investigating Taylor's murder. He passed the paper to his mother.

Pops pulled out his wallet. "Jimmy, what do I owe you?"

"Pops, please don't insult me," Jimmy replied. "You are my guest in this lovely abode. Keep your money."

"You don't have to tell me twice," Pops said, laughing, and put his wallet away.

"Let's get a move on. You two have a plane to catch," Easton said to his parents.

After a few hugs and kisses, they left Jimmy in tears.

* * *

During the drive to National Airport, Easton chatted about his plans for the holiday.

"I'll be home for Thanksgiving," Easton said. "I want to bring Ruth with me, if it's okay with you."

"Ruth is always welcome in our home," Pops said. "Naomi too."

"Thanksgiving is a perfect time to bring Ruth, with the family and all there," his mother chimed in.

On their way to the gate, Easton stopped and watched through the large plate glass windows, huge jet-propelled planes taking off, leaving a stream of smoke in the clear blue sky. The first time he flew on a plane, it scared him to death being up in the air so high, though the landing seemed worse; the noise so loud he thought they'd crash any minute.

As soon as they arrived at the gate, boarding commenced. Easton promised his parents he'd check in more often. He stayed and watched their plane taxi down the runway and lift off. In that moment, he feared what Ruth must be feeling, having loved then lost a father for a second time. Losing Pops . . . never.

* * *

Easton had rushed to cousin Bessie's without his briefcase and drove home to get it. When he took off his cap, he saw blood on the rim. He'd taken the Band-Aid off hoping no one would notice the sore on his head. He didn't want to lie about his injury and he didn't want to tell the truth either, especially to his mother, already believing someone might come after him. "Damn," he said. He washed the blood off and covered his sore with a small bandage.

"What on earth happened to you?" Mrs. Kelly asked, noticing the bandage on Easton's head when he sat at the kitchen table.

"Two men tried to rob me behind the Grille last night. I'd be dead if Jimmy hadn't fired his gun and scared them off," Easton replied.

Mrs. Kelly dropped down in a chair. "Jesus Christ. If folks don't start living by the gospel, we're all going to suffer at the hands of the Almighty."

Easton held his tongue, not wanting to disrespect Mrs. Kelly, nor did he want to hear about God's wrath upon the world this morning. He quickly drank the coffee Mrs. Kelly poured for him and raced off to work, leaving her alone and praying.

* * *

As he entered the *News* room, a copyboy handed Easton a photo of a young boy arrested for Taylor's murder.

"I be damned, it's Jeremiah," Easton said. "When did they arrest him?"

"Last night," the copyboy replied. "Lloyd told me to tell you he's at the Second precinct."

"Thanks," Easton replied. He looked over at the two small console televisions. On one screen, a newsclip talked about the Montgomery, Alabama, boycott—no mention of the arrest on the other TV screen. He dialed Ira's number.

"Ira, Easton here, you arrested Taylor's neighbor for his murder?"

"Yeah, we found the boy wearing Taylor's watch," Ira replied.

"His watch?" Easton asked, surprised.

"We can't divulge everything, Easton. Naomi swore Taylor had it on the night of the murder. She gave it to him for his birthday last year, and after he died, it disappeared."

"Expensive?" Easton asked.

"A Bulova," Ira answered. "Is that important?"

"I don't know," Easton replied. "It's kind of strange the day after Taylor's funeral you bring in a suspect, or is it just for show?"

"Come on, man . . . give them some credit," Ira said.

"Are you questioning Jeremiah?" Easton asked.

"I'll be in the room. Filmore, the officer who knocked you around, is going to take a go at him. So far the kid hasn't copped to the murder. We're checking his alibi now." Ira paused for a moment. "I just got word. The interrogation starts in thirty minutes. I need to go."

Easton called Odean next. "You're home!"

"Yeah, didn't sleep last night," Odean said. "I did my route this morning and came back to the crib to catch a few."

"What do you know about the kid they arrested for Taylor's murder?" asked Easton.

"A sixteen-year-old wannabe, scared of his own shadow. I used to deal heroin with his cousin. He lives on Taylor's block," Odean replied.

"I know," Easton said. "I interviewed him the morning Taylor was murdered."

“I saw his cousin this morning. It seems he and his buddies were on the corner, crooning, when an officer questioned them about Taylor’s murder. When he saw the boy’s watch, I guess he figured it didn’t belong to him. He made him take it off . . . Taylor’s name is engraved on the back. He told the officer he bought it from a soldier for five dollars. His family is all shook up. They’re trying to find a lawyer for him. Arrested with Taylor’s watch on hasn’t helped none. By the way, Israel Bailey is his uncle.”

“Do tell,” Easton responded. “Have they tried a public defender?” Easton asked.

“Public defender? Do you know one worth a damn?” Odean asked.

“Do you believe he killed Taylor?” Easton asked.

“Hell no,” Odean replied.

“Tell his family to call Samia Cox. She works in Judge Gabriel Hammond’s office, and don’t mention my name,” Easton said.

* * *

Newspaper reporters were huddled in front of the Second precinct, waiting for the chief of police to give a press conference about the arrest. Easton didn’t believe Jeremiah killed Taylor. He appeared scared to death in his mug shot. Cold-blooded killers don’t give a damn. It’s possible the boy might have stolen the timepiece from the house or found it somewhere—a killer he was not.

“Can you believe the chief is giving a press conference about the arrest of a black man’s killer?” Easton asked Lloyd, who was bracing himself on crutches.

“No,” Lloyd replied. “But Aaron told me to get over here just in case.”

Easton turned toward the station. “I hate these waiting games. I’m going to call Ruth.”

“She’s in the station with Mrs. Taylor,” Lloyd said. “I thought you knew.”

Easton’s face went blank. “No, I didn’t. See what happens when you start work late, you miss the important stuff. I wonder why they’re in there. I guess I’m playing the game after all.”

Easton puffed on his cigarette and glanced toward the station. Uniformed cops were standing front and center, screening people going in and out of the building. Cameras started flashing as Ruth and Naomi surfaced. Surrounded by cops, they were escorted to a squad car and driven away.

“Something’s not right,” Easton said, concerned. “I’ll be at Ruth’s.”

# Chapter 35

Four police cars were parked on Sixth Street by the time Easton got there. ***What the hell happened?*** He raced up steps to the front porch. A cop stood guard at the door. He asked Easton what business he had with the Taylor's.

"Ruth Johnson is my fiancée," Easton replied.

The cop knocked on the door. "Simms," he called out, "ask Ms. Johnson to come to the door, please."

Moments later, a very anxious Ruth appeared. "Ms. Johnson, do you know this man?"

"Yes, he's my boyfriend. Please let him in," she replied.

The cop moved to the side, and Easton went in.

"What happened?" Easton asked, trailing behind her to the kitchen, where Leroy and Naomi sat talking.

"Someone sent Mom a death threat!" Ruth yelled.

"Ruth, I'm still here, there's no need for hysterics," Naomi said.

"What am I supposed to do, just pray that no one kills you too?" Ruth yelled louder.

"Stop it, Ruth. Stop it." Naomi left her seat and grasped Ruth's arms. "I intend to be here for your wedding, and maybe even Leroy's wedding if he hurries and finds someone, and to help take care of my grandchildren. Whoever sent that letter has more to fear than we do."

Easton's eyes shifted from mother to daughter, surprised at this new revelation. "What did the threat say?" Easton asked.

"Mom won't live to see me get married." Ruth ran out of the room.

Easton followed her sobs to the parlor. He cradled her in his arms. "Why didn't you call me? I would have come right over."

"I didn't know about it until we were on our way to the precinct," Ruth responded. "Ira called this morning and said they had a suspect. He wanted us to come for the lineup, to see if we knew the boy. He sent a car for us, and Mom decided to read her mail on the way there. That's when she found it. Easton, I'm losing it. It'll be a miracle if I don't have a nervous breakdown."

Easton held Ruth close. All the insults that had chipped away at her—fear, hurt, pain, despair, sorrow—played out in a torrent of tears, charging down her face like a raging river. He held on to her trembling body until she relaxed, until she spoke without sputtering.

"You okay?" Easton asked her.

"No," she replied, soft-spoken. "They arrested Jeremiah Bailey for Dad's murder. He's just a kid, a good kid. I don't believe he killed Dad. He's always so polite and did anything Dad told him to do, and he's smart."

"I talked to him the morning your dad died. I don't believe he killed him either," Easton said. "But it bothers me that the death threat is written with crayons. Kids play with crayons, not adults."

* * *

Easton doubted that Taylor's killer sent the threat to Naomi—why would he? "Suffice it to say, he could've killed her the same night he knocked off Taylor, if he wanted her dead," Easton said to Aaron. "It doesn't add up. And the kid they arrested . . . he didn't send it either."

"How can you be so sure?" Aaron asked.

"He's not a street kid. He just doesn't fit a killer profile," Easton replied.

"By the way, the chief didn't have the press conference," Aaron said.

"No surprise," Easton responded, and went back to his desk to call Odean. "Did Samia Cox take Jeremiah's case?"

"From what I heard, she showed up with another lawyer, named Younger. She's kicking ass already," Odean replied.

"Jeremiah's mother needs to know that Mrs. Taylor received a death threat this morning," Easton said.

"No shit! We got one crazy fool out here," Odean said.

"Yes, we do. Have his mother tell Unger right away," Easton said. "I can't ask Ruth or Naomi Taylor to tell her. They need to stay clear of this mess. And don't tell the kid's family where you're getting information."

"My lips are sealed," Odean assured him.

Easton called Ira next.

"What's the plan to protect Naomi?" Easton asked.

"Cops are at the house for the rest of the day, just in case the bastard tries to execute the threat?" Ira replied.

"What about tomorrow?" Easton asked.

"No matter how light Naomi is, she's still black. She's not getting any special favors from the chief. She's on her own after today. Besides, no one physically attacked her," Ira replied. "But I'll tell the other brothas to stop by and check on her when they can."

"I don't know about you, but I'm not sitting around waiting for someone to come after Ruth or Naomi," Easton said.

"The handwriting experts are analyzing the death threat," Ira said. "Maybe we'll get a hit."

"A death threat written in red crayon, on construction paper," Easton commented.

"Yeah, it makes you wonder if the person has a kid or spends time with children," Ira said.

"You think children are in danger?" Easton asked.

"I don't want to know after it's too late," Ira replied. "This whole case is strange."

"I need to find Taylor's murderer before somebody else is killed," Easton said.

"It's not your job to find Taylor's killer. It's my job," Ira said. "Stick to reporting, before you get in over your head."

"Look, man, I'm already in over my head." Easton hung up and went in search of Lloyd. He found him lollygagging in the copy room.

"Lloyd, I need you to write another leader for the column since Aaron published the other one in the special edition. I'll be in the street, looking for a killer." Easton said.

"You're covered, man. I'll make you proud," Lloyd said.

# Chapter 36

It had been two days since Taylor's funeral, and Easton's nerves were on edge. He had been pounding the streets of the city pressing his contacts for information, talking with Taylor's business associates, and scaling every barber and beauty shop, carryout, and diner in the city for information. He'd even tried to talk with Family Life employees leaving work, though none would talk to him. He felt as if he'd been in a boxing ring, pushed up against the ropes then knocked down for the count. His efforts hadn't produced a clear motive or suspect, and now someone had threatened Naomi Taylor's life. To leave the matter of Taylor's death and Naomi's life in the hands of the DC police would scream defeat in his mind. Taylor's killer might fade into oblivion and remain on the street forever. Moreover, he sensed a terrible danger in not knowing who wanted the Taylor's dead and if Ruth was next.

Easton believed Ruth when she said Jeremiah was smart, although he didn't believe the boy had enough smarts to pull off a murder. What he did believe was the killer had entered Taylor's home, stabbed him to death in his kitchen, left through the front door without leaving a footprint or fingerprint, and somehow managed to remain at large. Although Taylor had a rock-hard body, like a wrestler, Easton believed the killer either had to be stronger or took him by surprise. The murder occurred in the early morning hours while his wife slept upstairs, no witnesses, and no weapon. An onerous case, and with little police support, Easton knew he'd have to do more. There was a growing sentiment in the Negro community that the killer might never be found—especially if a policeman or the Klan had got him. Aside from that, Easton believed Taylor had intimidated somebody he knew, somebody he let in the house that night.

* * *

Leaves swirled through the streets, and a drizzle fell over the city as Easton drove to the O Street Market. "Taylor's murder investigation isn't going too well," Easton said to the Bean Master.

"I thought they arrested a young boy last night," the Bean Master said, surprised.

"That boy didn't kill Taylor," Easton said. "He worked around Taylor's house, never been in trouble with the law, a good student. The police arrested him with Taylor's watch on. He said he bought it from a soldier on the street?"

"A soldier?" the Bean Master asked. "No wonder they arrested his behind. You know as well as I do, no soldier is going to be on the street selling nothing."

"They're interrogating him now. I say he's innocent," Easton said.

"Son, why don't you just say what's really on your mind," the Bean Master said.

"Taylor knew his killer," Easton said, emphatically. "He let him in the house. He had to. There was no forced entry."

"Who would you let in your house at that time of the morning?" the Bean Master asked.

Easton hesitated before answering. "People I'm close to—Ruth, family members, my best friend, people at the ***Negro News.***"

"Then that's who you need to talk to . . . people close to Taylor. People he'd let in his house at that time of the morning? The boy they arrested."

* * *

Later that evening, Easton met Toast for drinks. "Mrs. Taylor received a death threat yesterday."

"You bullshitting me," Toast responded.

Easton shook his head. "No, man, not about this."

"Oh noooo," Toast said, and took a swig of his drink.

"Can you believe Mrs. Taylor had police protection all day yesterday?"

"To make up for not finding her husband's killer," Toast replied.

Easton lowered his head, clutching a drink in both hands. "It's my fault Taylor died. I made a mistake exposing Family Life's corrupt shit. They stole from the dead. My clue to how sick they are. I missed it."

"Don't blame yourself," Toast said. "You did the right thing publishing that article. A whole lot of people will wake up tomorrow not worrying about their life insurance because of you."

"I don't know what I'd do if something happened to Ruth," Easton said. "Man, I love her so much."

"Nothing's going to happen to Ruth, because she has you," Toast assured him.

# Chapter 37

Sunday morning, Easton woke with a splitting headache. He'd fallen in bed drunk, feeling sorry for himself. He sat on the sofa, staring at the sunrays that spread across the faded wallpaper. He downed a couple of aspirins and clicked on his radio to "A Mighty Fortress Is Our God." When it came to religion, Easton accepted his role as sinner because he knew he hadn't lived a perfect life. However, his attendance at church this morning would be for the business of murder, not to ask for forgiveness. He decided to attend services at the Taylor family's place of worship. He hoped while sitting among people Taylor once worshipped with, God would point him to someone more sinful than he was, someone who might have killed Taylor, or perhaps just being in the place might spark some divine revelation about the murder he'd overlooked.

* * *

"Good morning," Easton said to Yancey, Dorothy, and Doc Nelson as they arrived at the church.

"Morning to you, son," Doc said. The others echoed his greeting. "Are Naomi and Ruth coming this morning?"

"Mrs. Taylor is not doing so well since she received a death threat," Easton responded.

"What you say. It's been one thing after another," Yancey said. "When she told Mildred about it, I didn't believe it. We're going by to see her today."

The organ prelude began. Easton slid into the back pew. The other's sat in a middle pew with Boone and Ivy, their usual Sunday morning seats, where on occasion Easton had joined Ruth, Taylor, and Naomi. He caught a glimpse of Mildred sitting with the choir. Others who attended the funeral and repast were scattered throughout the chapel. Doc Nelson didn't stay seated very long. He left his pew before the service started. Odean had told Easton, not one soul had witnessed or knows of ill will between Taylor and Doc Nelson. Although Easton had seen friendships end at the drop of a dime, especially when money or women were involved, if the breakup stayed close to the chest, no one would be the wiser if one friend died. Doc Nelson returned to his pew right after the clergy took their place in the pulpit.

Reverend Ford arranged papers on the lectern and addressed the congregation. "It's with deep sorrow that I announce the death of Ms. Cynthia Bailey, Jeremiah Bailey's mother." Everyone gasped, including Easton. "She died in her sleep last night. Most of you know she had surgery on her heart a couple of years ago, and she had been doing fine." He paused. "Most of us will never experience our sons or daughters arrested for murder, thank the Lord. We don't know what toll it took on her, knowing her son sat in jail accused of murder. What we do know—God is our savior and redeemer and he will not forsake us. Jeremiah will need us more than ever now. We will do what God wants us to do, what William Taylor would do if he were here, help Jeremiah." The reverend asked the church to pray for him and his family. The choir rose to sing, "Precious Lord, Take My Hand".

Not the revelation Easton had hoped for. He thought about how he'd treated Jeremiah when he last saw him. Now he's in jail and his mother is dead. He felt awful. He prayed for forgiveness and, after the service, headed for Ruth's house.

* * *

"Hub, is everything all right?" Easton asked the cop, one of the four Negro's on the police force, surprised to see him at the funeral home.

"Everything's fine," Hub replied. "Just stopped by to check on the Taylor women." Hub was taller than Easton at six foot four and 250 pounds, and his upper body appeared as wide as a three-by-five piece of pressed wood. The department had hired him a year ago, bringing the count of Negro cops to an all-time high of four.

Easton heard gospel music reverberating through the open door. Ruth or Naomi, Easton didn't know for sure which one sang along with Mahalia Jackson's rendition of "Amazing Grace." He paused for a moment to listen. "Heads or tails, who's singing with Mahalia, Ruth or Mrs. Taylor? Easton asked Hub, slapping a coin on the back of his hand.

"I already know who's blowing in there, 'cause she sang to me." Hub laughed as he skipped down the steps to his car.

Easton put the coin back in his pocket and followed the songster's voice to the kitchen. Ruth stood at the sink, washing greens, tapping her feet, and singing along with Mahalia. He stopped at the door and listened.

Ruth must've felt his presence. She turned around and smiled as he slinked toward her. He saw a sparkle in her eyes that he hadn't seen since Taylor died. He kissed her on the mouth.

"You feel better today?"

"A lot better," Ruth said. "Mom had a good night and a good morning, so I'm good."

"I can tell. You're singing again, and you have a little bounce in your step." Easton swung her around. "I went to your church this morning. Reverend Ford said Jeremiah Bailey's mother died last night."

"Yes, she did." Ruth's smile disappeared. "When we heard the ambulance early this morning, we ran outside. Her brother was on the porch, crying, and—"

Easton interrupted her. "I'll be right back." Easton ran to Jeremiah's house and knocked on the door. Israel Bailey opened it.

"Reverend Ford said Jeremiah's mother died last night," Easton said. "Please accept my condolences. I heard she was a wonderful woman."

"What's your name again?" Israel asked.

"Easton Priest."

"Oh yeah, the reporter. Cynthia is . . . was my sister, a good woman . . . good mother with a bad heart. She died too young. I told Jeremiah this morning. He just fell apart. Said he didn't want to live anymore." Israel pulled a handkerchief from his pants pocket and wiped his eyes. He stared down at the floor. "I need to go take care of business." He thanked Easton for stopping by and closed the door.

Israel's show of sadness surprised Easton. ***A hardened criminal, maybe not.***

* * *

"I wonder when Israel Bailey came back in town, or if he ever left," Easton said. "And why did his sister keep her maiden name?"

Ruth set a large pot of greens on the stove. "So that's where you ran off to." She turned the fire on under the pot. "His sister never married Jeremiah's father. Don't ask me why, I don't have a clue."

"I thought everybody knew everybody's business on Sixth Street," Easton said.

"All families have secrets. As a matter of fact, I know more about some of my patients' than their families," Ruth said. "I imagine your family has a few secrets too."

Easton grinned. "You may be right. It seems the Bailey family had one they've kept for a long time. To hear Jimmy and Ira tell it, something terrible happened to Israel his senior year in high school that led him astray. No one seems to know what happened."

"I bet Dad knew, and if he did, Dr. Nelson knows too," Ruth said.

"Why, thank you, baby, for your insightfulness. I'll make a point to ask Doc Nelson about Israel," Easton said. The sore on his head started itching. When he scratched it, dried blood collected under his fingernails. He decided to tell Ruth about the attempted robbery before she heard of it from someone else. DC was not a big city.

"You were supposed to go home!" she screeched. "Why on earth did you walk through the alley alone?" She examined the abraded area on his head. "It's dirty, don't move." She pranced out of the kitchen.

Easton took off his jacket, threw it on the back of his chair, and washed the blood from under his nails in the kitchen sink. Ruth returned with a first aid kit she kept in the powder room. She cleaned off the crusted blood, dabbed the sore with Mercurochrome, and covered it with a bandage.

"It may not stick to your hair very long. You want me to shave around it?" Ruth asked.

"No, thanks. I'll change it when it gets loose," Easton responded.

Ruth sashayed around the table to the pantry and trashed the dirty gauze pads. She started back toward Easton and noticed a piece of paper on the floor. She stooped down and picked it up. "Who's Louise?"

"Louise?" Easton asked, questioning why Ruth asked about her.

"Yes, her name and phone number is on this piece of paper," Ruth said.

Easton spun around to see her staring at the paper with Louise's phone number on it. It had fallen from his pocket when he took off his jacket. "Oh, Louise, she works for Family Life. I interviewed her about the company."

"You call her at home?" Ruth asked, glaring at him.

"Wait a minute, now." Easton grabbed Ruth's hands. "I have a business relationship with her, nothing more."

"You said that about Anna," she reminded him.

"Anna came on to me, I didn't encourage the woman." Easton swung Ruth around onto his lap. "I love you, Ruth, and no one else," he said, wrapping his arms around her.

"Dad's dead, Mom's received a death threat, you've been attacked, another woman's phone number appears on my kitchen floor—my nerves can't handle too much more," she murmured.

"I don't mean to cause more hurt for you, Ruth," Easton said. "Louise is important to my investigation. There'll always be women I need to interview. I thought you trusted my love for you."

All of a sudden, water from the pot of greens boiled over. Ruth leaped from Easton's lap and turned down the burner on the old gas stove. She heard the sound of footsteps on the stairs.

"Mom's coming."

Easton stood to greet Naomi as she came into the kitchen. "Good morning, Mrs. Taylor."

"Morning, Easton," Naomi said. "Okay, Ruth, I see you got the greens going. What do you want me to do?"

"We need dessert, cake or bread pudding," Ruth replied.

Although she forced herself to be pleasant, Easton heard the tension in Ruth's voice.

"Chocolate cake, please," Easton proposed.

Naomi placed her hand on the back of Easton's chair. "I take it you'll be here for dinner. By chance, did Mrs. Kelly put you out?"

Ruth and Easton laughed. “No, ma’am. I love your cooking and your daughter.”

“Oh boy, you know exactly what to say. Chocolate cake it is.”

Easton thought for a moment then asked, “Mrs. Taylor, had you seen Israel Bailey before this morning?”

“No,” Naomi answered, as she gathered ingredients for the cake. “When Cynthia’s mother died—it’s been years now—I didn’t attend the funeral, so I never met all her family.”

Naomi went into the pantry. Easton stared at Ruth’s rear end as she bent over to put a roast in the oven. His eyes quickly shifted to Naomi coming through the pantry door, carrying five-pound bags of flour and sugar in her arms. He got up and took the bags from her.

“I need to get a move on,” Easton said as he set the bags on the table. “What time do we eat?”

“Five o’clock,” Ruth replied. “I’ll walk out with you.”

“See you this evening, Mrs. Taylor,” Easton said, leaving the kitchen.

“Don’t be late. We don’t like warming up food in this house,” Naomi told him.

“Yes, ma’am,” Easton replied. Both Ruth and her mother could burn. In fact, he’d praised their cooking so much, his mother had gotten jealous. He had to play it down some around her.

* * *

Easton pulled into Family Life Insurance Company’s parking lot and spotted Doc Nelson’s Desoto. He quickly shifted his car in reverse and sped backward onto the street, praying that no one had seen him, circled the block, and drove into an alley across from the company’s building. He almost hit two mangy-haired dogs racing through the alleyway, where he parked on a grassy strip alongside a garage. He’d already planned what to say if someone questioned his presence in the narrow backstreet—his car cut off and he’d called for help. From Easton’s vantage point, he had a direct view of the parking lot and a side view of the three-story brick house the company advertised as its main office. They also had offices downtown and in Baltimore, Maryland.

Forty minutes into his stakeout, his throat became irritated. Smoke from burning one cigarette after another had scratched his gullet. He reached for a bottle of soda to douse the vapors and relieve the pain. When he opened the warm drink, it fizzled all over his shirt, pants, and the seat of his car. “Damn!” he bellowed. He hopped from the car and squatted down while he wiped off his clothes and seat with a handkerchief. He slid back in the car. Ten minutes later, Doc Nelson and Thomas surfaced from the building. Easton grabbed his camera and snapped pictures before the two men jumped into Doc’s car and drove off.

Easton tailed them up Seventh Street past the Wonder Bread Factory, where the aroma of fresh baked bread drifted in the air, reminding him of the homemade rolls his mother baked every Sunday. He wondered if Ruth planned to make rolls for dinner. A loud car horn startled him back to the matter at hand. He continued following the Desoto onto Howard Place, one of the main streets on the Howard University campus. Doc Nelson turned left at the dead end. Easton parked on Howard Place, grabbed his camera, jumped from his car, and fell into step with a group of students laughing and jonin' on a brotha's high-water pants. Easton laughed too. When he reached the corner, he saw Doc Nelson and Thomas going through the entrance to the gated campus.

Easton kept his distance and followed their movements through the stately wrought-iron fence. Doc stopped to talk with students sitting on the steps outside a building. Thomas hustled across the square to a group of boys congregating under a tree. He saw something change hands between Thomas and one of the boys. He didn't want to believe that something may have been drugs, then again, when Thomas slipped something in the hands of another boy and yet another, Easton about flipped. He opened the shutter covering his camera lens and captured the last exchange. Afterward, he glanced toward the building where he last saw Doc Nelson. He'd gone. He turned around and spotted him heading toward the open gate. Easton scrambled behind a nearby tree and waited until both men returned to Doc Nelson's car and sped away.

* * *

Easton hustled to his car and managed to pick up the Desoto's trail, which ended on the side street next to the Grille. Just as he drove past the Grille, he spotted Israel Bailey, dressed in a brown suit and a cap, stroll inside. Easton found a parking space a block away, dashed into a drugstore, and called his cuz on a pay phone.

"Jimmy, it's Easton. I'm across the street. Is Doc Nelson, Thomas, and Israel Bailey in there?" Easton asked.

"They just walked in."

"Doc Nelson and Thomas are selling drugs to kids on Howard's campus."

"No, they aren't!" Jimmy shrieked.

"Yes, they are," Easton said.

"No wonder some of these boys come in here acting like assholes, they're high as a kite. I'm gonna kick some ass in here today. I gotta go."

"No, Jimmy! Don't hang up!" Easton pleaded with his cousin. "Don't do anything, please don't. I need more evidence. I won't get it if you beat the shit out of them. Just keep an eye on the creeps. I'll call you later."

Easton trudged back to his car, concerned that Jimmy might blow his investigation. The whole thing had a chilling effect on Easton—the Godfather and his capos, godson, peddling drugs to kids. The more he thought about it, the angrier he got. He exited his car and headed back to the Grille. He wandered into a crowd of people at a bus stop across the street and pretended to wait for the bus. Five minutes later, he saw the bus inching its way up the street. ***All these people are getting on the bus,*** he thought. He'd have to find another place to stake out the restaurant.

As it were, Doc, Israel, and Thomas went out of the Grille before the bus reached the stop. Easton sprinted to his car, revved up the engine, maneuvered out of the tight parking space, and sped toward the corner, the yellow light changing to red by the time he reached the crossroads. Doc's car passed through the intersection right in front of him. Easton banged on the steering wheel. For a fleeting moment he considered running the red light. ***It'd be my luck to get caught or cause an accident.*** He dismissed the thought and waited for the green light. He hung a sharp right into heavy traffic and almost rammed into the back of a car. ***Calm down,*** he said to himself. ***Calm down.*** Cars were bumper to bumper. Once he passed the stretch of shops and restaurants, he knew traffic would clear and he'd have no problem catching up with the Desoto, as other cars would eventually turn off the busy thoroughfare.

A red light met him on every corner, it seemed. After four blocks of crawling in traffic, he spotted the shiny black car a couple of streets ahead, going through a light. He drove faster, trying to catch it. It made a left turn. He read the street signs and figured it had turned onto Seventh Street. He turned on Seventh Street and saw the car in the distance. It turned left onto Gresham Place, where Doc Nelson stopped at the end of the block. Easton pulled to the curb at the corner. Thomas crawled out of the car and stumbled into his mother's house. Once Doc drove away, Easton left his car and knocked on the door.

"Easton . . . surprise . . . surprise," said Thomas, his speech slurred, eyes glazed. His breath reeked of beer.

"You've been pretty busy today," Easton said.

"Yes, I have." Thomas spun around on his heels and almost fell down laughing. "Whatcha want?" he asked Easton, rubbing his eyes, still fidgeting.

"How long you been using?" Easton asked.

"Using. Whatcha talking about?" Thomas responded.

"Doc Nelson told me about your drug problem. He forgot to tell me that you two sell drugs to kids. I'm sure their parents would like to know why you frying their boys' brains." Easton pushed Thomas against the wall.

"What . . . you want to buy some too, Mr. Goody Two-shoes?" Thomas swung at Easton and missed, his eyelids fighting to stay open. He fell to the floor.

"You sorry ass, you belong under the jail," Easton said. "Call Doc and tell him you're not doing his dirt anymore."

"Oh no! I can't do that. I can't tell Uncle Nelson that. He'll kick my ass all over the place," Thomas whined.

"I'll kick your ass if you don't call him," Easton shouted.

"Come on, Easton. Somebody killed my old man. They killed him. I needed a little something to help me get through it, that's all."

"You don't have to hustle for Doc to get the help you need. Selling drugs is not how you honor your father's memory."

Thomas wept. "Easton, don't do this to me. I loved my daddy. I wanted to be just like him. That's why I played baseball."

"And Ruth said you were good too," Easton responded. "It's not helping you now, so get up and pack some clothes. I'm taking you to Saint Elizabeth's."

"No! I'm not going back there," Thomas whimpered like a scared puppy.

Easton knelt down and got in Thomas's face. "Thomas, we go now or I call the cops."

* * *

An hour later, Thomas, with Easton's help, signed himself into Saint Elizabeth's Hospital. Easton left him protesting, afraid of what Doc Nelson might do to him. He assured Thomas that he'd be safe in the hospital with all the nurses and orderlies running around. Easton had a half hour to lose before dinner, so he stopped at a pay phone and called Ira at work. He had the day off, so Easton called him at home.

"Ira, Easton here. Sorry to bother you on your off day." Easton reported what he'd observed on campus. "Maybe Taylor found out Doc Nelson and Thomas was dealing drugs, and Doc Nelson killed him or had someone else do it."

"It's a pretty big jump from selling drugs to murder. Doc Nelson is a respected businessman. You gotta give me more than this to bring him in," Ira said.

"Can't you follow him for a few days?" Easton asked. "He's bound to hit the streets again, with or without Thomas."

"I can tell you now, my boss is going to say we don't have the manpower to follow a hunch," Ira replied.

"Ira, right now your boss don't have diddly-squat," Easton said, annoyed. "You'd rather pin Taylor's murder on his wife, even though her life's been threatened, instead of finding the real killer. How much sense does that make?"

"I'll see what I can do," Ira said.

"What's the story on Jeremiah Bailey?" Easton asked.

"After he found out his mother died, he completely fell apart, blaming himself for getting in trouble. We put him on suicide watch after he threatened to kill himself," Ira said. "The chief is going to transfer him to Saint Elizabeth's. The only prints on the watch were Taylor's, Naomi's, and Bailey's. The soldier must have wiped his off before he sold it. But Bailey's prints didn't match any we collected from the kitchen. Maybe he wore gloves. Detectives finished searching his house, but they didn't find anything. His lawyer is threatening to sue the department for police brutality. The kid's face wasn't messed up before our boys arrested him, and he doesn't have a record either, an honor student in high school," Ira said.

"Well, how about that, a Negro boy with ambition," Easton said. "His college education may be paid for, compliments of the DC police department and a good lawyer." He hung up and dialed Louise's number.

"Easton, I'm so glad you called. Dr. Nelson and Thomas stopped meeting here," Louise said. "They're meeting at Dr. Nelson's drugstore. Mr. Daniels gave me the phone number, in case I need to call him."

"What about Thomas?" Easton asked, trying to find out if she'd seen or talked to him lately.

"We're supposed to go to a movie tonight, but I haven't heard from him yet," she responded.

Easton decided not to tell her about Thomas's whereabouts. He'd let her find out on her own. "Were you able to get names from the other cancelled policies?"

"No, like I told you before, my friend left and I don't have a reason to go in that office. I wouldn't know where to find the policies anyway."

"I understand. Thanks anyway," Easton said. Doc Nelson's behavior had sickened him. His head hurt, and it didn't help that the temperature had risen to an unseasonable high of eighty-two degrees either. He climbed back in his car and turned on the radio. Doc Nelson reminded him of a parasite, feeding off the young. He wondered what else the doctor was capable of. After today, he'd move his name to the top with Daniels as a suspect in Taylor's murder. He'd need to hurry and find some evidence before Doc Nelson destroyed Thomas or somebody else.

* * *

Easton's heart raced, trying to keep pace with his anger. He broke the speed limit, driving to Doc Nelson's house, only to realize the obvious when he got there . . . Doc Nelson's car no where in sight; not in the driveway or parked on the street. Easton kept going, weaving in and out of traffic, until he reached the Pharmacie, where Doc Nelson's car sat in front of it. Easton eased off the gas. He coasted to the corner, made a U-turn, and stopped near the entrance to a gas station up the block from the Pharmacie. He sprinted from his car to a payphone and called Ruth.

"I'm in the middle of something and can't leave now," Easton told Ruth. "I'll explain later."

Ruth expressed her disappointment. "Is this what I have to look forward to when we're married . . . eating Sunday dinner alone?"

"I'm investigating your father's murder," Easton replied.

"I'm sorry, Easton . . . I'm being selfish . . . I miss you," Ruth said.

"I'll be there soon. I love you," Easton said.

Since most of the small businesses on the block were closed on Sunday, Easton didn't see much foot traffic on the street, except for the people going in and out of the apartments above the enterprises. He watched the fans in the windows spin around at full speed and imagined the cool air blowing in his face. He looked in his rearview mirror and cringed when a car raced through the intersection, going so fast he just knew the driver would lose control and slam into his car. He sighed with relief when it flew past him.

Cigarette butts filled Easton's ashtray to the brim, and his car reeked from smoke. He'd become sluggish, sweat soaked through his shirt, and he longed for a cold drink to wet his mouth and throat, dry and parched from taking in hot air and cigarette smoke. He didn't want to leave, not yet. A police car zipped by, its siren blaring. Easton covered his ears to block out the piercing wail of an ambulance that followed close behind. After it passed, his eyebrows puckered at the sight of Daniels walking up to the Pharmacie door. He shot upright and took Daniels's picture before Doc Nelson let him in.

At dusk, Doc Nelson and Daniels emerged from the Pharmacie, and not a minute too soon for Easton, who'd thought about going in after them. They drove off in Doc's car. Easton pursued the loathsome two into southeast and onto Asylum Road, to Saint Elizabeth's Hospital, and the same building where he'd taken Thomas. ***Doc must have found out Thomas signed himself in,*** Easton thought. He held back until Doc Nelson parked and went inside. Daniels stayed in the car.

Darkness soon set in, although light from the spotlights on the building and lampposts in the parking lot made it easy to see people coming and going. Easton clenched his teeth and gripped the steering wheel. He'd promised Thomas he'd be safe in the hospital. Perspiration poured out of his brow from the stifling heat, maybe, or from the adrenaline racing through his body; he didn't know which. He wanted to believe that Doc Nelson hadn't been stupid enough to hurt Thomas. On the contrary, a licensed pharmacist selling drugs on the street was stupid. For whatever reason Doc Nelson went into the hospital, it didn't take long, twenty minutes, to be exact.

* * *

Rain started coming down so fast, Doc Nelson nearly collided with an oncoming car as he turned onto Asylum Road leaving the hospital. Easton saw it all—Doc skidding on the rain-slick road into oncoming traffic, which happened to be a big black Cadillac. It swerved to avoid hitting Doc's car and stopped short of slamming into a tree on the shoulder of the road. Doc Nelson jumped from his car and ran to the Cadillac. He talked with the driver, who stayed in the car, then he returned to his car and drove off. ***No one got hurt,*** Easton thought. He drove past the Cadillac still parked on the shoulder of Asylum road.

The drenching rain slowed traffic all the way across town. When they finally reached Doc's Pharmacie, Doc Nelson went inside. Daniels got in his car and drove off. Easton decided he'd seen enough and drove to Taylor's Funeral Home, over two hours late for dinner. He hoped Ruth would still feed him. The rain had cooled off the city, though not true of his anger, still sizzling inside. He believed Doc was a heathen—sitting in church on Sunday mornings, selling illegal drugs on Sunday afternoon, and with his godson no less. If that wasn't sacrilegious, he didn't know what was. Easton said to himself, ***Jail is too good for Doc Nelson. He needs to be thrown in a small boat, sent out to sea, and cut off from the rest of the world.*** He'd build the boat himself, if he knew how.

# Chapter 38

Easton rang the doorbell at the funeral home. Ruth greeted him with a hug.

"We're in the dining room," she said to Easton, who followed her, all the while wondering how to tell Naomi that her stepson was a druggie and her late husband's best friend his supplier.

"My gracious, Easton, you look like something the cat dragged in," Naomi said, giving him the once-over. "What happened to your shirt?"

Easton's shirt had wrinkled, and he'd wiped his wet hands on it, leaving smudge marks from the soda that had fizzled on him earlier. He hesitated before answering.

"Can't a hungry man get a plate of food after a hard day's work," Easton said, looking everywhere except at Ruth and Naomi.

Not his usual charismatic self, Ruth sensed that something wasn't right. "I'll get your plate. Have some iced tea." She poured him a tall glass of the sweet tea. Easton guzzled it all down before she left the room.

"Are you all right?" Naomi asked.

"Just hungry, thirsty, and tired," Easton replied, staring at the chocolate cake sitting in the middle of the table.

Ruth returned with Easton's food. "I kept it warm on the stove. I hope it tastes okay."

"Thank you, Ruth, it'll be fine." Easton said a quick prayer, picked up his fork, and started eating. "This is so good."

Ruth and Naomi watched him gobble down every morsel on his plate. When he finally put his fork down, Ruth spoke.

"The hospital called and asked me to work tonight. I'm leaving at ten thirty."

"You didn't say no?" Easton asked.

"I didn't want to. I can use the extra money to buy material for my wedding gown and other things I need," Ruth replied.

"Doc Nelson and Thomas are selling drugs on the street," Easton said.

Naomi and Ruth looked at each other.

"You can't be serious," Naomi said. "Doc will lose his license forever, if he's caught selling drugs. I don't think he's that dense."

"I followed him and Thomas to Howard's campus today. I saw Thomas selling drugs to some boys on campus. Doc Nelson waited for him. After they left, they met Israel Bailey at Jimmy's."

Naomi's face turned white as a ghost.

Ruth sighed. "I wonder if Dad knew, and if he did, why didn't he tell you, Mom?"

Naomi didn't answer.

"There's more," Easton said. "After Doc Nelson dropped Thomas off at his mother's, I found him inside stoned. I forced Thomas to sign himself in at Saint Elizabeth's, then I tracked down Doc Nelson at his drugstore. When Mr. Daniels showed and they drove off together, I followed them. Guess where they went."

"Saint Elizabeth's?" Ruth asked.

"Yes," Easton replied.

"Oh lord," Naomi shouted.

"Doc Nelson went inside. Daniels stayed in the car," Easton said. "Mrs. Taylor, please call the hospital and ask about Thomas. Since you're his stepmother, they'll tell you how he's doing. I want to make sure Doc Nelson didn't hurt him."

Naomi scurried to Taylor's office and called the hospital.

Ruth massaged Easton's neck. "Have you told Ira yet?"

"Yeah," Easton replied. "He's talking with the chief tomorrow."

A few minutes later, Naomi returned. "The nurse just made rounds, and Thomas is okay. She wouldn't let me talk to him though."

Easton heaved a sigh. "Be leery of Doc Nelson. I don't trust him. Who's to say he isn't behind the death threat or the dudes that tried to rob me." This was an awkward moment for Easton. "Mrs. Taylor, even though Doc Nelson has been a part of your family for a long time, I don't believe he's your friend."

* * *

At ten thirty, Easton and Ruth left the house in separate cars. Ruth drove the Packard to the hospital, and Easton headed home, his stomach ready to explode from the two helpings of roast beef, four biscuits, greens, and two slices of chocolate cake he'd wolfed down. He parked a couple of houses down from the house. Tired and weary, he inched out of the car. He took a couple of steps and fell hard onto the sidewalk, his left arm pinned under his chest. He rolled over. A man wearing a dark jacket and a stocking cap covering his face leaned toward him. Half the weight of the man's body gravitated down his leg to the heavy boot, crushing Easton's chest, the pressure so fierce, Easton scarcely took in enough air to breathe. Easton yanked the man's ankle, not enough to topple him though.

The man lunged at Easton with a long knife.

Easton threw up his right arm to block the blow. The knife sliced through his arm. Easton yelled from the excruciating pain.

One by one, porch lights flicked on.

"What's going on down there?" one of the neighbors hollered from his porch. He saw the two men wrestling on the ground and fired his pistol. The blast sent the attacker scrambling, but not before he twisted the knife from Easton's arm. Easton, barely able to speak, whimpered like an injured dog left in the road to die.

Mr. and Mrs. Kelly had heard the commotion, went outside, and was kneeling beside Easton.

"Mrs. Kelly," Easton whispered, reaching his left hand out to her. "Help me."

Mrs. Kelly gasped at the sight of Easton's bloody shirt. "Oh god!" she said, and turned to her husband. "Call an ambulance and bring me those towels at the bottom of the closet. He's about to bleed to death." Mrs. Kelly, hands trembling, wrapped Easton's arm with the towels, her voice quavering as she prayed. "Jesus, please help him, please help him."

Easton passed out right before the ambulance arrived. After the paramedics took him away, a hysterical Mrs. Kelly hurried inside and called Ruth. Naomi answered the phone. Mrs. Kelly told her what happened to Easton and then blurted out, "He's not dead yet."

Naomi dropped the receiver.

# Chapter 39

Ruth parked in the hospital's employee parking lot and rode the elevator to the fourth floor. Her colleagues thanked her for going in on such short notice. She went to work changing dressings on her three postsurgical patients. She felt at home on the unit, doing the two things she enjoyed most—nursing and nurturing.

"Ruth, line 2," the unit clerk announced over the intercom.

Ruth waited until her patient swallowed his pills, then hurried to the nurses' station to answer the phone. "This is Ruth Johnson, how can I help you?"

"Ruth, this is Marion in the emergency room. Dr. Zette asked me to call you. Do you have a friend named Easton Priest?"

"Yes, he's my boyfriend."

"He's been stabbed pretty badly and he's here. You need to come down now. He's in cubicle 3," Marion said.

Ruth hung up the phone and slid down onto the floor, shaking. She knew the drill. When a doctor says "Come now," you can bet the situation is dire. She wanted to get up and run, but couldn't. Her legs felt like rubber.

"Ruth, what happened!" the unit clerk screamed. Other nurses nearby rushed to her.

"Easton's been stabbed. He's in the ER. Dr. Zette said I should come down now. Please help me," she said to her colleagues. "I feel weak."

"I'll take her down," Mrs. Frederick, the head nurse, said. "The rest of you get back to your patients. Make sure Ruth's are covered." Mrs. Fredrick and the unit clerk helped Ruth to her feet. She folded her arms around Ruth, and they rode the service elevator to the first floor. Once they reached the ER, Ruth pulled away and raced to cubicle 3.

* * *

Two cops were standing in front of the curtain drawn across cubicle 3. Ruth eyed them, daring them to stop her from entering the cubicle. She jerked open the curtain. Easton lay on a stretcher, his eyes closed, his breathing shallow. Blood ran from a plastic bag through clear tubing and into a needle in his left arm. Leads on his chest were attached to gray cables hooked to a machine that monitored his heart, and oxygen flowed through a cannula in his nose. Dr. Zette was pulling jagged pieces of flesh from the open wounds in Easton's right arm. Blood dripped from the massive wounds like water from a broken spigot. Ruth reared back, tears rolling down her face. She stumbled to his side.

"Easton," Ruth spoke in his ear. He didn't answer. "Easton."

Easton turned toward the sound of Ruth's voice. He peered at her, trying to focus, and whispered, "Ruth."

"It's me, love. Who did this to you?" Ruth asked, fighting the urge to scream. "Who did this?"

Easton didn't answer. He drifted off to sleep. Ruth held her hands over her heart.

"He's semiconscious," Dr. Zette said. "He lost a lot of blood, and he's had a heavy dose of morphine for pain, so it may be a while before he responds." Dr. Zette finished suturing Easton's wounds.

Naomi stepped into the small cubicle with Leroy. She squeezed past a nurse to reach Ruth, who collapsed in her arms, shaking. Naomi guided her out of the cubicle.

"Ruth, you've got to pull yourself together. If you fall apart, who's going to help Easton? You can't go back in there like this."

"Somebody's trying to kill him, just like they killed Dad." The slew of tears continued.

"Ruth, look at me," Naomi said.

Ruth gazed up at her mother through tear-filled eyes.

"Easton needs you now. None of us can control what hateful, evil people do. All we can do is take care of the people we love and ask the Lord to protect them," Naomi said. "Whoever killed your father may be trying to kill Easton too." Naomi jeered at the two policemen waiting to interview Easton. "Maybe they'll finally find the bastard."

"We'll do our best," one of the cops said.

Dr. Zette opened the curtain. "Fortunate for Mr. Priest, his attacker missed the main artery, not by much though."

The police approached Dr. Zette to interview Easton.

"I'm afraid not. He's had a heavy dose of morphine, and he's going in and out of consciousness. Besides, I can't guarantee what he says is reliable while he's under the influence."

"Talk to me," Ruth shouted. "I'll tell you who did this, Dr. A. C. Nelson, and he may try to hurt me and my mother."

"Do you have proof?" the other cop asked.

"Maybe if you talk to him, you'll find some," Ruth replied, anger and hurt in her voice. She stormed into the cubicle, Naomi behind her. The cops left the area.

Easton's eyes were open. "Doc," Easton murmured.

Naomi, shaken by the prospect that Doc Nelson stabbed Easton, fled the cubicle.

"I'm scared, Easton," Ruth said. "I don't want you killed investigating Dad's murder."

Easton closed his eyes and nodded off again. Ruth waited a few minutes to see if he'd rouse. When he didn't, she went in search of Naomi. She found her in the waiting room with Leroy.

"Mom, it's going to be a long night. Go home with Leroy. I'll stay with Easton."

"You sure you don't want me to keep you company?" Naomi asked.

"I'll be fine," Ruth replied.

"I'll get Thomas's room ready for Easton. Mrs. Kelly is so shook up, I don't think she'll be able to take care of him when he leaves here," Naomi said.

"Leroy, please stay with Mom until I get home," Ruth said. "I don't trust anyone with her but you."

"I'm a big girl, Ruth. I can take care of myself," Naomi said. "But Leroy can help me in the house."

Leroy hugged Ruth then hustled Naomi to his car.

* * *

Ruth curled up in a chair beside Easton's bed and draped her body with a white hospital blanket. During the night she napped between nurses checking Easton's heart monitor and hanging pints of blood because he'd lost so much of his own.

"We don't have a bed for Mr. Priest yet," a nurse said to Ruth, as she checked Easton's dressing.

"Maybe this morning," Ruth responded. She left the cubicle while the nurse took Easton's blood pressure and temperature, and went to the bathroom. She passed by the emergency room entrance. The early morning light shone through the double glass doors. The day shift would be in soon and Dr. Zette too. She splashed water on her face, combed her hair, and brushed her teeth with a toothbrush a nurse had given her. She returned to cubicle 3 feeling refreshed. Easton fixed his eyes on her as she went closer to his bed.

"Good morning," she said, kissing him on the cheek.

Easton smiled. "Good morning."

"You okay?" Ruth asked him.

"Pain," Easton replied, still groggy.

Dr. Zette walked into the cubicle. "Mr. Priest, I'm Dr. Zette, the surgical resident. You are a lucky man. You survived a pretty vicious attack, and you're dating the most beautiful nurse in the hospital." He gazed at Ruth. "You can't ask for more than that."

Easton winked at Ruth.

Dr. Zette flipped through Easton's chart. "Your wounds are quite extensive, but I don't think you need surgery at this time. I cleaned the wounds before I sewed you up, and you have antibiotics dripping through your IV. You may need more blood and medication, so I'm admitting you to the hospital. You'll be here for several days. A room will be free soon."

"Thank you," Easton said, grimacing.

"The nurse will bring you something for pain," Dr. Zette said. "I'll come see you later."

Right after Easton received a shot for pain, two orderlies transported him on a gurney to the unit where Ruth worked. At Ruth's request, Dr. Zette had called hospital admissions to make the arrangements. As Easton rolled through the hospital corridors on a gurney, he thought about Taylor's killer moving about somewhere in the city and there wasn't a damn thing he could do about it in his present condition. He groaned as the orderlies transferred him from the gurney to a bed, the intravenous tubing in his left arm tangled in the bedsheets. Ruth unraveled the tubing and helped him get comfortable. Before long, he dozed off.

* * *

Easton heard the loud thud of footsteps nearing his bed. His eyelids were so heavy, they barely opened wide enough to see who had walked in his room.

"What did they give you, man?" Ira asked him. "You're about as lifeless as a piece of wood."

"Morphine," Easton answered.

"Did you save some for me?"

Easton moaned. "No . . . you can't have any. You gotta bring in Doc Nelson and his crew first."

"His crew . . . you mean Daniels and Israel Bailey?" Ira asked.

"The executioners," Easton replied.

"What about Thomas?" Ira asked.

"No," Easton replied. "He didn't kill his father. He needs to be at Saint Elizabeth's."

"I'll check on him," Ira said. "By the way, we interviewed your neighbors. Nobody got a good look at your attacker . . . too dark, they said. I'm glad you're going to be all right."

"I have the best nurse," Easton said, as Ruth sauntered in the room.

Ira hugged Ruth. "Don't get jealous now, I won't take her away from you while you're on your sickbed."

They laughed.

After Ira left, Easton had Ruth dial Aaron's number. He told Aaron he'd been stabbed and admitted to the hospital.

"Naomi Taylor told me. It's over for you," Aaron said. "You're not dying on my watch. The police will have to find Taylor's killer . . . it's their job anyway."

"Aaron, they won't," Easton said. "I'm this close." Easton attempted to lift his right hand to no avail. "Let me finish. I can't go into the field now anyway. Please don't give the investigation to someone else."

Aaron grumbled his reporter's objection. Easton supposed he heard the urgency in his reporter's voice.

"I'll stop by later," Aaron said, and hung up.

Ruth saw the disappointment in Easton's face. "Love, he won't take the investigation from you. You've earned the right to finish it."

"If I can't work soon, he'll assign it to someone else," Easton said.

* * *

When Aaron went by later that evening, Easton had dropped off into a deep sleep. Aaron didn't want to wake him, Ruth did.

"Mr. Holt, Easton needs to know your decision. He needs to have a reason to get better," Ruth said, and roused Easton from sleep.

Easton opened his eyes to Aaron looking down at him.

"How you doing?" Aaron asked.

"I'm almost as good as new," Easton replied, not wanting Aaron to know how bad he really felt.

Aaron saw right through Easton. "It doesn't look like it to me," he said, perusing the intravenous infusion, the heart monitor, and the oxygen setup behind his bed. "You gonna bring all this to the office with you?"

Easton smiled. "I need more time. In a week or so, I'll be up and about, and Lloyd said he'd come by the house and help me with the investigation and the column, if it's all right with you."

"How can I, in good faith, keep you on this case after this?" Aaron asked.

"It comes with the territory and a risk I'm willing to take," Easton replied. "Investigative reporting is all I know. I can do it, Aaron."

"I believe you," Aaron said. "Let me know when you're ready to work."

# Chapter 40

Every morning for five days, nurses went into Easton's hospital room around eight o'clock in the morning to change his bandages. Ruth changed it if she happened to be on duty. When she or another nurse peeled off the gauze to clean and dress his wounds, a stinging, often burning pain seemed to linger forever. He'd bite his lip so hard he'd draw blood. "Tell me that what you're doing is going to save me and not kill me," Easton said to Ruth one morning.

Ruth smiled. "I promise, it will save you."

When she'd finish with him, the physical therapist took his turn torturing him, at least that's how Easton saw it, repeatedly stretching his arm to keep it loose and mobile. And finally, Dr. Zette, poking and jabbing at his arm, "checking for infection and nerve damage," he'd said. Easton told him, "Doc, trust me, the nerves aren't damaged, I can feel you pushing on me." By ten o'clock in the morning, Easton's whole right side throbbed with pain, unleashed from the constant manipulation of his injured limb. He hurt so bad, he'd call on Jesus until a nurse came with a narcotic and shot it in his behind. She didn't have to tell him to turn on his side. He'd already be in position when she went through the door. "Take me out of my misery," he'd say, urging the drug to work its magic.

Easton's parents had arrived the day after the attack and stayed four days. They had wanted to stay longer, however, Pops had to get back to the farm. Since Dr. Zette had upgraded Easton from critical to stable, they felt comfortable leaving him in Ruth's hands.

* * *

Later that afternoon, Ira went to see Easton. He told Easton that Thomas had signed himself out of Saint Elizabeth's.

"Where is he?" Easton asked.

"His mother said Doc Nelson sent him to South Carolina on business," Ira replied. "When I asked her about Thomas's drug use, she damn near took my head off. She had no idea he was using. I told her to call Saint Elizabeth's if she didn't believe me."

"Did she call?" Easton asked.

"She called Doc Nelson then called me back. He claimed he didn't know Thomas had a drug problem. She said she was going to call Thomas and get to the bottom of it."

"Doc is a sleazebag," Easton said. "I bet Thomas told him that I'm onto their drug dealing and Doc set me up."

"I'll talk to Doc. If Thomas did tell him, he's already disposed of any evidence," Ira said. "I haven't told the chief that we suspect Doc's involvement. I don't want to implicate him in Taylor's murder yet, in case we're wrong."

"Okay," Easton said.

* * *

November 4th, day 7 of Easton's hospitalization, Dr. Zette entered his room with Ruth and another nurse.

"We're going to change your dressing, and if there're no signs of infection and your blood tests are normal, you can go home," Dr. Zette said.

The nurse set up a dressing tray, and Dr. Zette removed Easton's bandages, cleaned the incision line, and covered it with a new bandage. When Easton's blood tests came back normal, Dr. Zette wrote his discharge orders, which included a sling to immobilize his arm. Ruth helped Easton into a clean pair of pajamas. They waited an hour before the physical therapist appeared with the sling. Soon after, an orderly wheeled Easton to the front entrance of the hospital. He stayed with him while Ruth darted off to retrieve the Packard. He helped Easton into the car, careful not to stress his arm. The roads were not so kind. Each time the car rolled over uneven pavement or a steel plate in the road, Easton flinched. His arm felt like a fireball hit it. At the sight of Taylor's funeral home, he sighed with relief. He staggered into the house, and Ruth helped him upstairs.

# Chapter 41

Before taking Easton to Thomas's old bedroom, Ruth helped him to the phone in her mother's room. He called Mrs. Kelly and his parents to say he'd been discharged from the hospital and planned to stay with Ruth. Easton's mother cried on the phone. His father stayed quiet.

"Ma, I'm okay. Ruth and Mrs. Taylor will take care of me."

"Easton, I'm your mother. It's my job to care for you," she cried.

Easton grimaced. His pain medicine had worn off, and he'd become agitated. He handed Ruth the phone.

"Mrs. Priest, Easton's in a lot of pain right now. I promise I'll take good care of him," Ruth said.

"I know you will, Ruth. I won't come unless you need me. Tell Easton I love him. I'll call him tomorrow," Mrs. Priest said.

While Ruth talked with Easton's mother, he'd made his way to Thomas's room. Ruth helped him into bed, gave him a pain pill, and held him in her arms until he fell asleep. She slipped away to her room, frantic that someone wanted her mother and Easton dead. She squeezed her pillow and stared at pictures of Easton and her mother, wondering how she'd ever live without them, the two people she loved the most. She saturated her pillow with tears.

* * *

Easton woke four hours later, sore and hungry. Naomi had made chicken soup, and although Easton dropped the spoon a couple of times, struggling to eat with his left hand, he managed to put away two bowls of soup, a slice of chocolate cake Ruth surprised him with, and two glasses of iced tea. When he finished, he felt as if he'd won the jackpot.

"You're spoiling me," Easton said.

"I promised your mother I'd take care of you," Ruth responded. "That includes feeding you."

Easton stared into Ruth's eyes. "I can't wait until we're married."

Ruth leaned over and kissed him on the mouth. She eased down on the bed, snuggled close to him, and rambled on about plans for their wedding, including the choice of colors for the wedding party. "What color shirt are you wearing with your tux?" Ruth asked.

Easton didn't answer. She sat up. He had fallen asleep. She wondered if he heard anything she said.

* * *

The first day at Ruth's, Easton hibernated in Thomas's room, without a cigarette or a real bath. It's not that he didn't appreciate Ruth's bed baths; he just wanted to soak in a hot tube of water and let the steam open his mind and the water soothe his soul. Glad to be alive and kicking, he wanted to start living a normal life again, believing one day his arm would heal and his pain would become a lost memory.

"You know, a hot tub of water might help me feel better," Easton said after waking up one morning.

"I think that can be arranged," Ruth said playfully. She filled the tub with hot water and summoned Easton to the bathroom. She covered his bandages with saran wrap to keep them dry. "I'll wait here. Holler if you need help. No, holler if it's an emergency."

Easton laughed, not for long though. When he lifted his right hand to wash, his arm throbbed with pain, and the soap kept slipping from his hand, so he gave in, rinsed off, and covered himself with a robe. He opened the door. Ruth hadn't moved from her seat at the top of the stairs. She gripped his waist and helped him to the room and into his pajamas. He swallowed a pain pill and soon fell asleep.

* * *

Around one o'clock that afternoon, Easton woke up perspiring from a bizarre dream.

***Easton saw himself sitting in Taylor's kitchen with Ruth and Naomi and Taylor went walking through the pantry door, dressed in his black suit and striped tie, like the murder had never occurred and asked Easton what happened to his arm, and when Easton told him he was stabbed, Taylor said probably some woman Easton had pissed off did it and not to worry because the police would catch her; then he kissed Naomi on the mouth and begged her not to marry anyone else because he would be back but he had something to settle with his friend Doc and wanted to know when Ruth and Easton were getting married so he wouldn't be late walking her down the aisle, and he saw Thomas at Saint Elizabeth's and said he'd be fine, not to worry about him, then waved good-bye, going out the pantry door Naomi running after him, yelling, "Who killed you?" He said he'd tell her later, so Easton and Ruth stood with Naomi laughing as they watched him ride off down the alley on a black stallion.***

"I must be losing my mind," Easton said out loud, remembering the dream. He slid his feet into his house shoes and took a few short steps to the window, where small droplets of rain covered the windowpane. He watched the fine spray blow around in the air. As much as he enjoyed being with Ruth, he didn't like being confined to a room; even a walk in the rain would be a welcome change. And he wanted a cigarette.

From her room, Ruth heard Easton stirring about. She finished folding clothes and joined him. "Do you want to go downstairs for lunch?"

Easton smiled. "Yeah, I'd like that."

* * *

Before Easton sat down to eat, he headed for the pantry to smoke, not one, but two cigarettes. When he finished, he joined Ruth and Naomi at the kitchen table.

"Mrs. Taylor, thanks for letting me stay here. Ruth's taking very good care of me." Easton started munching on a roast beef sandwich Naomi had made for him.

"I'm sure she has," Naomi said. "You're a lucky young man. Not everyone has their own private nurse."

Naomi heard a knock at the door. "I'll get it," she said. Not one minute later, she'd run back into the kitchen.

"He's here, Doc's here," she said in an anxious voice.

"Should we let him in?" Ruth asked.

"He may have killed Taylor, sent me a death threat, got Thomas strung out on drugs, and tried to kill Easton. What do you think?" Naomi replied, pissed off.

"Wait," Easton said. "Let's hear what he has to say."

Another knock at the front door. Naomi, not happy with the idea, agreed to let him in. "Doc, come on in. We're in the kitchen, having lunch."

Doc Nelson followed behind Naomi. "I just came by to see how you're doing, if you need anything."

"We're fine," Naomi said, entering the kitchen.

"Well, I see you've moved in," Doc said, tugging at Easton's robe. "Did you two get married and didn't tell anyone?"

"Not yet," Easton said, his eyes fixed on Doc. "Someone tried to kill me over a week ago. I'm here recovering."

"I heard you were robbed. I didn't know they tried to kill you," Doc said.

"In front of my house," Easton responded.

"Anybody arrested?" Doc asked.

"No, the coward came at me from behind, wearing a stocking cap," Easton replied. "My neighbors couldn't finger him."

"The hoodlums that tried to rob you wore stocking caps," Ruth said. "Are stocking caps the latest attire for criminals these days?"

"Someone tried to rob you and somebody else tried to kill you?" Doc Nelson asked Easton.

"Yes, sir, I don't believe it myself," Easton answered.

The room fell silent. All eyes were on Doc Nelson.

"To answer your question, Ruth, criminals have used stocking caps for years," Doc Nelson said. He turned to Naomi. "Is there anything you need or anything I can do to help?"

"No, we're fine. I think the worst is over. Tell Dorothy to call me later. We're supposed to go shopping downtown one of these days," Naomi said.

"Well, you all be careful. I hope you feel better, young man, and the cops find the person who stabbed you. I'll keep you in my prayers."

"Before you go, Dr. Nelson, do you remember an Israel Bailey from your high school days?" Easton asked.

"Why, yes," Doc replied. "I saw him at his sister's funeral."

Easton, confined to the hospital, had missed Cynthia Bailey's funeral. "I was told that something terrible happened to him in his senior year of high school that changed his life. Do you know what happened?"

"He had a fledging career in baseball, I know that, but I don't know what turned him around," Doc replied. He said his good-byes, and Naomi escorted him to the door.

When Naomi returned to the kitchen, Easton said, "I didn't say the person stabbed me. I said someone tried to kill me."

Ruth and Naomi exchanged looks.

"The newspaper, maybe he read about it," Ruth offered.

"I've read the ***Negro News*** and the ***Star*** every day since Easton's attack, from front to back. I didn't see it in there," Naomi countered.

"TV or radio?" Ruth asked.

"I doubt it," Easton replied. "I don't rate that kind of coverage. Plus, I told Aaron not to put anything in the ***Negro News***, because I want to write about the attack myself."

Easton asked Ruth to dial Ira's number. He'd gone out on patrol.

"Ruth, I've been meaning to ask you. When I interviewed Doc, every now and then, his hand jerked. What's it from?" asked Easton.

"Maybe Parkinson's disease or some other neurological disorder. I never noticed it, have you, Mom?" Ruth asked.

"No," Naomi replied.

"Well, I doubt he stabbed Mr. Taylor with his hand jerking the way it does, but it doesn't mean he wasn't involved," Easton said. He turned to Ruth. "I want you to go with me to Tennessee Thanksgiving. We need a break, and it's quiet on the farm, and safe."

Ruth faced her mother then Easton. "I can't leave Mom by herself, Easton."

"Sweetie pie, don't worry about me. You go with Easton, I'll be fine," Naomi said. "Besides, I'm not supposed to leave town anyway, I'm a suspect."

"We can all go," Easton said. "Mrs. Taylor, the police won't object to you leaving the city for a few days."

"You and Ruth go without me." Naomi left the room.

Ruth was about to follow her, then Easton said, "Let me." He faltered while walking to Taylor's office, where Naomi sat flipping through papers on the desk. "Mrs. Taylor, we need to get away for a spell. All this pressure gets to you after a while. Besides, if Ruth goes with me Thanksgiving, I'm asking her to marry me. I don't want to wait until Christmas. Most of my family will be there, and it will mean a lot to both of us if you're there too, even though Ruth doesn't know, and please don't tell her."

Naomi stopped flipping papers. "You're proposing? I can't miss that moment in my baby's life. I'll go, Easton. Thank you." She hugged him ever so gently. "Now, go be with your future bride."

Easton hobbled back to the kitchen, smiling, thinking how fast Naomi changed her mind when he mentioned proposing to Ruth.

"She's going. We'll leave the day before Thanksgiving."

"What about Leroy?" Ruth asked.

"Leroy?" Easton replied.

"You know he spends Thanksgiving with us," Ruth said.

"Okay, okay. Leroy can tag along. He can help Pops repair the barn for winter since I can't," Easton said.

"I'll ask him if he wants to go. Maybe he'll find his ***adageyudi*** down there," Ruth said.

"His what?" Easton asked.

"His love," Ruth answered.

"What about Thomas?" Easton asked.

"Thomas always eats Thanksgiving dinner with his mother, and dessert with us," Ruth replied. "Since you can't drive and Mom doesn't like driving, I guess Leroy and I can switch off, if he goes."

"Let's go by train or fly," Easton replied.

Naomi returned to the kitchen. "Fly on what?" she asked.

"A jet," Ruth replied. "I've never been on one. We'll arrive a lot sooner than a train and have more time to visit."

"Ruth, do you remember when those two planes crashed into each other over the Grand Canyon in July? Everybody on board died. Now, give me a good reason why I should fly to Tennessee, other than the fact you've never been on a plane," Naomi asked her.

"In January, a train derailed in Los Angeles, killing people. Nothing is foolproof, not even a car. We either go by plane or train," Ruth said.

The telephone rang. Ruth answered it then handed the receiver to Easton. "Ira."

Easton told Ira about Doc Nelson's visit. "I didn't say I was stabbed. How did he know? Mrs. Taylor and Ruth didn't tell him, and nothing has been in the paper about the attack."

"You're scaring me, man. Doc Nelson is supposed to be the good guy," Ira said.

"You just don't want to believe Doc Nelson is bad blood," Easton said. "It is what it is."

"Okay . . . okay . . . I'm still not ready to implicate Doc Nelson," Ira said, disappointment in his voice.

Easton put down the receiver. He shook his head, his mouth turned down. "I wish Doc Nelson wasn't involved either. Sooner or later, Ira's got to accept the fact that Doc is, at best, a criminal, at worse, a killer."

"I can't accept it either," Naomi said, sounding angry, and stomped out of the kitchen.

"I need a cigarette," Easton said. "I'll be in the pantry."

"It won't ease the hurt," Ruth said.

Easton looked at Ruth. "No, it won't, but seeing Daniels or Doc Nelson in jail will."

# Chapter 42

Later that day, Easton woke from a nap and sat on the side of the bed. He stretched his injured arm, and to his surprise, it didn't hurt as much. He remembered Ruth's promise, when she'd left him crazy in pain after changing his bandage in the hospital, "I promise it will save you." He felt as if a huge weight had been lifted from his shoulders and arm and his mind. He felt too that soon he'd be typing his column again instead of dictating it to Lloyd. He felt saved. He stood in front of the bathroom mirror. Since he hadn't shaved since the attack, he'd grown a full beard and a mustache. ***Not bad,*** he said to himself.

He treaded softly downstairs to find Ruth. The house seemed unusually quiet, except for the wood floors creaking as he stepped through the house. He glanced at the hall clock—after three o'clock. He wondered why Ruth didn't wake him before she left for work. He strolled into the kitchen. No sign of Naomi. He opened the pantry door leading to the morgue. "Mrs. Taylor," he called. She didn't answer. He hurried to the front of the house and opened the door—no one on the porch and no one in sight. He returned to the kitchen to call Ira for an update on Taylor's murder investigation.

"I told the chief I wanted to work full-time on Taylor's case, that I'd find his killer and bring him in," Ira said. "He laughed in my face, called me a boy, threatened to close the investigation, then said, and get this, if I didn't bring in somebody soon, my ass is his."

"Hallelujah!" Easton yelled.

"I said the same thing."

"You didn't call," Easton said.

"You were asleep," Ira said.

"When you hauling Doc Nelson's ass in there?"

"Tomorrow."

* * *

The next morning, Easton and Naomi took a cab to the Second precinct.

"I knew you'd want to be here in case we got a confession from him. You don't need to worry. He doesn't know you're here. You'll be able to see him, but he can't see you," Ira said to Naomi. "Easton, you can sit with her."

Ira directed a detective to escort Naomi and Easton to an observation room. Not much bigger than a closet, the room was darkened by a black curtain hanging on one wall. When the detective opened the curtain, Easton and Naomi looked through the one-way mirror at Doc Nelson, his attorney sitting bedside him. Naomi gasped and covered her mouth at the sight of him. She sat down, her body trembling like a leaf fluttering in the wind.

Easton moved closer to the mirror. Doc Nelson didn't seem down in the mouth at all, not one worry line on his face. His eyes seemed to laugh when he did, and when he spoke his mouth moved in slow motion, his normal way of talking, which sometimes took him longer than most to finish a sentence.

"I want to hate Doc," Naomi said. "But I can't. He let Ruth and I stay in his home when we first moved here, and because of him, I met and fell in love with Taylor."

"I understand," Easton said.

"Mrs. Taylor, they're starting now," said the detective. He clicked on the intercom.

Ira's voice echoed through the small room. "I appreciate you coming in, Dr. Nelson. This won't take long." Ira sat across the table from the doctor. "What do you know about William Taylor's murder?"

"What I read in the paper . . . what Naomi told me," Doc Nelson answered.

Ira eyed him closely. "Before he died, did Taylor tell you he feared for his life?"

"No," Doc replied, turning away from Ira.

"Did you know his son, Thomas, sold drugs on the street?"

"No."

"You didn't! Oh, but you knew Thomas had signed himself into Saint Elizabeth's, because you went to see him," Ira said. "And before that, you took him to Howard's campus to sell drugs."

Doc Nelson stayed silent for a moment. When he spoke, he said, "Thomas called me from Saint Elizabeth's. He'd gotten hold of some bad drugs. He needed help. Who told you I took him to Howard's campus?"

"This is how it works, Dr. Nelson. I ask the questions, you answer them."

Doc Nelson took a handkerchief out of his jacket pocket and wiped his brow. "It's warm in here."

Ira turned to his partner. "Get the doctor some water, please." He continued interrogating Doc. "Did you take Thomas to Howard's campus?"

"Yes, he said his car broke down and he had to meet someone about a job," Doc Nelson replied. "I don't know what he said or gave to the boy he met with."

"Did you stab Easton Priest?"

Doc Nelson looked at Ira like he had two heads. "Absolutely not!" He shook his head and clenched his hands together on the table.

"Do you know who did?"

"No." Doc Nelson sipped on the tepid water and frowned.

"Are you selling drugs on the street, Dr. Nelson?"

"Are you crazy? I'm a pharmacist, not a drug dealer."

"Dr. Nelson, did you kill William Taylor?"

"All right, that's enough," said the doctor's attorney. "This interview is over." Doc Nelson and his attorney headed for the door.

"Dr. Nelson, don't leave town anytime soon. I'm not done with you yet," Ira said.

* * *

Ira met Easton and Naomi at his desk, where the detective had taken them.

"I guess you heard, no confession," Ira said.

"I've known Doc for over twenty years, but I can't tell if he's lying," Naomi said, her arms crossed.

"I don't care what he said in there, he's involved in Mr. Taylor's murder," Easton spoke in an angry tone, his disgust toward Doc Nelson made clear.

"We need to know his handle," Ira said.

"We already know his handle . . . murder and drugs," Easton responded.

"He'll slip up soon, they all do, and we'll be waiting. I need to get back to work," Ira said.

"I'm not waiting," Easton said. "Mrs. Taylor, are you ready?"

Naomi nodded.

They walked out the precinct and down the steps to the sidewalk. Doc Nelson glanced at them as he drove by in his Desota.

"Damn," Easton said. "He saw us."

* * *

Ira kept Easton informed about all the interviews he'd conducted with Taylor's close friends, acquaintances, and people in the city he'd done business with. Naomi had supplied Ira with most of the names. During the interviews, he'd learned of others who had forged some kind of relationship with Taylor and interviewed them too.

"Louise Palmer came in today," Ira said to Easton, laughing. "A nervous wreck. She held her pocketbook so tight I thought it might pop open."

"I wonder what she had in it," Easton said.

"Don't know. I didn't have a reason to search it. She didn't hand me anything I didn't know. When I asked her about her friend Georgia Reed, she looked at me like she'd seen a ghost and then started bawling. She swears she doesn't know where she is. She started crying, afraid she's going to lose her job and not be able to work the elections. When I told her she was free to go, she flew out of here."

# CHAPTER 43

It was the eve of the presidential election and, Easton and Ruth went back and forth with Naomi about whom to vote for.

"Why on earth should I vote Republican?" Naomi asked. "They don't care about Negroes. I bet the chief of police is a Republican, and that's why Taylor's killer is still running around free."

"Mom, Adlai Stevenson is in cahoots with segregationists," Ruth said. "Democracy might end in the United States and set Negroes back fifty years or more, if he wins."

"I'm not convinced," Naomi said.

"Mrs. Taylor, Ruth is right," Easton said. "If we don't reelect Eisenhower, we stand to lose a lot of ground. We have four Negroes on the police force, more than what we had four years ago, and one is leading Mr. Taylor's murder investigation. That says a lot."

"You sound like Taylor." Naomi smiled and started out the kitchen. "Come on now, no more talk about the election. Nat King Cole's show is coming on." The fifteen-minute weekly variety show debuted that night. Cole was the first black performer in America to host a network variety show. It came about in the aftermath of a beating he'd suffered at the hands of four white men while performing on stage in Birmingham, Alabama. He lay stunned on the stage before being helped off. Eventually, his attackers were subdued and taken to jail.

* * *

On Election Day, many Negroes went to the polls believing as Easton and Ruth did, afraid if they didn't vote Republican, Negroes might lose the foothold so many had fought and died for. After Naomi and Ruth voted, Ruth drove Easton to the designated place near his house to vote.

That evening, Easton and Ruth invited friends over to wait for the election results—Caroline and her boyfriend and Toast and his wife and son, who'd fallen asleep in Naomi's bed. As it turned out, the Eisenhower-Nixon Republican ticket won, although the Democrats prevailed, winning the majority in both houses of Congress.

"At least I won't have to sit in the back of the bus again," Ruth said.

"And I won't have to tell my son he has to use a 'colored only' bathroom," Toast said. "Speaking of my son, let's go, honey. We need to get this boy home."

Caroline and her boyfriend left too.

Easton and Ruth closed up the house and went to bed.

* * *

Easton and Ruth had gotten into a routine of eating meals together, watching TV, listening to the radio in the parlor, and on occasion, Naomi joined them. She'd plunk her 45s on the record player, and they'd listen to jazz late into the evening. On the days Ruth worked seven to three thirty, they'd eat dinner and then sit in the parlor with Naomi, glued to the six o'clock news. They'd watch clips of Negro students from colored colleges and universities in the South being arrested for sitting in at restaurant counters reserved for whites only, and in Montgomery, Alabama, Negroes were still walking and carpooling to work. It had been over a year since the bus boycott started. Negroes in Alabama had refused to ride the buses unless the laws changed. They walked, rode in cabs or on bicycles to get around.

A bulletin interrupted the normally scheduled news program. It was November 13, 1956, "The United States Supreme Court today affirmed a three-judge US District Court declaring Alabama's state and local laws requiring segregation on buses unconstitutional."

Naomi jumped out of her seat. She danced and sang "All Hail the Power of Jesus's Name." Ruth and Easton got up and danced too. Naomi ran to the refrigerator and grabbed a bottle of champagne left from the party the night Taylor died. She handed it to Easton, and he popped it open. Though they knew the struggle wasn't over, they wept for their forefathers and raised their glasses to the men and women who refused to ride the buses. It was a day for the history books—no more sitting in the back of the bus or giving up their seat for a white person.

After the news went off, Easton and Ruth put away the dinner dishes left drying in the dish rack and joined Naomi in the parlor. She stared at Taylor's picture sitting on the end table. "Taylor, we won. Negroes can sit anywhere on the bus we want, now," Naomi said. She pressed her hand hard to her chest then slid onto the piano stool and played Nat King Cole's version of "Smile."

* * *

Two days later, Easton packed his things to go home, yet he wanted to stay. He'd gotten comfortable in the house. However, with Ruth's help, he'd recovered enough to care for himself and didn't want to overstay his welcome.

Naomi stepped out on the porch with the couple as they prepared to leave. She'd enjoyed watching Easton devour the meals she cooked. With all that he ate, he still managed to keep a healthy physique, just like Taylor. He'd eat anything he wanted and never gained a pound. She, on the other hand, had to count every ounce of food she ate.

"I'll miss you eating all my food," Naomi said to Easton, smiling.

"Me too." Easton laughed. "Thanks again for letting me stay here."

"You're welcome, son. Just don't overdo it. I'm still here to help if I can." Naomi hugged him.

* * *

A bleak November sky and strong winds foreshadowed a storm forecasted for the DC area. Ruth, unnerved by leaves and broken limbs flying through the air, steered the Packard to the boarding house where Easton lived.

"I'll come by in the morning before work to check your arm," Ruth said.

"You don't have to, I know what to do," Easton responded. "You taught me well."

"Mrs. Kelly doesn't know that," Ruth said, laughing. "It'll be an excuse for you to entertain me in your room." She bumped the curb, backing into a space in front of the house. Easton's injured arm hit the door.

"Ouch!" Easton yelped. He rested his arm close to his body, clenching his teeth.

"Sorry," Ruth exclaimed. She cut the engine, leaned over, and kissed him.

"It's better already," he said.

Mr. Kelly opened the front door, smiling. "I was wondering if you were coming back here. How you feel?"

"Much better," Easton replied. "Where is Mrs. Kelly?"

"She's out shopping," Mr. Kelly replied. "If she'd known you were coming home today, she'd be here. Let me help you upstairs."

"Thank you, Mr. Kelly, but I can make it by myself," Easton said.

* * *

Mrs. Kelly had tidied up Easton's room. Ruth fluffed up the pillows on the sofa, and they cuddled together.

"Will Mrs. Kelly come up here when she comes home?" Ruth asked.

"She might," Easton replied.

Ruth stayed anyway. They watched ***Alfred Hitchcock Presents*** on TV. After it ended, Ruth said, "I can't believe I didn't get kicked out."

"They like you," Easton said. "And so do I."

"Well, I want them to keep liking me." Ruth kissed Easton good-bye and left for home.

* * *

Ruth returned the next morning before the sun rose, and inspected Easton's arm. Satisfied that there were no changes since yesterday, she took off for work.

Later that morning, Easton moseyed into the ***Negro News*** room. His coworkers cheered and clapped, delighted to see him. Lloyd walked over to him. He had dropped by the hospital and Ruth's house to talk about Taylor's murder investigation and help Easton write his column. "Looking good, Mr. Priest," shaking Easton's hand. "Glad you're back."

"Thank you," Easton said to his colleagues. "And thanks for all the cards and letters. They almost made me cry."

Aaron went out of his office at the sound of Easton's voice. "Are you ready to rock and roll?" He reached out to shake Easton's hand.

"Will you settle for the cha-cha?" Easton stepped forward then back and to the right. His colleagues roared with laughter and started humming and singing "Life Is but a Dream" and did the cha-cha along with him.

"You got it," Aaron said. "Come on, I've got a few stories that need editing."

Easton followed Aaron to his office. He handed Easton a stack of papers. "Welcome back."

"Whoa! It's been busy around here," Easton said.

"Yes, it has."

Easton took the papers to his desk, emptied an ashtray full of old cigarette butts, lit a cigarette, leaned back in his chair, and began reading. When he got to the third story, he straightened up. The title was "William Taylor Speaks from the Grave." After he read it, he pounded the floor to Aaron's office, knocked on the open door, and marched in.

"Who wrote this?" Easton asked, dropping the manuscript on Aaron's desk.

Aaron noted the initials on the byline. "Dominic wrote this. I didn't assign it to him."

"Dominic, the copyboy?" Easton asked.

"Yes."

Easton sighed. For a second he felt embarrassed. "I have to give him his due, it's good. As a matter of fact, it's real good."

Aaron glanced at Easton. "What do you want to do?"

"Print it," Easton replied. "We don't have anything finished for the column. Maybe somebody will be inspired and tell us who killed Taylor after they read it."

"All right, it's a go," Aaron said.

By the time Easton finished editing the other stories, the muscles in his injured arm had tightened. He groaned from the pain. Aaron and Dominic were talking outside Aaron's office. Easton praised Dominic on his article, encouraging him to write more. He shook the young boy's hand and left him grinning like a Cheshire cat. He headed home while he'd still be able to maneuver his arm to drive.

* * *

Raindrops pounded Easton's windshield, remnants of a storm that had passed through the city the night before. Water had pooled in the street, and when cars sped through the large puddles, water sprayed on people standing near the curb. Out of nowhere, a dog scampered into the path of Easton's car. He slammed on the brakes, skidded on the wet pavement, and jumped the curb, almost hitting a woman standing at a bus stop. Cars behind him screeched to a halt. Easton shaken, hunched over the steering wheel, grimacing in pain. Two men ran up to his window.

"You okay, son?" one of the men asked.

"Yeah," Easton responded, even though his arm was hurting something fierce. He regained his composure and backed down into the street, all the while speculating about the damage to his car. He got out and inspected the front fender and the tire.

The other man got down on the ground and looked under Easton's car with a flashlight. "I don't see anything loose or broken. You're in good shape, son."

The dread Easton had sensed disappeared. He smiled at the man. "I got an angel watching over me." He steered his car slowly at first to make sure nothing loosened and fell to the street, then he increased his speed. He'd come to rest on his arm when he hit the curb. Now it felt as if someone had punched it. It quivered in pain. As soon as he got home, he downed two pain pills and lay on the sofa facing the window. The sun blazing bright, just as it did at Taylor's burial, was the last thing he remembered before passing out.

* * *

Ruth called and woke Easton. "Did you have a good day?" she asked.

"I've had better days," Easton answered, half-awake. When he became more alert, he told her about the dog that almost got both of them killed, how miserable he'd been because of the pain, and how his injury had threatened his livelihood. "Writing, that's all I know."

"Give it time, Easton. Your cuts were deep. You may have pain in that arm for a long time," Ruth said. "Are you wearing the sling?"

It's not what he wanted to hear, even if it were true, although he didn't expect anything less from Ruth. She'd never forsake the truth to tell him just what he wanted to hear.

"Yeah, I'm wearing it. I'm going to work on my column before the pain comes again," Easton said. "Can I call you later?"

"Yes, love," Ruth replied. "Don't work too hard."

Before Easton started typing, he opened the window in his room and puffed on a cigarette. He blew smoke through the screen and watched it fade into the air.

He imagined his pain simply vanishing in the air with the smoke. He wondered where he'd be if the knife had cut his wrist a millimeter to the left and severed his radial artery, the one people cut when they're trying to kill themselves, Ruth had told him. He picked up a pen and rolled it in his fingertips, desperate to put his story on paper. ***One day, one day.*** The aroma of sweet potato pie roused him from self-pity and lured him to the kitchen like a baited animal. He filled his stomach with the longing he wanted to fill with his pen.

# Chapter 44

The days leading up to Thanksgiving were busy. Easton worked long hours, trying to find the key to Taylor's murder that continued to elude him and the police, although he doubted the police were losing sleep looking for the killer. Some days he'd drive to Sixth Street for dinner, even if Ruth was at work. Leroy would be puttering around the place, raking leaves, cleaning gutters, and putting in storm windows. Naomi didn't want to wait. "Five inches of snow might fall before we get back from Tennessee," she had told them. Unable to help, Easton felt useless.

* * *

The evening before Easton left for Tennessee, he phoned Ira to make sure he had his parents' telephone number, if by some stroke of luck the police arrested Taylor's killer or his attacker, while he was gone.

"Tomorrow! Telling me sooner would have been better and safer for the Taylors," Ira shouted.

Easton moved the receiver away from his ear and stared at it. All the times they'd talked, Ira had never raised his voice to him. "Hold up, Ira. Mrs. Taylor told Sergeant Currie about the trip and gave her my daddy's phone number," Easton retorted. "Something told me to call you before I left."

"I be damned. Nobody tells me shit. See what I mean," Ira said. "I'm sorry, man. I'm walking on a tightrope here. I promised the chief a collar, and he wants it now. I'll be in a soup line if I don't find Taylor's killer soon. Anyway, I don't know anyone in Tennessee to look out for the Taylors or you."

"None of us would need looking after if the sick bastard was behind bars," Easton said, annoyed. "Besides, what are the chances he shows up in Tennessee? Take down this number. I have a column to finish before I leave."

Easton turned up the sound on his radio. The Dells, a rhythm and blues group, were singing "Oh, What a Night." He sang along as he hunt-and-pecked an editorial for his column, "A Brush with Death." It took him twice as long to type using one hand. He paused for a break, rolled up his sleeves, and checked the time on his watch. Almost midnight. He drank half of his soda and resumed typing. Around one o'clock in the morning, he left the editorial on Aaron's desk and sped home to pack. Ruth expected him at her door before daybreak. The train was scheduled to leave Union Station at seven o'clock in the morning and arrive in Harrington, Tennessee, around seven o'clock in the evening.

Easton tucked away Ruth's engagement ring in his trench coat pocket. He wanted to keep the ring on his person, in case his luggage got lost or stolen. It struck him that he hadn't planned how to pop the question, what he'd say. He lay in bed trying to decide how he'd propose to Ruth; made drowsy by the pain pill he'd swallowed, he soon fell asleep.

* * *

The telephone rang several times before Easton opened his eyes to the jingling sound. Half-asleep, he sat upright and switched on the light.

"Hello."

"Are you up?" Ruth asked.

"I am now," Easton replied.

"Breakfast is on the stove. See you."

Easton lay down until the beeping from his alarm clock resonated in the room. It reminded him of the constant beep-beep from the heart monitor the nurse had connected him to during his hospital stay. He rolled out of bed, showered, dressed, and threw his comb and his toothbrush in the suitcase.

* * *

Ruth stood right where she said she'd be, at the front door. Easton seized the moment and kissed her.

"Food's getting cold," Naomi called out.

"Nothing's cold where I'm standing," Easton said, grinning at Ruth.

"Shush, Easton," Ruth said. "Coming." She straightened her clothes, and they joined Naomi and Leroy in the kitchen.

When they were ready to leave, Leroy loaded the luggage in the taxicab's trunk. Easton helped Ruth and Naomi into coats Naomi had made over the summer. Naomi wore a three-quarter-length light blue tweed with large square buttons, and Ruth's, the color of her dark brown hair, stopped right below the knee with a green braided trim along the hemline. Ruth covered her head with a green beret.

"Did you buy your hat from Leslie Ann Penny at the market?" Easton asked.

"I did. You like?"

"Yes, I do," Easton replied. "You won't need it in Tennessee though. The temperature is always ten or fifteen degrees warmer than DC. We'll be out and about in our short sleeves."

* * *

The cab driver earned a healthy tip helping Leroy cart the heavy luggage inside. The wait for check-in lasted twenty minutes, not bad for the day before Thanksgiving, considering all the people that sat waiting for a train. There weren't too many seats left.

Easton stopped at the newsstand and bought cigarettes and cigars.

"You smoke cigars too?" Naomi asked.

"No, they're for Pops and my uncles."

After a short while, the announcer belted out their train over the loudspeaker, "Old Dominion number 508 to Knoxville, Tennessee, now boarding on track 3. Please have your tickets ready."

Ruth scampered to the track door to be first in line. People glared at Easton, Leroy, and Naomi as they joined her. When the doors opened, they followed Ruth past several cars to the first-class car. The Pullman porter stood at the door. His starched white jacket, spick-and-span, seemed whiter than snow next to his ebony-colored skin, a black bow tie clipped to his shirt collar. Ruth handed him their tickets.

"Enjoy your trip, madam," he said to Naomi and Ruth.

"Enjoy your trip, sir," he said to Easton and Leroy.

When Naomi found their seats. "How much did you pay for these tickets?"

"Mom, don't worry about it," Ruth answered. "This is my first time going South and I didn't want to drive, and I didn't expect Leroy to drive by himself. Besides, tomorrow isn't promised to any of us. After all we've been through, let's enjoy the ride."

Naomi looked around. Her concern wasn't all about the money spent on the tickets. "I don't see any other Negroes in this car?"

"The Interstate Commerce Commission said that all segregation on trains and buses must end by January 1956. It's November now," Easton informed her.

"You think Jim Crow cares about what the Interstate Commerce Commission says? They didn't care in the South, now, did they? I'm glad I updated my will," Naomi responded.

The porter came by and handed pillows and a blanket to each of them. Naomi peeked at Ruth, as she got comfortable in her seat. "Thank you, sweetie pie."

"Are you all in the right car?" A white man with gray hair, wearing wire-rimmed glasses and dressed in a gray tweed suit, stood over them.

"Our tickets say we are," Easton replied, observing him.

"You don't say. Three colored people and a redskin. Let me see your tickets," he demanded.

"You work on this train?" Easton asked.

"I'll have you know, I'm an attorney for the Commonwealth of Virginia," the man said, raising his voice. Murmuring in the car stopped as people listened in.

"Then you know we don't have to show you anything," Easton said. He picked up a newspaper and started reading it.

"You spooks are despicable. You don't belong in this car," he said.

Naomi stood and faced him. "Mr. Attorney from the Commonwealth of Virginia, I think you better go sit down before I show you how despicable I can be."

"You don't tell me what to do," he said.

Just then the porter stepped between the two. "Sir, can I help you to your seat, sir? The train is about to pull out of the station. Let me carry your briefcase for you, sir."

The man stared at Naomi. She stared back. Riders gawked at the two, uncertain how things might end.

"Sir, this way, please," the porter pleaded. The man handed the porter his briefcase. He proceeded down the aisle, mumbling something under his breath.

Murmuring throughout the car grew louder.

The man glanced back at Naomi.

"What did I tell you?" Naomi said, staring back at the man.

# Chapter 45

Six thirty in the evening, the train arrived in Knoxville, Tennessee, the closest station to Harrington, which happened to be in Roane County, forty miles away. Pops and Easton's mother were waiting. After hugs, kisses, and a few tears, they rode the thirty minutes to the farm where Easton grew up.

A long gravel driveway led to a two-story white farmhouse with a tin roof that sat about a hundred yards from the road. Its cement porch was wrapped around to the back of the house, and stems from a grapevine sprawled along its foundation. Two gliders and four chairs were positioned across it. A walnut tree, taller than the house, sat in the middle of the front lawn. Four-foot hedges traced its perimeter. They laughed at the sight of chickens scurrying across the yard, clucking up a storm, their feathers ruffled from a three-legged dog teetering after them.

Pops parked in the driveway.

Ruth and Naomi shed their coats in the eighty-degree heat and gazed at the mountainous terrain.

"We're in the valley, at the base of the Cumberland Plateau, that's why you see so many trees bearing down on us," Easton said. "Indian summer goes well into December here. It's cool now, compared to some years when we've had temperatures in the hundreds."

"It's beautiful," Ruth said, holding Easton's hand.

"Yes, it is. But you have to be careful. Sometimes, wolves come out of the woods, barking and pouncing on livestock and people."

Ruth and Naomi glared at him.

"Easton, shame on you," his mother said. "Stop trying to scare them."

Pops and Leroy laughed as they toted the luggage inside.

"I'll show you where you're bedding down," Pops said. He led Ruth and Naomi up a steep wooden staircase to a room with twin beds and set their luggage in a corner. "This is it. Thelma will have your supper warmed up soon." He went back downstairs.

Easton and Leroy were reconciling where they'd sleep. "Let's flip a coin for the bedroom," Easton said to Leroy, who'd walked into the front room from the kitchen.

"No need," Leroy said. "I'll sleep on the back porch. I can stargaze before I fall asleep."

* * *

Ruth and Naomi surveyed their quaint sleeping quarters. The walls were papered with pink roses, and white lace curtains covered the two windows overlooking the front yard. Ruth opened the windows, hoping a breeze might come through and cool off the room. She'd already started perspiring.

"Wow, the carving on this dressing table is beautiful. I've never seen anything like it," Ruth said, tracing the outline of the design with her fingers. She sat on a stool in front of the mirror attached to the ornate brown-and-gold table. A framed photo of a young couple sat on it. "Easton's parents, I bet." She showed the photo to her mother.

"What a beautiful picture," Naomi said. "And this bedspread." Naomi rubbed her hand across the pink-and-white crocheted cover. "It's handmade. Those quilts folded on that rocking chair are too." Naomi pointed to a brown rocker in the corner.

"How do you know?" Ruth asked.

"I can recognize a homemade quilt anywhere. I watched my grandmother make quilts until she died," Naomi said.

They hung up their dresses and left the rest to put away later.

* * *

The men were at the dining room table, chewing the fat. Naomi thanked Pops for letting her retreat to his home and went into the kitchen. Ruth asked Pops about the picture on the dresser.

"That's us," Pops replied. "I was twenty-four and Thelma twenty-one when we married. Two years later, Easton came along, and two years after that, Thelma Junior. We don't see much of her since she moved to Germany. She's a nurse too. Maybe she'll come home for Christmas," Pops said, his voice cracking.

Easton had told Ruth how Thelma Junior's fiancé had run off with another woman. Thelma, devastated, joined the army, did her stint, and for the last four years had lived in Germany. She hadn't come home since she moved, not even to visit.

Naomi and Thelma went in the dining room with trays of food: meat loaf, baked potatoes, turnip greens, and corn bread. Pops blessed the table, and they dug in. They stuffed themselves silly. When they finished, no one wanted to move.

Easton talked about the town of Harrington. "It only takes five minutes to go from one side of town to the other. We have one department store, a couple of grocery stores, and five colored churches. Roane County is a dry county, so if you want wine or beer, you have to go to Kingston. There's no nightlife here either. We have to drive to Knoxville if you want to go clubbing."

Naomi and Thelma must've been reading each other's mind. They both got up and headed for the kitchen at the same time to put away leftovers and clean the kitchen.

*  *  *

Thanksgiving morning, inside the farmhouse, Easton woke to the sound of the cock crowing. This day he'd ask Ruth to marry him. He had wanted it to be a perfect day, with both families present though for Naomi it might be bittersweet. He was certain Taylor's murder would loom in silence amid the joy.

The house smelled like fried bacon. He imagined his mother in the kitchen, juggling between basting the twenty-pound turkey and frying the bacon. Pops and Leroy would be in the holler by now tending to the cows, where Easton would be too if it weren't for his bum arm. He rolled out of bed, got dressed, and joined his mother in the kitchen.

"Morning," he said to her.

"Morning, son," she replied, not looking up from the dough she was rolling out on the kitchen table. "It's going to be a hot one today. Temperature's supposed to be in the eighties by noon. With the oven going all day and the family piling in here later on, we'll all be like the turkey . . . roasted."

"And you're going to love every minute of it," Easton said, pouring himself a cup of coffee.

Easton's parents had hosted Thanksgiving dinner for more than twenty years. The majority of the extended family had left the Tennessee Valley. With the exception of a few, they'd return and spend Thanksgiving Day at Easton's house, recounting memories of past gatherings and creating new ones. It became a day and a place to escape from the hurts of the world, to reflect on the good, and to embrace the unconditional love from elder family members who'd been through it all, to hear them tell it, and to eat some good old Southern cooking. But not before attending Thanksgiving Day church services at Tabernacle Baptist Church, the Priest family's place of worship.

Easton walked through the back porch and into the yard and lit a cigarette. Soon the sun would rise and its scorching rays would harden the already dry earth. Easton kicked at the dirt. ***We sure can use some rain,*** he said to himself.

"Fresh coffee for you," Easton's mother said, handing him a cup. "Breakfast is ready, if you want it."

"I'll wait for Pops and Leroy, if it's okay with you," Easton responded.

"Okay." She turned to go inside, then she said, "You got a lot on your mind, I can tell. I got a few minutes to listen."

"I don't want to trouble you," Easton said.

"It's too late, Easton, you brought it home with you," she responded.

Easton sighed. "Taylor's murder—the killer is getting away scot-free. I believe he's still in the city somewhere, laughing at me."

The heat was slowly rising with the sun, and sweat dribbled from Easton's mother's head. She wiped her brow with a handkerchief and asked, "What's troubling you more . . . the killer still loose in the city or he's laughing at you?" She went in the house, the screen door clapping behind her.

Easton, taken aback at her question, realized how stupid he sounded. Yes, he'd blamed the killer for being free. What man or woman alive would want to face the electric chair? He'd be hiding somewhere too. Yet he'd become bitter believing the killer might be mocking him. He'd made the murder investigation about him.

He glanced over at the hill beside the dirt road leading to the neighbor's house. All kinds of flowers covered the knoll: buttercups, snapdragons, blue chicory, snakeroots, scarlet sage, coneflowers with lavender and purple petals, and daffodils. At some point between the bread baking and the gravy simmering, his mother would gather a bunch and put them in a vase on the dining room table.

* * *

Later that afternoon, Ruth, Naomi, and Leroy joined the Priest family at Tabernacle Baptist Church. The one-story church painted white may well fit inside the House of Worship with room to spare. Blackbirds were crouched on the black wrought-iron steeple atop the roof. Easton had told Ruth that his great-grandparents, now deceased, had helped build the church almost a hundred years ago. It looked like a small house nestled among the tall oaks that soared above the thick brush alongside the road, their branches creating a bridge across the sky like a trestle, rays of sunlight beaming through. White pines towered over the oaks and all the other trees in the brush. Pine needles from the mammoth trees were scattered about on the dirt road in front of the church, giving off a pleasant fragrance.

"I wish I could bottle up this pine scent and carry it home. It smells so fresh," Ruth said.

"It's from pine oil in the needles," Easton said. "Folks down here burn pinewood for pine tar and then mix it with beer to get rid of tapeworms. They use the sap to make turpentine and treat infections, and the pulp to heal wounds."

"We didn't learn anything about pine tar for healing in nursing school," Ruth said.

"Scholars don't believe in the natural things God has given us for healing, like the pine tree. You won't hear anyone lecturing on the subject, not in this day and time," Easton said.

A big brown rabbit jumped from the bushes and hopped across the road, startling Ruth.

"We have snakes too," Easton said.

Ruth stood still and scoured the road.

Easton and the others chuckled.

"That's not funny," Ruth said, squeezing Easton's hand, trying not to laugh too.

Cars driving by honked their horns. Birds were singing, and the sound of their shoes pressing on the gravel walkway gave off the only other sound.

* * *

"Reverend Rodger Samuels is the preacher and my mother's cousin. You'll meet him at dinner," Easton told Ruth and Leroy, as they went through the wooden doors and into the sanctuary. The room sweltered from the heat. The four narrow windows in the chapel were open, and portable fans were running at maximum speed. It didn't help.

Ruth and Leroy followed Easton to the second pew, where his family always sat. The choir stood in the loft opposite the lectern, wearing red robes. Pops donned a robe and joined them. The pianist played the melody to "We Gather Together," and they began to sing. Reverend Samuels marched down the aisle to the pulpit, in front of him a boy carrying a large gold-colored cross. Smoke from incense burning at the altar rose to the ceiling and floated above the chancel like a cloud.

The sermon called attention to the blessings that God had bestowed upon each person in the room.

"Be thankful for his countless gifts of love," Reverend Samuels said.

The collection plate went around once, unlike in the House of Worship, where the plate would have gone around at least three times during a two-hour service, taking in hundreds of dollars.

"That incense on the altar, it didn't hide the smell of turkey and baked bread coming from the Lyles' place. Did you see Reverend Samuels's mouth drooling? He was hungry," Easton said, laughing, as Pops drove the five minutes back home.

"Shame on you, Easton, talking about your uncle like that," Easton's mother said. "Who's on the porch already?"

"Reverend Samuels," Easton replied. They all laughed, including Easton's mother.

Pops coasted up the driveway. A woman rose from a glider and ran to the edge of the porch. Pops and Easton's mother climbed out of the car and stared at the woman.

They all started walking toward the woman. As Ruth got closer, she turned toward Easton, smiling.

"She doesn't look like Reverend Samuels to me. She looks like your twin."

"Thelma Junior," Easton murmured, "my sister."

Shorter than Easton at five foot ten, his sister had the same slender build, dark eyes, cleft in her chin, and full lips—hers painted a dark rose. A gold-feathered hat covered black ringlets of hair resting on her shoulders. Her bronze skin seemed to glow in the yellow dress she wore, a gold chain dangling around her neck. She stood tall, arms by her side, chin in the air. She ran down the porch steps and almost knocked her mother to the ground, hugging her. She then swung around to Pops and embraced him. His body sagged in her arms like a mighty oak tree sickened at the roots. He started slipping from her grip, the dead weight from his body too heavy to support. Easton reached him just in time, grabbed his waist, and he and Leroy helped Pops in the house and into his armchair.

Easton watched Pops, whose eyes were now fixed on Thelma Junior. She had appeared out of the blue after four years. She sat at Pops's feet, and every now and then he'd stroke her hair. It bothered Easton that Pops hadn't said a word since he sat down. He'd offered Pops a shot of whiskey; he drank a glass of water instead. By the time everyone else arrived and the biscuits were ready, Pops began speaking again. Easton stopped worrying.

"Thelma Junior, you okay down there?" Easton asked her.

"I'm fine," she replied, leaning against Pops's leg.

* * *

Easton ran upstairs to retrieve Ruth's diamond ring from his coat pocket. When he rejoined the family, he wasted no time putting his plans in motion. "Attention, please," he yelled above all the chatter. "Before Reverend Samuels says the grace, I want to share something with you all. Mom, Mrs. Taylor, please come here for a minute." They hurried into the living room from the kitchen. "Thelma Junior, welcome home," Easton said. "We're all thankful you're here with us today. We missed you."

"Amen to that," Jimmy said.

"Praise the Lord," others shouted.

Thelma Junior nodded.

Easton continued. "And you're here on a very special day in my life." He turned to Ruth, got down on one knee, and drew in a deep breath. "Ruth, will you marry me?" he asked, sliding a one-and-a-half-carat diamond ring on her finger. Other than cameras flashing and a few gasps, no one spoke.

Overwhelmed, Ruth stared at the ring. Her hand quivered in Easton's hand.

"Yes," she whispered.

"We can't hear you," Naomi shouted.

"Yes, I'll marry you," she spoke louder. Easton stood and kissed her lips.

"All right, lover boy," Jimmy hollered.

The room erupted in laughter.

Naomi rubbed her finger over the precious stone. "I'm so happy for you, sweetie pie." Naomi kissed Ruth on the cheek and hugged her tight. And then she said, "I wish your daddy was here to see this." Naomi darted to the kitchen.

Ruth started after her.

"Let her go, she'll be okay," Easton said, holding Ruth's hand.

They turned their attention to Pops and Easton's mother, who sat on the armrest of his chair. Pops rose to his feet. He threw his arms around Easton and his future daughter-in-law.

"I love both of you, son. When you were stabbed, I asked God to take me and spare you. I didn't want to live without you." The emotional strain caused his voice to tremble.

"Pops, I plan to be around for a long time," Easton said. "I'll have a wife to care for pretty soon." He winked at Ruth.

"What a glorious day," Easton's mother said to Pops. "Now come on so the reverend can say grace before the food gets cold."

The family gathered two-deep around the dining room table, holding hands, while the reverend blessed the food. Afterward, folks piled plates high with food and ate until their bodies were numb.

* * *

Easton left Ruth and went to the kitchen for a drink. He laughed when he saw Jimmy at the kitchen table, sucking on a chicken bone with one hand, a glass of moonshine in the other hand.

"Please don't get cut up again before you tie the knot. I'm not sure I'd want to lay up with someone all sliced and bruised on my honeymoon," Jimmy said. "That reminds me, your bachelor party is going to be at the Grille. I got it all planned. I'll close the restaurant at ten o'clock, and we'll party all night then drag your behind to the altar."

"You're too much, man," Easton said. "Who's minding the restaurant while you're here?"

"Joe. He'll be here Christmas, and I'll stay in DC, unless Mama comes to DC, which I doubt," Jimmy said. "Big Mama is too frail to travel, and Mama is scared to death to leave her with anyone else. That's why they're not here." Big Mama was Jimmy's grandmother.

"What are you boys doing in here?" Aunt Minnie asked, strolling into the kitchen.

"Waiting for you, Auntie," Jimmy replied.

"Let me have a taste of that," she said, pointing to Jimmy's drink.

"Here, you can have it. I'll pour myself another one," Jimmy said.

"Thank you, son." She winked at him and left.

"I love Auntie. I swear she can smell liquor a mile away." Jimmy hit the table with his fist and laughed.

"Every family has one," Easton said, laughing with Jimmy.

* * *

Over the next couple of days, Pops and Leroy woke before dawn and worked on the farm. By noon they'd all hop in the car and take off to some place. The Great Smoky Mountains were their first stop. Pops navigated the narrow roads to Clingmans Dome, the highest point in the mountains and in Tennessee. The views expanded over one hundred miles and into seven states.

"This is amazing," Ruth exclaimed. "It looks like a picture painted on a canvas."

"Nature is, without a doubt, showing off for you city folks today," Easton said.

"Even Skyline Drive doesn't have a magnificent view like this," Naomi said. "I see colors I've never seen before, and it's late November."

After a few more minutes of gazing at the spectacular scene, they piled back in the car. Pops negotiated bends and curves through the mountain to an area where members of the Cherokee Nation lived and worked, dressed in their native attire, peacock-feathered headpieces and all. The Cherokees had migrated from different parts of the United States and settled in the Smokey Mountains. Reminiscent of a small town out of the Old West, the natives had saddled and tied their horses to wooden rails outside the small gift shops, and the women carried their papoose in pouch-like bags strapped on their back. Leroy talked with the Cherokee men perched in front of the shops, who were smoking pipes and cigars, while the others shopped.

The next day they visited Jimmy and his mother in Foley Hills, a colored section of Knoxville, Tennessee. Jimmy and his mother had the same light brown eyes, the only feature the two had in common. A slender five foot five, she had a lean face, a narrow nose, wide lips, and skin darker than the night. She wore her thick salt-and-pepper hair combed back in one long plait. Large silver hoop earrings hung from her ears.

They feasted on barbecue ribs, turnip greens, potato salad, and corn muffins Jimmy's mother had made from scratch. Jimmy entertained them with stories about patrons who frequented the Grille. Some stories were so outrageous, they didn't know whether to believe him or not. They laughed so hard, their sides hurt.

* * *

That evening, Easton called Ira. "Tell me you caught a killer."

"Man, I'm going to lose my job if I don't arrest somebody soon," Ira said.

"The chief giving you a hard time?" Easton asked.

"Screaming at me like a scorned woman," Ira replied. "Somebody's hiding the bastard or covering for him. We should have him by now."

"I believe Doc Nelson is involved. Can't you arrest him for peddling drugs?" Easton said.

"Not enough evidence," Ira replied.

"What about Daniels?" Easton asked.

"Maybe after the audit, we'll have something to move on," Ira responded.

"No news is bad news," Easton said.

"What time is your train coming in?" Ira asked.

"Around six thirty tomorrow evening," Easton replied.

"If I'm on patrol, I might come by the station. Maybe I'll have some good news."

"You're a detective leading the investigation, why are you going on patrol?" Easton asked.

"Because I'm still as black as an ace of spades."

# Chapter 46

By the time the train pulled into Union Station, Sunday, November 25, the sun had disappeared below the horizon. The city sky had faded from blue to red, and the imposing presence of the US Capitol stood outlined against the evening glow. At the gate, Ira waited for their arrival. Easton saw two Caucasian men dressed in black suits standing beside him. They approached Naomi.

"Mrs. Naomi Taylor . . . you're under arrest for the murder of William Taylor." One of the men shoved the arrest warrant in Naomi's face. The other snatched her overnight case and forced both arms behind her back to cuff her.

Ruth screamed, "Stop! Stop! Leave her alone!" She grabbed the man's arm. Too late, he'd already locked the metal bracelets around Naomi's wrist. He knocked Ruth away so hard she slammed against Easton's injured arm.

Easton grimaced in pain, holding his arm, anger seething inside. He heaved toward the man, his heart racing, his fist ready to strike.

"Back off!" the man's partner warned, clutching his standard-issue pistol.

Ruth leaped in front of Easton. She tried to shove him backward. He pressed forward. "Easton, no, he'll shoot you!" Ruth shrieked.

Onlookers watched in horror.

Ira and Leroy quickly dragged Easton away from the man. "He's a detective. Don't make it any worst than what it is," Ira said. "You're no good to anybody dead."

"He manhandled my woman," Easton bellowed.

"And he'll kill you, if you get in his way," Leroy said.

The detectives, still clutching their weapons, escorted Naomi, misty-eyed, her face ashen, out of Union Station.

"Did you know about this?" Easton asked Ira as they marched behind Naomi.

"No . . . they just showed up, told me to stand back, not to interfere. I thought they were here for somebody else," Ira answered, visibly shaken.

The detectives helped Naomi into the backseat of a squad car double-parked in front of the train station. As soon as the detective closed the door, it sped off.

"Let's go!" Easton said. They ran to Ira's car. "Ruth, we'll call your mother's lawyer at the precinct. Do you have his phone number with you?

"No . . . I'll get it from information," she responded, her voice trembling, fear etched in her face. He placed his hand around her waist and held her close.

"Don't worry, your mother will be released in a little while," Easton said.

"How long is a little while, Easton? How long?" She pushed off from him and eased into Ira's car.

Ira turned on his siren and sped to the Second precinct. A crowd had already gathered outside. News traveled fast in the city, especially when it involved a favorite daughter. Ira parked in a lot behind the precinct.

"The phone booth is over there." Ira pointed toward a covered entrance and ran inside.

Ruth walked briskly toward the phone booth, her cheeks turning red from the sting of cold air. With the windchill factor, the forty-five-degree temperature felt like twenty degrees. Her narrow eyes squinted to see through tears caused by the frigid air. The telephone operator gave her two numbers for the lawyer. She reached him at the first listing. He promised to meet her at the precinct right away.

* * *

"Where is Mrs. Naomi Taylor?" Easton asked the cop at the sign-in desk.

"Who's asking?" asked the cop.

"I'm her daughter," Ruth answered.

"She's being processed, you can't see her now."

"I have to see her!" Ruth cried.

Just then Ira plodded out of the squad room. Ira faced Ruth and clasped her hand in his. "Your mother is going to be arraigned soon. Where's her lawyer?"

"On his way," Ruth replied.

"Who ordered the arrest?" Easton asked. "No, let me guess . . . the chief."

"Yeah, and I cursed his ass out," Ira said.

"Ira . . . no!" Easton shouted.

"Yeah, the nincompoop fired me," Ira responded. "I have ten minutes before they throw me off the premises. I'm going to clean out my locker. I'll meet you in court."

"This can't be happening," Easton said.

"It is what it is," Ira said, and raced off.

Easton, Ruth, and Leroy gathered in a corner of the lobby, waiting for Naomi's lawyer. Easton held his peace, while Ruth quietly sobbed in his arms, though he knew Taylor's murder and Naomi's arrest would forever haunt him. Had he not investigated Family Life Insurance Company and published their atrocities, he and Ruth might be in some cozy spot, planning their wedding, rather than in a police station with Naomi's future at stake.

* * *

An hour later, through the shadows of the narrow corridor, Naomi's lawyer went scurrying toward them.

"Ruth, I've already met with your mother. She's holding up pretty good. She'll be taken to District Court at any moment. I'll request bail, and since she doesn't have any previous arrests, I don't believe the judge will deny it. You need to be prepared to put up quite a bit of money. Do you know how to get to it?"

Ruth didn't speak. She was barely breathing. She nodded.

The lawyer shook hands with Easton and Leroy. "Take Ruth to the courthouse, I'll see you all there."

He left just as quickly as he came.

# Chapter 47

Easton, Ruth, and Leroy dashed to District Court. A line of people stretched from the receptionist desk around a corner and into a waiting room. One woman sat behind the desk to service all the people in line. Easton wondered what brought so many people into the courthouse on a Sunday evening. He walked up to the desk. "Where's the arraignment courtroom?"

"Down the hall, on the right," the woman answered without looking up.

They hustled down the hallway crowded with people moving in both directions. Dark-wood baseboards separated the dingy white walls from the ceramic tile worn down from scores of people, like Ruth and Easton, walking through the corridors to hear the fate of their loved ones. Although Naomi had been charged with murder, Easton believed she'd make bail too. According to Ruth, she'd never been arrested in her life, never even received a parking ticket. He prayed the judge would give Naomi the benefit of the doubt and let her go home tonight. He worried that anything less would push Ruth over the edge.

* * *

They sat on the second row in the courtroom. Easton and Leroy stood as Naomi walked in with her lawyer. Naomi glanced over at Ruth then quickly looked away.

The judge read the charges against Naomi. "Mrs. Naomi Taylor, you're being charged with first-degree murder. How do you plead?"

Naomi straightened her body. "Not guilty," she answered with a determined expression on her face.

The prosecuting attorney interjected. "Mrs. Taylor was the only person in the house the night of her husband's murder. When the police arrived, her clothes were covered with his blood."

Naomi's attorney offered a rebuttal. "Mrs. Taylor is an upstanding citizen in this community. She did not kill her husband and is not a threat to anyone. As a matter of fact, she received a death threat after her husband's murder. Whoever killed her husband wants to kill her. Or do you think she sent the death threat to herself?"

"Save it for the trial, counselor," said the judge.

"Your Honor, I'd like to request bail for my client," Naomi's attorney put forward.

"Any objection?" the judge asked the prosecutor.

"Yes, Your Honor. I request that Mrs. Taylor be remanded into custody. We have enough evidence to prove she murdered her husband."

"Good, then bring it to trial with you. Bail is set at ten thousand dollars. I'll see you in four weeks."

Ruth jumped from her seat and ran toward her mother. The guard whisked Naomi away before she reached her.

"Ruth, you need to arrange for bail. Your mother has to remain in custody until you do," Naomi's lawyer said. "Your mother said to use the house."

"What do I do?" Ruth asked helplessly.

"Come with me." Ira motioned to Easton and Ruth to follow him. "Bailin' won't take long." Ira drove the couple to the funeral home to get the deed for the house and Easton's car. He wrote down the name and address of a bail bondsman and gave it to Easton. "Tell him I sent you."

* * *

"Open All Night," the sign said on the bail bondsman's business on Fourteenth Street. Three other customers were in the place. It took almost two hours to post the bond, using the house as collateral. The bondsman made it very clear to Ruth that if Naomi skipped town, they'd send a bounty hunter after her. "Man, woman, or child, we don't care, we comin' after you."

Ruth looked at Easton. "Mom isn't going anywhere. She's so mad now she's ready to kick somebody's behind for putting her through this."

"I hope not," Easton said. "We don't want to come back here again."

They sprinted to Easton's car. Neither took a deep breath until the clerk of courts accepted the bond. By midnight, Naomi sat with Easton and Ruth in the funeral parlor, trying to make sense of what had happened.

# Chapter 48

Easton left the funeral home around one o'clock Monday morning, November 26. The playing field had changed again with Naomi's arrest; the focus turned to proving Naomi's innocence rather than vindicating Taylor's murder. He poured himself a shot of bourbon and smoked a cigarette before crashing. Around ten o'clock the next morning, he dragged himself out of bed.

* * *

"Detectives arrested Naomi Taylor at Union Station yesterday for her husband's murder," Easton said to Aaron.

"I know . . . I got the call late last night," Aaron said. He rose from his chair. "I didn't want to print anything until I talked to you. What evidence do they have against her?"

"Alone in the house with Taylor, covered in his blood when police arrived on the scene," Easton replied. "She's out on bail. I'll put something together for the column. Oh . . . and the chief fired Ira. That'll be in the column too."

Aaron patted Easton's shoulder. "Ira called me. He wants me to put in a good word for him with a security company he's interviewing with, and I will. I don't believe Naomi killed Taylor. She has too much class to dirty her hands with a murder."

"She is a bit siddity," Easton grinned. "Like mother, like daughter."

"You said it," Aaron said jokingly. "How is Ruth?"

"I talked to her this morning, and she's calmed down," Easton replied. "We're engaged. I proposed to her in Tennessee."

"Congratulations!" Aaron reached out and grabbed Easton's hand. "Ruth is a fine young lady. When's the big day?"

"Sometime in May," Easton replied.

"I've got something for you," Aaron said.

Easton followed Aaron into the ***News*** room. Aaron rolled a chair to the middle of the room and stood in it. "Listen up, everyone. Easton and Ruth got engaged over the holiday . . . time to celebrate."

Everyone in the office cheered and clapped at the good news. Aaron jumped from the chair, ran back to his office, and returned with two bottles of champagne and paper cups. He moved from person to person, pouring champagne.

"To Easton and Ruth," Aaron said, holding up his cup of bubbly. He drank it down in one gulp. "Now it's payday." He took a piece of paper from his pocket and read from it. "The winner is . . . Dominic." Aaron handed Dominic twenty dollars. Everyone in the room clapped and whistled except Easton.

"What's going on?" Easton asked.

"Brotha, we had an engagement pool on you," Lloyd said, laughing. "The month you'd pop the question. It seems young Dominic's got your number, Mr. Priest."

"The way you snoop around, we weren't sure we'd pull it off," Aaron said.

Easton laughed, drank champagne, thanked his colleagues, and retreated to his desk. He lit a cigarette and called Ira at home. "Naomi Taylor is out on bail."

"I heard," Ira said.

"Any chance of getting your job back?" Easton asked.

"I'm not waiting around to find out. I got an interview with a security company tomorrow," Ira replied.

"I'm sorry, man. It wasn't supposed to go down like this," Easton said.

"It's not your fault," Ira said. "The chief is a mean, spiteful son of a bitch. I'm not worried, he's gonna get his."

"Anything new on the case?" Easton asked.

"A boy hanging around Sixth Street while you were gone. Taylor's neighbor called us because no one recognized him. Turns out he's a friend of Jeremiah Bailey and was waiting for him to come home."

"You still tailing Doc and Daniels?" Easton asked.

"They've been squeaky clean. I think they're on to us," Ira said.

"What about Thomas, have you heard from him?" Easton inquired.

"His mother talked to him. He told her he's still doing work for Doc. He won't say what," Ira replied.

"Selling drugs," Easton said.

"I hope not," Ira responded.

"We've got to find Taylor's killer to clear Naomi's name and for you to get your job back," Easton said.

"You got a plan?" Ira asked.

# Chapter 49

Easton's eyes moved across the room from one reporter's desk to another. He observed the copyboys waiting to launch on cue for a finished story or to take orders for coffee or food. Voices competed with phones ringing; smoke clouded the air. A loud thud startled Easton. He spun around in his chair. Dominic had dropped a box of steno pads on the floor. On the wall above him hung a photo of Mary Ann Shadd Cary, lawyer, abolitionist, and the first black newspaperwoman in North America. When Easton told Ruth her story, at first she questioned it. "I thought you told me that Fay Jackson was the first black newspaper reporter," Ruth had said. Easton reminded her that Fay Jackson came on the scene long after Mary Ann Shadd Cary died. Even so, it had been no surprise to Ruth that Negro women had led the way in a lot of things. And she'd say it again when Rosa Parks refused to give up her seat on the bus.

Next to Mary Ann Shadd Cary's picture hung a group photo of Negro journalists who'd made a name for themselves over the years. Easton studied the picture. He reached for a file from his desk drawer and reread an article written by Samuel Rupert, a journalist in the photo, who said Negroes weren't vigorous enough about righting wrongs against their own people. They were color struck. Too busy creating boundaries within their own race, separating the haves and the have-nots and the light-skinned and the dark-skinned, no different from how white people treated Negroes. Rupert believed it had played out contrary to the struggle for equal rights so as not to distract from the bigger issue that affected all Negroes—racial inequality.

Easton picked up the phone and called his cousin Jimmy. "What you got going tomorrow?" he asked Jimmy.

"Tomorrow is Tuesday, cuz. You know we have our foot-long special," Jimmy replied.

"No, I mean, what are your plans for tomorrow?" Easton clarified himself.

"I'll be here. Why, what's going on?" Jimmy asked.

"We need the people in Shaw to help us find Taylor's killer. I've been begging for help in my column every week and no one's come forward, so I want to meet the people where they are . . . in front of your restaurant, with a big sign in the window and fliers asking for help. If it works for the civil rights protesters, maybe it will work for us."

"Bring it on," Jimmy said. "What time you coming by?"

"When the biscuits come out the oven," Easton replied.

Easton hung up and raced to Aaron's office. He knocked on his door and went in before Aaron invited him in.

"Sorry, Aaron . . . we need help finding Taylor's killer, and I have a plan." Easton went on to tell Aaron that he wanted to arouse the Shaw community to help find Taylor's killer. He'd post a sign in Jimmy's window and hand out fliers to merchants and people on the street.

"Well, I don't see a reason not to try," Aaron said. "You can take one reporter with you, I can't spare anybody else."

"I'll take Lloyd," Easton said.

* * *

There were plenty of people strolling up and down Rhode Island Avenue when Easton and Lloyd arrived at the Grille Tuesday morning, November 27. Jimmy and Lloyd stood outside and watched Easton position a twenty-four-by-thirty-six-inch poster in the restaurant's window. When it appeared straight, Jimmy gave Easton a thumbs-up, and he joined them outside. The poster read as follows:

William Thomas Taylor III
Undertaker and Embalmer
Murdered October 13, 1956
Killer Still at Large—We Need Your Help!
Call the ***Negro News*** with any information that may help us
find the killer: Tuckerman 28943

"You didn't tell me you were going to hang a curtain in my window," Jimmy said. "That's an awfully big poster. I don't think anybody walking by will miss it unless they're blind. I do like the colors—red, black, and green. How creative. Well, back to work." He went inside.

Jimmy had provided a small table and a chair for Lloyd to sit in while he distributed the fliers. Easton didn't need to sit, Jimmy had said.

"You need to hustle these people to make them stop and listen to you. You can't do that if your behind is in a chair. And send some customers inside, business has been slow."

Easton pursued people up and down the block, begging for help in finding Taylor's killer. More women stopped to listen than men did. When he talked about Naomi's arrest and how she feared for her life because of the death threat she received, they looked at him in disbelief, their eyes opened almost as wide as their mouth. It didn't make sense to them. They'd shake their head, curse the police, cry, grab a flier from Easton's hand, and hurry off. They didn't even ask questions.

They just took off, as if they were on a mission, at least that's what Easton hoped—a mission to find information about Taylor's murder.

Many of the people knew Easton worked for the ***Negro News*** and had broken the story about Family Life. Those who didn't, he'd suggest they read his weekly column to stay up-to-date on the murder investigation and reminded them that his newspaper published stories they'd never read anywhere else.

By lunchtime, over half of the fliers had been distributed. Easton had to call the ***News*** office to have more sent over to Jimmy's. By ten o'clock that night, there were none left. At times during the day, Easton had crossed over Rhode Island Avenue to appeal to folks walking on the other side of the street. His feet hurt, and because he had talked nonstop all day, his voice sounded raspy. Even when he had paused to eat or go to the john, he'd ask anybody nearby to help find Taylor's killer.

Easton thanked Jimmy for letting him and Lloyd petition people outside his restaurant.

"Anytime, cuz," Jimmy said. "As a matter of fact, I'm keeping the poster in the window until Taylor's murder is solved. It seems I picked up some business helping you. God is good when you do right, isn't he?"

Easton smiled. "Yes, he is."

"What do we do now?" Lloyd asked.

"Tonight we go home and sleep," Easton replied. "Tomorrow we wait . . . patiently."

# Chapter 50

By seven o'clock Wednesday morning, November 28, Easton had completed the draft for his next column, "There by the Grace of God Go I: The Shaw Community Rallies to Find William Taylor's Killer." ***If people had not considered helping before, after yesterday maybe they'd reconsider,*** he surmised. Easton tossed the draft on Lloyd's desk for his review. As soon as he returned to his desk, the phone rang.

"Easton . . . somebody attacked Ruth at the hospital!" Naomi shrieked in the phone.

Easton jumped from his seat. "What . . . is she all right?" Easton asked.

"I don't know," Naomi cried. "They won't tell me anything over the phone."

Easton slammed down the receiver. "No! Not Ruth! No!" He dropped into his chair.

Everyone in the room heard him bellow like a bull in pain. Aaron ran to him. "Easton, what happened?"

"Ruth . . . somebody attacked her at the hospital!" Papers flew from his desk as Easton rummaged for his car keys. When he found them, he darted out the door to his car and sped through the streets, swerving in and out of traffic, until he reached the hospital where Ruth worked.

* * *

"Where's Ruth Johnson?" Easton asked the emergency room clerk. She remembered Easton and directed him to curtain 2. The hospital had hired Ira as a security guard, and he stood steadfast in front of curtain 2.

"Get out of my way!" Easton screamed. "Let me see her!" He pushed forward.

Ira held him back. "The doctor is with her."

"Is she alive? Just tell me she's alive, man," Easton pleaded with Ira, his body trembling with such force that Ira had to hold on to him to keep him from falling.

"She's alive, Easton," Ira replied. "Stay with me now."

A nurse opened the white curtains. Easton straightened his body and turned to look at Ruth. The right side of her face had swelled to twice its original size, and Dr. Zette had sutured an open cut above her left eye, now closed shut.

"Oh god . . . no!" Easton yelled, jerking away from Ira. Ruth's eyes were already small; now they looked like slits on her puffy face. "Ruth!" Easton choked back tears, gripped her hand in his, and kissed her swollen face. "It's me . . . Easton. It's my fault. They hurt you to get to me. I can't do this anymore." He wept.

Naomi ran into the cubicle, Leroy behind her. She stopped in her tracks. Each time she blinked, a tear dropped.

"My baby! My baby! You can't stop now, Easton, someone hurt my baby." Naomi staggered toward the bed. She smothered Ruth in her arms. "I'll look for the bastard myself . . . if you and the police won't."

Leroy, pained by the sight of Ruth, ran from the cubicle and flipped over a chair.

"Leroy, take it easy," Ira said, wiping the sweat from his face. "Mrs. Taylor, we'll get the person who did this."

"You haven't found the person who killed my husband. You think I'm going to sit around and wait for you to find the person who did this?" Naomi asked. "Do you?"

Ira turned away, not answering. He moved toward Dr. Zette. "Doc, can I talk to Ruth? We need a description of the attacker."

"She's unconscious. She had a serious blow to her head and face. It may be days before she wakes up, if she does. I'm sending her for tests to check for brain damage," Dr. Zette said. "The good thing . . . she's breathing on her own. Did you talk to Nurse Caroline and her boyfriend? They witnessed the attack."

"No, where are they?" Ira asked.

"Ask the clerk to page them. I told them not to leave until you and the police arrived," Dr. Zette replied.

Ira ran off to the clerk's desk.

"Mrs. Taylor, I'm going after the son of a bitch," Easton said. "Ruth, I'll be back, baby." Easton kissed her hand.

"Easton, he's dangerous," Naomi said. "Take Leroy with you."

Easton left the cubicle. He spotted Leroy sitting in a chair in a corner of the emergency room. "Come with me," Easton said. They walked past the clerk's desk.

"You're leaving?" Ira asked Easton, surprised he'd left Ruth's side so soon.

"I'll be back," Easton replied.

* * *

"Leroy, I wasn't sure at first, now I am. Taylor's murder, everything, it's about the funeral home, the business," Easton said, as they drove to Doc's Pharmacie.

"Where did that come from?" Leroy asked.

"Taylor's already gone. With Ruth and her mother out of the way, he'd only have Thomas to deal with," Easton replied. "Why would the killer go after Ruth and Naomi if he only had a beef with Taylor? It doesn't make sense."

"It doesn't have to make sense to us, just to the killer," Leroy responded. "Maybe we'll find proof at Doc's Pharmacie to bear out your motive."

Easton parked in the alley behind the Pharmacie. It opened for customers at nine o'clock. Easton checked his watch. "From what I'm told, Doc is here at eight thirty every morning. If we're lucky, we have ten minutes. We have to move fast," Easton said.

The door had a deadbolt lock on it, not easy to pick. Leroy pried open a window instead. They climbed into Doc Nelson's office. The room had a basement smell-musty and dank.

"It didn't smell in here when I interviewed Doc Nelson last month," Easton said. He stepped behind the partition where the scent almost knocked him over, though it didn't smell as bad as the rotten meat and the blood spatter in Taylor's kitchen. He noticed a pair of dungarees and a black T-shirt hanging from a hook next to the sink. Easton grasped the clothes. The shirt, wrinkled and soiled, and the pants, stiff like they'd been drenched in starch. He held up the pants.

"It's these clothes we smell. The pants are way too short for Doc's long legs." He pulled a pair of black boots from under the sink and held them above his head. "Doc can't get his toes in these boots either. I wonder if they're the ones that almost crushed my chest."

"Over here." Leroy motioned to Easton. He had moved the refrigerator away from the wall. Behind it, a wall safe, a mercenary's knife taped next to it.

I'll call Ira," Easton said.

"You can't. We're breaking and entering," Leroy said. "Besides, he doesn't work for the department anymore. Where's your camera?"

Easton snapped several pictures of the knife, boots, clothes, and random pictures of Doc's office. A creak from a door opening somewhere in the building startled the two men. Easton glanced at his watch then proceeded to jump through the window. Leroy pushed the refrigerator back in place, lunged through the window, and closed it shut right when Doc went through his office door.

* * *

"I wonder who those clothes and boots belong to. I'd like to ask Doc Nelson," Easton said as he drove back to the hospital.

Leroy shook his head. "You can't."

"You're right," Easton said. How would Easton explain what he saw without incriminating himself? He grew silent. The sight of Ruth's marred face tormented him, causing his insides to hurt. He labored to breathe.

"Are you all right?" Leroy asked.

"Ruth . . . I can't . . ."

"Pull over," Leroy shouted.

Easton coasted to the curb. Leroy jumped from the car and ran to the driver's side. "Easton, take a deep breath. Again." Leroy continued to prompt Easton to breathe deeply until he relaxed. Afterward, he said, "Slide over, I'm driving."

"What have I done?" Easton asked. He sat forward, his head bowed, squeezing his hands together so tight, he cut off blood to his fingers, now numb.

"Talk to me," Leroy said.

"Ruth should be planning our wedding, instead of laying in the hospital, beat up," Easton exclaimed.

"Stop blaming yourself," Leroy said. "Whoever is tormenting you and Ruth and Etsi will not stop until he gets what he wants. Pray to the god of your making. Your enemy will be revealed, and peace will come."

"Ruth's in a coma, Leroy. I don't care about peace right now. I just want her to wake up." Easton reached in his shirt pocket for a cigarette. He glared out the car window and gritted his teeth between puffs. "He may want Ruth, but he'll have to kill me first."

"Me too," Leroy said.

* * *

By the time they returned to the hospital, Ruth had been transported to the fourth floor, the unit where she worked. Naomi sat quietly listening to Dr. Zette report on Ruth's test results.

"No bones were broken in Ruth's face, and no signs of brain damage were seen on x-ray," Dr. Zette reported. "I'll check on her later."

"Thank you, Jesus," Naomi prayed, squeezing Ruth's hand.

"Did she wake up?" Easton asked, walking in the room.

"No," Naomi replied. "Do you know who did this?"

"We think so," Easton said. "I need to talk with Ira."

"Did Doc do this?" Naomi asked, nettled with anger.

"Etsi, we don't have proof he did anything," Leroy replied.

"What I saw is enough proof for me," Easton said.

"You can't use what you saw," Leroy reminded him. "We broke into his office."

Naomi cried out, "Why, Lord, why? Taylor loved him like a brother."

Leroy embraced Naomi. They both wept.

Easton kissed Ruth on the forehead and caressed her face. She didn't move. He left the room and went to the phone booth.

* * *

Ira had left the hospital, so Easton called him at home.

"He's with Hub," Ira's wife said.

Easton called the precinct, looking for Hub. "I just dropped him off at Keith's Barbershop," Hub said.

Easton called the barbershop. "Keith, put Ira on the phone."

Ira picked up the phone.

"Someone needs to search Doc's Pharmacie," Easton told Ira

"Why?" Ira asked.

"When I interviewed him for Taylor's story, I saw things that might link him to Taylor's murder and the attacks on us," Easton responded.

"Why are you telling me now? What kinds of things?" Ira asked.

Easton lied. "I don't remember."

"What do you mean, you don't remember? You're a reporter, brotha, you're supposed to remember everything you see and hear," Ira said.

"Look behind the refrigerator and the partition in his office."

"Easton, please tell me you didn't do anything to compromise the case," Ira exclaimed.

"No, not me," Easton responded.

"Make sure you don't. You need to keep it together and let Hub do the policing, before you screw up something. The department can't go in without a search warrant, but maybe Hub can convince the chief to give him one." Ira hung up.

* * *

Easton called his parents next. "Ruth's in a coma. Somebody attacked her in the hospital parking lot. She doesn't look like herself, and the doctor won't say if or when she's going to wake up." Then he shouted, "God . . . please don't take her from me!"

"Easton!" his mother yelled, trying to get his attention. "Easton, listen to me. Pray over her, pray hard, son, God will hear you."

"I'm so sorry, son," Pops said on the other end of the phone. "We'll come, if you need us."

Easton had quieted. "I'll call you." He put down the receiver and closed his eyes. The attack on Ruth, far worse than his, had plunged her into another world. He felt as if he'd lost her. He recalled their recent visit to Hains Point, how he'd held Ruth's face in his hands, telling her that she couldn't leave him, that she couldn't fly away on a jet to some faraway place. She didn't leave him by jet. It didn't matter, she'd left him anyway. He wanted her back.

When he opened his eyes, he leaned against the telephone booth, shaking his head, wondering if he'd survive his broken heart. He called Jimmy. It hadn't taken long for word to get around about the attack on William Taylor's daughter. Jimmy had already heard about it and had tried to reach Easton. He offered to send food to the hospital, and that wasn't all he offered.

"I know you don't pack, but I do," Jimmy said. "I have a piece, if you want it."

"Hold it for me." Easton thanked Jimmy.

Easton made one more call. “Odean, I need your help,” Easton said. Odean had also heard about the attack on Ruth.

“I’m already on it,” Odean said. “How is she?”

“In a coma,” Easton said.

“I’m sorry, man,” Odean said. “Keep the faith. I’ll call you when I get something.”

# Chapter 51

On December 3, two weeks before Naomi's trial and five days after Ruth's attack, she remained in a deep sleep, not even responding to the sharp needles the nurses and doctors used to prick her skin. Naomi held vigil over Ruth for twenty of the twenty-four hours each day, leaving her bedside just long enough to go home, bathe, change clothes, and tend to urgent business issues. Leroy went every evening after work, and Easton, well, Easton set up shop in a corner of Ruth's room since Aaron didn't press him to go into the office. He took his typewriter from home, worked on Taylor's story and his column, used Ruth's shower, and ate at her bedside, never too far away.

Ruth's and Naomi's friends visited often, sometimes twice in one day. When Doc Nelson showed with Dorothy, he'd stand by Ruth's bed and stare at her. He never said anything or reached out to touch her.

Naomi, however, seemed pensive, focusing solely on Ruth, not giving Doc much more than a nod. Her lawyer had convinced the judge to postpone her trial until after Christmas in light of the vicious attack on Ruth. A pattern of violence toward the Taylor women had emerged that no judge dare refute.

Reverend Ford visited almost every day, offered comfort to Naomi, and pleaded with Jesus to awaken Ruth. And she did on December 6, 1956, when they were all deep in prayer, surrounding her bed.

"Mom," Ruth murmured, "Easton."

Reverend Ford stopped praying. Everyone opened their eyes at the faint sound of Ruth's voice. She peered through her swollen eyes as she slowly moved her head around.

Leroy ran from the room.

"Praise the Lord!" the reverend shouted.

"Thank you, Jesus," Naomi hollered. She fell to her knees, grabbed Ruth's hand, rested her head on Ruth's bed, and flooded the sheet with her tears.

Easton gripped Ruth's other hand, tears streaming down his face. At that moment, he owned no pride.

"Easton," Ruth whispered again.

Easton leaned close to hear her.

"He wants to . . . rape me."

"Over my dead body," Easton remarked.

Leroy returned with a nurse.

"Welcome back, Ruth. Dr. Zette's on his way," the nurse said. "I need to take your vital signs."

Easton and Naomi reluctantly stepped away to let the nurse check Ruth. When Dr. Zette arrived, he asked everyone to leave, except Naomi and the nurse. After he examined Ruth, he smiled. "Everything is working fine, except your right eye. I'll ask an ophthalmologist to look at it. You're still on bed rest. We'll start you off with ice chips to see how you tolerate . . ." Dr. Zette stopped talking in the middle of his sentence and smiled. "Am I preaching to the choir?" He turned to Naomi. "Is that how you say it?"

"No, Doctor, you're not preaching to the choir, and yes, you said it right. Ruth needs to hear this from you, so keep talking," Naomi said.

Dr. Zette completed his plan of care for Ruth and left.

Once Ruth's colleagues learned she'd aroused from her coma, it seemed as if every nurse in the hospital dropped by, four or five at a time. The room became so crowded at one point, the head nurse told everybody to get out, including Easton. Naomi didn't budge, and the head nurse didn't make her.

* * *

After Ruth's attack, the chief of police had expressed doubts about Naomi's guilt. He rehired Ira, though he didn't apologize for firing him in the first place. Easton called Ira.

"She's awake."

Ira rushed to the hospital. Ruth gave a very vague description of the man who attacked her. Mumbling, she described him, "Skinny . . . tall . . . brown skinned . . . black jacket . . . baseball cap covered his eyes." She started coughing.

"Okay, enough for now," Easton said.

"Ruth, you did good," Ira said, smiling. "I'll come back in a couple of days, and we'll talk again, when you feel better." He shook Easton's hand and left.

* * *

The puffiness in Ruth's face subsided a little each day. She managed to open her left eye, once swollen shut, and was able to chew solid food without a lot of pain. She begged Dr. Zette to let her go home.

"Ruth, you're not out of the woods yet, you know that," Dr. Zette said.

"Mom and Easton will take care of me and Caroline too," Ruth pleaded.

* * *

On the fourteenth day of her hospitalization, Wednesday, December 12, Dr. Zette discharged Ruth to home. "Don't overdue it. I want to see you in my office next week."

"Thank you, Dr. Zette," Ruth said.

Naomi hugged the doctor. "Thank you for taking such good care of my baby."

"You're welcome." Dr. Zette squeezed Ruth's hand and hurried out the room.

"I'm taking you home right now." Easton kissed Ruth on the lips. "I missed you, baby. I almost lost my mind."

Ruth's laugh was muffled, her slightly swollen face still making it difficult to talk, let alone laugh. "I would have married you anyway."

A nurse went into the room with a wheelchair. "Ruth, you have prescriptions to be filled, an antibiotic and pain pill. Are you allergic to any medications?"

Ruth smiled and replied, "No."

"I have to ask," the nurse said.

"I know," Ruth replied. She handed Naomi the prescriptions. "The pharmacy downstairs. We'll wait in the lobby."

Naomi left for the pharmacy.

Easton picked up Ruth, sat her in the wheelchair, and rolled her to the nurse's station to say good-bye to her colleagues, who smothered her with tears, hugs, and kisses for what seemed like eternity—fifteen minutes. Afterward, they headed for the elevator, smiling, a far cry from the days leading up to this one.

* * *

When they arrived at the funeral home, Easton helped Ruth into bed and stayed with her until she fell asleep. He started down the stairs. Naomi stood at the bottom.

"I love my baby more than my own life. Please help us," Naomi said to Easton, as he went down the steps. She ran into the parlor and unleashed a mournful sound unlike any he'd ever heard. Easton hurried to Naomi and embraced her.

"I love Ruth too, and I promise, we'll find the scum who hurt her," Easton said.

"Taylor is gone, and you and Leroy are the only people I trust right now," Naomi said, weeping. "Ruth's first-aid kit is empty. Here's a list of things we need." Naomi handed Easton the list.

"I'll go now while Ruth is asleep," Easton said. "Call Leroy and let him know you're home. Lock the door behind me."

Before he went to the Pharmacie, he stopped at home. He'd run out of clean clothes and needed to pick up a few things. While there, he called his parents with the good news. "Ruth's home."

"Thank the Lord," his mother said.

"You need to protect her and Naomi," Pops said. "As long as Taylor's killer is still out there, they're not safe and neither are you."

As far back as Easton remembered, Pops had always kept a rifle by his armchair. Easton had always felt safe knowing Pops would protect him. He wondered if that's what Pops meant, for him to arm himself. Seeing as how he was about to face Doc Nelson, he thought it better not to have a loaded pistol on him. He might be inclined to pull the trigger. To date, no one had been able to disprove Doc's involvement in Taylor's murder.

* * *

The intern who'd worked the day Easton interviewed Doc stood behind the Pharmacie counter. He sized him up. For a man his height and size, around five-feet-ten and chunky, he'd never fit into the clothes and boots Easton found behind the partition. Easton had never met anyone that tall with small feet.

"Is Doc Nelson in?" Easton asked.

"Yes." The young man glimpsed at the phone lines. "He's on a call, if you want to wait."

"I'll wait." Easton killed time by taking pictures inside and outside the drugstore.

Leslie Ann Penny went out of the beauty salon next door, her hair full of waves. "Why, what a surprise. You taking pictures for your scrapbook?" she asked Easton.

"No," Easton responded. "They're for a story about William Taylor. How are you?"

She smirked. "I'm fine, thank you. I hear trouble is following you around town, and you didn't tell me you were engaged to Ruth Johnson. She's one of my best customers."

"At the time you and I talked, we weren't engaged," Easton said, perusing her uniform. "You're in the army?"

"Yes, my third year," she answered, smiling.

"How did you hear about the attack on Ruth?" Easton asked.

"Attack on Ruth?"

"Yes, at the hospital, two weeks ago," Easton replied.

"When I mentioned trouble following you, I meant the attack on you. I didn't know about Ruth's attack," Leslie said. "How is she?"

"Beat up."

"Who did it?"

"Don't know yet," Easton replied. "The SOB is still cowering somewhere."

"I'm so sorry to hear this," Leslie said. "Please give Ruth my regards. I have to go. Good luck to you both."

Easton watched Leslie drive off in a black 1956 Chevy. ***Driving a new car, the army must be awfully good to her,*** he thought. He started back inside the store. Doc Nelson had surfaced from the back room and greeted Easton with a handshake.

"Easton . . . how's Ruth?" Doc asked.

"After being pistol-whipped into a coma, I'd say she's doing well. She's home," Easton said, stepping back into the store.

Doc Nelson planted his hands on the counter. He bowed his head. "Thank you, Lord," he said, shaking his head.

"Ruth used all her first-aid supplies on me," Easton said. "We need to restock them." He handed him the list. Doc Nelson's right hand jerked like it did when Easton interviewed him. As much as he wanted to, Easton restrained himself from knocking his ass through the window. He waited while Doc and his intern gathered the items on the list. When they finished, Doc refused to accept payment from Easton, sending him off with two of everything for the kit.

"I'm calling Naomi right now. I need to help more," he said, slumbering back toward his office.

"You need to be in jail," Easton said, under his breath.

Doc didn't hear him. The intern did. He looked at Easton and didn't say a word.

* * *

"Doc's Pharmacie?" Naomi asked Easton, reading the store's name on the bag of supplies.

"Yes, ma'am," Easton replied.

"He called, asking about Ruth," Naomi said.

"I know." Easton skipped steps up to Ruth's room. He sat on the bed, caressing her hand, the way she had his, and watched her take in air and slowly let it out through pursed lips. He touched her swollen face and leaned closer to kiss her lips. She stirred yet stayed asleep. Up until now, he never believed he'd want to kill somebody, on the contrary, what happened to Ruth had him straddling that fine line between good and evil, and most days the devil himself reigned, trampling through his soul, causing pain so deep inside, he didn't believe he'd survive another minute. He'd never prayed as hard as he had since Ruth's attack, the only thing that kept him going. He went downstairs to find Naomi.

* * *

"Sit, you need to eat," Naomi said. "My neighbor brought over a whole ham, macaroni and cheese, greens, and your favorite—chocolate cake. You know Ruth and I can't eat all this food before it goes bad."

Easton hadn't eaten all morning. At the sight and smell of the fare spread across the table, he began to drool. "No need to worry. Between me and Leroy, it won't be around long enough to go bad."

"I forgot about Leroy," Naomi said. "I guess he'll be by later."

"I talked to him this morning. He's coming after work," Easton said. "I'm going in the office when I finish here. I need to check in with Aaron. Will you be okay until then?"

"I'll be fine," Naomi replied. "I have plenty to keep me busy."

Easton devoured his meal and got up to leave. "Thanks, Mrs. Taylor. That hit the spot." He kissed Naomi on the cheek and started out the kitchen. He turned, and before he opened his mouth to speak . . .

"I know, I know . . . Lock the door behind you," Naomi said. She followed Easton to the front door and saw him out.

* * *

As Easton hoped, Aaron hadn't gone in the office yet. It gave him a moment to rest his mind. He tried to remember the last time he'd slept all night. Since the attack on Ruth, he'd wake up two or three times during the night, the sight of her marred face imprinted in his mind. He slumped over on his desk and shut his eyes.

"Easton, man . . . you all right?" Lloyd asked, tapping Easton on his arm.

Easton raised his head. "He beat her, he threatened to come back and rape her. If I get to him before the police, it's over for him."

"Mr. and Mrs. Taylor, you and Ruth. If you ask me, I'd say it's a family thing, except ***you*** aren't family . . . yet," Lloyd said. "How do you explain that?"

"If I could explain it, I'd know who killed Taylor, who threatened Naomi, and who roughed up me and Ruth," Easton replied. "He'd be in jail or cremated by now."

"Don't do anything crazy, man. We need you here," Lloyd said.

"Like you said, it's a family thing, and families take care of each other." Easton reared back in his chair and lit a cigarette. Lloyd rolled back to his desk.

Easton thought about the clothes, boots, and knife in Doc's office. He wondered if they were still there, if the intern knew about them, or better yet, whom they belonged to. Breaking and entering, as it were, would get him a year or two behind bars, maybe more since he was a colored man. He took a long drag off his cigarette. He'd take his chances and tell Ira he might have something to help with the case, and hope he would not throw him jail when he told him what he saw.

"What knife, clothes, and boots?" Ira asked.

"In Doc's office," Easton replied. "His intern may know who they belong to."

"When were you in his office?" Ira asked.

"Remember, I interviewed him for Taylor's story," Easton replied. Easton didn't lie, though he didn't tell Ira the whole truth either.

"Okay, I'll question the young man. It'll give me a chance to look around the place. What days does Doc work at Saint Elizabeth's?" Ira asked.

"I don't know, but the intern knows," Easton replied.

"Calling the intern may raise suspicion. I'll call Saint Elizabeth's," Ira said. "They answer calls all day about doctors' schedules. They won't care why I'm asking and won't be suspicious."

Easton hung up the phone and sighed. ***That didn't go bad at all.*** He felt positive the suspicious items sealed Doc Nelson's involvement in Taylor's murder and maybe the attack on him, Ruth, and Naomi. The more he thought about it, the angrier he got. He called Doc's Pharmacie. Doc had gone to Saint Elizabeth's for the rest of the day. He'd return to the Pharmacie tomorrow. He called Ira with Doc's schedule.

"Easton, I told you not to call the intern," Ira screeched. "Are you losing your mind?"

"I'm trying to help you, Ira," Easton exclaimed. "I don't want anyone else sliced up, beat to death, or threatened again. A maniac is on the loose, and we have to find him."

"Easton, listen to me. I know you want to help, but I don't need your help right now. Let me do my job," Ira said. "Please back off."

"Okay, Ira, have it your way," Easton said, and slammed down the receiver. "Lloyd, the column, let's finish it."

Over the next two hours, Easton and Lloyd wrote the lead for his weekly column, "The Taylor Chronicles: The Ghost of Death and Despair.

"Not bad, not bad," Lloyd said when they finished.

"Why, because you wrote most of it?" Easton asked.

"You my teacher, sir," Lloyd teased.

Easton laughed. "If I don't review these manuscripts, Aaron's going to have my hide. I won't be teaching anybody, anything."

After Easton edited the manuscripts Aaron had left for him, he hurried to his car, jumped inside, and jerked the door shut. He revved the engine and took off. His mind, never free of Ruth's marred face, had catapulted into images of Doc Nelson's unscathed face, smiling and joking with his customers. No matter what happens, he'd tell Doc what he thought of him—a low-life, murdering piece of scum. It didn't matter that no tangible proof of Doc's guilt existed. He'd somehow force him to admit his role in the Taylors' misfortunes and the attack on him, and afterward, he'd call Ira to arrest him. Too bad for Doc, Easton had no one else to unleash his pain onto.

* * *

The December temperatures hovered in the low fifties, with bright sunshine most days and crisp, cool nights. If it weren't for the Christmas displays in the windows of the major department stores and the Salvation Army bell ringers on the corners downtown, Easton would never know Christmas was right around the corner. He drove down Seventh Street, glancing at the window displays, thankful that he would spend the holidays with Ruth at her house instead of in a hospital room.

By the time he reached Asylum Road, dusk had set in. He slowed while negotiating the sharp curves in the road leading to Saint Elizabeth's main building, which housed the pharmacy. He saw Doc Nelson's Desota parked in a space reserved for doctors. He glanced at his watch, five thirty. According to the hospital switchboard, the pharmacy closed at five-thirty. Easton waited in his car. At seven o'clock, Doc had not appeared. Easton left his car and walked to a pay phone near the front entrance. He rang Ira. "While Ruth was in a coma, I lost my focus for minute and—"

"A minute!" Ira interrupted. "More than that, brotha." They both chuckled.

"I'm at Saint Elizabeth's, waiting for Doc," Easton said.

"What are you talking about?" Ira yelled. "Get out of there, now!"

"Listen, Ira, I gotta motive for all this shit," Easton said.

"No, you listen to me," Ira said. "You're out-of-bounds, Easton. Go home to Ruth and let me handle this. Did you hear me? Go . . . home . . . now!"

"Please, Ira, just hear me out and I'll go home," Easton pleaded with him.

"Okay, okay . . . I'm listening."

"Taylor's funeral home," Easton said.

"What about it?" Ira asked.

"It's a valuable piece of property, a successful business. Naomi, Thomas, and Ruth are his heirs, and I'd bet money Naomi won't sell the place even if she gives up the business. The killer wants Naomi and Ruth permanently out of the way. No telling what's planned for Thomas. He may be in the crosshairs too, for all we know."

"So . . . why attack you?" Ira asked. "You aren't a family member."

"Lloyd said the same thing," Easton replied. "It's simple, the killer doesn't want me to marry Ruth and become a family member."

"Easton, you're stretching things a bit," Ira said. "Who's the suspect? Where's the evidence?"

Easton grew silent. "I'll have it soon."

"Easton, I'm not going to tell you again, go home," Ira said.

"I can't." Easton hung up. He strolled back to his car and lit a cigarette. "Tutti Frutti," one of his favorite songs, played on the radio. He sang to the top of his lungs along with Little Richard. He bounced in his seat and tapped his fingers on the steering wheel, and when the song ended, he leaned back, laughing. He had immersed himself into the liveliness and cheerful tempo of the music, and slowly the shackles of anger and hate had loosened. He felt free for a moment then news on the radio announced another lynching down South. It quickly brought him back to reality.

Easton stared at the building like he was daring Doc to come out. ***I ain't leaving till I'm done with you, nigga,*** he said to himself. He watched people come and go in wheelchairs, on stretchers, and babies in the arms of adults. They were not close enough for him to see their pain, fear, sadness, or joy, yet he remembered experiencing all of these feelings after his attack, and again after Ruth was bludgeoned.

By seven thirty, Doc Nelson still hadn't emerged, and Easton had not checked in on Ruth. He left the car again, this time to call her; that's when he noticed the black Chevy straddling a parking space near the building. He hadn't seen it before because other cars had surrounded it. Doc Nelson climbed out of the car from the driver's seat.

"Easton Priest, I thought I saw you over there on the telephone. What brings you to the hospital?" Doc asked.

Easton looked back toward Doc's Desota and then to the Chevy. ***How did I miss him?*** he asked himself. "I'm investigating a murder?"

"A murder . . . whose murder?" Doc asked.

"Your best friend, or did you forget?" Easton asked him.

Doc turned toward the Chevy and straightened the brim of his hat. When he turned to face Easton, he had a big smile on his face. "Well, the investigation is over for you, Easton Priest."

Leslie Ann Penny and Rutherford Daniels jumped from the backseat of the Chevy.

Easton stepped back and stared wide-eyed at the three. He shoved his left hand in his jacket pocket. Empty. He glanced toward his car. He'd left the pistol Jimmy gave him on the front seat. Leslie moved toward Easton and pulled a knife from the pocket of her black jacket. She held it at her side. "The truth is, Easton, you're in my way," Leslie said.

"What? What is this?" Easton yelled. He stared at the knife and back at her. "You killed Taylor." He took another step backward.

She nodded.

"Doc, did you help her?" Easton asked, glaring at Doc Nelson.

Doc looked away.

"Why?" Easton asked him.

"You wouldn't understand," Doc replied.

"Try me," Easton said.

"Too late," Daniels said. "We're through talking."

"Don't worry, Easton. I'll take care of Ruth for you." Leslie leered at Easton like a tiger ready to leap on its prey.

He stepped sideways toward the building, not knowing where else to give ground. Even though he towered over Leslie, she had the knife, a mercenary's knife, like the one taped behind the refrigerator in Doc's office, and she was a soldier, trained to confront any man or woman. She also had Daniels and Doc standing by her.

"You stabbed me too, didn't you? You dress up well as a man. Yeah . . . now I see . . . ***you*** planned to rape Ruth. You go both ways?"

Doc grabbed Easton's injured arm and jerked it behind his back. Easton slid to the ground, yelling in pain, trying to ply Doc's hand loose. The harder he tried, the tighter Doc twisted his arm. Sweat poured from his face, and his whole body trembled. He raised his head; his vision blurred. Leslie knelt beside him. As she raised the knife to stab him, he closed his eyes and whispered, "God help me."

Sirens from three police cars came out of nowhere, their bright lights illuminating the three men and Leslie. Ira jumped from one of the moving cars and pointed his gun at Leslie's head.

"Drop it," Ira demanded.

She hesitated.

"Drop the knife . . . now!" Ira pressed the revolver hard into her cheek.

Leslie grimaced and dropped the knife.

"I guess you didn't want to die tonight, after all, though I would have been glad to oblige you. On the ground," Ira said, shoving her to the pavement. He kicked the knife away and cuffed her.

Daniels had tried to run, still he was no match for the young cop who tackled him to the ground. Doc Nelson had dropped to his knees, his hands up without any prompting. He sighed, as if relieved it was all over.

"You're all under arrest for attempted kidnapping and murder," Ira said to the three.

Ira helped Doc up. "What the hell happened to you, Dr. Nelson?"

Doc gritted his teeth, refusing to answer Ira. He was thrown in a paddy wagon with the others and taken to the Second precinct.

* * *

Easton drove to the precinct, the pain in his battered arm almost unbearable. Ira rode with him and sensed Easton's discomfort.

"Since you didn't want a doctor at Saint Elizabeth's to look at your arm, stop at Freedman's and have them call your doctor," Ira said. "We have plenty of time. The posse's not going anywhere."

"I have pain medicine at home," Easton replied. "I'll be fine."

"Suit yourself," Ira said.

"That's the second time in two months my life flashed by me," Easton said.

"When you told me you were at Saint Elizabeth's, I figured I'd better get over here. I didn't expect to see Daniels and Leslie with Doc," Ira said.

"You know her?" Easton asked.

"She goes to my church. I swear, you think you know people, and then something like this happens," Ira said.

"Leslie killed Taylor," Easton said.

"We'll find out soon enough," Ira responded.

"I didn't see it," Easton said.

"Me neither," Ira said.

Easton reached into his glove compartment. He handed Ira a white envelope. "Put this on the cops' desk that knocked me out. Don't let anyone see you do it."

"What's in here?" Ira asked.

"It's best you don't know," Easton said.

* * *

By the time Easton left the police station at midnight, Doc Nelson and Daniels had fingered Leslie Penny for Taylor's murder, although they didn't say why she killed him, at least not while Easton was there.

Leslie had refused to talk. Not surprising, there was nothing mild mannered about her. She'd trained well in the army, like a man; her assault tactics were so skillful she'd stabbed Taylor to death and almost crushed Easton's chest with force from the heavy combat boots she wore.

When Easton reached home, he took two pain pills, a hot shower, and crawled into bed. He felt the sheet quiver from his battered arm trembling under it. Even the pillow he propped it on moved to the rhythm of his pain. He dare not move. He saw himself on the ground, Doc Nelson twisting his arm so tight, he'd forgotten to breathe. He still heard the sirens blaring, growing louder, coming closer, and Ira's voice next to him. His eyes burned. He squeezed them shut, trying to hold back the tears. It didn't help. They rolled down the side of his face. His mouth trembled like his arm. He opened his eyes and faced the open blinds, the moon faded in and out of the clouds, the rain came, rolling down the windowpane. Then sleep.

# Chapter 52

Later that morning, Easton woke in a cold sweat. His arm had swelled and the throbbing pain more intense. He flinched when he touched it. He swallowed two more pain pills, hobbled to the bathroom, and drenched his sore arm with hot water from the shower, hoping for some relief. It didn't help. While it usually took him thirty minutes to dress, an hour went by and he still hadn't tied his shoes. He couldn't. He changed to his loafers.

Easton barely made the drive to Ruth's house; dizzy with pain, he thought he'd pass out any moment. He rolled to the curb in front of the funeral home and parked, so grateful he didn't have to go into reverse or squeeze into a space. He sat for a few minutes, trying to regain his composure before seeing Ruth. She hadn't completely recovered herself, and he didn't want to add to her woes. When he finally went inside, he broke the news about the arrests.

Naomi looked up toward the ceiling and raised her hands in the air. "Another blessing!"

Ruth hugged Easton. He grabbed his arm and screamed. She reared back. "Easton, what's wrong?"

Easton barely spoke. "Doc twisted my arm . . . it's killing me."

Ruth rolled up his shirtsleeve. "Oh god . . . no!"

Easton's arm, red, hot, and tender, had blown up like a balloon. He had an open wound the size of a fifty-cent piece at the bend in his elbow.

"This just happened!" Easton said, surprised to see the wound. "I swear, it wasn't there this morning."

Ruth rushed to the parlor for a thermometer and took his temperature—104 degrees Fahrenheit. She covered the wound with gauze, ran to the phone, and called the hospital. Dr. Zette answered his page in no time. Ruth described the condition of Easton's arm, and he directed her to take him in right away.

"We'll take a cab," Ruth said.

"No, I'll drive," Naomi said. It had been years since she sat behind a wheel. She didn't like driving. She'd walk, take the bus, or have someone drive her where she needed to go. She'd almost lost Ruth. She'd do anything for her now.

* * *

Dr. Zette had reserved a bed for Easton on the fourth floor. Within the hour, he'd drained almost a cup of pus from his arm. He cleaned and dressed the wound, still weeping the yellow fluid. Afterward, Easton received massive doses of penicillin that dripped from intravenous tubing through a needle into his good arm. Ruth insisted on staying with him overnight, although she still required care herself.

Early the next morning, Dr. Zette drained more of the foul fluid from Easton's arm. He also examined Ruth's face and her eye. "It looks good. Keep putting ice on it. I'll be back this afternoon."

Naomi brought lunch for Ruth and Easton and stayed around for a while.

Around one thirty that afternoon, Dr. Zette returned with Easton's chart in hand. "Your temperature is normal, and I see your pain has eased. How do you feel?" Dr. Zette asked.

"Much better," Easton replied. "For a minute, I thought I was dying."

"You were in serious condition," Dr. Zette informed him. "I'm going to order another blood test to make sure the infection is subsiding. If it's normal, you can go home today."

Easton smiled. "Thank you, Doctor."

"If that's the case, I won't leave now. I'll wait for the test results," Naomi said. "If you need me, I'll be in the chapel, praying. Leroy will be here soon."

Easton and Ruth dozed off, exhausted from lack of sleep. Nurses had rushed past one another in the night, like a revolving door, monitoring Easton's temperature, drawing blood, and hanging bags filled with penicillin.

Two hours later, Dr. Zette returned to Easton's room. "Mr. Priest, you can go home if you have someone to change your dressing."

Easton smiled at Ruth.

"I can change it," Ruth said.

"How can you take care of yourself and him too?" Dr. Zette asked. "Your vision is still poor."

"Dr. Zette, I can change a dressing with my eyes closed," Ruth exclaimed. "My mother will help me too."

"Very well, I will discharge Mr. Priest into your care."

Soon after, a nurse went and removed the tubing and needle from Easton's arm and handed Ruth prescriptions the doctor had left for him. Ruth took the prescriptions to the pharmacy. A candy striper went in with a wheelchair.

Naomi walked in Easton's room with Leroy. They'd run into each other in the lobby. "We must be going home," Naomi said at the sight of the wheelchair.

"Yes, we are," Easton said, "as soon as Ruth comes back with my prescriptions."

Leroy helped Easton into the wheelchair. When Ruth returned, they all left for the funeral home.

* * *

Easton made his way to Thomas's old room again. He insisted on going in it alone. Leroy followed him upstairs anyway. Ruth sat in the kitchen with her mother.

"Taylor's killer is behind bars," Naomi said. "We don't have to be afraid anymore."

Ruth said nothing, then she said, "Easton will lose his arm, if it doesn't heal."

"Stop worrying and pray," Naomi said.

Leroy went in the kitchen. "He wants a glass of cold water."

Ruth filled a pitcher with ice water and carried it on a tray with two glasses. Easton drank half the pitcher before he dozed off. Ruth sat in a chair by his bed and slept too.

* * *

Two hours later, Thelma Junior walked in the room and roused the two from sleep. "I hear you and Ruth are taking turns at this."

"Thelma!" Easton said, surprised.

"Pops called and told me about Ruth. Leroy didn't tell me about you until I got here. I would have come sooner. Trying to close up shop took me longer than I thought. I expected to see Ruth laying in bed, recuperating, not you," Thelma said.

Easton managed a weak smile. He saw Leroy and Naomi standing in the doorway. For a brief moment in time, it seemed they'd all been held hostage by Taylor's killer, even Leroy, whose kindred spirit suffered along with them. Easton closed his eyes and quietly prayed for healing.

# Chapter 53

Doc Nelson wanted to spare his wife the humiliation of a trial and confessed to selling drugs, walking in on Leslie when she stabbed Taylor to death, and plotting to kill Easton. He claimed he didn't know about her plan to kill Naomi and Ruth once she disposed of Easton. He described all the sordid details. Dorothy, his lawyer, and Ira were present in the room. Easton watched through a one-way mirror. Naomi chose to stay away this time.

Doc clenched his hands together. As he spoke, he looked away from Dorothy. "Daniels and I had sex with Leslie on several occasions. Afterward, she extorted money from us, threatening to tell our wives if we didn't give her what she wanted."

Dorothy gasped.

Doc continued. "She said Taylor wouldn't sleep with her, that she'd never measure up to Naomi. She insisted on seducing him anyway. After Taylor's party, I took Dorothy home and drove back to Sixth Street to meet Leslie. I told Dorothy that I'd forgotten my wallet. Leslie arrived at Taylor's before I did. She claimed she saw him close the blinds and wanted to go inside. The plan was to get him outside to persuade him to have sex with her. I told her to go to hell. She threatened to call Dorothy if I didn't help her get inside." Doc lifted a handkerchief from his pocket and wiped his brow. "Taylor had given me a key to the front door, in case of emergencies. I let her in. We heard noise coming from the kitchen, and before I knew it, she'd run to the kitchen. I waited in the hallway. When I heard glass breaking, I ran to the kitchen. Leslie was standing in front of Taylor, laughing. I didn't hear him say anything. She called him an asshole and pushed him against the wall. That's when I saw the blood dripping from the knife in her hand. I tried to grab the knife from her. She was too quick. She jabbed me in the groin with her knee. It hurt so bad, I fell to my knees. When I looked up . . . she'd already cut Taylor's throat." The room grew silent except for Doc weeping.

"What happened next?" Ira asked.

"I got the hell out of there."

"Why didn't you call an ambulance for Taylor? Did you want him to die?" Ira asked.

Doc was still weeping. "No, no . . . I was in shock."

"Dr. Nelson, you left your best friend for dead," Ira said. "You're a doctor . . . why did you leave him to die?"

"My head was messed up. I'd been under a lot of pressure, afraid I'd lose everything I owned from poor investments I'd made. I got sucked into selling drugs, trying to pay off my debts, then got tangled up with Leslie. When she killed Taylor, I believed her when she said she'd kill Dorothy." He looked at his wife, tears pouring down her face, her whole body shaking. "I'm sorry, Dorothy."

"Why did Leslie go after Easton and the Taylor women?" Ira asked.

"She wanted Taylor's funeral home. She thought it would be easier to get to Ruth and Naomi if she got rid of Easton."

"Who beat up Ruth?" Ira asked.

"Quentin, Leslie's boyfriend."

"Damn, a family affair," Ira said. "What about Israel Bailey?"

"He supplied Daniels with heroin. Daniels didn't want to take a chance buying it off the street in DC," Doc replied. "He thought he might get caught."

"Why did you send Thomas away?"

"So Leslie wouldn't kill him," Doc said, glancing at Dorothy. "I love Thomas like my own son."

"You don't give dope to people you love," Ira said.

Dorothy's face went blank. She looked at Doc and said, "Saint Elizabeth's said Thomas had drugs in his blood after Taylor died. I know you didn't give him those drugs. Tell me I'm right."

Doc covered his face with both hands. "I'm sorry."

* * *

Ira would later say to Easton, "I don't know if Doc is a prick or a damn fool. I would've taken my chances with Dorothy finding out about an affair and kicking my ass out the house, rather than being bullied by that broad."

"Except she threatened to kill Dorothy," Easton said.

"An empty threat, if Doc had come to me," Ira said.

Ira was right. Taylor would be alive today if Doc hadn't been so weak-minded, so stupid.

With Doc Nelson's confession, Naomi's lawyer moved quickly to get the murder charges against her dropped.

* * *

During Doc Nelson's arraignment later that morning, the judge denied him bail. He denied bail for Daniels and Leslie too. Like Doc, Daniels had rolled over on Leslie. It didn't help him. The prosecuting attorney accused him of corporate fraud, drug trafficking, and conspiracy to kidnap and murder Easton. Easton predicted he might get out of jail in time to enjoy his great-grandchildren.

Easton learned that being tried in a US District Court and the army's criminal court for conduct of unbecoming an officer, was a double whammy for Leslie. It didn't matter that killing Taylor was a civilian offense; she'd be court-martialed too. The US Army had worked with DC District Court to arrange for Leslie to be tried in District Court.

# Chapter 54

It's nothing no worse than going through the Christmas holidays with grief and sorrow hanging over you like a sprig of mistletoe, except it wasn't a reason to kiss anybody. The good news, the judge dropped the murder charge against Naomi, so the Taylor and Priest families made the best of it and spent Christmas together in DC. They wore themselves out shopping, taking in a few clubs, visiting friends, and trying not to dwell on all the suffering they had endured.

Easton and his family attended Christmas Eve services at the House of Worship with Naomi and Ruth. On Christmas Day, Naomi cooked dinner, and on New Year's Eve, they all went to church for watch night services to thank God for helping them through all the turmoil. Dorothy joined them. It had been a sad time, yet they found solace in knowing that the gospel promised joy and salvation with the coming of Christ, a reason to celebrate, at least until January 15, 1957. On that day, Doc Nelson stood before the judge for sentencing, and Leslie Ann Penny was tried for Taylor's murder.

Doc's attorney had asked for leniency, since he tried to intervene in Taylor's murder. The judge didn't buy it. Naomi, Yancey, and Mildred sat with Dorothy on the edge of their seats. Easton, Ruth, Leroy, Thelma Junior, Thomas, and his mother sat behind them.

"You have disappointed me and this court, Dr. Nelson. You were given a gift of an education that many won't ever attain. You were a role model for the young people in the community, and you let them down. You sold drugs to children and across state lines, you conspired to kidnap and murder Easton Priest, and you opened the door to your best friend's house to allow your mistress to kill him. What do you have to say for yourself?" the judge asked.

"I'm sorry for all the hurt and pain I've caused my wife and friends. I let things get out of control. I deserve whatever comes to me," Doc Nelson said, lowering his head.

Not moved by his remorse, the judge sentenced Doc Nelson to fifteen years in the penitentiary. Dorothy slid out of her seat, wailing. Yancey and Naomi pulled her up.

Doc yelled to Naomi to see after Dorothy, as guards led him out the door he went through.

Thomas shouted to him, "Why? Why? Why'd you do it? He loved you, I loved you."

The door closed behind Doc Nelson.

* * *

Thomas had returned to DC from South Carolina after learning of his godfather's arrest. He had cried on the phone when his mother told him why his father had to die. He'd been torn up inside all the while believing he caused his daddy's death. He'd fallen to his knees, thanking Jesus, over and over again that his drug use had not lead to his father's murder.

The moment he reached the city, he'd hailed a cab to Sixth Street. He hadn't talked much to Naomi since his father's murder. Had he known the real reason for his death, he'd gone home sooner. He told her about his drug addiction, how he'd tried to quit, and how Doc kept supplying him with drugs. Some days he'd stagger about the city in a daze, not sure of his surroundings, bedding down in strange places, and with strange people, and he always managed to quit jobs before he got fired. Taylor suspected drug use and beat the truth out of him.

"Daddy went head-on with Uncle Nelson," he'd told Naomi. "I never for one second believed he would hurt Daddy or let anyone else hurt him."

"I wish Taylor had told me about your problem. I might have been able to help you and him," Naomi had said. "We may well have helped each other."

* * *

The clerk of the court directed Naomi to the courtroom where Leslie's trial was about to start, a different judge presiding. "It'll all be over soon," Naomi said to her family and friends. "Dorothy, are you sure you're up to this?"

"I want to see that heifer in chains," Dorothy said, weeping. She blamed Leslie for Doc's demise.

Naomi, Ruth, and Easton went to meet with Naomi's lawyer. The others passed the time in the cafeteria. Twenty minutes before the trial, they all joined other spectators in the courtroom. Ira was already there. Leslie wore an orange jumpsuit just like Doc's, no makeup. Her hair braided in cornrows, she appeared younger than her thirty years. She smiled at Naomi and Dorothy.

"Murderer!" Naomi hollered.

"Bitch," Dorothy yelled out.

"Order in the court!" shouted the judge, the pounding of his gavel vibrating through the room. "Anymore outbursts and I'll throw all of you out of my courtroom."

Ruth grasped Naomi's arm. She whispered to her to calm down.

The judge read the charges against Corporal Leslie Ann Penny. Afterward, the prosecutor presented his case against her. His first witness, Dr. A. C. Nelson. Dorothy smiled at the sight of him.

After Doc Nelson's testimony, Leslie's lawyer pounded him with questions about their relationship, accusing Doc of rape and abuse. He denied any such thing and gave names of other married men she had blackmailed after sleeping with them.

Daniels also took the stand, telling the court how Leslie had bragged about killing Taylor in a plot to take over his funeral business and how she'd sliced up Easton Priest. "'His wife and daughter are next,' she'd said. She'd get her boyfriend to take care of them."

The defense portrayed her as a patriot, a soldier in the army who loved her country, who'd become a victim of abuse. Her commanding officer took the stand and spoke of her exemplary record since enlisting three years ago. Several of her army buddies said the same. Even her minister spoke well of her.

"I guess they forgot we caught her with a blade ready to cut your ass up," Ira said to Easton.

"Don't remind me," Easton said.

After cross-examination, Naomi's lawyers rested their case. They hoped the jury would see through the façade and find her guilty. They deliberated for three hours and went back with a verdict—guilty of all charges. The guards carted Leslie off to jail. Naomi and Dorothy cried in each other's arms, their friends and family looking on.

* * *

A month later, February 15, 1957, they were in the courtroom again for Leslie's sentencing.

"Corporal Leslie Ann Penny, do you have anything you'd like to say to the court before your sentencing?" the judge asked.

"Your Honor, Mr. Daniels and doctor Nelson took advantage of me. They raped me and forced me to kill William Taylor. I didn't want to. I'm innocent."

"Corporal Penny, the jury of your peers didn't think so. It's obvious you don't want to take responsibility for murdering William Taylor, planning the attacks on his wife and daughter, attempting to murder Easton Priest, and extorting money from your lovers. Nor have you shown any remorse for the pain you've caused these families," the judge said. "I'm sentencing you to life in prison without parole."

The room erupted in cheers. People stood and clapped, as the woman who'd killed a favorite son, terrorized his family, blackmailed her lovers, and eluded police smirked as the guards hustled her out of the room.

* * *

Before leaving District Court, Dorothy had to meet with Doc's lawyer. "It won't take long to hand him a check," she said.

Easton and Ruth waited with Naomi in the foyer near the exit. Twenty minutes later, Leslie Ann Penny shuffled down the corridor, cuffed and flanked by guards. Dorothy came from around a corner, advancing in a path toward her.

"Lord, I hope Dorothy doesn't have a gun in her purse," Naomi said.

Easton and Ruth turned toward Dorothy. They watched Dorothy walk like a woman on a mission, steadfast and determined. As Dorothy and Leslie got closer to each other, Naomi, fearing the worse, raced to embrace Dorothy, holding her until Leslie passed by.

Dorothy screamed at Leslie, calling her every name in the book. Leslie laughed at Dorothy, firing her up even more. Dorothy tried to wrestle from Naomi's grip. Easton helped hold her. Enraged and sobbing, she fell limp in their grip.

"Doc's coming out soon," Dorothy whimpered. "They're taking him to Lorton. I want to see him again."

No sooner had the words left her mouth than Doc appeared in the corridor, towering over the guards in front and behind him, his hands and ankles shackled together with a chain. Dorothy bawled like a child who'd lost her favorite toy, as she watched Doc walk out of her life.

"I love you," Doc said to Dorothy as he toddled past her.

Dorothy followed him outside, Naomi next to her.

Doc Nelson descended the stairs toward a crowd on the sidewalk, shouting and cursing at him. What sounded like a firecracker silenced them. Easton and Leroy knew the difference between a firecracker and a gunshot. So did the guards, who were now poised like hunting dogs, their guns pointing straight ahead.

Doc Nelson fell back. Blood splattered on one of the guards. Dorothy shrieked. She broke free of Naomi and Mildred, ran down the steps, and fell on top of Doc. "Doc! Doc!" she cried. He didn't answer. Blood ran down the side of his head and trickled down the steps.

Easton and Ruth pushed forward to get closer. "I'm a nurse," Ruth said to a policeman. He let her through the human barrier formed by the police within seconds. Doc had a faint pulse. She felt his breath on her face. She pulled a handkerchief from her purse and covered the bloody hole in Doc's head, pressing down hard to stop the bleeding. When the paramedics arrived, they placed an oxygen mask on Doc's face and rushed him to the hospital.

* * *

Easton, Leroy, and Yancey, who'd been waiting outside, hurried to retrieve their cars. They sped to Freedman's Hospital, where they took Doc Nelson. Forty-five minutes after they arrived in the emergency room, a doctor and a nurse appeared from behind a curtain, where two policemen stood guard.

"He's gone," Ruth whispered to Easton.

"Mrs. Nelson?" the doctor asked, not knowing which of the women to approach.

Dorothy stood up.

"I'm sorry, Mrs. Nelson. We tried to save him, but—"

A sudden shrill sound came from Dorothy's mouth. She collapsed in Yancey's arms. The nurse ran for a wheelchair. Yancey and the doctor helped Dorothy in it. By the time the doctor finished examining her, she'd settled down. She had a peculiar aura about her though—a quiet, almost shy demeanor.

"Do you want to see your husband?" the doctor asked.

"Yes."

"Okay. As soon as the nurses clean him up, they'll come for you. I've ordered a Valium to calm your nerves. I want you take it now and see your doctor tomorrow," he said.

Not long after, a nurse summoned Dorothy to her husband's deathbed. Yancey wheeled her to him. She stayed with Doc close to an hour. Mildred and Naomi had to talk her into leaving. Murphy's men were arriving soon to take his body to the funeral home.

Naomi decided to ride home with Dorothy in Yancey's car. The plan was for Dorothy to stay with Yancey and Mildred since "You already got your hands full," Mildred had said to Naomi. They rode the short distance to Naomi's house in silence, except for Dorothy moaning and weeping. Before Naomi left the car, she told Dorothy, "We'll get through this, and don't you worry about Doc and Taylor, they'll work things out and be friends again up there, dancing with the angels." She kissed Dorothy on the cheek and slid out the car. She stood on the sidewalk and watched them drive away.

* * *

Quentin King, Leslie's boyfriend, had been arrested for beating Ruth. They'd find out later that Quentin's lawyer had bailed him out of jail. It's believed the lawyer paid someone to say Quentin was working at the time of Ruth's attack. It didn't help that Ruth and Caroline failed to identify him in a lineup. He'd changed his appearance using makeup and a cap, the brim pulled down to hide his face. Distressed over Leslie's sentence, he'd shot and killed Doc. When the police went to his apartment to question him later that day, he had the barrel of a gun pressed against his temple, ready to pull the trigger. They disarmed him without much fanfare, took him to jail, and locked him away with the others.

# Chapter 55

February 22, a week after Doc Nelson died, he was laid to rest. Easton covered the funeral, and the ***Negro News*** sent a photographer. Easton observed fewer people at the graveside service, compared to the throngs at Taylor's funeral. Everyone there seemed to be supportive of Dorothy and Doc's extended family, though Easton believed most of them felt sorry for her. He did.

Even Thomas attended the funeral. "Because my godmother didn't do anything to hurt me. She loves me," he said. "I'm going for her."

Naomi, Ruth, and Leroy were there too. As a matter of fact, Naomi helped Dorothy plan the whole thing, something small, respectable. "I love Dorothy, she's my blood. We'll grieve together as a family and help each other through this madness."

* * *

The next day, Naomi made lunch for Ruth, Easton, Leroy, and Thelma Junior, whom Leroy had taken a liking to.

"I'm giving up the funeral business," she announced at the dining room table. "I start teaching home economics next week at Dubois."

Ruth dropped her fork on the table. "You can't. It's a family institution."

"That I don't want to keep and neither does Thomas," Naomi said. "Do you want it?"

Taken off guard, Ruth said, "I don't know. I need to think about it."

"Let me know what you decide and soon," Naomi said.

Ruth finished her meal and reminded Easton about his doctor's appointment, in an hour.

"After I eat. I always have to wait an hour before I'm seen anyway," Easton said.

* * *

"What do you think, should I take over the funeral business?" Ruth asked Easton on their way to the doctor's office.

"Is it in your heart, Ruth? I'd say no since you had to ask me rather than tell me that's what you want," Easton replied.

Ruth smiled. "No, its not."

"I guess you answered your own question," Easton responded.

Ruth pulled into the hospital parking lot. "Mom is good with people. She's patient, caring, and smart. I think she'll make an excellent teacher."

"Your mother is a strong woman. I'm surprised she went to Doc's funeral," Easton said as they walked into the hospital. "To support her cousin is one thing, to mourn the person who helped kill her husband, I don't know. It takes a special person to do that."

"She is special," Ruth said.

Easton signed in to see the surgeon Dr. Zette trained under. An hour later a nurse called his name. He followed her to a room where he waited another fifteen minutes. When the surgeon finally examined him, he decided to admit Easton to the hospital again.

"There's more pus we need to get rid of," the surgeon said. "I want to give this arm every chance to heal before I consider amputating it."

Easton studied him like he had two heads. "This arm is staying right where it is. You can drain it all day and all night, you can't cut it off though. It still has a lot of writing to do. It'll heal."

"I know it's frightening to think you might lose your arm. If it means saving your life, we may not have a choice," the surgeon said.

"My arm is my life, it's how I feed myself, how I'm going to feed my wife and children. It's staying right here," Easton said, pointing to his arm. "Now what floor do I go to?"

* * *

Easton stayed in Thomas's old room between his hospitalizations, four at the last count. Thelma Junior had moved to town and got a job working in the operating room at Freedman's Hospital. She and Ruth switched off days and nights, depending on their work schedule, to care for Easton, fueled by the possibility he might lose his arm. His parents had visited him twice and called several times a week. By the end of March, his arm had healed; he moved back to his rented room and returned to work full-time.

Easton and Ruth went on a fast track to plan their wedding for the last weekend in May, an even smaller affair than they had originally agreed to. They bought a big, airy house in upper Northwest and a used car for Ruth. Naomi enjoyed the independence that came with driving herself around so much that she decided to keep the Packard.

It had all started in the warmth and calm of an indian summer—shades of splendor, long days, and cool nights—hunting season as it were. However, there was no mistake about it. Easton had come very close to being devoured by the game. What a sobering revelation. He wrote a twenty-page exposé about Taylor's murder investigation. The ***Negro News***, along with other Negro-owned newspapers, published it. A few television stations read excerpts from it on the eleven o'clock news, mostly in defense of the police department; however, the Justice Department took notice and investigated the DC police department, forcing them to change their ways. They'd shown indifference in their efforts to solve William Taylor's murder because they didn't care about Negroes violating one another. They didn't take the case seriously until after the Taylor women were attacked.

Easton had been attacked twice and almost lost his arm, yet no efforts had been made to flush out the person responsible. In spite of the trauma he endured, his career took off. He lectured at Negro colleges and universities throughout the country about investigative reporting and, in particular, William Taylor's case. At the end of each lecture, he'd close with "Although I almost lost my life and endured a considerable amount of pain, I'd do it all over again if I had to, because I believe every man, woman, and child on this great earth has a responsibility to take care of their own. If they're not able, the rest of us need to pick up the pieces. I did through investigative reporting. You all may find other ways. It doesn't matter how you heed your brothers' call, as long as you take up their cross and do right by them. Thank you."

Edwards Brothers Malloy
Oxnard, CA USA
July 8, 2014